Dean Koontz was born into a very poor family and learned early on to escape into fiction – though books were scorned by his parents as a waste of time. He won an *Atlantic Monthly* fiction competition in 1965 at the age of twenty. Since then seventeen of his novels have appeared in national and international bestseller lists and have sold over ninety million copies worldwide.

He lives in Southern California with his wife Gerda.

Critical acclaim for

HIDEAWAY
'Fiercely exciting. A grandly melodramatic morality play that will have Koontz's fans – both here and in heaven – cheering' *Kirkus Reviews*

COLD FIRE
'His most enjoyable book to date' *The Times*

THE BAD PLACE
'In his imaginative new novel, Koontz soars beyond the limits of *Midnight* and his other bestsellers . . . [He] should lure even more readers to his myriad following with his terrifyingly credible fantasy' *Publishers Weekly*

Dragon Tears

Dean Koontz

First published in Great Britain in 1993
by HEADLINE BOOK PUBLISHING

First published in paperback in 1993
by HEADLINE BOOK PUBLISHING

A HEADLINE FEATURE paperback

14

ISBN 0 7472 4167 8

Printed and bound in Great Britain by
Clays Ltd, St Ives plc

HEADLINE BOOK PUBLISHING
A division of Hodder Headline PLC
338 Euston Road
London NW1 3BH

This book is for some special people
who live too far away—

Ed and Carol Gorman

—with the wish that our modern world
really *had* shrunk to one small town,
as the media philosophers insist it has.
Then we could meet at the little cafe
down on Main Street at Maple Avenue to
have lunch, talk, and laugh.

Part One

THIS OLD HONKYTONK OF FOOLS

You know a dream is like a river
Ever changing as it flows.
And a dreamer's just a vessel
That must follow where it goes.
Trying to learn from what's behind you
And never knowing what's in store
Makes each day a constant battle
Just to stay between the shores.

— The River
Garth Brooks, Victoria Shaw

Rush headlong and hard at life
Or just sit at home and wait.
All things good and all the wrong
will come right to you: it's fate.

Hear the music, dance if you can.
Dress in rags or wear your jewels.
Drink your choice, nurse your fear
In this old honkytonk of fools.

— The Book of Counted Sorrows

ONE

·1·

Tuesday was a fine California day, full of sunshine and promise, until Harry Lyon had to shoot someone at lunch.

For breakfast, sitting at his kitchen table, he ate toasted English muffins with lemon marmalade and drank strong black Jamaican coffee. A pinch of cinnamon gave the brew a pleasantly spicy taste.

The kitchen window provided a view of the greenbelt that wound through Los Cabos, a sprawling condominium development in Irvine. As president of the homeowner's association, Harry drove the gardeners hard and rigorously monitored their work, insuring that the trees, shrubs, and grass were as neatly trimmed as a landscape in a fairy tale, as if maintained by platoons of gardening elves with hundreds of tiny shears.

As a child, he had enjoyed fairy tales even more than children usually did. In the worlds of the Brothers Grimm and Hans Christian Andersen, springtime hills were always flawlessly green, velvet-smooth. Order prevailed. Villains invariably met with justice, and the virtuous were rewarded – though sometimes only after hideous suffering. Hansel and Gretel didn't die in the witch's oven; the crone herself was roasted alive therein. Instead of stealing the queen's newborn daughter, Rumpelstiltskin was foiled and, in his rage, tore himself apart.

In real life during the last decade of the twentieth century, Rumpelstiltskin would probably get the queen's daughter. He would no doubt addict her to heroin, turn her out as a prostitute, confiscate her earnings, beat her for pleasure, hack her to pieces, and escape justice by claiming that society's intolerance for bad-tempered, evil-minded trolls had driven him temporarily insane.

Harry swallowed the last of his coffee, and sighed. Like a lot of people, he longed to live in a better world.

Before going to work, he washed the dishes and utensils, dried them, and put them away. He loathed coming home to mess and clutter.

At the foyer mirror by the front door, he paused to adjust the knot in his tie. He slipped into a navy-blue blazer and checked to be sure the weapon in his shoulder holster made no telltale bulge.

As on every workday for the past six months, he avoided traffic-packed freeways, following the same surface streets to the Multi-Agency Law Enforcement Special Projects Center in Laguna Niguel, a route that he had mapped out to minimize travel time. He had arrived at the office as early as 8:15 and as late as 8:28, but he had never been tardy.

That Tuesday when he parked his Honda in the shadowed lot on the west side of the two-story building, the car clock showed 8:21. His wristwatch confirmed the time. Indeed, all of the clocks in Harry's condominium and the one on the desk in his office would be displaying 8:21. He synchronized all of his clocks twice a week.

Standing beside the car, he drew deep, relaxing breaths. Rain had fallen overnight, scrubbing the air clean. The March sunshine gave the morning a glow as golden as the flesh of a ripe peach.

To meet Laguna Niguel architectural standards, the Special Projects Center was a two-story Mediterranean-style building with a columned promenade. Surrounded by lush azaleas and tall melaleucas with lacy branches, it bore no resemblance to most police facilities. Some of the cops who worked out of Special Projects thought it looked too effete, but Harry liked it.

The institutional decor of the interior had little in common with the picturesque exterior. Blue vinyl-tile floors. Pale-gray walls. Acoustic ceilings. However, its air of orderliness and efficiency was comforting.

Even at that early hour, people were on the move through the lobby and hallways, mostly men with the solid physique and self-confident attitude that marked career cops. Only a few were in uniform. Special Projects drew on plainclothes homicide detectives and undercover operatives from federal, state, county, and city agencies to facilitate criminal investigations spread over numerous jurisdictions. Special Projects teams – sometimes whole task forces – dealt with youth-gang killings, serial murders, pattern rapists, and large-scale narcotics activities.

Harry shared a second-floor office with Connie

Gulliver. His half of the room was softened by a small palm, Chinese evergreens, and the leafy trailers of a pothos. Her half had no plants. On his desk were only a blotter, pen set, and small brass clock. Heaps of files, loose papers, and photographs were stacked on hers.

Surprisingly, Connie had gotten to the office first. She was standing at the window, her back to him.

'Good morning,' he said.

'Is it?' she asked sourly.

She turned to him. She was wearing badly scuffed Reeboks, blue jeans, a red-and-brown-checkered blouse, and a brown corduroy jacket. The jacket was one of her favorites, worn so often that the cords were threadbare in places, the cuffs were frayed, and the inner-arm creases in the sleeves appeared to be as permanent as river valleys carved in bedrock by eons of flowing water.

In her hand was an empty paper cup from which she had been drinking coffee. She wadded it almost angrily and threw it on the floor. It bounced and came to rest in Harry's half of the room.

'Let's hit the streets,' she said, heading toward the hall door.

Staring at the cup on the floor, he said, 'What's the rush?'

'We're cops, aren't we? So let's don't stand around with our thumbs up our asses, let's go do cop stuff.'

As she moved out of sight into the hall, he stared at the cup on *his* side of the room. With his foot, he nudged it across the imaginary line that divided the office.

He followed Connie to the door but halted at the threshold. He glanced back at the paper cup.

By now Connie would be at the end of the corridor, maybe even descending the stairs.

Harry hesitated, returned to the crumpled cup, and tossed it in the waste can. He disposed of the other two cups as well.

He caught up with Connie in the parking lot, where she yanked open the driver's door of their unmarked Project sedan. As he got in the other side, she started the car, twisting the key so savagely that it should have snapped off in the ignition.

'Have a bad night?' he inquired.

She slammed the car into gear.

He said, 'Headache?'

She reversed too fast out of the parking slot.

He said, 'Thorn in the paw?'

The car shot toward the street.

Harry braced himself, but he was not worried about her driving. She could handle a car far better than she handled people. 'Want to talk about whatever's wrong?'

'No.'

For someone who lived on the edge, who seemed fearless in moments of danger, who went sky-diving and breakneck dirt-biking on weekends, Connie Gulliver was frustratingly, primly reticent when it came to making personal revelations. They had been working together for six months, and although Harry knew a great many things about her, sometimes it seemed he knew nothing *important* about her.

'It might help to talk about it,' Harry said.

7

'It wouldn't help.'

Harry watched her surreptitiously as she drove, wondering if her anger arose from man problems. He had been a cop for fifteen years and had seen enough of human treachery and misery to know that men were the source of most women's troubles. He knew nothing whatsoever of Connie's love life, however, not even whether she had one.

'Does it have to do with this case?'

'No.'

He believed her. She tried, with apparent success, never to be stained by the filth in which her life as a cop required her to wade.

She said, 'But I sure do want to nail this sonofabitch Durner. I think we're close.'

Doyle Durner, a drifter who moved in the surfer subculture, was wanted for questioning in a series of rapes that had grown more violent incident by incident until the most recent victim had been beaten to death. A sixteen-year-old schoolgirl.

Durner was their primary suspect because he was known to have undergone a circumferential autologous penile engorgement. A plastic surgeon in Newport Beach liposuctioned fat out of Durner's waist and injected it into his penis to increase its thickness. The procedure was definitely not recommended by the American Medical Association, but if the surgeon had a big mortgage to pay and the patient was obsessed with his circumference, the forces of the marketplace prevailed over concerns about post-operative complications. The circumference of Durner's manhood had

been increased fifty percent, such a dramatic enlarge-
ment that it must have caused him occasional discom-
fort. By all reports, he was happy with the results, not
because he was likely to impress women but because
he was likely to hurt them, which was the whole point.
The victims' description of their attacker's freakish
difference had helped authorities zero in on Durner
– and three of them had noted the tattoo of a snake
on his groin, which had been recorded in his police file
upon his conviction for two rapes in Santa Barbara eight
years ago.

By noon that Tuesday, Harry and Connie had spoken
with workers and customers at three hangouts popular
among surfers and other beach habitues in Laguna: a
shop that sold surfboards and related gear, a yogurt and
health food store, and a dimly lighted bar in which a
dozen customers were drinking Mexican beers at eleven
o'clock in the morning. If you could believe what they
said, which you couldn't, they had never heard of Doyle
Durner and did not recognize him in the photo they
were shown.

In the car between stops, Connie regaled Harry with
the latest items in her collection of outrages. 'You hear
about the woman in Philadelphia, they found two infants
dead of malnutrition in her apartment and dozens of
crack-cocaine vials scattered all over the place? She's so
doped up her babies starve to death, and you know all
they could charge her with? Reckless endangerment.'

Harry only sighed. When Connie was in the mood
to talk about what she sometimes called 'the continuing crisis' – or when she was more sarcastic, 'the

pre-millennium cotillion'; or in her bleaker moments, 'these new dark ages' – no response was expected from him. She was quite satisfied to make a monologue of it.

She said, 'A guy in New York killed his girlfriend's two-year-old daughter, pounded her with his fists and kicked her because she was dancing in front of the TV, interfering with his view. Probably watching "Wheel of Fortune," didn't want to miss a shot of Vanna White's fabulous legs.'

Like most cops, Connie had an acute sense of black humor. It was a defense mechanism. Without it you'd be driven crazy or become terminally depressed by the endless encounters with human evil and perversity that were central to the job. To those whose knowledge of police life came from half-baked television programs, real-life cop humor could seem crude and insensitive at times – though no good cop gave a rat's ass for what anybody but another cop thought of him.

'There's this Suicide Prevention Center up in Sacramento,' Connie said, braking for a red traffic light. 'One of the counselors got sick of getting calls from this depressive senior citizen, so he and a friend went to the old guy's apartment, held him down, slashed his wrists and throat.'

Sometimes, beneath Connie's darkest humor, Harry perceived a bitterness that was *not* common to cops. Perhaps it was worse than mere bitterness. Maybe even despair. She was so self-contained that it was usually difficult to determine exactly what she was feeling.

Unlike Connie, Harry was an optimist. To remain an

optimist, however, he found it necessary not to dwell on human folly and malevolence the way she did.

Trying to change the subject, he said, 'How about lunch? I know this great little Italian trattoria with oilcloth on the tables, wine bottles for candleholders, good gnocchi, fabulous manicotti.'

She grimaced. 'Nah. Let's just grab tacos at a drive-through and eat on the fly.'

They compromised on a burger joint half a block north of Pacific Coast Highway. It had about a dozen customers and a Southwest decor. The tops of the whitewashed wood tables were sealed beneath an inch of acrylic. Pastel flame-pattern upholstery on the chairs. Potted cacti. Gorman and Parkison lithographs. They ought to have been selling black-bean soup and mesquite-grilled beef instead of burgers and fries.

Harry and Connie were eating at a small table along one wall – a dry, grilled-chicken sandwich for him; shoestring fries and sloppy, aromatic cheeseburger for her – when the tall man entered in a flash of sunlight that flared off the glass door. He stopped at the hostess station and looked around.

Although the guy was neatly groomed and well dressed in light-gray cords, white shirt, and dark-gray Ultrasuede jacket, something about him instantly made Harry uneasy. His vague smile and mildly distracted air gave him a curiously professorial look. His face was round and soft, with a weak chin and pale lips. He looked timid, not threatening. Nevertheless, Harry's gut tightened. Cop instinct.

·2·

Sammy Shamroe had been known as 'Sam the Sham' back when he was a Los Angeles advertising-agency executive blessed with a singular creative talent – and cursed with a taste for cocaine. That had been three years ago. An eternity.

Now he crawled out of the packing crate in which he lived, trailing the rags and crumpled newspapers that served as his bedding. He stopped crawling as soon as he moved beyond the drooping boughs of the oleander bush which grew at the edge of the vacant lot and concealed most of the crate. For a while he stayed on his hands and knees, his head hanging down, staring at the alley pavement.

Long ago he had ceased to be able to afford the high-end drugs that had so thoroughly ruined him. Now he suffered from a cheap-wine headache. He felt as if his skull had fallen open while he slept, allowing the wind to plant a handful of prickly burrs in the surface of his exposed brain.

He was not in the least disoriented. Because the sunlight fell straight down into the alley, leaving shadows only close along the back walls of the buildings on the north side, Sammy knew it was nearly noon. Although he hadn't worn a watch, seen a calendar, held a job, or had an appointment to keep in three years, he was always aware of the season, the month, the day. Tuesday. He was acutely cognizant of where he was (Laguna Beach), of how he had gotten there (every mistake, every self-indulgence, every stupid self-destructive act retained in vivid detail), and of what he could expect for the rest of his life (shame, deprivation, struggle, regret).

The worst aspect of his fall from grace was the stubborn clarity of his mind, which even massive quantities of alcohol could pollute only briefly. The prickly burrs of his hangover headache were a mild inconvenience when compared to the sharp thorns of memory and self-awareness that bristled deeper in his brain.

He heard someone approaching. Heavy footsteps. A faint limp: one foot scraping lightly against the pavement. He knew that tread. He began to tremble. He kept his head down and closed his eyes, willing the footsteps to grow fainter and recede into silence. But they grew louder, nearer . . . then stopped directly in front of him.

'You figured it out yet?'

It was the deep, gravelly voice that had recently begun to haunt Sammy's nightmares. But he was not asleep now. This was not the monster of his turbulent dreams. This was the *real* creature that inspired the nightmares.

Reluctantly Sammy opened his grainy eyes, and looked up.

The ratman stood over him, grinning.

'You figured it out yet?'

Tall, burly, his mane of hair disordered, his tangled beard flecked with unidentifiable bits and chunks of matter too disgusting to contemplate, the ratman was a terrifying figure. Where his beard did not conceal it, his face was gnarled by scars, as if he had been

13

poked and slashed with a white-hot soldering iron. His large nose was hooked and crooked, his lips spotted with weeping sores. Upon his dark and diseased gums, his teeth perched like broken, age-yellowed marble tombstones.

The gravelly voice grew louder. 'Maybe you're already dead.'

The only ordinary thing about the ratman was his clothes: tennis shoes, charity-shop khakis, cotton shirt, and a badly weathered black raincoat, all stained and heavily wrinkled. It was the uniform of a lot of street people who, some by their own fault and some not, had fallen through the cracks in the floorboards of modern society into the shadowy crawlspace beneath.

The voice softened dramatically as the ratman bent forward, leaned closer. 'Already dead and in Hell? Could it be?'

Of all the extraordinary things about the ratman, his eyes were the most disturbing. They were intensely green, unusually green, but the queerest thing was that the black pupils were elliptical like the pupils of a cat or reptile. The eyes made the ratman's body seem like merely a disguise, a rubber suit, as if something unspeakable peered out of a costume at a world on which it had not been born but which it coveted.

The ratman lowered his voice even further to a raspy whisper: 'Dead, in Hell, and me the demon assigned to torture you?'

Knowing what was coming, having endured it before, Sammy tried to scramble to his feet. But the ratman, quick as wind, kicked him before he could get out of the way. The kick caught him in the left shoulder, just missing his face, and it didn't feel like a sneaker but like a jackboot, as if the foot inside was entirely of bone or horn or the stuff of which a beetle's carapace was formed. Sammy curled into the fetal position, protecting his head with his folded arms as best he could. The ratman kicked him again, again, left foot, right foot, left foot, almost as if doing a little dance, a sort of jig, one-kick-anduh-two-kick-anduh one kick anduh-two, not making a sound, neither snarling in rage nor laughing scornfully, not breathing hard in spite of the exertion.

The kicking stopped.

Sammy drew into an even tighter ball, like a pill bug, curling around his pains.

The alleyway was unnaturally silent except for Sammy's soft weeping, for which he loathed himself. The traffic noise from the nearby streets had completely faded. The oleander bush behind him no longer rustled in the breeze. When Sammy angrily told himself to be a man, when he swallowed his sobs, the quietude was death-perfect.

He dared to open his eyes and peek between his arms, looking toward the far end of the alley. Blinking to clear his tear-veiled vision, he was able to see two cars halted in the street beyond. The drivers, visible only as shadowy shapes, waited motionlessly.

Closer, directly in front of his face, an inch-long wing-less earwig, strangely out of its environment of rotting wood and dark places, was frozen in the process of crossing the alley. The twin prongs on the insect's back end appeared wicked, dangerous, and were curled up like the stinging tail of a scorpion, though in reality it was harmless. Some of its six legs touched the pavement, and others were lifted in mid-stride. It didn't move even one of its segmented antennae, as if frozen by fear or poised to attack.

Sammy shifted his gaze to the end of the alley. Out in the street, the same cars were stalled in the same spots as before. The people in them sat like mannequins.

The insect again. Unmoving. As still as if dead and pinned to an entomologist's specimen board.

Warily Sammy lowered his crossed arms from his head. Groaning, he rolled onto his back and looked up reluctantly at his assailant.

Looming, the ratman seemed a hundred feet tall. He studied Sammy with solemn interest. 'Do you want to live?' he asked.

Sammy was surprised not by the question but by his inability to answer it. He was caught between the fear of death and the need to die. Each morning he was disappointed when he woke and found that he was still among the living, and each night when he curled up in his rag-and-paper bedding, he hoped for endless sleep. Yet day after day he struggled to obtain sufficient food, to find a warm place on those rare cold nights when California's climatic grace deserted it, to stay dry when it rained so as to avoid pneumonia, and he looked both ways before crossing a street.

Perhaps he did not want to live, but wanted only the punishment of living.

'I'd like it better if you wanted to live,' the ratman said quietly. 'More fun for me.'

Sammy's heart was beating too thunderously. Each pulse throbbed hardest in the bruised flesh that marked the impact points of the ratman's ferocious kicks.

'You've got thirty-six hours to live. Better do something, don't you think? Hmmmm? The clock is running. Ticktock, ticktock.'

'Why are you doing this to me?' Sammy asked plaintively.

Instead of replying, the ratman said, 'Midnight tomorrow the rats will come for you.'

'I've never done anything to you.'

The scars on the tormentor's brutal face grew livid. '. . . chew out your eyes . . .'

'Please.'

His pale lips tightened as he spoke, revealing more of his rotting teeth: '. . . strip away your lips while you scream, nibble your tongue . . .'

As the ratman grew increasingly agitated, his demeanor became not more feverish but cold. His reptilian eyes seemed to radiate a chill that found its way into Sammy's flesh and into the deepest reaches of his mind.

'Who are you?' Sammy asked, not for the first time.

The ratman did not answer. He swelled with rage. His thick, filthy fingers curled to form fists, uncurled, curled, uncurled. He kneaded the air as if he hoped to squeeze blood from it.

What are you? Sammy wondered but dared not ask.

'Rats,' hissed the ratman.

Afraid of what was about to happen, although it

17

had happened before, Sammy scooted backward on his butt, toward the oleander bush that half concealed his packing crate, trying to put some distance between himself and the towering hobo.

'Rats,' the ratman repeated, and he began to tremble. It was starting.

Sammy froze, too terrified to move.

The ratman's trembling became a shudder. The shudder escalated into violent shaking. His oily hair whipped about his head, his arms jerked, his legs jigged, and his black raincoat flapped as if he were in a cyclone, but no wind huffed or howled. The March air was as preternaturally still as it had been since the hulking vagrant's appearance, as if the world were but a painted stage and the two of them the only actors upon it.

Becalmed on reefs of blacktop, Sammy Shamroe finally stood. He was driven to his feet by fear of the roiling tide of claws, sharp teeth, and red eyes that would soon rise around him.

Beneath his clothes, the ratman's body churned like a burlap sack full of angry rattlesnakes. He was . . . *changing*. His face melted and re-formed as if he stood in a forge controlled by some mad deity intent on molding a series of monstrosities, each of which would be more terrible than the one before it. Gone were the livid scars, gone were the reptilian eyes, gone the wild beard and tangled hair, gone the cruel mouth. For a moment his head was nothing but a mass of undifferentiated flesh, a lump of oozing mush, red with blood, then red-brown and darker, glistening, like something that had been poured out of a dog-food can. Abruptly the tissue solidified, and his head was composed of rats clinging to one another, a ball of rats, tails drooping like Rastafarian dreadlocks, fierce eyes as scarlet as drops of radiant blood. Where hands should have hung from his sleeves, rats bristled out of frayed cuffs. The heads of other rodents began to poke from between the buttons of his bulging shirt.

Though he had seen all of this before, Sammy tried to scream. His swollen tongue stuck to the roof of his dry mouth, so he made only a panicky muffled sound in the back of his throat. A scream wouldn't help anyway. He had screamed before, during other encounters with his tormentor, and no one had responded.

The ratman came apart as if he were a rickety scarecrow in a sundering storm, pieces of his body dropping away. When each part hit the pavement, it was an individual rat. Whiskered, wet-nosed, sharp-toothed, squealing, the repellent creatures swarmed over one another, long tails lashing left and right. More rats poured out of his shirt and from under the cuffs of his trousers, far more than his clothes could possibly have contained: a score of them, two score, eighty, more than a hundred.

Like a deflating balloon that had been crafted in the form of a man, his clothes settled slowly to the pavement. Then each garment was transformed as well. The wrinkled lumps of cloth sprouted heads and limbs and produced more rodents, until both the ratman and his reeking wardrobe had been replaced by a seething mound of vermin squirming over and under one another with the boneless agility that made their kind so repulsive.

Sammy could not get his breath. The air grew even more leaden than it had been. Whereas the wind had died earlier, an unnatural stillness now seemed to settle over deeper levels of the natural world, until the fluidity of oxygen and nitrogen molecules declined drastically, as if the atmosphere had begun to thicken into a liquid, which he could draw into his lungs only with the greatest effort.

Now that the ratman's body had disintegrated into scores of squirming beasts, the transformed corpus abruptly dispersed. The fat, sleek rats erupted out of the mound, fleeing in all directions, scuttling away from Sammy but also swarming around him, over his shoes and between his legs. That hateful, living tide spilled into the shadows along the buildings and into the vacant lot, where it either drained into holes in the building walls and in the earth – holes that Sammy could not see – or simply vanished.

A sudden breeze harried crisp dead leaves and scraps of paper ahead of it. The swish of tires and the rumble of engines arose as cars on the main street moved past the mouth of the alley. A bee buzzed by Sammy's face.

He was able to breathe again. He stood for a moment in the bright noon light, gasping.

The worst thing was that it had all happened in sunshine, in the open air, without smoke and mirrors and clever lighting and silk threads and trapdoors and the standard tools of a magician's craft.

Sammy had crawled out of his crate with the good

intention of starting his day in spite of his hangover, maybe look for discarded aluminum cans to redeem at a recycling center, maybe do a little panhandling along the boardwalk. Now the hangover was gone, but he still didn't feel like facing the world.

On unsteady legs, he returned to the oleander bush. The boughs were heavily laden with red flowers. He pushed them aside and stared at the large wooden crate under them.

He picked up a stick and poked at the rags and newspapers inside the big box, expecting a couple of rats to erupt from hiding. But they had gone elsewhere.

Sammy dropped to his knees and crawled into his haven, letting the draperies of oleander fall shut behind him.

From his pile of meager possessions in the back of the crate, he removed an unopened bottle of cheap burgundy and unscrewed the cap. He took a long pull of the warmish wine.

Sitting with his back against the wooden wall, clutching the bottle in both hands, he tried to forget what he had seen. As far as he could see, forgetting was his only hope of coping. He could not manage the problems of everyday life any more. So how could he expect to deal with something as extraordinary as the ratman?

A brain steeped in too many grams of cocaine, peppered with too many other drugs, and marinated in alcohol could produce the most amazing zoo of hallucinated creatures. And when his conscience got the better of him and he struggled to fulfill one of his periodic pledges of sobriety, withdrawal led to delirium tremens, which were populated by an even more colorful and threatening phantasmagoria of beasts. But none of them was as memorable and as deeply disturbing as the ratman.

He took another generous swallow of wine and leaned his head back against the wall of the crate, holding fast to the bottle with both hands.

Year by year, day by day, Sammy had found it increasingly difficult to distinguish between reality and fantasy. He had long ago ceased to trust his perceptions. Yet of one thing he was dismayingly certain: the ratman was real. Impossible, fantastical, inexplicable – but real.

Sammy expected to find no answers to the questions that haunted him. But he could not stop asking: what was this creature; where did it come from; why did it want to torment and kill a grizzled, beaten-down street person whose death – or continued existence – was of little or no consequence to the world?

He drank more wine.

Thirty-six hours. Ticktock. Ticktock.

·3·

Cop instinct.

When the citizen in the gray cords, white shirt, and dark-gray jacket entered the restaurant, Connie noticed him and knew he was bent in some way. When she saw that Harry had also noticed, her interest in the guy increased dramatically because Harry had a nose that would make a bloodhound envious.

Cop instinct is less instinct than a sharply honed talent for observation and the good sense to interpret correctly whatever is observed. With Connie it was more a subconscious awareness than a calculated monitoring of everyone who crossed her line of sight.

The suspect stood just inside the door, near the cash register, waiting while the hostess seated a young couple at a table near one of the big front windows.

He appeared ordinary at first glance, even harmless. But on closer inspection, Connie could identify the incongruities that had caused her subconscious to recommend a closer look at the man. No signs of tension were visible in his rather bland face, and his posture was relaxed – but his hands were fisted tightly at his sides, as if he could barely control an urgent need to strike at someone. His vague smile reinforced the air of absentmindedness that clung to him – but the smile kept coming and going, flickering uncertainly, a subtle testament to inner turmoil. His sport coat was buttoned, which was odd because he wasn't wearing a tie and because the day was warm. More important, the coat did not hang properly; its outer and inner pockets seemed filled with something heavy that pulled it out of shape, and it bulged over his belt buckle – as if concealing a handgun jammed under the waistband of his pants.

Of course, cop instinct wasn't always reliable. The coat might just be old and out of shape. The guy might actually be the absentminded professor he appeared to be; in which case his coat might be stuffed with nothing more sinister than a pipe, tobacco pouch, slide rule, calculator, lecture notes, and all sorts of items he had slipped into his pockets without quite realizing it.

Harry, whose voice had trailed off in mid-sentence, slowly put down his chicken sandwich. He was intently focused on the man in the misshapen coat.

Connie had picked up a few shoestring french fries. She dropped them onto the plate instead of eating them, and she wiped her greasy fingers on her napkin, all the while trying to watch the new customer without obviously staring at him.

The hostess, a petite blonde in her twenties, returned to the reception area after seating the couple by the window, and the man in the Ultrasuede coat smiled. She spoke to him, he replied, and the blonde laughed politely as if what he'd said was mildly amusing.

When the customer said something more and the hostess laughed again, Connie relaxed slightly. She reached for a couple of fries.

The newcomer seized the hostess by her belt, jerked her toward him, and grabbed a handful of her blouse. His assault was so sudden and unexpected, his moves so cat-quick, that he had lifted her off the floor before she began to scream. As if she weighed nothing, he threw her at nearby diners.

'Oh, shit.' Connie pushed back from the table and came to her feet, reaching under her jacket and behind to the revolver that was holstered in the small of her back.

Harry rose, too, his own revolver in hand. 'Police!'

His warning was drowned out by the sickening crash of the young blonde slamming into a table, which tipped

24

sideways. The diners toppled out of their chairs, and glasses shattered. All over the restaurant people looked up from their food, startled by the uproar.

The stranger's flamboyance and savagery might just mean he was on drugs – or he might also be genuinely psychotic.

Connie took no chances, dropping into a crouch as she brought her gun up. 'Police!'

Either the guy *had* heard Harry's first warning or he had seen them out of the corner of his eye, because he was already scuttling toward the back of the restaurant, between the tables.

He had a handgun of his own – maybe a Browning 9mm, judging by the sound and by the glimpse she got. He was using it, too, firing at random, each shot thunderous in the confines of the restaurant.

Beside Connie, a painted terracotta pot exploded. Chips of glazed clay showered onto her. The dracaena margenata in the pot toppled over, raking her with long narrow leaves, and she crouched even lower, trying to use a nearby table as a shield.

She wanted in the worst way to get a shot at the bastard, but the risk of hitting one of the other customers was too great. When she looked across the restaurant at child's level, thinking maybe she could pulverize one of the creep's knees with a well-placed round, she could see him scrambling across the room. The trouble was, between her and him, a scattering of panicked, wide-eyed people had taken refuge under their tables.

'Shit.' She pursued the geek while trying to make as

small a target of herself as possible, aware that Harry
was going after him from another direction.

People were screaming because they were scared, or
had been shot and were in pain. The crazy bastard's
gun boomed too often. Either he could change clips
with superhuman speed or he had another pistol.

One of the big windows took a direct hit and came
down in a jinglejangle clangor. A waterfall of glass
splashed across the cold Santa Fe tile floor.

As Connie crept from table to table, her shoes picked
up mashed french fries, ketchup, mustard, bits of oozing
cacti, and crunching-tinkling pieces of glass. And as she
passed the wounded, they cried out or pawed at her,
desperate for help.

She hated to ignore them, but she had to shake them
off, keep moving, try to get a shot at the walking
phlegm in the Ultrasuede coat. What meager first-aid
she might be able to provide wasn't going to help them.
She couldn't do anything about the terror and pain the
sonofabitch had already wrought, but she might be able
to stop him from doing more damage if she stayed on
his ass.

She raised her head, risking a bullet in the brain, and
saw the scumbag was all the way at the back of the
restaurant, standing at a swinging door that had a glass
porthole in the center. Grinning, he squeezed off rounds
at anything that caught his attention, apparently equally
pleased to hit a potted plant or a human being. He was
still unnervingly ordinary in appearance, round-faced
and bland, with a weak chin and soft mouth. Even his
grin failed to make him look like a madman; it was more

the broad and affable smile of someone who had just seen a clown take a pratfall. But there was no doubt he was crazy-dangerous, because he shot a big saguaro cactus, then a guy in a checkered shirt, then the saguaro again, and he *did* have two guns, one in each hand.

Welcome to the 1990s.

Connie rose from shelter far enough to line up a shot.

Harry was equally quick to take advantage of the lunatic's sudden obsession with the saguaro. He came to his feet in another part of the restaurant and fired. Connie fired twice. Chunks of wood exploded from the door frame beside the psycho's head, and the glass blew out of the porthole; they had bracketed him by inches with their first shots.

The geek vanished through the swinging door, which took both Harry's and Connie's next rounds and kept swinging. Judging by the size of the bullet holes, the door was hollow-core, so the slugs might have gone through and nailed the sonofabitch on the other side.

Connie ran toward the kitchen, slipping a little on the food-strewn floor. She doubted they were going to be lucky enough to find the creep wounded and squirming like a half-crushed cockroach on the other side of that door. More likely, he was waiting for them. But she couldn't rein herself in. He might even step through the door from the kitchen and cut her down as she approached. But her juices were up; she was jazzed. When her juices were up, she couldn't help but do everything full-bore, and it didn't even matter that her juices were up most of the time.

God, she *loved* this job.

·4·

Harry *hated* this cowboy stuff.

When you were a cop, you knew violence might come down sooner or later. You might suddenly find yourself up to your neck in wolves a lot nastier than any Red Riding Hood ever had to deal with. But even if it was part of the job, you didn't enjoy it.

Well, maybe you did if you were Connie Gulliver. As Harry rushed the kitchen door, going in low and fast with his revolver ready, he heard her behind him, feet slapping-crunching-squishing on the floor, coming full-tilt. He knew that if he looked back at her, she would be grinning, not unlike the maniac who had shot up the restaurant, and although he knew she was on the side of the angels, that grin never failed to unnerve him.

He skidded to a halt at the door, kicked it, and instantly jumped to one side, expecting an answering hail of bullets.

But the door slammed inward, swung back out, and no gunfire followed. So when it swung inward again, Connie burst past him and went into the kitchen with it. He followed her, cursing under his breath, which was the only way he ever cursed.

In the humid, claustrophobic confines of the kitchen, burgers sizzled on a grill and fat bubbled in a deep-fryer. Pots of water boiled on a stove top. Gas ovens creaked and popped from the intense heat they contained, and a bank of microwave ovens hummed softly.

Half a dozen cooks and other employees, dressed in white slacks and T-shirts, their hair tucked under white string-tied caps, pale as dead men, stood or cowered midst the culinary equipment. They were wrapped by curling tendrils of steam and meat smoke, looking less like real people than like ghosts. Almost as one they turned toward Connie and Harry.

'Where?' Harry whispered.

One of the employees pointed toward a half-open door at the back of the kitchen.

Harry led the way along a narrow aisle flanked on the left by racks of pots and utensils. On the right was a series of butcher blocks, a machine used to cut well-scrubbed potatoes into raw french fries and another that shredded lettuce.

The aisle widened into a clear space with deep sinks and heavy-duty commercial dishwashers along the wall to the left. The half-open door was about twenty feet directly ahead, past the sinks.

Connie moved up to his side as they drew near the door. She kept enough distance between them to assure they couldn't both be taken out by one burst of gunfire.

The darkness past that threshold bothered Harry. A windowless storeroom probably lay beyond. The smiling, moon-faced perp would be even more dangerous once cornered.

After flanking the door, they hesitated, taking a moment to think. Harry would gladly have taken half the day to think, giving the perp plenty of time to stew in there. But that wasn't how it worked. Cops were expected to act rather than react. If there was a way out of the storeroom, any delay on their part would allow the perp to escape.

Besides, when your partner was Connie Gulliver, you did not have the luxury of dawdling or ruminating. She was never reckless, always professional and cautious – but so quick and aggressive that it seemed sometimes as if she had come to homicide investigations by way of a SWAT team.

Connie snatched up a broom that was leaning against the wall. Holding it near the base, she poked the handle against the half-open door, which swung inward with a protracted squeak. When the door was all the way open, she threw the broom aside. It clattered like old bones on the tile floor.

They regarded each other tensely from opposite sides of the doorway.

Silence in the storeroom.

Without exposing himself to the perp, Harry could see just a narrow wedge of darkness beyond the threshold.

The only sounds were the chuckling and sputtering of the pots and deep fryers in the kitchen, the hum of the exhaust fans overhead.

As Harry's eyes adjusted to the gloom beyond the door, he saw geometric forms, dark gray in the threatening black. Suddenly he realized it wasn't a storeroom. It was the bottom of a stairwell.

He cursed under his breath again.

30

Connie whispered: 'What?'

'Stairs.'

He crossed the threshold, as heedless of his safety as Connie was of hers, because there was no other way to do it. Stairways were narrow traps in which you couldn't easily dodge a bullet, and dark stairways were worse. The gloom above was such that he couldn't see if the perp was up there, but he figured he made a perfect target with the backlighting from the kitchen. He would have preferred to blockade the stairwell door and find another route onto the second floor, but by then the perp would be long gone or barricaded so well that it might cost a couple of other cops' lives to root him out.

Once committed, he took the stairs as fast as he dared, slowed only by the need to stay to one side, against the wall, where the floorboards would be the tightest and the least likely to sag and squeak underfoot. He reached a narrow landing, moving blindly with his back to the wall.

Squinting up into utter lightlessness, he wondered how a second floor could be as perfectly dark as a basement.

From above came soft laughter.

Harry froze on the landing. He was confident that he was no longer backlit. He pressed tighter to the wall.

Connie bumped into him and also froze.

Harry waited for the queer laugh to come again. He hoped to get a fix precise enough to make it worth risking a shot and revealing his own location.

Nothing.

He held his breath.

Then something thumped. Rattled. Thumped again. Rattled. Thumped again.

He realized some object was rolling and bouncing down the steps toward them. What? He had no idea. His imagination deserted him.

Thump. Rattle. Thump.

Intuitively he knew that whatever was coming down the stairs was not good. That's why the perp had laughed. Something small from the sound of it, but deadly in spite of being small. He was infuriated with himself for being unable to *think*, to visualize. He felt stupid and useless. A foul sweat suddenly sheathed him.

The object hit the landing and rolled to a stop against his left foot. It bumped his shoe. He jerked back, then immediately squatted, blindly felt the floor, found the damn thing. Larger than an egg but roughly egg-shaped. With the intricate geometric surface of a pinecone. Heavier than a pinecone. With a lever on top.

'Get down!' He stood and threw the hand grenade back into the upper hall before following his own advice and dropping as flat as possible on the landing.

He heard the grenade clatter against something above.

He hoped his throw had sent the damn thing all the way into the second-floor hall. But maybe it bounced off a stairwell wall and was arcing down even now, the timer ticking off the last second or two before detonation. Or maybe it had barely landed in the upstairs hall and the perp had kicked it back at him.

The explosion was loud, bright, cataclysmic. His ears rang painfully, every bone seemed to vibrate as the blast wave passed through him, and his heartbeat accelerated even though it had been racing already. Chunks of wood, plaster, and other debris rained over him, and the stairwell was filled with the acrid stench of burnt powder like a Fourth of July night after a big fireworks display.

He had a vivid mental picture of what might have happened if he had been two seconds slower: his hand dissolving in a spray of blood as he gripped the grenade upon detonation, his arm tearing loose of his body, his face crumpling in on itself . . .

'*What the hell?*' Connie demanded, her voice close yet far away, distorted because Harry's ears were still ringing.

'Grenade,' he said, scrambling to his feet.

'Grenade? Who *is* this bozo?'

Harry had no clue as to the guy's identity or motivation, but he now knew why the Ultrasuede jacket had hung so lumpily. If the perp had been packing one grenade, why not two? Or three?

After the brief flash of the explosion, the darkness on the stairs was as deep as ever.

Harry discarded caution and clambered up the second flight, aware that Connie was coming close behind him. Caution didn't seem prudent under the circumstances. You always had a chance of dodging a bullet, but if the perp was carrying grenades, all the caution in the world wouldn't count when the blast hit.

Not that they were accustomed to dealing with grenades. This was a first.

He hoped the lunatic had been waiting to hear them die in the explosion – and had instead been caught unawares when the grenade boomeranged on him. Any time a cop killed a perp, the paperwork was horrendous, but Harry was willing to sit at a typewriter happily for *days* if only the guy in the Ultrasuede coat had been transformed into wet wallpaper.

The long upstairs corridor was windowless and must have been night-black before the explosion. But the grenade had blown one door off its hinges and had torn holes in another. Some daylight filtered through the windows of unseen rooms and into the hallway.

Damage from the explosion was extensive. The building was old enough to have lath and plaster construction instead of drywall, and in places the lath showed through like brittle bones between ragged gaps in the desiccated flesh of some ancient pharaoh's mummified body. Splintered floorboards had torn loose; they were scattered half the length of the corridor, revealing the subfloor and in some places the charred beams beneath.

No flames had sprung up. The snuffing force of the blast had prevented anything from catching fire. The thin haze of smoke from the explosion didn't reduce visibility, except that it stung his eyes and made them water.

The perp was not in sight.

Harry breathed through his mouth to avoid sneezing. The acrid haze was a bitterness on his tongue.

Eight doors opened off the hall, four on each side,

including the one that had been blown entirely from its hinges. With no more direct communication than a glance, Harry and Connie moved in concert from the top of the stairs, careful not to step in any of the holes in the floor, heading toward the open doorway. They had to inspect the second level quickly. Every window was potentially an escape route, and the building might have back stairs.

'*Elvis!*'

The shout came from the doorless room they were approaching.

Harry glanced at Connie, and they both hesitated because there was a weirdness about the moment that was unsettling.

'*Elvis!*'

Though other people might have been on the second floor before the perp had arrived, somehow Harry knew it was the perp shouting.

'*The King! The Master of Memphis!*'

They flanked the doorway as they had done at the foot of the stairs.

The perp began shouting titles of Presley hits: '*Heartbreak Hotel, Blue Suede Shoes, Hound Dog, Money Honey, Jailhouse Rock . . .*'

Harry looked at Connie, raised one eyebrow. She shrugged.

'*Stuck On You, Little Sister, Good Luck Charm . . .*'

Harry signaled to Connie that he would go through the door first, staying low, relying on her to lay down a suppressing fire over his head as he crossed the threshold.

'*Are You Lonesome Tonight, A Mess of Blues, In the Ghetto!*'

As Harry was about to make his move, a grenade arced out of the room. It bounced on the hall floor between him and Connie, rolled, and disappeared into one of the holes made by the first explosion.

No time to fish for it under the floorboards. No time to get back to the stairs. If they delayed, the corridor would blow up around them.

Contrary to Harry's plan, Connie rushed first through the blasted doorway into the room with the perp, staying low, squeezing off a couple of rounds. He followed her, firing twice over her head, and both of them clattered across the shattered door that had been torn off its hinges and blown down in the first explosion. Boxes. Supplies. Stacked everywhere. No sign of the perp. They both dropped to the floor, *threw* themselves down and between piles of boxes.

They were still dropping, scrambling, when the hallway went to pieces in a flash and crash behind them. Harry tucked his head under his arm and tried to protect his face.

A brief hot wind brought a storm of debris through the doorway, and a lighting fixture on the ceiling dissolved into glass hail.

Breathing the fireworks stink again, Harry raised his head. A wicked-looking piece of wooden shrapnel – as big as the blade of a butcher's knife, thicker, almost as sharp – had missed him by two inches and embedded itself in a large carton of paper napkins.

The thin film of sweat on his face was as cold as ice-water.

He tipped the expended cartridges from the revolver, fumbled the speedloader from its pouch and slipped it in, twisted it, dropped it, snapped the cylinder shut.

'*Return to Sender, Suspicious Minds, Surrender!*'

Harry was pierced by a longing for the simple, direct, and comprehensible villains of the Brothers Grimm, like the evil queen who ate the heart of a wild boar, thinking it was really the heart of her stepdaughter, Snow White, whose beauty she envied and whose life she had ordered forfeited.

·5·

Connie raised her head and glanced at Harry, who was lying beside her. He was covered with dust, chips of wood, and glimmering bits of glass, as she no doubt was herself.

She could see that he wasn't getting off on this the way she was. Harry liked being a cop; to him a cop was a symbol of order and justice. Madness like this pained him because order could be imposed only through violence equal to what the perpetrator dealt out. And real justice for the victims could never be extracted from a perp who was so far gone that he couldn't feel remorse or fear retribution.

The geek shouted again. '*Long Legged Girl, All Shook Up, Baby Don't Get Hooked on Me!*'

37

Connie whispered: 'Elvis Presley didn't sing "Baby Don't Get Hooked on Me."'

Harry blinked. 'What?'

'That was Mac Davis, for God's sake.'

'*Rock-a-Hula Baby, Kentucky Rain, Flaming Star, I Feel So Bad!*'

The geek's voice seemed to be coming from overhead.

Cautiously Connie eased up from the floor, revolver in hand. She peered between the stacked boxes, then over them.

At the far end of the room, near the corner, a ceiling trapdoor was open. A folding ladder extended from it.

'*A Big Hunk O' Love, Kiss Me Quick, Guitar Man!*'

The walking piece of dog vomit had gone up that ladder. He was shouting at them from the dark attic above.

She wanted to get hold of the geek and smash his face in, which was not a measured police response, perhaps, but heartfelt.

Harry spotted the ladder when she did, and as she rose to her feet, he stood beside her. She was tense, ready to hit the floor again fast if another grenade dropped out of that overhead trap.

'*Any Way You Want Me, Poor Boy, Running Bear!*'

'Hell, that wasn't Elvis, either,' Connie said, not bothering to whisper any more. 'Johnny Preston sang "Running Bear."'

'What does it matter?'

'The guy's an asshole,' she said angrily, which was not exactly an answer. But the truth was, she didn't know *why* it bothered her that this loser couldn't get his Elvis trivia correct.

'*You're the Devil in Disguise, Don't Cry Daddy, Do the Clam!*'

'"Do the Clam"?' Harry said.

Connie winced. 'Yeah, I'm afraid that *was* Elvis.'

As sparks squirted from the shorting wires in the damaged light fixture overhead, they crossed the room on opposite sides of a long waist-high row of boxes, closing in on the attic access.

From the world beyond the dust-streaked window, faraway sirens wailed. Backup and ambulances.

Connie hesitated. Now that the geek had gone into the attic, it might be best to flush him out with tear gas, lob up a concussion grenade to stun him senseless, and just wait for reinforcements.

But she rejected the cautious course. While it would be safer for her and Harry, it could be riskier for everyone else in downtown Laguna Beach. The attic might not be a dead end. A service door to the roof would give the creep a way out.

Evidently Harry had the same thought. He hesitated a fraction of a second less than she did, and started up the ladder first.

She didn't object to his leading the way because he was not acting out of some misguided protective urge, not trying to spare the lady cop from danger. She'd come through the previous doorway first, so he led this time. They intuitively shared the risk, which was one thing that made them a good team in spite of their differences.

Of course, though her heart was pounding and her gut was clenched, she would have *preferred* to go first.

Crossing a solid bridge was never as satisfying as walking on a high wire.

She followed him up the ladder, and he hesitated at the top only briefly before disappearing into the gloom above. No shot rang out, no explosion shook the building, so Connie went into the attic, too.

Harry had moved out of the gray light that came up through the trap. He crouched a few feet away, beside a naked dead woman.

On second glance, it proved to be a mannequin with permanently staring, dust-coated eyes and an eerily serene smile. She was bald, and her plaster skull was marred by a water stain.

The attic was dark but not impenetrable. Pale daylight sifted through a series of screened ventilation cut-outs in the eaves and through larger vane-capped vents in the end walls, revealing cobweb-festooned rafters under a peaked roof. The center offered enough headroom for even a tall man to stand erect, though nearer the wide walls it was necessary to crouch. Shadows loomed everywhere, while piles of storage trunks and crates offered numerous hiding places.

A congregation seemed to have gathered in that high place to conduct a secret Satanic ceremony. Throughout the long, wide chamber were the partial silhouettes of men and women, sometimes lit from the side, sometimes backlit, more often barely visible, standing or leaning or lying, all silent and motionless.

They were mannequins similar to the one on the floor beside Harry. Nevertheless, Connie felt their stares, and her skin grew pebbly with gooseflesh.

One of them actually might be able to see her, one who was made not of plaster but of blood, flesh, and bone.

·6·

Time seemed suspended in the high redoubt of the mannequins. The humid air was tainted with dust, the crisp aroma of age-yellowed newspapers, moldering cardboard, and pungent mildew that had sprung up in some dark corner and would perish with the end of the rainy season. The plaster figures watched, breathless.

Harry tried to remember what businesses shared the building with the restaurant, but he couldn't recall to whom the mannequins might belong.

From the east end of the long chamber came a frantic hammering, metal on metal. The perp must be pounding on the larger vent in the end wall, trying to break out, willing to risk a drop to the alley, serviceway, or street below.

Half a dozen frightened bats erupted from their roosts and swooped back and forth through the long garret, seeking safety but reluctant to trade the gloom for bright daylight. Their small voices were shrill enough to be heard over the rising shriek of the sirens. When they passed close enough, the leathery flap of their wings and an air-cutting *whoosh* made Harry flinch.

He wanted to wait for backup.

The perp hammered harder than before.

Metal screeched as if giving way.

41

They couldn't wait, didn't dare.

Remaining in a crouch, Harry crept between piles of boxes toward the south wall, and Connie slipped away in the opposite direction. They would take the perp in a pincer move. When Harry went as far to the south side of the room as the sloping ceiling allowed, he turned toward the east end, where the heavy hammering originated.

On all sides, mannequins struck eternal poses. Their smooth, round limbs seemed to absorb and amplify the meager light that passed through the narrow vents in the eaves; where not clothed by shadows, their hard flesh had a supernatural alabaster glow.

The hammering stopped. No clang or pop or final wrenching noise indicated that the vent had been knocked loose.

Harry halted, waited. He could hear only the sirens a block away and the squealing of the bats when they swooped near.

He inched forward. Twenty feet ahead, at the terminus of the musty passageway, dim ash-gray light issued from an unseen source to the left. Probably the big vent on which the perp had been hammering. Which meant it was still firmly in place. If the vent had been knocked out of its frame, daylight would have flooded that end of the attic.

One by one, the sirens expired down in the street. Six of them.

As Harry crept forward, he saw a pile of severed limbs in one of the shadowy niches in the eaves between two rafters, spectrally illuminated. He flinched and almost cried out. Arms cut off at the elbows. Hands amputated at the wrists. Fingers spread as if reaching for help, pleading, seeking. Even as he gasped in shock, he realized the macabre collection was only a heap of mannequin parts.

He proceeded in a duckwalk, less than ten feet from the end of the narrow passageway, acutely aware of the soft but betraying scrape of his shoes on the dusty floorboards. Like the sirens, the agitated bats had fallen silent. A few shouts and the crackling transmissions of police-band radios rose from the street outside, but those sounds were distant and unreal, as if they were the voices in a nightmare from which he was just waking or into which he was slipping. Harry paused every couple of feet, listening for whatever revealing noises the perp might be making, but the guy was ghost-quiet.

When he reached the end of the aisle, about five feet from the east wall of the attic, he stopped again. The vent on which the perp had been hammering must be just around the last stack of boxes.

Harry held his breath and listened for the breathing of his prey. Nothing.

He eased forward, looked around the boxes, past the end of the passageway into the clear area in front of the east wall. The perp was gone.

He had not left by the yard-square attic vent. It was damaged but still in place, emitting a vague draft and thin, uneven lines of daylight that striped the floor where the perp's footprints marred the carpet of dust.

Movement at the north end of the attic caught Harry's attention, and his trigger finger tensed. Connie peered around the corner of the boxes piled on that side of the garret.

Across the wide gap, they stared at each other.

The perp had circled behind them.

Though Connie was mostly in shadows, Harry knew her well enough to be certain of what she was mouthing silently: *shit, shit, shit.*

She came out of the northern eaves and crept across the open space at the east end, moving toward Harry. She peered warily into the mouths of other aisles between rows of boxes and mannequins.

Harry started toward her, squinting into the gloomy aisles on his side. The garret was so wide, so packed with goods, that it was a maze. And it harbored a monster to rival any in mythology.

From elsewhere in the high room came the now-familiar voice: '*All Shook Up, I Feel So Bad, Steamroller Blues!*'

Harry squeezed his eyes shut. He wanted to be somewhere else. Maybe in the kingdom of 'The Twelve Dancing Princesses,' with its twelve gorgeous young heirs to the throne, subterranean castles of light, trees with leaves of gold, others with leaves of diamonds, enchanted ballrooms filled with beautiful music . . . Yeah, that would be all right. It was one of the Grimm Brothers' gentler tales. Nobody in it got eaten alive or hacked to death by a troll.

'Surrender!'

It was Connie's voice this time.

Harry opened his eyes and frowned at her. He was afraid she would give away their position. True, he had not been able to pinpoint the perp by listening to him; sounds bounced around the attic in strange ways, which was a protection for them as well as for the madman. Nevertheless, silence was wiser.

The perp shouted again: '*A Mess of Blues*, *Heartbreak Hotel!*'

'Surrender!' Connie repeated.

'*Go Away Little Girl!*'

Connie grimaced. 'That wasn't Elvis, you peabrain! That was Steve Lawrence. Surrender.'

'*Stay Away.*'

'Surrender.'

Harry blinked sweat out of his eyes and studied Connie with incomprehension. He had never felt less in control of a situation. Something was going down between her and the lunatic, but Harry didn't have a clue as to what it was.

'*I Don't Care If the Sun Don't Shine.*'

'Surrender.'

Suddenly Harry remembered that 'Surrender' was the title of a Presley classic.

'*Stay Away.*'

He thought that might be another Presley song.

Connie slipped into one of the aisles, out of Harry's sight, as she called out: 'It's Now or Never.'

'*What'd I Say?*'

Moving away into the maze, Connie answered the perp with two Presley titles: 'Surrender. I Beg of You.'

'*I Feel So Bad.*'

After a hesitation, Connie responded: 'Tell Me Why.'

'*Don't Ask Me Why.*'

A dialogue had been established. In Presley song titles. Like some bizarre television quiz-show contest with no prizes for correct answers but plenty of peril for wrong ones.

In a crouch, Harry eased into a different aisle from the one that Connie had taken. A spider's web wrapped his face. He pulled it off and crept deeper into the mannequin-guarded shadows.

Connie resorted to a previously used title: 'Surrender.'

'*Stay Away*.'

'Are You Lonesome Tonight?'

After a hesitation, the perp admitted: '*Lonely Man*.'

Harry still couldn't get a fix on the voice. Sweat was really pouring off him now, wispy remnants of the spider web clung to his hair and tickled his brow, his mouth tasted like the bottom of a pestle in Frankenstein's laboratory, and he felt as if he'd stepped out of reality into some drug addict's dark hallucinations.

'Let Yourself Go,' Connie advised.

'*I Feel So Bad*,' the perp repeated.

Harry knew he shouldn't be so disoriented by the peculiar twists this pursuit kept taking. These were the 1990s, after all, an age of unreason if ever there had been one, when the bizarre was so common as to establish a new definition of normality. Like the holdup men who had recently taken to threatening convenience-store clerks not with guns but with syringes full of AIDS-tainted blood.

Connie called to the perp, 'Let Me Be Your Teddy Bear,' which seemed, to Harry, an odd turn in the song-title conversation.

But the perp came right back at her in a voice full of yearning and suspicion: '*You Don't Know Me.*'

Connie needed only a few seconds to find the right follow-up: 'Doncha Think It's Time?'

And talk about bizarre: Richard Ramirez, the serial killer known as the Night Stalker, was visited regularly in prison by a stream of attractive young women who found him appealing, exciting, a romantic figure. Or what about that guy in Wisconsin not long ago, cooking parts of his victims for dinner, keeping rows of severed heads in his refrigerator, and neighbors said, well, yeah, there had been bad smells coming from his apartment for years, and now and then they heard screams and high-powered electric saws, but the screaming never lasted long, and anyway the guy seemed so nice, he seemed to *care* about people. The 1990s. No decade like it.

'*Too Much,*' the perp finally said, evidently disbelieving Connie's professed romantic interest.

'Poor Boy,' she said with apparently genuine sympathy.

'*Way Down.*' The perp's voice, now annoyingly whiny, echoed off the cobwebbed rafters as he admitted his lack of self-esteem, a very '90s sort of excuse.

'Wear My Ring Around Your Neck,' Connie said, romancing him as she prowled through the maze, no doubt intending to blow him away the moment she caught sight of him.

The perp didn't reply.

Harry kept on the move, too, diligently searching each shadowy niche and byway, but feeling useless. He had never imagined that in the last decade of this strange century, he might have to be an expert on rock-'n'-roll trivia to be an effective cop.

He hated crap like this, but Connie loved it. She embraced the chaos of the times; there was something dark and wild in her.

Harry reached an aisle that was perpendicular to his. It was deserted – except for a couple of naked mannequins that had toppled over long ago, one atop the other. Hunkered down, shoulders hunched protectively, Harry moved on.

'Wear My Ring Around Your Neck,' Connie called out again from elsewhere in the maze.

Maybe the perp was hesitating because he thought it was an offer that a guy should make to a gal, not the other way around. Though definitely a '90s man, maybe the bastard still had an old-fashioned sense of gender roles.

'Treat Me Nice,' Connie said.

No answer.

'Love Me Tender,' Connie said.

The perp still did not respond, and Harry was alarmed that the conversation had become a monologue. The creep might be close to Connie, letting her talk so he could get a better, final fix on her.

Harry was about to shout a warning when an explosion shook the building. He froze, crossing his arms protectively over his face. But the blast had not occurred in the attic; there had been no flash.

From the floor below came cries of agony and terror, confused voices, shouts of anger.

Evidently other cops had entered the lower room

where the ladder gave access to the attic, and the perp had heard them. He'd dropped a grenade through the trapdoor.

The gruesome screams conjured an image in Harry's mind: some guy trying to keep his intestines from spilling out of his belly.

He knew that he and Connie were in a rare moment of total agreement, experiencing the same dread and fury. For once he didn't give a damn about the perp's legal rights, excessive use of force, or the proper way of doing things. He just wanted the bastard dead.

Above the screams, Connie tried to re-establish the dialogue: 'Love Me Tender.'

'*Tell Me Why*,' the perp demanded, still doubting her sincerity.

'My Baby Left Me,' Connie said.

The screams were subsiding on the floor below. Either the injured man was dying, or others were moving him out of the room where the grenade had detonated.

'Anyway You Want Me,' Connie said.

The perp was silent for a moment. Then his voice echoed through the room, infuriatingly directionless, '*I Feel So Bad*.'

'I'm Yours,' Connie said.

Harry couldn't get over the speed with which she thought of the appropriate titles.

'*Lonely Man*,' the perp said, and indeed he sounded miserable.

'I've Got a Thing About You Baby,' Connie said.

She's a genius, Harry thought admiringly. And seriously obsessed with Presley.

Counting on the perp being pretty much distracted by Connie's weird seduction, Harry risked showing himself. Because he was directly under the peak of the roof, he rose slowly to his full height, and surveyed the garret on all sides.

Some piles of boxes were shoulder-high, but many others were only a few inches higher than Harry's waist. A lot of human forms stared back from the shadows, tucked in among the boxes and even sitting on them. But all of them must have been mannequins because none moved or shot at him.

'*Lonely Man. All Shook Up*,' the perp said despairingly.

'There's Always Me.'

'*Please Don't Stop Loving Me.*'

'Can't Help Falling in Love,' Connie said.

Standing, Harry had a slightly better sense of the direction from which the voices arose. Both Connie and the perp were ahead of him, but at first he couldn't discern if they were close to each other. He could not see over the boxes into any of the other avenues of the maze.

'*Don't Be Cruel*,' the perp pleaded.

'Love Me,' Connie urged.

'*I Need Your Love Tonight*.'

They were at the west end of the attic, the south side, and they *were* close to each other.

'Stuck on You,' Connie insisted.

'*Don't Be Cruel.*'

Harry sensed an escalation in the intensity of the dialogue, subtly conveyed in the gunman's tone, in

the speed of responses, and in his repetition of the
same title.

'I Need Your Love Tonight.'

'*Don't Be Cruel.*'

Harry stopped putting caution first. He hurried
toward the voices, into an area more densely populated
by mannequins, groups clustered in niches between
boxes. Pale shoulders, graceful arms, hands pointing
or raised as if in greeting. Painted eyes sightless in
the gloom, painted lips eternally parted in half-formed
smiles, in greetings never vocalized, in passionless
erotic sighs.

More spiders lived there, too, evidenced by webs that
tangled in his hair and stuck to his clothes. As he moved,
he wiped the gossamer off his face. Wispy rags of it
dissolved on his tongue and lips, and his mouth flooded
with saliva as nausea gripped him. He choked down his
gorge and expelled a wad of spittle and spider stuff.

'It's Now or Never,' Connie promised from somewhere nearby.

The familiar answering three words had become less
of a plea than a warning: '*Don't Be Cruel.*'

Harry had the feeling the guy wasn't being lulled at
all but was ticking toward a new explosion.

He proceeded another few feet and stopped, turning
his head from side to side, listening intently, afraid he
would miss something because the booming of his own
heart was so loud in his ears.

'I'm Yours, Puppet on a String, Let Yourself Go,'
Connie urged, voice falling to a stage whisper to foster
a false sense of intimacy with her prey.

51

Although Harry respected Connie's skills and instincts, he was afraid that her eagerness to sucker the perp was distracting her from the realization that the perp might not be responding out of his confusion and longing but out of a similar desire to sucker *her*.

'Playing for Keeps, One Broken Heart for Sale,' Connie said.

She sounded as if she was right on top of Harry, in the next aisle, surely no farther than two aisles away, and parallel with him.

'Ain't that Loving You Baby, Crying in the Chapel.' Connie's whisper had grown more fierce than seductive, as if she was also aware that something had gone wrong with the dialogue.

Harry tensed, waiting for the perp's response, squinting into the gloom ahead, then turning to look back the way he had come when he imagined the smiling, moon-faced killer stealing up behind him.

The attic seemed to be not merely silent but the source of all silence, as the sun was the source of light. The unseen spiders moved with perfect stealth through all the dark corners of that high room, and millions of dust motes drifted as soundlessly as planets and asteroids in the airless void of space, and on both sides of Harry, gatherings of mannequins stared without seeing, listened without hearing, posed without knowing.

Forced between clenched teeth, hard as a threat, Connie's whisper had ceased to be an invitation, had become a challenge; and song titles no longer constituted her entire rap: 'Anyway You Want Me, you toad, come on, come to mama. Let Yourself Go, dirtbag.'

No reply.

The attic was silent but also eerily still, filled with less motion than a dead man's mind.

Harry had the strange feeling that he was becoming one of the mannequins that stood around him, his flesh transformed into plaster, his bones into steel rods, sinews and tendons changing into bundles of wire. He let only his eyes move, and his gaze slid across the inanimate citizens of the garret.

Painted eyes. Pale breasts with permanently erect nipples, round thighs, tight buttocks, curving away into darkness. Hairless torsos. Men and women. Bald heads or matted wigs caked with dust.

Painted lips. Puckered as if to plant a kiss, or in a playful pout, or parted slightly as if in erotic surprise at the electricity of a lover's touch, others formed into shy smiles, some coy, some with a broader curve, the dull gleam of teeth, here a more thoughtful smile, and there a full and perpetual laugh. No. Wrong. The dull gleam of teeth. Mannequin teeth don't gleam. No saliva on mannequin teeth.

Which one, there, there, in the back of the niche, behind four true mannequins, one clever mime, peering out between bald and bewigged heads, almost lost in shadows but moist eyes glistening in the dimness, no more than six feet away, face to face, the smile opening wider as Harry watched, wider but as humorless as a wound, the weak chin, the moon face, and one more song title so soft as to be barely audible, '*Blue Moon*,'

Harry taking in all of this in an instant, even as he was bringing up the muzzle of his revolver and squeezing the trigger.

The perp opened fire with his Browning 9mm maybe a fraction of a second before Harry did, and the attic was filled with the crashes and echoes of shots. He saw the flash of the pistol's muzzle, which seemed to be directly in front of his chest, oh God please, and he emptied his revolver faster than seemed possible, all in a blink if he'd dared to blink, the weapon bucking so hard that it seemed likely to fly out of his grip.

Something hit him hard in the gut, and he knew he had been shot, though he had no pain yet, just a sharp pressure and a flare of heat. And before the pain could follow, he was knocked backward, mannequins toppling into him, driving him against the wall of the aisle. The stacked boxes rocked, and some were dislodged into the next branch of the maze. Harry was carried to the floor in a clatter of plaster limbs and hard pale bodies, trapped under them, gasping for breath, trying to shout for help, able to make no sound louder than a wheeze. He smelled the distinct metallic odor of blood.

Someone snapped on the attic lights, a long string of small bulbs hanging just under the peak of the roof, but that improved visibility only for a second or two, just long enough for Harry to see that the perp was part of the weight that held him on the floor. The moon face peered down from the top of the heap, between the naked interlocking limbs and past the hairless skulls of the mannequins, his eyes now as sightless as theirs. His smile was gone. His lips were painted, but with blood.

54

Although Harry knew that the lights were not actually going out, it seemed as though they were on a dimmer being cycled off. He tried to call out for help but still could only wheeze. His gaze shifted from the moon face toward the fading lightbulbs overhead. The last thing he saw was a rafter streaming with tattered cobwebs. Cobwebs that fluttered like the flags of long-lost nations. Then he slipped into darkness as deep as a dead man's dream.

·7·

Out of the west-northwest, ominous clouds rolled like silent battalions of war machines, driven by a high-altitude wind. Though the day was still calm and pleasantly warm at ground level, the blue sky steadily vanished behind those thunderheads.

Janet Marco parked her broken-down Dodge at one end of the alleyway. With her five-year-old son Danny and the stray dog that had recently attached itself to them, she walked along that narrow back-street, examining the contents of one garbage can after another, seeking survival in the discards of others.

The east side of the alley was flanked by a deep but narrow ravine filled with immense eucalyptus trees and a tangle of dried brush, while the west side was defined by a series of two- and three-car garages separated by wrought-iron and painted-wood gates. Beyond some of the gates, Janet glimpsed small patios and cobbled courtyards shaded by palms, magnolias, ficuses, and

Australian tree ferns that flourished in the ocean air. The houses all faced the Pacific over the roofs of other houses on lower tiers of the Laguna hills, so they were mostly three stories tall, vertical piles of stone and stucco and weathered cedar shingles designed to make maximum use of the expensive real estate.

Though the neighborhood was affluent, the rewards of scavenging were pretty much the same there as anywhere else: aluminum cans that could be returned to a recycling center for pennies, and redeemable bottles. However, once in a while she found a treasure: bags of clothes that were out of style but looked unworn, broken appliances that would fetch a couple of dollars from a second-hand shop if they needed only minor repairs, unwanted costume jewelry, or books and old-fashioned phonograph records that could be resold to specialty shops for collectors.

Danny toted a plastic garbage bag into which Janet dropped the aluminum cans. She carried another bag to hold the bottles.

As they progressed along the alleyway, under a rapidly darkening sky, Janet repeatedly glanced back at the Dodge. She worried about the car and tried never to get more than two blocks from it, keeping it in sight as much as possible. The car was not only a means of conveyance; it was their shelter from the sun and the rain, and a place to store their meager belongings. It was home.

She lived in dread of a mechanical breakdown severe enough to be irreparable – or irreparable within their means, which was the same thing. But she was most afraid of theft, because with the car gone they would have no roof over their heads, no safe place to sleep.

She knew that no one was likely to steal such a rolling wreck. The thief's desperation would have to exceed Janet's own, and she could not conceive of anyone more desperate than she was.

From a large brown plastic trash can, she extracted half a dozen aluminum cans that someone had already flattened and that ought to have been separated for recycling. She put them in Danny's garbage bag.

The boy watched solemnly. He said nothing. He was a quiet child. His father had intimidated him into being the next thing to a mute, and in the year since Janet had cut that domineering bastard out of their lives, Danny had become only slightly less withdrawn.

Janet glanced back at the car. Still there.

Cloud shadows fell over the alleyway, and a soft salt-scented breeze arose. From far out over the sea came a low peal of thunder.

She hurried to the next can, and Danny followed her.

The dog, which Danny had named Woofer, sniffed at the trash containers, padded to a nearby gate, and poked his snout between the iron bars. His tail wagged continuously. He was a friendly mutt, reasonably well behaved, the size of a golden retriever, with a black and brown coat, and a cute face. But Janet tolerated the cost of feeding him only because he had drawn so many smiles from the boy in the past few days. Until Woofer came along, she had almost forgotten what Danny's smile was like.

Again, she glanced at the battered Dodge. It was all right.

She looked toward the other end of the alley, and then toward the brush-choked ravine and peeling trunks of the huge eucalyptuses across the way. She was afraid not just of car thieves, and not merely of residents who might object to her rummaging through their garbage. She was also afraid of the cop who had been harassing her lately. No. Not a cop. Something that pretended to be a cop. Those strange eyes, the kind and freckled face that could change so swiftly into a creature out of a nightmare . . .

* * *

Janet Marco had one religion: fear. She had been born into that cruel faith without being aware of it, as full of wonder and the capacity for delight as any child. But her parents were alcoholics, and their sacrament of distilled spirits revealed in them an unholy rage and a capacity for sadism. They vigorously instructed her in the doctrines and dogmas of the cult of fear. She learned of only one god, which was neither a specific person nor a force; to her, god was merely power, and whoever wielded it was automatically elevated to the status of deity.

That she had fallen under the thrall of a wife-beater and control freak like Vince Marco, as soon as she was old enough to escape her parents, was no surprise. By then she was devoted to victimhood, had a need to be oppressed. Vince was lazy, shiftless, a drunkard, a gambler, a womanizer, but he was highly skilled and energetic when it came to crushing the spirit of a wife.

For eight years they had moved around the West, never staying longer than six months in any town, while Vince made a subsistence living – although not always an honest one. He didn't want Janet to develop friendships. If he remained the only consistent presence in her life, he had total control; there was no one to advise and encourage her to rebel.

As long as she was utterly subservient and wore her fear for him to see, the beatings and torments were less severe than when she was more stoical and denied him the pleasure of her anguish. The god of fear appreciated visible expressions of his disciples' devotion every bit as much as did the Christian God of love. Perversely, fear became her refuge and her only defense against even greater savageries.

And so she might have continued until she was no better than a shivering, terrorized animal cowering in its burrow . . . but Danny came along to save her. After the baby was born, she began to fear for him as much as for herself. What would happen to Danny if Vince went too far some night and, in an alcoholic frenzy, beat her to death? How would Danny cope alone, so small, so helpless? In time she feared harm to Danny *more* than to herself – which should have added to her burden but which was strangely liberating. Vince didn't realize it, but he was no longer the only consistent presence in her life. Her child, by his very existence, was an argument for rebellion and a source of courage.

She still might never have become courageous enough

to throw off her yoke if Vince had not raised his hand to the boy. One night a year ago, in a dilapidated rental house with a desert-brown lawn on the outskirts of Tucson, Vince had come home reeking of beer and sweat and some other woman's perfume, and had beaten Janet for sport. Danny was four then, too small to protect his mother but old enough to feel that he ought to defend her. When he appeared in his pajamas and tried to intervene, his father slapped him repeatedly, viciously, knocked him down, and kicked at him until the boy scrambled out of the house into the front yard, weeping and terrified.

Janet had endured the beating, but later, when both her husband and her boy were asleep, she'd gone to the kitchen and taken a knife from a wall rack near the stove. Utterly fearless for the first – and perhaps last – time in her life, she returned to the bedroom and stabbed Vince repeatedly in the throat, neck, chest, and stomach. He woke as the first wound was inflicted, tried to scream, but only gurgled as his mouth filled with blood. He resisted, briefly and ineffectually.

After checking on Danny in the next room to be sure he had not awakened, Janet wrapped Vince's body in the blood-stained bed sheets. She tied the shroud in place at his ankles and neck with clothesline, dragged him through the house, out of the kitchen door, and across the backyard.

The high moon grew alternately dim and bright as clouds like galleons sailed eastward across the sky, but Janet was not concerned about being seen. The shacks along that stretch of the state route were widely spaced, and no lights glowed in either of the two nearest homes.

Driven by the grim understanding that the police could take her from Danny as surely as Vince might have done, she hauled the corpse to the end of the property and out into the night desert, which stretched unpopulated to the far mountains. She struggled between mesquite shrubs and still-rooted tumbleweeds, across soft sand in some places and hard tables of shale in others.

When the cold face of the moon shone, it revealed a hostile landscape of stark shadows and sharp alabaster shapes. In one of the deeper shadows – an arroyo carved by centuries of flash floods – Janet abandoned the corpse.

She stripped the sheets off the body and buried those, but she didn't dig a grave for the cadaver itself because she hoped that night scavengers and vultures would pick the bones clean quicker if it was left exposed. Once the denizens of the desert had chewed and pecked the soft pads of Vince's fingers, once the sun and the carrion eaters got done with him, his identity might be deduced only by dental records. Since Vince had rarely seen a dentist, and never the same one twice, there were no records for the police to consult. With luck, the corpse would go undiscovered until the next rainy season, when the withered remains would be washed miles and miles away, tumbled and broken and mixed up with piles of other refuse, until they had essentially disappeared.

That night Janet packed what little they owned and drove away in the old Dodge with Danny. She was not even sure where she was going until she had crossed the state line and driven all the way to Orange County. That *had* to be her final destination because she couldn't afford to spend more money on gasoline just to get farther away from the dead man in the desert.

No one back in Tucson would wonder what had happened to Vince. He was a shiftless drifter, after all. Cutting loose and moving on was a way of life to him.

But Janet was deathly afraid to apply for welfare or any form of assistance. They might ask her where her husband was, and she didn't trust her ability to lie convincingly.

Besides, in spite of carrion-eaters and the dehydrating ferocity of the Arizona sun, maybe someone had stumbled across Vince's body before it had become unidentifiable. If his widow and son surfaced in California, seeking government aid, perhaps connections would be made deep in a computer, prompting an alert social worker to call the cops. Considering her tendency to succumb to anyone who exerted authority over her – a deeply ingrained trait that had been only slightly ameliorated by the murder of her husband – Janet had little chance of undergoing police scrutiny without incriminating herself.

Then they would take Danny away from her.

She could not allow that. *Would* not.

On the streets, homeless but for the rusted and rattling Dodge, Janet Marco discovered that she had a talent for survival. She was not stupid; she had just never before had the freedom to exercise her wits. From a society whose refuse could feed a significant portion of the Third World, she clawed a degree of precarious security, feeding herself and her son with recourse to a charity kitchen for the fewest possible meals.

She learned that fear, in which she had long been steeped, did not have to immobilize her. It could also motivate.

*   *   *

The breeze had grown cool and had stiffened into an erratic wind. The rumble of thunder was still far away but louder than when Janet had first heard it. Only a sliver of blue sky remained to the east, fading as fast as hope usually did.

After mining two blocks of trash containers, Janet and Danny headed back to the Dodge with Woofer in the lead.

More than halfway there, the dog suddenly stopped and cocked his head to listen for something else above the fluting of the wind and the chorus of whispery voices that were stirred from the agitated eucalyptus leaves. He grumbled and seemed briefly puzzled, then turned and looked past Janet. He bared his teeth, and the grumble sharpened into a low growl.

She knew what had drawn the dog's attention. She didn't have to look.

Nevertheless she was compelled to turn and confront the menace for Danny's sake if not her own. The Laguna Beach cop, *that* cop, was about eight feet away.

He was smiling, which is how it always started with

him. He had an appealing smile, a kind face, and beautiful blue eyes.

As always, there was no squad car, no indication of how he had arrived in the alleyway. It was as if he had been lying in wait for her among the peeling trunks of the eucalyptuses, clairvoyantly aware that her scavenging would bring her to this alley at this hour on this very day.

'How're you, Ma'am?' he asked. His voice was initially gentle, almost musical.

Janet didn't answer.

The first time he approached her last week, she had responded timidly, nervously, averting her eyes, as excruciatingly respectful of authority as she had been all her life – except for that one bloody night outside of Tucson. But she had quickly discovered that he was not what he appeared to be, and that he preferred a monologue to a dialogue.

'Looks like we're in for a little rain,' he said, glancing up at the troubled sky.

Danny had moved against Janet. She put her free arm around him, pulling him even closer. The boy was shivering.

She was shivering too. She hoped Danny didn't notice.

The dog continued to bare his teeth and growl softly.

Lowering his gaze from the stormy sky to Janet again, the cop spoke in that same lilting voice: 'Okay, no more farting around. Time to have some real fun. So what's going to happen now is . . . you've got till dawn. Understand? Hmmmmm? At dawn, I'm going to kill you and your boy.'

His threat did not surprise Janet. Anyone with authority over her had always been as a god, but always a savage god, never benign. She *expected* violence, suffering, and imminent death. She would have been surprised only by an exhibition of kindness from someone with power over her, for kindness was infinitely rarer than hatred and cruelty.

In fact, her fear, already nearly paralyzing, might have been made even greater only by that unlikely show of kindness. Kindness would have seemed, to her, nothing more than an attempt to mask some unimaginably evil motive.

The cop was still smiling, but his freckled, Irish face was no longer friendly. It was chillier than the coolish air coming off the sea in advance of the storm.

'Did you hear me, you dumb bitch?'

She said nothing.

'Are you thinking that you ought to run, get out of town, maybe go up to L.A. where I can't find you?'

She was thinking something rather like that, either Los Angeles or south to San Diego.

'Yes, please, try to run,' he encouraged. 'That'll make it more fun for me. Run, resist. Wherever you go, I'll find you, but it'll be a lot more *exciting* that way.'

Janet believed him. She had been able to escape her parents, and she had escaped Vince by killing him, but now she had come up against not merely another of the many gods of fear who had ruled her but *the* God of fear whose powers exceeded understanding.

His eyes were changing, darkening from blue to electric green.

Wind suddenly gusted strongly through the alley, whipping dead leaves and a few scraps of paper ahead of it.

The cop's eyes had become so radiantly green, there seemed to be a light source behind them, a fire within his skull. And the pupils had changed, too, until they were elongated and strange like those of a cat.

The dog's growl became a frightened whine.

In the nearby ravine the eucalyptus trees shook in the wind, and their soft soughing grew into a roar like that of an angry mob.

It seemed to Janet that the creature masquerading as a cop had commanded the wind to rise to lend more drama to his threat, though surely he did not have so much power as that.

'When I come for you at sunrise, I'll break open your bodies, eat your hearts.'

His voice had changed as completely as had his eyes. It was deep, gravelly, the malevolent voice of something that belonged in Hell.

He took a step toward them.

Janet backed up two steps, pulling Danny along. Her heart was hammering so hard, she knew her tormentor could hear it.

The dog also retreated, alternately whining and growling, his tail tucked between his legs.

'At dawn, you sorry bitch. You and your snot-nosed little brat. Sixteen hours. Only sixteen hours, bitch. Ticktock . . . ticktock . . . ticktock . . .'

The wind died in an instant. The whole world fell silent. No rustling of trees. No distant thunder.

A twig, bristling with half a dozen long eucalyptus leaves, hung in the air a few inches to her right and a foot in front of her face. It was motionless, abandoned by the whooping wind that had supported it, but still magically suspended like the dead scorpion in the souvenir acrylic paperweight that Vince had once bought at an Arizona truckstop.

The cop's freckled face stretched and bulged with amazing elasticity, like a rubber mask behind which a great pressure had been exerted. His green, catlike eyes appeared ready to pop out of his wildly deformed skull.

Janet wanted to run for the car, her haven, home, lock the door, safe in their home, and drive like hell, but couldn't do it, dared not turn her back on him. She knew she would be brought down and torn apart in spite of the promised sixteen-hour headstart, because he wanted her to watch his transformation, demanded it, and would be furious if ignored.

The powerful were intensely proud of their power. The gods of fear needed to preen and to be admired, to see how their power humbled and terrified those who were powerless before them.

The cop's distended face melted, his features running together, eyes liquefying into red pools of hot oil, the oil soaking into his doughy cheeks until he was eyeless, nose sliding into his mouth, lips spreading out across his chin and cheeks, then no chin or cheeks any more, just an oozing mass. But his waxlike flesh didn't steam or drip to the ground, so the presence of heat was probably an illusion.

Maybe all of it was an illusion, hypnosis. That would explain a lot, raise new questions, yes, but explain a lot.

His body was pulsing, writhing, changing inside his clothes. Then his clothes were dissolving into his body, as if they had never been real clothes but just another part of *him*. Briefly the new form he assumed was covered with matted black fur: an immense elongated head began taking shape on a powerful neck, hunched and gnarled shoulders, baleful yellow eyes, a ferocity of wicked teeth and two-inch claws, a movie werewolf.

On each of the four previous occasions this thing had appeared before her, it had manifested itself differently, as if to impress her with its repertoire. But she was unprepared for what it became now. It relinquished the wolf incarnation even before that body had completely taken form, and assumed a human guise once more, though not the cop. Vince. Even though the facial features were less than half developed, she believed it was going to become her dead husband. The dark hair was the same, the shape of the forehead, the color of one malevolent pale eye.

The resurrection of Vince, buried beneath Arizona sands for the past year, shook Janet more than anything else the creature had done or become, and at last she cried out in fear. Danny screamed, too, and clung even more tightly to her.

The dog did not have the fickle heart of a stray. He stopped whining and responded as if he had been with them since he was a pup. He bared his teeth, snarled, and snapped at the air in warning.

Vince's face remained less than half formed, but his body took shape, and he was naked as he had been when she had overwhelmed him in his sleep. In his throat, chest, and belly, she thought she saw the wounds left by the kitchen knife with which she had killed him: gaping gashes that were bloodless, but dark and raw and terrible.

Vince raised one arm, reaching toward her.

The dog attacked. Collarless life on the streets had not left Woofer weak or sickly. He was a strong, well-muscled animal, and when he launched himself at the apparition, he seemed to take flight as readily as a bird.

His snarl was clipped off, and he was miraculously halted in mid-air, body in the arc of attack, as if he were only an image on a videotape after someone pushed the 'pause' button. Flash-frozen. Foamy slaver shone like frost on his black lips and in the fur around his muzzle, and his teeth gleamed as coldly as rows of small sharp icicles.

The eucalyptus twig, clothed in silvery-green leaves, hung unsupported to Janet's right, the dog to her left. The atmosphere seemed to have crystallized, trapping Woofer for eternity in his moment of courage, yet Janet was able to breathe when she remembered to try.

Still half formed, Vince stepped toward her, passing the dog.

She turned and ran, pulling Danny with her, expecting to freeze in mid-step. What would it feel like? Would darkness fall over her when she was paralyzed or would she still be able to see Vince walk into view from behind her and come eye to eye again? Would she drop into a well of silence or be able to hear the dead man's hateful voice? Feel the pain of each blow that he rained on her or be as insensate as the levitated eucalyptus twig?

Like flood waters, a tide of wind roared through the alleyway, nearly knocking her over. The world was filled with sound again.

She spun around and looked back in time to see Woofer return to life in mid-air and finish his interrupted leap. But there was no longer anyone for him to attack. Vince was gone. The dog landed on the pavement, slipped, skidded, rolled over, and sprang to his feet again, snapping his head around in fear and confusion, looking for his prey as if it had vanished before his eyes.

Danny was crying.

The threat seemed to have passed. The backstreet was deserted but for Janet, her boy, and the dog. Nevertheless, she hurried Danny toward the car, eager to get away, glancing repeatedly at the brush-filled ravine and at the deep shadows between the huge trees as she passed them, half expecting the troll to climb out of its lair again, ready to feed on their hearts sooner than it had promised.

Lightning flickered. The roar of thunder was louder and closer than before.

The air smelled of the rain to come. That ozone taint reminded Janet of the stink of hot blood.

·8·

Harry Lyon was sitting at a corner table at the rear of the burger restaurant, clasping a water glass in his right hand, his left hand fisted on his thigh. Now and then he took a sip of water, and each sip seemed colder than the one before it, as if the glass absorbed a chill, instead of heat, from his hand.

His gaze traveled over the toppled furniture, ruined plants, broken glass, scattered food, and congealing blood. Nine wounded had been carried away, but two dead bodies lay where they had fallen. A police photographer and lab technicians were at work.

Harry was aware of the room and the people in it, the periodic flash of the camera, but what he saw more clearly was the remembered moon face of the perpetrator peering down at him through the tangled limbs of the mannequins. The parted lips wet with blood. The twin windows of his eyes and the view of Hell beyond.

Harry was no less surprised to be alive now than when they had pulled the dead man and the department-store dummies off him. His stomach still ached dully where the plaster hand of the mannequin had poked into him with the full weight of the perp behind it. He'd thought he'd been shot. The perp had fired twice at close range, but evidently both rounds had been deflected by the intervening plaster torsos and limbs.

Of the five rounds that Harry had fired, at least three had done major damage.

Plainclothes detectives and techs passed in and out of the nearby, bullet-torn kitchen door, on their way to or from the second floor and attic. Some spoke to him or clapped him on the shoulder.

'Good work, Harry.'

'Harry, you okay?'

'Nice job, man.'

'You need anything, Harry?'

'Some shitstorm, huh, Harry?'

He murmured 'thanks' or 'yes' or 'no' or just shook his head. He wasn't ready for conversation with any of them, and he certainly wasn't ready to be a hero.

A crowd had gathered outside, pressing eagerly against police barriers, gawking through both broken and unbroken windows. He tried to ignore them because too many of them seemed to resemble the perp, their eyes shining with a fever glaze and their pleasant everyday faces unable to conceal strange hungers.

Connie came through the swinging door from the kitchen, righted an overturned chair, and sat at the table with him. She held a small notebook from which she read. 'His name was James Ordegard. Thirty-one. Unmarried. Lived in Laguna. Engineer. No police record. Not even a traffic citation.'

'What's his connection with this place? Ex-wife, girl-friend work here?'

'No. So far we can't find a connection. Nobody who works here remembers ever seeing him before.'

'Carrying a suicide note?'

'Nope. Looks like random violence.'

'They talk to anyone where he works?'

She nodded. 'They're stunned. He was a good worker, happy— '

'The usual model citizen.'

'That's what they say.'

The photographer took a few more shots of the nearer corpse – a woman in her thirties. The strobe flashes were jarringly bright, and Harry realized that the day beyond the windows had grown overcast since he and Connie had come in for lunch.

'He have friends, family?' Harry asked.

'We have names, but we haven't talked to them yet. Neighbors either.' She closed the notebook. 'How you doin'?'

'I've been better.'

'How's your gut?'

'Not bad, almost normal. It'll be a lot worse tomorrow. Where the hell did he get the grenades?'

She shrugged. 'We'll find out.'

The third grenade, dropped through the attic trapdoor into the room below, had caught a Laguna Beach officer by surprise. He was now in Hoag Hospital, desperately clinging to life.

'Grenades.' Harry was still disbelieving. 'You ever hear anything like it?'

He was immediately sorry he had asked the question. He knew it would get her started on her favorite subject – the pre-millennium cotillion, the continuing crisis of these new dark ages.

Connie frowned and said, 'Ever hear anything like it? Not like, maybe, but just as bad, worse, lots worse. Last year in Nashville, a woman killed her

73

handicapped boyfriend by setting his wheelchair on fire.'

Harry sighed.

She said, 'Eight teenagers in Boston raped and killed a woman. You know what their excuse was? They were bored. Bored. The city was at fault, you see, for doing so little to provide kids with free leisure activities.'

He glanced at the people crowding the crime-scene barriers beyond the front windows – then quickly averted his eyes.

He said, 'Why do you collect these nuggets?'

'Look, Harry, it's the Age of Chaos. Get with the times.'

'Maybe I'd rather be an old fogey.'

'To be a good cop in the '90s, you've gotta be *of* the '90s. You gotta be in sync with the rhythms of destruction. Civilization is coming down around our ears. Everyone wants a license, no one wants responsibility, so the center won't hold. You've gotta know when to break a rule to save the system – and how to surf on every random wave of madness that comes along.'

He just stared at her, which was easy enough, much easier than considering what she had said, because it scared him to think she might be right. He couldn't consider it. Wouldn't. Not right now, anyway. And the sight of her lovely face was a welcome distraction.

Although she did not measure up to the current American standard of ultimate gorgeousness set by beer-commercial bimbos on television, and though she did not possess the sweaty exotic allure of the female rock stars with mutant cleavage and eight pounds of stage makeup who unaccountably aroused a whole generation of young males, Connie Gulliver was attractive. At least Harry thought so. Not that he had any romantic interest in her. He did not. But he was a man, she was a woman, and they worked closely together, so it was natural for him to notice that her dark-brown-almost-black hair was beautifully thick with a silken luster though she cropped it short and combed it with her fingers. Her eyes were an odd shade of blue, violet when light struck them at a certain angle, and might have been irresistibly enticing if they had not been the watchful, suspicious eyes of a cop.

She was thirty-three, four years younger than Harry. In rare moments when she let her guard down, she looked twenty-five. Most of the time, however, the dark wisdom acquired from policework made her seem older than she was.

'What're you staring at?' she asked.

'Just wondering if you're really as hard inside as you pretend to be.'

'You ought to know by now.'

'That's just it – I ought to.'

'Don't get Freudian on me, Harry.'

'I won't.' He took a sip of water.

'One thing I like about you is, you don't try to psychoanalyze everyone. All that stuff's a load of crap.'

'I agree.'

He wasn't surprised to find they shared an attitude. In spite of their many differences, they were enough alike to work well as partners. But because Connie avoided self-revelation, Harry had no idea whether they had arrived at their similar attitudes for similar – or totally opposed – reasons.

Sometimes it seemed important to understand why she held certain convictions. At other times Harry was equally sure that encouraging intimacy would lead to a messier relationship. He hated messiness. Often it was wise to avoid familiarity in a professional association, keep a comfortable distance, a buffer zone – especially when you were both carrying firearms.

In the distance, thunder rolled.

A cool draft slipped across the jagged edges of the big broken window and all the way to the back of the restaurant. Discarded paper napkins fluttered on the floor.

The prospect of rain pleased Harry. The world needed to be cleansed, freshened.

Connie said, 'You going to check in for a mind massage?'

Following a shooting, they were encouraged to take a few sessions of counseling.

'No,' Harry said. 'I'm fine.'

'Why don't you knock off, go home?'

'Can't leave you with everything.'

'I can handle it here.'

'What about all the paperwork?'

'I can do that too.'

'Yeah, but your reports are always full of typos.'

She shook her head. 'Your clock's wound too tight, Harry.'

'It's all computers, but you don't even bother to run the spell-check program.'

'I just had grenades thrown at me. Fuck spell-check.'

He nodded and got up from the table. 'I'll go back to the office and start writing up the report.'

Accompanied by another long, low rumble of thunder, a couple of morgue attendants in white jackets approached the dead woman. Under the supervision of an assistant coroner, they prepared to remove the victim from the scene.

Connie handed her notebook to Harry. For his report, he would need some of the facts she had collected.

'See you later,' she said.

'Later.'

One of the attendants unfolded an opaque body bag. It had been doubled so tightly upon itself that the layers of plastic separated with a sticky, crackling, unpleasantly organic noise.

Harry was surprised by a wave of nausea.

The dead woman had been facedown with her head turned away from him. He had heard another detective say that she had been shot in the chest and face. He didn't want to see her when they rolled her over to put her into the bag.

Quelling his nausea with an effort of will, he turned away and headed for the front door.

Connie said, 'Harry?'

Reluctantly he looked back.

She said, 'Thanks.'

'You too.'

That was probably the only reference they would ever make to the fact that their survival had depended on being a good team.

He continued toward the front door, dreading the crowd of onlookers.

From behind him came a wet, suction-breaking sound as they lifted the woman out of the congealing blood that half glued her to the floor.

Sometimes he could not remember why he had become a cop. It seemed not a career choice but an act of madness.

He wondered what he might have become if he had never entered police work, but as always his mind blanked on that one. Perhaps there *was* such a thing as destiny, a power infinitely greater than the force which drove the earth around the sun and kept the planets in alignment, moving men and women through life as if they were only pieces on a game board. Perhaps free will was nothing more than a desperate illusion.

The uniformed officer at the front door stepped aside to let him out. 'It's a zoo,' he said.

Harry wasn't sure if the cop was referring to life in general or just to the mob of onlookers.

Outside, the day was considerably cooler than when Harry and Connie had gone into the restaurant for lunch. Above the screen of trees, the sky was as gray as cemetery granite.

Beyond police sawhorses and a barrier of taut yellow crime-scene tape, sixty or eighty people jostled one another and craned their necks for a better view of the carnage. Young people with new-wave haircuts stood shoulder to shoulder with senior citizens, businessmen in suits next to beachboys in cutoffs and Hawaiian shirts. A few were eating huge chocolate-chip cookies bought at a nearby bakery, and they were generally festive, as if none of *them* would ever die.

Harry was uncomfortably aware that the crowd took an interest in him when he stepped out of the restaurant. He avoided meeting anyone's gaze. He didn't want to see what emptiness their eyes might reveal.

He turned right and moved past the first of the large windows, which was still intact. Ahead was the broken pane where only a few toothlike shards still bristled from the frame. Glass littered the concrete.

The sidewalk was empty between the police barriers and the front of the building – and then a young man of about twenty slipped under the yellow tape where it bridged the gap between two curbside trees. He crossed the sidewalk as if unaware that Harry was approaching, his eyes and attention fixed intently on something inside the restaurant.

'Please stay behind the barrier,' Harry said.

The man – more accurately a kid in well-worn tennis shoes, jeans, and a Tecate beer T-shirt – stopped at the shattered window, giving no indication that he had heard the warning. He leaned through the frame, fiercely focused on something inside.

Harry glanced into the restaurant and saw the body of the woman being maneuvered into a morgue bag.

'I told you to stay behind the barrier.'

They were close now. The kid was an inch or two

shorter than Harry's six feet, lean, with thick black hair. He stared at the corpse, at the morgue attendants' glistening latex gloves which grew redder by the moment. He seemed unaware that Harry was at his side, looming over him.

'Did you hear me?'

The kid was unresponsive. His lips were parted slightly in breathless anticipation. His eyes were glazed, as though he'd been hypnotized.

Harry put a hand on the boy's shoulder.

Slowly the kid turned from the slaughter, but he still had a faraway look, staring *through* Harry. His eyes were the gray of lightly tarnished silver. His pink tongue slowly licked his lower lip, as if he had just taken a bite of something tasty.

Neither the punk's failure to obey nor the arrogance of his blank stare was what set Harry off. Irrationally, perhaps, it was that tongue, the obscene pink tip leaving a wet trail on lips that were too full. Suddenly Harry wanted to hammer his face, split his lips, break out his teeth, drive him to his knees, shatter his insolence, and teach him something about the value of life and respect for the dead.

He grabbed the kid, and before he quite knew what was happening, he was half shoving and half carrying him away from the window, back across the sidewalk. Maybe he hit the creep, maybe not, he didn't think so, but he manhandled him as roughly as if he had caught him in the act of mugging or molesting someone, wrenched and jerked him around, bent him double, and forced him under the crime-scene tape.

The punk went down hard on his hands and knees, and the crowd moved back to give him a little room. Gasping for breath, he rolled onto his side and glared up at Harry. His hair had fallen across his face. His T-shirt was torn. *Now* his eyes were in focus and his attention won.

The onlookers murmured excitedly. The scene in the restaurant was passive entertainment, the killer dead by the time they arrived, but this was real action right in front of their eyes. It was as if a television screen had expanded to allow them to step through the glass, and now they were part of a real cop drama, right in the middle of the thrills and chills; and when he looked at their faces, Harry saw that they were hoping the script was colorful and violent, a story worth recounting to their families and friends over dinner.

Abruptly he was sickened by his own behavior, and he turned from the kid. He walked fast to the end of the building, which extended to the end of the block, and slipped under the yellow tape at a spot where no crowd was gathered.

The department car was parked around the corner, two-thirds of the way along the next tree-lined block. With the onlookers behind him and out of sight, Harry began to tremble. The trembling escalated into violent shivering.

Halfway to the car he stopped and leaned one hand against the rough trunk of a tree. He took slow deep breaths.

A peal of thunder shook the sky above the canopy of trees.

A phantom dancer, made of dead leaves and litter, spun down the center of the street in the embrace of a whirlwind.

He had dealt much too harshly with the kid. He'd been reacting not to what the kid had done but to everything that had happened in the restaurant and the attic. Delayed-stress syndrome.

But more than that: he had needed to strike out at something, someone, God or man, in frustration over the stupidity of it all, the injustice, the pure blind cruelty of fate. Like some grim bird of despair, his mind kept circling back to the two dead people in the restaurant, the wounded, the cop clinging to a thread of life at Hoag Hospital, their tortured husbands and wives and parents, bereaved children, mourning friends, the many links in the terrible chain of grief that was forged by each death.

The kid had just been a convenient target.

Harry knew he ought to go back and apologize, but couldn't. It was not the kid he dreaded facing as much as that ghoulish crowd.

'The little creep needed a lesson anyway,' he said, justifying his actions to himself.

He had treated the kid more like Connie might have done. Now he even sounded like Connie.

. . . you've gotta be in sync with the rhythms of destruction . . . civilization is coming down around our ears . . . gotta know when to break a rule to save the system . . . surf on every random wave of madness that comes along . . .

Harry loathed that attitude.

Violence, madness, envy, and hatred would not consume them all. Compassion, reason, and understanding
would inevitably prevail. Bad times? Sure, the world had
known plenty of bad times, hundreds of millions dead
in wars and pogroms, the official murderous lunacies
of fascism and communism, but there had been a few
precious eras of peace, too, and societies that worked
at least for a while, so there was always hope.

He stopped leaning on the tree. He stretched, trying
to loosen his cramped muscles.

The day had started out so well, but it sure had gone
to hell in a hurry.

He was determined to get it back on track. Paperwork
would help. Nothing like official reports and forms
in triplicate to make the world seem ordered and
rational.

Out in the street, the whirlwind had gathered more
dust and detritus. Earlier the ghost dancer had appeared
to be waltzing along the blacktop. Now it was doing
a frantic jitterbug. As Harry took a step away from
the tree, the column of debris changed course, zigged
toward him, and burst upon him with startling power,
forcing him to shut his eyes against the abrasive grit.

For one crazy moment he thought he was going to
be swept up as Dorothy had been, and spun off to Oz.
Tree limbs rattled and shook overhead, shedding more
leaves on him. The huffing and keening of the wind
briefly swelled into a shriek, a howl – but in the next
instant fell into graveyard stillness.

Someone spoke directly in front of Harry, voice low
and raspy and strange: 'Ticktock, ticktock.'

83

Harry opened his eyes and wished he hadn't.

A hulking denizen of the streets, fully six feet five, odious and clad in rags, stood before him, no more than two feet away. His face was grossly disfigured by scars and weeping sores. His eyes were narrowed, little more than slits, and gummy white curds clogged the corners. The breath that came between the hobo's rotten teeth and across his suppurating lips was so foul that Harry gagged on the stench.

'Ticktock, ticktock,' the vagrant repeated. He spoke quietly, but the effect was like a shout because his voice seemed to be the only sound in the world. A preternatural silence draped the day.

Feeling threatened by the size and by the extravagant filthiness of the stranger, Harry took a step backward. The man's greasy hair was matted with dirt, bits of grass, and leaf fragments; dried food and worse was crusted in his tangled beard. His hands were dark with grime, and the under side of every ragged, overgrown fingernail was tar-black. He was no doubt a walking petri dish in which thrived every deadly disease known to man, and an incubator of new viral and bacterial horrors.

'Ticktock, ticktock.' The hobo grinned. 'You'll be dead in sixteen hours.'

'Back off,' Harry warned.

'Dead by dawn.'

The hobo opened his squinched eyes. They were crimson from lid to lid and corner to corner, without irises or pupils, as if there were only panes of glass where eyes should have been and only a store of blood within the skull.

'Dead by dawn,' the hobo repeated.

Then he exploded. It wasn't anything like a grenade blast, no killing shockwaves or gush of heat, no deafening boom, just a sudden end to the unnatural stillness and a violent influx of wind, *whoosh!* The hobo appeared to disintegrate, not into particles of flesh and gouts of blood but into pebbles and dust and leaves, into twigs and flower petals and dry clods of earth, into pieces of old rags and scraps of yellowed newspapers, bottle caps, glittering specks of glass, torn theater tickets, bird feathers, string, candy wrappers, chewing-gum foil, bent and rusted nails, crumpled paper cups, lost buttons . . .

The churning column of debris burst over Harry. He was forced to close his eyes again as the mundane remains of the fantastic hobo pummeled him.

When he could open his eyes without risk of injury, he spun around, looking in every direction, but the airborne trash was gone, dispersed to all corners of the day. No whirlwind. No ghost dancer. No hobo: he had vanished.

Harry turned around again in disbelief, gaping.

His heart knocked fiercely.

From another street, a car horn blared. A pickup truck turned the corner, approaching him, engine growling. On the other side of the street, a young couple walked hand in hand, and the woman's laughter was like the ringing of small silver bells.

Suddenly Harry realized just *how* unnaturally quiet the day had become between the appearance and departure of the rag-clothed giant. Other than the gravelly and malevolent voice and what few sounds of movement the hobo made, the street had been as silent as any place a thousand leagues beneath the sea or in the vacuum of space between galaxies.

Lightning flashed. The shadows of tree limbs twitched on the sidewalk around him.

Thunder drummed the fragile membrane of the sky, drummed harder, the heavens grew blacker as if lightning-burnt, the air temperature seemed to drop ten degrees in an instant, and the laden clouds split. A scattering of fat raindrops snapped against the leaves, *ponged* off the hoods of parked cars, painted dark blotches on Harry's clothes, splattered his face, and drove a chill deep into his bones.

TWO

·1·

The world appeared to be dissolving beyond the windshield of the parked car, as if the clouds had released torrents of a universal solvent. Silver rain sluiced down the glass, and the trees outside seemed to melt as readily as green crayons. Hurrying pedestrians fused with their colorful umbrellas and deliquesced into the gray downpour.

Harry Lyon felt as if he would be liquefied as well, rendered into an insensate solution and swiftly washed away. His comfortable world of granite reason and steely logic was eroding around him, and he was powerless to halt the disintegration.

He could not decide whether he had actually seen the burly vagrant or merely hallucinated him.

God knew, an underclass of the dispossessed wandered the American landscape these days. The more money the government spent to reduce their numbers, the more of them there were, until it began to seem as if they were not the result of any public policy or lack of it but a divine scourge. Like so many people, Harry had learned to look away from them or through them because there seemed to be nothing he could do to help them in any significant way . . . and because their very existence raised disturbing questions about the stability of his own future. Most were pathetic and harmless. But some were undeniably strange, their faces enlivened by the ticks and twitches of neurotic compulsions, driven by obsessive needs, the gleam of madness in their eyes, the capacity for violence evident in the unremitting coiled tension of their bodies. Even in a town like Laguna Beach – portrayed in travel brochures as a pearl of the Pacific, one more California paradise – Harry could no doubt find at least a few homeless men whose demeanor and appearance were as hostile as that of the man who had seemed to come out of the whirlwind.

He could not, however, expect to find one of them with scarlet eyes lacking irises and pupils. He was not confident, either, about the probability of locating any street person who could manifest himself out of a dust devil, or explode into a collection of mundane debris and fly away on the wind.

Perhaps he had imagined the encounter.

That was a possibility Harry was loath to consider. The pursuit and execution of James Ordegard had been traumatic. But he didn't believe being caught in Ordegard's bloody rampage was sufficiently stressful to cause hallucinations replete with dirty fingernails and killer halitosis.

If the filthy giant was real, where had he come from? Where had he gone, who had he been, what disease or birth defect had left him with those terrifying eyes?

Ticktock, ticktock, you'll be dead by dawn.

He twisted the key in the ignition and started the engine.

Paperwork awaited him, soothingly tedious, with blanks to fill in and boxes to check. A neatly typed file would reduce the messy Ordegard case to crisp paragraphs of words on clean white paper, and then none of it would seem as inexplicable as it did at that moment.

He wouldn't include the crimson-eyed hobo in his report, of course. That had nothing to do with Ordegard. Besides, he didn't want to give Connie or anyone else in Special Projects a reason to make jokes at his expense. Dressing for work unfailingly in a coat and tie, being disdainful of foul language in a profession rife with it, going by the book at all times, and being obsessive about the neatness of his case files already made him a frequent target of their humor. But later, at home, he might type up a report about the hobo, just for himself, as a way of bringing order to the bizarre experience and putting it behind him.

'Lyon,' he said, meeting his own eyes in the rearview mirror, 'you *are* a ridiculous specimen.'

He switched on the windshield wipers, and the melting world solidified.

The afternoon sky was so overcast that the street lamps, which were operated by a solar-sensitive switch, were deceived by the false twilight. The pavement glistened, shiny black. All of the gutters were full of fast-moving, dirty water.

He went south on Pacific Coast Highway, but instead of turning east on Crown Valley Parkway toward Special Projects, he kept going. He passed Ritz Cove, then the turn-off for the Ritz-Carlton Hotel, and drove all the way into Dana Point.

When he pulled up in front of Enrique Estefan's house, he was somewhat surprised, although subconsciously he had known where he was headed.

The house was one of those charming bungalows built in the '40s or early '50s, before soulless stucco tract homes had become *the* architecture of choice. Decoratively carved shutters, scalloped fascia, and a multiple-pitch roof gave it character. Rain drizzled off the fronds of the big date palms in the front yard.

During a brief lull in the downpour, he left the car and ran up the walkway. By the time he climbed the three brick steps onto the porch, the rain was coming down hard again. There was no wind any more, as if the great weight of the rain suppressed it.

Shadows waited like a gathering of old friends on the front porch, among a bench-style swing and white wooden chairs with green canvas cushions. Even on a sunny day the porch would be comfortably cool, for it was sheltered by densely interwoven, red-flowering bougainvillaea that festooned a trellis and spread across the roof.

He put his thumb on the bell push and, above the drumming of the rain, heard soft chimes inside the house.

A six-inch lizard skittered across the porch floor to the steps, and out into the storm.

Harry waited patiently. Enrique Estefan – Ricky to his friends – did not move very fast these days.

When the inner door swung open, Ricky squinted out through the screen door, clearly not happy to be disturbed. Then he grinned and said, 'Harry, good to see you.' He opened the screen door, stepped aside. '*Really* good to see you.'

'I'm dripping,' Harry said, pulling off his shoes and leaving them on the porch.

'That's not necessary,' Ricky said.

Harry entered the house in his stocking feet.

'Still the most considerate man I ever met,' Ricky said.

'That's me. Ms Manners of the gun-and-handcuff set.'

They shook hands. Enrique Estefan's grip was firm, although his hand was hot, dry, leathery, padded with too little flesh, almost withered, all knuckles and metacarpals and phalanges. It was almost like exchanging greetings with a skeleton.

'Come on in the kitchen,' Ricky said.

Harry followed him across the polished-oak floor. Ricky shuffled, never entirely lifting either foot.

The short hallway was illumined only by the light spilling in from the kitchen at the end and by a votive candle flickering in a ruby glass. The candle was part of a shrine to the Holy Mother that was set up on a narrow table against one wall. Behind it was a mirror in a silver-leafed frame. Reflections of the small flame glimmered in the silver leaf and danced in the looking glass.

'How've you been, Ricky?'

'Pretty good. You?'

'I've had better days,' Harry admitted.

Although he was Harry's height, Ricky seemed several inches shorter because he leaned forward as if progressing against a wind, his back rounded, the sharp lines of his shoulder blades poking up prominently against his pale-yellow shirt. From behind, his neck looked scrawny. The back of his skull appeared as fragile as that of an infant.

The kitchen was bigger than expected in a bungalow and a lot cheerier than the hallway: Mexican-tile floor, knotty-pine cabinetry, a large window looking on to a spacious backyard. A Kenny G number was on the radio. The air was heavy with the rich aroma of coffee.

'Like a cup?' Ricky asked.

'If it's not any trouble.'

'No trouble at all. Just made a fresh pot.'

While Ricky got a cup and saucer from one of the cabinets and poured coffee, Harry studied him. He was worried by what he saw.

Ricky's face was too thin, drawn, with deeply carved lines at the corners of his eyes and framing his mouth. His skin sagged as if it had lost nearly all elasticity. His eyes were rheumy. Maybe it was only a backsplash of color from his shirt, but his white hair had an unhealthy yellow tint, and both his face and the whites of his eyes exhibited a hint of jaundice.

He had lost more weight. His clothes hung loosely on him. His belt was cinched to the last hole, and the seat of his pants drooped like an empty sack.

Enrique Estefan was an old man. He was only

thirty-six, one year younger than Harry, but he was an old man just the same.

·2·

Much of the time, the blind woman lived not merely in darkness but in another world quite apart from the one into which she had been born. Sometimes that inner realm was a kingdom of brightest fantasy with pink and amber castles, palaces of jade, luxury high-rise apartments, Bel Air estates with vast verdant lawns. In these settings she was the queen and ultimate ruler – or a famous actress, fashion model, acclaimed novelist, ballerina. Her adventures were exciting, romantic, inspiring. At other times, however, it was an evil empire, all shadowy dungeons, dank and dripping catacombs full of decomposing corpses, blasted landscapes as gray and bleak as the craters of the moon, populated by monstrous and malevolent creatures, where she was always on the run, hiding and afraid, neither powerful nor famous, often cold and naked.

Occasionally her interior world lacked concreteness, was only a domain of colors and sounds and aromas, without form or texture, and she drifted through it, wondering and amazed. Often there was music – Elton John, Three Dog Night, Nilsson, Marvin Gaye, Jim Croce, the voices of her time – and the colors swirled and exploded to accompany the songs, a light show so dazzling that the real world could never produce its equal.

Even during one of those amorphous phases, the magic country within her head could darken and become a fearful place. The colors grew clotted and somber, the music discordant, ominous. She felt that she was being swept away by an icy and turbulent river, choking on its bitter waters, struggling for breath but finding none, then breaking the surface and gasping in lungsful of sour air, frantic, weeping, praying for delivery to a warm dry shore.

Once in a while, as now, she surfaced from the false worlds within her and became aware of the reality in which she actually existed. Muffled voices in adjacent rooms and hallways. The squeak of rubber-soled shoes. The pine scent of disinfectant, medicinal aromas, sometimes (but not now) the pungent odor of urine. She was swaddled in crisp, clean sheets, cool against her fevered flesh. When she disentangled her right hand from the bedding and reached out blindly, she found the cold steel safety railing on the side of her hospital bed.

At first she was preoccupied by the need to identify a strange sound. She did not try to rise up, but held fast to the railing and was perfectly still, listening intently to what initially seemed to be the roar of a great crowd in a far arena. No. Not a crowd. Fire. The chuckling-whispering-hissing of an all-consuming blaze. Her heart began to pound, but at last she recognized the fire for what it was: its opposite, the quenching downpour of a major storm.

She relaxed slightly – but then a rustle arose nearby, and she froze again, wary. 'Who's there?' she asked, and was surprised that her speech was thick and slurred.

'Ah, Jennifer, you're with us.'

Jennifer. My name is Jennifer.

The voice had been that of a woman. She sounded past middle-age, professional but caring.

Jennifer almost recognized the voice, knew she had heard it before, but she was not calmed.

'Who are you?' she demanded, disconcerted that she was unable to rid herself of the slur.

'It's Margaret, dear.'

The tread of rubber-soled shoes, approaching.

Jennifer cringed, half expecting a blow but not sure why.

A hand took hold of her right wrist, and Jennifer flinched.

'Easy, dear. I only want to take your pulse.'

Jennifer relented and listened to the rain.

After a while, Margaret let go of her wrist. 'Fast but nice and regular.'

Memory slowly seeped back into Jennifer. 'You're Margaret?'

'That's right.'

'The day nurse.'

'Yes, dear.'

'So it's morning?'

'Almost three o'clock in the afternoon. I go off duty in an hour. Then Angelina will take care of you.'

'Why am I always so confused when I first . . . wake up?'

'Don't worry about it, dear. There's nothing you can do to change it. Is your mouth dry? Would you like something to drink?'

'Yes, please.'

'Orange juice, Pepsi, Sprite?'

'Juice would be nice.'

'I'll be right back.'

Footsteps receding. A door opening. Left open. Above the sound of the rain, busy noises from elsewhere in the building, other people on other errands.

Jennifer tried to shift to a more comfortable position in the bed, whereupon she rediscovered not merely the extent of her weakness but the fact that she was paralyzed on her left side. She could not move her left leg or even wiggle her toes. She had no feeling in her left hand or arm.

A deep and terrible dread filled her. She felt helpless and abandoned. It seemed a matter of the utmost urgency that she recall how she had gotten in this condition and into this place.

She lifted her right arm. Although she realized that it must be thin and frail, it felt heavy.

With her right hand, she touched her chin, her mouth. Dry, rough lips. They had once been otherwise. Men had kissed her.

A memory glimmered in the darkness of her mind: a sweet kiss, murmured endearments. It was but a fragment of a recollection, without detail, leading nowhere.

She touched her right cheek, her nose. When she explored the left side of her face, she could feel it with her fingertips, but her cheek itself did not register her touch. The muscles in that side of her face felt . . . twisted.

After a brief hesitation, she slid her hand to her eyes.

She traced their contours with her fingertips, and what she discovered caused her hand to tremble.

Abruptly she remembered not only how she had wound up in this place but everything else, her life back to childhood all in a flash, far more than she wanted to remember, more than she could bear.

She snatched her hand away from her eyes and made a thin, awful sound of grief. She felt crushed under the weight of memory.

Margaret returned, shoes squeaking softly.

The glass clinked against the nightstand when she put it down.

'I'll just raise the bed so you'll be able to drink.'

The motor hummed, and the head of the bed began to lift, forcing Jennifer into a sitting position.

When the bed stopped moving, Margaret said, 'What's wrong, dear? Why, I'd think you were trying to cry . . . if you could.'

'Does he still come?' Jennifer asked shakily.

'Of course he does. At least twice a week. You were even alert on one of his visits a few days ago. Don't you remember?'

'No. I . . . I . . .'

'He's very faithful.'

Jennifer's heart was racing. A pressure swelled across her chest. Her throat was so tight with fear that she had trouble speaking: 'I don't . . . don't . . .'

'What's the matter, Jenny?'

'. . . don't want him here!'

'Oh, now, you don't mean that.'

'Keep him out of here.'

'He's so devoted.'

'No. He's . . . he's . . .'

'At least twice a week, and he sits with you for a couple of hours, whether you're with us or wrapped up inside yourself.'

Jennifer shuddered at the thought of him in the room, by the bed, when she was not aware of her surroundings.

She reached out blindly, found Margaret's arm, squeezed it as tightly as she could. 'He's not like you or me,' she said urgently.

'Jenny, you're upsetting yourself.'

'He's *different*.'

Margaret put her hand on Jennifer's, gave it a reassuring squeeze. 'Now, I want you to stop this, Jenny.'

'He's inhuman.'

'You don't mean that. You don't know what you're saying.'

'He's a monster.'

'Poor baby. Relax, honey.' A hand touched Jennifer's forehead, began to smooth away the furrows, brush the hair back. 'Don't get yourself excited. Everything'll be all right. You're going to be fine, baby. Just settle down, easy now, relax, you're safe here, we love you here, we'll take good care of you . . .'

After more of that, Jennifer grew calmer – but no less afraid.

The aroma of oranges made her mouth water. While Margaret held the glass, Jennifer drank through a straw. Her mouth didn't work quite right. Occasionally she had minor difficulty swallowing, but the juice was cold and delicious.

When she emptied the glass, she let the nurse blot her mouth with a paper napkin.

She listened to the soothing fall of the rain, hoping that it would settle her nerves. It did not.

'Should I turn the radio on?' Margaret asked.

'No, thank you.'

'I could read to you if you'd like. Poetry. You always enjoy listening to poetry.'

'That would be nice.'

Margaret drew a chair to the side of the bed and sat in it. As she sought a certain passage in a book, the turning of the pages was a crisp and pleasant sound.

'Margaret?' Jennifer said before the woman could begin to read.

'Yes?'

'When he comes to visit . . .'

'What is it, dear?'

'You'll stay in the room with us, won't you?'

'If that's what you want, of course.'

'Good.'

'Now, how about a little Emily Dickinson?'

'Margaret?'

'Hmmmmm?'

'When he comes to visit and I'm . . . lost inside myself . . . you never let me alone with him, do you?'

Margaret was silent, and Jennifer could almost see the woman's disapproving frown.

'Do you?' she insisted.

'No, dear. I never do.'

Jennifer knew the nurse was lying.

'Please, Margaret. You seem like a kind person. Please.'

'Dear, really, he loves you. He comes so faithfully because he loves you. You're in no danger from your Bryan, none at all.'

She shivered at the mention of the name. 'I know you think I'm mentally disturbed . . . confused . . .'

'A little Emily Dickinson will help.'

'I *am* confused about a lot of things,' Jennifer said, dismayed to hear her voice growing rapidly weaker, 'but not about this. I'm not the least bit confused about this.'

In a voice too full of artifice to convey the powerful, hidden sinewiness of Dickinson, the nurse began to read: '*That Love is all there is, Is all we know of Love . . .*'

·3·

Half of the large table in Ricky Estefan's spacious kitchen was covered with a dropcloth on which were arranged the small-scale power tools he used to craft silver jewelry: a hand-held drill, engraving instrument, emery wheel, buffer, and less easily identifiable equipment. Bottles of fluids and cans of mysterious compounds were neatly arranged to one side, as were small paint brushes, white cotton cloths, and steel-wool pads.

He had been at work on two pieces when Harry interrupted: a strikingly detailed scarab brooch and a massive belt buckle covered with Indian symbols, maybe Navajo or Hopi. His second career.

His forge and mold-making equipment were in the garage. But when he worked on the finishing details of his jewelry, he sometimes liked to sit by the kitchen window, where he could enjoy a view of his rose garden.

Outside, even in the dreary gray deluge, the plentiful blooms were radiant yellow and red and coral, some as big as grapefruits.

Harry sat at the uncluttered part of the table with his coffee, while Ricky shuffled to the other side and put his cup and saucer down among the cans, bottles, and tools. He lowered himself into his chair as stiffly as an octogenarian with severe arthritis.

Three years ago, Ricky Estefan had been a cop, one of the best, Harry's partner. He'd been a good-looking guy, too, with a full head of hair, not yellow-white as it was now, but thick and black.

His life had changed when he had unwittingly walked into the middle of a robbery at a convenience store. The strung-out gunman had a crack habit for which he needed financing, and maybe he smelled cop the moment Ricky stepped through the door or maybe he was in the mood to waste anyone who even inadvertently delayed the transfer of the money from the cash register to his pockets. Whichever the case, he fired four times at Ricky, missing him once, hitting him once in the left thigh and twice in the abdomen.

'How's the jewelry business?' Harry asked.

'Pretty good. I sell everything I make, get more orders for custom belt buckles than I can fill.'

Ricky sipped his coffee and savored it before swallowing. Coffee was not on his approved diet. If he drank much, it played hell with his stomach – or what was left of his stomach.

Getting gut-shot is easy; surviving is a bitch. He was lucky that the perp's weapon was only a .22 pistol, unlucky that it was fired at close range. For beginners, Ricky lost his spleen, part of his liver, and a small section of his large intestine. Although his surgeons took every precaution to keep the abdominal cavity clean, the slugs spread fecal matter, and Ricky quickly developed acute, diffuse, traumatic peritonitis. Barely survived it. Gas gangrene set in, antibiotics wouldn't stop it, and he underwent additional surgery in which he lost his gallbladder and a portion of his stomach. Then a blood infection. Temperature somewhere near that on the sunward surface of Mercury. Peritonitis again, too, and the removal of another piece of the colon. Through it all he had maintained an amazingly upbeat mood and, in the end, felt blessed that he had retained enough of his gastrointestinal system to be spared the indignity of having to wear a colostomy bag for the rest of his life.

He had been off-duty when he'd walked into that store, armed but expecting no trouble. He had promised Anita, his wife, to pick up a quart of milk and tub of soft margarine on his way home from work.

The gunman had never come to trial. The distraction provided by Ricky had allowed the store owner – Mr Wo Tai Han – to pick up a shotgun that he kept behind the counter. He'd taken off the back of the perp's head with a blast from that 12-gauge.

Of course, this being the last decade of the millennium, that had not been the end of it. The mother and father of the gunman sued Mr Han for depriving them of the affection, companionship, and financial support of their deceased son, and never mind that a crack addict was incapable of providing any of those things.

Harry drank some coffee. It was good and strong. 'You hear from Mr Han lately?'

'Yeah. He's real confident about winning on appeal.'

Harry shook his head. 'Never can tell what a jury will do these days.'

Ricky smiled tightly. 'Yeah. I figure I'm lucky I didn't get sued too.'

He hadn't been lucky in much else. At the time of the shooting, he and Anita had been married only eight months. She stayed with him another year, until he was on his feet, but when she realized he was going to be an old man for the rest of his days, she called it quits. She was twenty-six. She had a life to live. Besides, these days, the clause of the matrimony vows that mentioned 'in sickness and in health, till death do us part' was widely regarded as not binding until the end of a lengthy trial period of, say, a decade, sort of like not being vested in a pension plan until you had worked with the company for five years. For the past two years, Ricky had been alone.

It must be Kenny G Day. Another of his tunes was on the radio. This one was less melodic than the first. It made Harry edgy. Maybe any song would have made him edgy just then.

'What's wrong?' Ricky asked.

103

'How'd you know something's wrong?'

'You'd never in a million years go visiting friends for no reason during work hours. You always give the taxpayer his money's worth.'

'Am I really that rigid?'

'Do you really need to ask?'

'I must've been a pain in the ass to work with.'

'Sometimes.' Ricky smiled.

Harry told him about James Ordegard and the death among the mannequins.

Ricky listened. He spoke hardly at all, but when he did have something to say, it was always the right thing. He knew how to be a friend.

When Harry stopped and stared for a long while at the roses in the rain, apparently finished, Ricky said, 'That's not everything.'

'No,' Harry admitted. He fetched the coffee pot, refreshed their cups, sat down again. 'There was this hobo.'

Ricky listened to that part of it as soberly as he had listened to the rest. He did not seem incredulous. No slightest doubt was visible in his eyes or attitude. After he had heard it all, he said, 'So what do you make of it?'

'Could've been seeing things, hallucinating.'

'Could you? *You?*'

'But for God's sake, Ricky, how could it have been real?'

'Is the hobo really weirder than the perp in the restaurant?'

The kitchen was warm, but Harry was chilled. He

folded both hands around the hot coffee cup. 'Yeah. He's weirder. Not by much, maybe, but worse. The thing is . . . you think maybe I should request psychiatric leave, take a couple of weeks for counseling?'

'Since when did you start believing those brainflushers know what they're doing?'

'I don't. But I wouldn't be happy about some other cop walking around with a loaded gun, hallucinating.'

'You're no danger to anyone but yourself, Harry. You're going to worry yourself to death sooner or later. Look, as for this guy with red eyes – everybody has something happen to him sometime in his life that he can't explain, a brush with the unknown.'

'Not me,' Harry said firmly, shaking his head.

'Even you. Now if this guy starts driving up in a whirlwind every hour on the hour, asking if he could have a date, wants to tongue-kiss you – then maybe you have a problem.'

Armies of rain marched across the bungalow roof.

'I'm a tightly wound customer,' Harry said. 'I realize it.'

'Exactly. You're tight. Not a loose bolt in you, my man.'

He and Ricky watched the rain for a couple of minutes, saying nothing.

Finally Ricky put on a pair of protective goggles and picked up the silver belt buckle. He switched on the hand-held buffer, which was about the size of an electric toothbrush and not loud enough to hinder conversation, and began cleaning tarnish and minute silver shavings out of one of the etched designs.

After a while Harry sighed. 'Thanks, Ricky.'

'Sure.'

Harry took his cup and saucer to the sink, rinsed them off, and put them in the dishwasher.

On the radio, Harry Connick Jr was singing about love.

Over the sink was another window. The hard rain was beating the hell out of the roses. Bright petals, like confetti, were scattered across the soaked lawn.

When Harry returned to the table, Ricky turned off the buffer and started to get up. Harry said, 'It's okay, I'll let myself out.'

Ricky nodded. He looked so frail.

'See you soon.'

'Won't be too long till the season starts,' Ricky said.

'Let's take in an Angels game opening week.'

'I'd like that,' Ricky said.

They both enjoyed baseball. There was a comforting logic in the structure and progression of every game. It was an antidote for daily life.

On the front porch, Harry slipped into his shoes again and tied the laces, while the lizard that he had frightened upon arrival – or one just like it – watched him from the arm of the nearest chair. Slightly iridescent green and purple scales glimmered dully along each serpentine curve of its body, as if a handful of semiprecious stones had been discarded there on the white wood.

He smiled at the tiny dragon.

He felt back in balance again, calm.

As he came off the last step onto the sidewalk and into

the rain, Harry looked toward the car and saw someone sitting in the front passenger seat. A shadowy, hulking figure. Wild hair and a tangled beard. The intruder was facing away from Harry, but then he turned his head. Even through the rain-spotted side window and from a distance of thirty feet, the hobo was instantly recognizable.

Harry swung back toward the house, intending to shout for Ricky Estefan, but changed his mind when he recalled how suddenly the vagrant had vanished before.

He looked at the car, expecting to discover that the apparition had evaporated. But the intruder was still there.

In his bulky black raincoat, the man seemed too large for the sedan, as if he were not in a real car but in one of those scaled-down versions in a bumper-car pavilion at a carnival.

Harry moved quickly along the front walk, slopping through gray puddles. Drawing nearer the street, he saw the well-remembered scars on the maniacal face – and the red eyes.

As he reached the car, Harry said, 'What're you doing in there?'

Even through the closed window, the hobo's reply was clearly audible: 'Ticktock, ticktock, ticktock . . .'

'Get out of there,' Harry ordered.

'Ticktock . . . ticktock . . .'

An indefinable but unnerving quality of the derelict's grin made Harry hesitate.

' . . . ticktock . . .'

107

Harry drew his revolver, held it with the muzzle skyward. He put his left hand on the door handle.

'. . . ticktock . . .'

Those liquid red eyes daunted Harry. They looked like blood blisters that might burst and stream down the grizzled face. The sight of them, so inhuman, was enervating.

Before his courage could drain away, he jerked open the door.

He was almost knocked over by a blast of cold wind, and staggered backward two steps. It came out of the sedan as if an arctic gale had been stored up in there, stung his eyes and drew forth tears.

The wind passed in a couple of seconds. Beyond the open car door, the front passenger seat was empty.

Harry could see enough of the sedan interior to know for certain that the vagrant was not in there anywhere. Nevertheless, he circled the vehicle, looking through all of the windows.

He stopped at the back of the car, fished his keys out of his pocket, and unlocked the trunk, covering it with his revolver as the lid swung up. Nothing: spare tire, jack, lug wrench, and tool pouch.

Surveying the quiet residential neighborhood, Harry slowly became aware of the rain again, of which he'd been briefly oblivious. A vertical river poured out of the sky. He was soaked to the skin.

He slammed the trunk lid, and then the front passenger door. He went around to the driver's side and got in behind the steering wheel. His clothes made wet squishing noises as he sat down.

Earlier, on the street in downtown Laguna Beach, the hobo had reeked of body odor and had expelled searingly bad breath. But there was no lingering stink of him in the car.

Harry locked the doors. Then he returned his revolver to the shoulder holster under his sodden sport coat.

He was shivering.

Driving away from Enrique Estefan's bungalow, Harry switched on the heater, turned it up high. Water seeped out of his soaked hair and trickled down the nape of his neck. His shoes were swelling and tightening around his feet.

He remembered the softly radiant red eyes staring at him through the car window, the oozing sores in the scarred and filthy face, the crescent of broken yellow teeth – and abruptly he was able to identify the unnerving quality in the hobo's grin which had halted him as he had first been about to yank open the door. Gibbering lunacy was not what made the strange derelict so threatening. It was not the grin of a madman. It was the grin of a predator, cruising shark, stalking panther, wolf prowling by moonlight, something far more formidable and deadly than a mere deranged vagrant.

All the way back to Special Projects in Laguna Niguel, the scenery and the streets were familiar, nothing mysterious about the other motorists that he passed, nothing otherworldly about the play of headlights in the nickel-bright rain or the metallic clicking that the cold droplets made against the skin of the sedan, nothing eerie about the silhouettes of palm trees against the iron sky. Yet he was overcome by a feeling of the uncanny, and he struggled to avoid the conclusion that he had brushed up against something . . . supernatural.

Ticktock, ticktock . . .

He thought about the rest of what the hobo had said after appearing out of the whirlwind: *You'll be dead by dawn.*

He glanced at his watch. The crystal was still filmed with rainwater, the face distorted, but he could read the time: twenty-eight minutes past three.

When was sunrise? Six o'clock? Six-thirty? Thereabouts, somewhere between. At most, fifteen hours away.

The metronomic thump of the windshield wipers began to sound like the ominous cadence of funeral drums.

This was ridiculous. The derelict couldn't have followed him all the way to Enrique's house from Laguna Beach – which meant the hobo was not real, merely imagined, and therefore posed no threat.

He was not relieved. If the hobo was imaginary, Harry was in no danger of dying by dawn. But as far as he could see, that left a single alternative explanation, and not one that was reassuring: he must be having a nervous breakdown.

·4·

Harry's side of the office was comforting. The blotter and pen set were perfectly squared with each other and precisely aligned with the edges of the desk. The brass clock showed the same time as did his wristwatch. The leaves of the potted palm, Chinese evergreens, and pothos were all clean and glossy.

The blue screen of the computer monitor was soothing, as well, and all the Special Projects forms were installed as macros, so he could complete them and print them without resort to a typewriter. Uneven spacing inevitably resulted when one attempted to fill in the blanks on forms with that antiquated technology.

He was an excellent typist, and he could compose case narrative in his head almost as fast as he could type. Anyone was capable of filling in blank spaces or making Xs in boxes, but not everyone was skilled at the part of the job he liked to call the 'essay test.' His case narratives were written in language both more vivid and succinct than that of any other detective he had ever known.

As his fingers flew across the keyboard, crisp sentences formed on the screen, and Harry Lyon was more at peace with the world than he had been at any time since he had sat at his breakfast table that morning, eating English muffins with lemon marmalade and enjoying the view of the meticulously trimmed condominium greenbelt. When James Ordegard's killing spree was summarized in spare prose stripped of value-weighted verbs and adjectives, the episode didn't seem half as bizarre as when Harry actually had been a part of it. He hammered out the words, and the words soothed.

He was even feeling sufficiently relaxed to allow himself to get more casual in the office than was his habit. He unbuttoned the collar of his shirt and slightly loosened the knot of his tie.

He took a break from the paperwork only to walk down the hall to the vending-machine room to get a cup of coffee. His clothes were still damp in spots and hopelessly wrinkled, but the frost in his marrow had melted.

On his way back to the office with the coffee, he saw the hobo. The hulking vagrant was at the far end of the hall, crossing the intersection, passing left to right in another corridor. Facing forward, never looking toward Harry, the guy moved purposefully, as if in the building on other business. In a few long strides he was through the intersection and out of sight.

As Harry hurried along the hall to see where the man had gone, trying not to spill the coffee, he told himself that it hadn't been the same person. There had been a vague resemblance, that was all; imagination and frayed nerves had done the rest.

His denials were without conviction. The figure at the end of the corridor had been the same height as his nemesis, with those bearish shoulders, that barrel chest, the same filthy mane of hair and tangled beard. The long black raincoat had spread around him like a robe, and he'd had that leonine self-possession, as if he were some mad prophet mystically transported from the days of the Old Testament and dropped into modern times.

Harry braked at the end of the hallway by sliding into the intersection, wincing as hot coffee slopped out of the cup and stung his hand. He looked right, where the vagrant had been headed. The only people in that corridor were Bob Wong and Louis Yancy, loan-outs from the Orange County Sheriff's Department, who were consulting over a manila file folder.

Harry said, 'Where'd he go?'

They blinked at him, and Bob Wong said, 'Who?'

'The hairball in the black raincoat, the hobo.'

The two men were puzzled.

Yancy said, 'Hobo?'

'Well, if you didn't see him, you had to *smell* him.'

'Just now?' Wong asked.

'Yeah. Two seconds ago.'

'Nobody came through here,' Yancy said.

Harry knew they weren't lying to him, weren't part of some immense conspiracy. Nevertheless, he wanted to walk past them and inspect all of the rooms along the corridor.

He restrained himself only because they were already staring at him curiously. He suspected he was something of a sight – disheveled, pale, wild-eyed.

He could not tolerate the idea that he was making a spectacle of himself. He'd built a life on the principles of moderation, orderliness, and self-control.

Reluctantly he returned to his office. He took a cork coaster from his top desk drawer, put it on the blotter, and set the dripping cup of coffee on it.

He kept a roll of paper towels and a spray bottle of Windex in the bottom drawer of one of the filing cabinets. He used a couple of the towels to blot his coffee-damp hands, then wiped off the wet cup.

He was pleased to see that his hands were not shaky.

Whatever the hell was happening, he would eventually figure it out and deal with it. He could deal with anything. Always had. Always would. Self-control. That was the key.

He took several slow, deep breaths. With both hands he smoothed his hair back from his forehead.

Heavy as a slab of slate, the lowering sky had pressed twilight into an earlier appearance. It was only a few minutes after five o'clock, an hour until sunset, but the day had surrendered to a protracted dusk. Harry turned on the overhead fluorescent lights.

For a minute or two he stood at the partially fogged window, watching tons of rain crash straight down on the parking lot. The thunder and lightning were long past, and the air was too heavy to permit wind, so the deluge had a tropical intensity, a grueling relentlessness that led the mind to ancient myths involving divine punishment, arks, and lost continents vanished beneath swollen seas.

Calmed somewhat, he returned to his desk chair and swung around to the computer. He was about to call up the case-narrative document that he had saved before going down the hall for coffee, when he realized that the screen was not blank, as it should have been.

Another document had been created in his absence. It consisted of a single word centered on the screen: TICKTOCK.

·5·

It was nearly six o'clock when Connie Gulliver returned to the office from the crime scene, having caught a ride in a Laguna Beach Police Department black-and-white. She was grousing about the media, one television reporter in particular who had dubbed her and Harry 'Batwoman and Batman,' for God-alone-knew what reason, maybe because their desperate pursuit of James Ordegard involved so much derring-do, or maybe just because there had been a flock of bats in the attic where they had nailed the bastard. Electronic journalists did not always have discernibly logical reasons or credible justifications for doing and saying some of the things they did and said. Reporting the news was neither a sacred trust nor a public service to them, it was show business, where you needed flash and splash more than facts and figures. Connie had been around long enough to know all of that and to be resigned to it, but she was hot about it anyway, haranguing Harry from the moment she walked through the door.

He was just finishing the paperwork when she arrived, having dawdled during the past half an hour, waiting for her. He'd decided to tell her about the tramp with the blood-red eyes, in part because she was his partner and he was loath to conceal anything significant from a partner. He and Ricky Estefan had always shared everything, which was one reason he had gone to see Ricky before returning to Special Projects, the other reason being that he valued Ricky's insights and advice. Whether the threatening hobo was real

115

or a symptom of mental collapse, Connie had a right to know about him.

If that filthy, spectral figure *was* imaginary, perhaps just talking about him with someone would puncture the balloon of delusion. The hobo might never appear again.

Harry also wanted to tell her because telling her gave him a reason to spend some off-duty time with her. At least a little socializing between partners was advisable, helped strengthen that special bond between cops who had to put their lives on the line for each other. They needed to talk about what they had been through that afternoon, relive it together, and thereby transform it from a traumatic experience into a polished anecdote with which to annoy rookies for years to come.

And in truth, he wanted to spend some time with Connie because he had begun to be interested in her not only as a partner but as a woman. Which surprised him. They were such opposites. He had spent so much time telling himself that she drove him nuts. Now he couldn't stop thinking about her eyes, the luster of her hair, the fullness of her mouth. Though he had not wanted to admit it, this change in his attitude had been building up speed for some time, and today gears had finally shifted in his head.

No mystery about that. He'd nearly been killed. More than once. A brush with death was a great clarifier of thoughts and feelings. He'd not only had a brush with death; he'd been embraced by it, hugged tight.

He had seldom harbored so many intense emotions all at once: loneliness, fear, aching self-doubt, joy at just being alive, desire so acute that it weighed upon his heart and made breathing just a little more difficult than usual.

'Where do I sign?' Connie asked, when he told her he had completed the paperwork.

He spread out all the requisite forms on his desk, including Connie's own official statement. He had written it for her, as he always did, which was against department policy and one of the few rules he had ever broken. But they split chores according to their skills and preferences, and he just happened to be better at this part than she was. Her own case narratives tended to be angry in tone instead of solemnly neutral, as if every crime was the most grievous personal affront to her, and sometimes she used words like 'asshole' or 'shithead' instead of 'suspect' or 'arrestee,' which was guaranteed to send the defendant's attorney into rapturous spasms of self-righteousness in the courtroom.

Connie signed all of the forms that he put in front of her, including the cleanly typed statement attributed to her, without reading any of them. Harry liked that. She trusted him.

As he watched her scribble her signature, he decided they should go somewhere special, even with him rumpled and damp, a cozy bar with plushly padded booths and low lighting and candles on the tables, a pianist making cocktail music – but not one of those slick guys who did polyester-lounge versions of good tunes and sang 'Feelings' once every half hour, the anthem of sentimental inebriates and mush-heads in all fifty states.

Connie couldn't stop fuming about being labeled Batwoman, and other abuses suffered at the hands of the media, so Harry had difficulty finding a moment to insert an invitation to drinks and dinner, which gave him too much time to look at her. Not that she looked any less appealing the longer he watched her. Just the opposite: when he took the time to study her face feature by feature, she proved to be more attractive than he had ever realized. The problem was, he also began to see just how tired she was: red-eyed, pale, large dark smudges of weariness beneath her eyes, shoulders slumped under the weight of the day. He began to doubt that she would want to have a drink and rehash the events of the lunch hour. And the more aware he became of her exhaustion, the more profoundly weary he felt himself.

Her bitterness over the electronic news media's tendency to turn tragedy into entertainment reminded Harry that she had *begun* the day angry, as well, troubled by something she had refused to discuss.

As his ardor cooled, he wondered whether it was really such a good idea to have a romantic interest in a partner in the first place. Department policy was to split up teams who developed more than a friendly relationship when off-duty, whether gay or straight. Long-enforced policies were usually based on a wealth of hard experience.

Connie finished signing the papers and gave him a once-over. 'This is the first time you've ever looked as if you might consider shopping at The Gap instead of exclusively at Brooks Brothers.' Then she actually

118

hugged him, which might have stirred his passion again except that it was a buddy hug. 'How's your gut feel?'

Just a dull ache, that's all, thank you, nothing that would inhibit me from making passionate, hot, sweaty love to you.

He said, 'I'm fine.'

'You sure?'

'Yeah.'

'God, I'm tired.'

'Me too.'

'I think I'll sleep a hundred hours.'

'At least ten.'

She smiled and, to his surprise, affectionately pinched his cheek. 'See you in the morning, Harry.'

He watched her as she walked out of the office. She was still wearing badly scuffed Reeboks, blue jeans, a red-and-brown-checkered blouse, and a brown corduroy jacket – and the outfit was worse for the wear of the past ten hours. Yet he could not have found her more alluring if she had been shoehorned into a clinging, sequined gown with canyonesque decolletage.

The room was dreary without her. The fluorescent light painted hard, cold edges on the furniture, on every leaf of every plant.

Beyond the steamed window, the premature twilight was giving way to night, but the stormy day had been so somber that the phase of demarcation was excruciatingly subtle. Rain hammered on the anvil of darkness.

Harry had come full circle from physical and mental exhaustion to thoughts of passion to exhaustion once more. It was almost like being an adolescent boy again.

He shut down the computer, switched off the lights, closed the office door, and filed copies of the reports in the front office.

Driving home in the depressingly leaden fall of rain, he hoped to God that he *could* sleep, and that his sleep would be without dreams. When he woke refreshed in the morning, perhaps the answer to the mystery of the crimson-eyed hobo would be apparent.

Halfway home he almost switched on the radio, wanting music. Just before he touched the controls, he stayed his hand. He was afraid that, instead of some top-forty number, he would hear the voice of the vagrant chanting: *ticktock, ticktock, ticktock* . . .

·6·

Jennifer must have dozed off. It was ordinary sleep, however, not the delirium of the fantasy worlds that so frequently offered her escape. When she woke, she did not have to shake off clinging visions of emerald-diamond-sapphire temples or cheering audiences enthralled with her vocal virtuosity in a Carnegie Hall of the mind. She was sticky because of the humidity, with a sour taste in her mouth – stale orange juice and heavy sleep.

Rain was still falling. It drummed complicated rhythms on the roof of the hospital. Private sanitarium, actually. But not rhythms alone: chuckling-gurgling-burbling atonal melodies as well.

Sightless, Jennifer had no easy way to know with certainty the hour of the day or the season. However, blind for twenty years, she had developed a refined awareness of her circadian rhythms and was able to guess the time of year and day with surprising accuracy.

She knew that spring was drawing near. Perhaps it was March, the end of the rainy season in southern California. She knew not the day of the week, but she suspected it was early evening, between six and eight o'clock.

Perhaps she'd eaten dinner, though she did not remember it. Sometimes she was barely conscious enough to swallow when they spoon-fed her, but not sufficiently aware to enjoy what she ate. On other occasions, when in a deeper catatonic state, she received nutrients intravenously.

Although the room was cast in silence, she was aware of another presence, either because of some indefinable peculiarity of the air pressure or an odor only subconsciously perceived. She remained motionless, trying to breathe as if sound asleep, waiting for the unknown person to move or cough or sigh and, thereby, provide her with a clue to identity.

Her companion did not oblige her. Gradually, Jennifer came to suspect that she was alone with *him*.

She knew that a pretense of sleep was safest.

She struggled to stay perfectly still.

Finally she could no longer tolerate continued ignorance. She said, 'Margaret?'

No one responded.

She knew the silence was false. She strove to recall the name of the swing-shift nurse. 'Angelina?'

No reply. Only the rain.

He was torturing her. It was psychological torture, but that was by far the most effective weapon that could be used against her. She had known so much physical and emotional pain that she had developed defenses against those forms of abuse.

'Who's there?' she demanded.

'It's me,' he said.

Bryan. Her Bryan.

His voice was soft and gentle, even musical, in no way threatening, yet it caused ice to form in her blood.

She said, 'Where's the nurse?'

'I asked her to leave us alone.'

'What do you want?'

'Just to be with you.'

'Why?'

'Because I love you.'

He sounded sincere, but she knew that he was not. He was congenitally incapable of sincerity.

'Go away,' she pleaded.

'Why do you hurt me?'

'I know what you are.'

'What am I?'

She did not respond.

He said, 'How can you know what I am?'

'Who better to know?' she said harshly, consumed by bitterness, self-loathing, loathing, and despair.

Judging by the sound of his voice, he was standing

near the window, closer to the plink and paradiddle of the rain than to the faint noises in the corridor. She was terrified that he would come to the bed, take her hand, touch her cheek or brow.

She said, 'I want Angelina.'

'Not yet.'

'Please.'

'No.'

'Then go away.'

'Why do you hurt me?' he asked again. His voice remained as gentle as ever, melodic as that of a choirboy, untouched by anger or frustration, only sorrow. 'I come twice a week. I sit with you. Without you, what would I be? Nothing. I'm aware of that.'

Jennifer bit her lip and did not reply.

Suddenly she sensed that he was moving. She could hear no footsteps, no rustle of garments. He could be quieter than a cat when he wished to be.

She *knew* he was approaching the bed.

Desperately she sought the oblivion of her delusions, either the bright fantasies or dark terrors within her damaged mind, she cared not which, anything other than the horror of reality in that too, too private sanitarium room. But she could not retreat *at will* into those interior realms; periodic involuntary consciousness was, perhaps, the greatest curse of her pathetic, debilitated condition.

She waited, trembling.

She listened.

He was ghost-silent.

The thunderous pummeling of rain on the roof was

cut off from one second to the next, but she understood that the rain had not actually ceased to fall. Abruptly the world was clutched in the grip of an uncanny silence, stillness.

Jennifer brimmed with fear, even into the paralyzed extremities of her left side.

He took hold of her right hand.

She gasped and tried to pull away.

'No,' he said, and tightened his grip. He was strong.

She called for the nurse, knowing it was useless to do so.

He held her with one hand and caressed her fingers with the other. He tenderly massaged her wrist. He stroked the withered flesh of her forearm.

Blindly, she waited, trying not to speculate upon what cruelties would ensue.

He pinched her arm, and a wordless plea for mercy escaped her. He pinched harder, then again, but probably not hard enough to leave a bruise.

Enduring, Jennifer wondered what his face was like, whether ugly or plain or handsome. She intuited that it would not be a blessing to recover her sight if she were required, just once, to gaze into his hateful eyes.

He pushed one finger into her ear, and his nail seemed as long and pointed as a needle. He twisted it and scraped, pressed harder still, until the pressure-pain was unbearable.

She screamed, but no one responded.

He touched her pancake breasts, deflated from long years of supine existence and intravenous nourishment.

Even in her sexless condition, her nipples were a source of pain, and he knew how to deliver agony.

However, it was not so much anything he did to her that mattered . . . but what he might think to do next. He was endlessly inventive. True terror lay in the anticipation of the unknown.

She screamed for someone, anyone, help, surcease. She begged God for death.

Her shrieks and cries for help fell into a void.

Finally she was silent and endured.

He released her, but she was acutely aware that he was still at her bedside.

'Love me,' Bryan said.

'Please go away.'

Softly: 'Love me.'

If Jennifer had been capable of producing tears, she would have wept.

'Love me, and I won't have any reason to hurt you again. All I want is for you to love me.'

She was no more capable of loving him than she was of producing tears from her ruined eyes. Easier to love a viper, a rock, or the cold indifferent blackness between the stars.

'I only need to be loved,' he insisted.

She knew that he was incapable of love. Indeed, he had no concept whatsoever of the meaning of the word. He wanted it only because he could not have it, could not feel it, because it was a mystery to him, a great unknown. Even if she were able to love him and convince him of her love, she would not be saved, for he would be unmoved by love when at last it was given to him, would deny its existence, and would continue to torture her out of habit.

Suddenly the rain sound resumed. Voices in the corridor. Squeaking wheels on the tiered cart that carried dinner trays.

The torment was over. For now.

'I can't stay long this evening,' Bryan said. 'Not the usual eternity.'

He chuckled at that remark, amused by himself, but to Jennifer it was only an offensive wet sound in his throat, humorless.

He said, 'I've had an unexpected increase in business. So much to do. I'm afraid I've got to run.'

As always, he marked his departure by bending over the bed railing and kissing the numb left side of her face. She could not feel the pressure or texture of his lips against her cheek, only a butterfly-wing touch of coolness. She suspected that his kiss might have felt no different, maybe only colder, if planted on the still-sensitive right side of her face.

When he left, he chose to make noise, and she listened to his receding footsteps.

After a while, Angelina came to feed her dinner. Soft foods. Mashed potatoes with gravy. Pureed beef. Pureed peas. Apple sauce with a sprinkling of cinnamon and brown sugar. Ice cream. Things she would have no difficulty swallowing.

Jennifer said nothing about what had been done to her. From grim experience, she had learned that she would not be believed.

He must have the appearance of an angel, because

everyone but her seemed disposed to trust him on first sight, attributing to him only the kindest motives and noblest intentions.

She wondered if her ordeal would ever end.

·7·

Ricky Estefan emptied half the box of rigatoni into the big pot of boiling water. A head of foam rose instantaneously, and an appealing starchy smell wafted up in a cloud of steam. On another burner stood a smaller pot of fragrantly bubbling spaghetti sauce.

As he adjusted the gas flames, he heard a strange noise toward the front of the house. A thump, not especially loud but solid. He cocked his head, listened. Just when he decided that he'd imagined the noise, it came again: *thump*.

He went down the hall to the front door, switched on the porch light, and looked through the fish-eye lens in the peephole. As far as he could see, no one was out there.

He unlocked the door, opened it, and cautiously leaned outside to look both ways. None of the outdoor furniture had fallen over. The night was windless, so the bench swing hung motionless on its chains.

The rain continued to fall hard. In the street, the vaguely purplish light of the mercury-vapor lamps revealed rivers along both gutters, nearly to the tops of the curbs, churning toward the drains at the end of the block, glistening like streams of molten silver.

He was concerned that the thump had signaled storm damage of some kind, but that seemed unlikely without a good wind.

After he closed the door, he twisted the dead-bolt into place and slid the security chain home. Since being gutshot and struggling back from the brink, he had developed a healthy paranoia. Well, healthy or unhealthy, it was a damned fine example of paranoia, shiny from use. He kept the doors locked at all times, and with nightfall he drew the drapes shut at every window so no one could peer inside.

His fear embarrassed him. He had once been so strong, capable, and self-confident. When Harry had left earlier, Ricky had pretended to stay at the kitchen table, working on the belt buckle. But as soon as he heard the front door close, he shuffled down the hall to slip the dead-bolt quietly into place while his old friend was still on the front porch. His face had been burning with shame, but he'd been uneasy about leaving a door unlocked even for a few minutes.

Now, as he turned away from the door, the mysterious noise came again. *Thump*.

This time he thought it was located in the living room. He stepped through the archway to find the source.

Two table lamps were on in the living room. A warm amber glow suffused that cozy space. The coved ceiling was patterned with twin circles of light broken by the shadows of lampshade wires and finials.

Ricky liked light throughout the house in the evening until he went to bed. He was no longer comfortable entering a dark room and *then* flicking a switch.

Everything was in order. He even peered behind the sofa to be sure . . . well, to be sure that nothing was amiss back there.

Thump.

His bedroom?

A door in the living room opened on a small vestibule with a simply but charmingly coffered ceiling. Three other doors ringed the vestibule: guest bath, a cramped guest bedroom, and a master bedroom of modest dimensions, one lamp aglow in each. Ricky checked everywhere, closets too, but found nothing that could have caused the thumping.

He pulled the drapes aside at each window to see if the latches were engaged and all the panes of glass intact. They were.

Thump.

This time it seemed to come from the garage.

From the nightstand beside his bed, he got a revolver Smith & Wesson .38 Chief's Special. He knew it was fully loaded. He flipped the cylinder out and checked anyway. All five rounds were there.

Thump.

He developed a stitch in his lower left abdomen, a painful stretching-twitching sensation with which he was too familiar, and although the bungalow was small, he needed more than a minute to reach the connecting door to the garage. It was off the hallway, just before the kitchen. He leaned against it, one ear to the crack of the jamb, listening.

Thump.

The sound had definitely come from the garage.

He pinched the dead-bolt turn between thumb and forefinger . . . then hesitated. He didn't want to go into the garage.

He became aware of a dew of perspiration on his brow.

'Come on, come on,' he said, but he didn't respond to his own urging.

He hated himself for being afraid. Although he remembered the terrible pain of the bullets smacking through his belly and scrambling his guts, although he could recall the agony of all the subsequent infections and the anguish of the months in the hospital under the shadow of death, although he knew that many other men would have given up when he persevered, and although he knew that his caution and fear were justified by all that he had experienced and survived, he hated himself nonetheless.

Thump.

Cursing himself, he disengaged the lock, opened the door, found the light switch. He stepped across the threshold.

The garage was wide enough for two cars, and his blue Mitsubishi was parked on the far side. The half nearer the house was occupied by his long workbench, racks of tools, cabinets filled with supplies, and the gas-fired forge in which he melted small ingots of silver to pour into the jewelry and buckle molds that he created.

The rataplan of the rain was louder here because there was no drop ceiling and the garage roof was not insulated. A damp chill rose off the concrete floor.

No one was in the nearer half of the large chamber.

None of the storage cabinets had a compartment big enough to hide a man.

With the .38 in hand, he circled the car, looked inside it, even eased down onto his creaking knees and peered under it. Nobody was hiding there.

The exterior man-size door of the garage was locked from the inside. So was the only window, which in any case was too small to admit anyone older than five.

He wondered if the noise had originated on the roof. For a minute, two minutes, he stood beside the car, staring up at the rafters, waiting for the thump to come again. Nothing. Just the rain, rain, rain, an unceasing tattoo.

Feeling foolish, Ricky returned to the house and locked the connecting door. He took the revolver into the kitchen with him and put it on the built-in secretary beside the telephone.

The flames under both the pasta and sauce had gone out. For a moment he thought the gas service had failed, but then he saw that the knobs in front of both burners were in the OFF position.

He knew they had been on when he left the kitchen. He turned them on again, and blue flames came to life with a *whoosh* under the pots. After adjusting them to the right intensity, he stared at them for a while; the flames did not subside of their own accord.

Somebody was playing games with him.

He returned to the secretary, picked up the gun, and considered searching the house again. But he had already inspected every inch of the place, and knew for certain that he was alone.

Following a brief hesitation, he searched it again – with the same result as the first time.

When he returned to the kitchen, no one had turned off the gas. The sauce was boiling so rapidly, it had begun to stick to the bottom of the pot. He put the gun aside. He speared a piece of rigatoni with a large fork, blew on it to cool it, tasted. It was slightly overcooked but okay.

He drained the pasta into a colander in the sink, shook the colander, dumped the pasta on a plate, and added sauce.

Somebody was playing games with him.

But who?

·8·

Rain drizzled through the leafy oleander bushes, en-countered the layers of plastic garbage bags that Sammy had draped across the packing crate, and drained off the plastic into the vacant lot or out into the alleyway. Under the rags that served as bedding, the floor of the crate was also lined with plastic, so his humble home was relatively dry.

Even if he had been sitting in water up to his waist, Sammy Shamroe might not have noticed, for he had already finished one double-liter jug of wine and had started a second. He was feeling no pain – or at least that's what he told himself.

He had it pretty good, really. The cheap wine kept him warm, temporarily purged him of self-hatred and

remorse, and put him in touch with certain innocent feelings and naive expectations of childhood. Two
fat blueberry-scented candles, salvaged from someone
else's garbage and anchored now in a pie pan, filled
his sanctuary with a pleasant fragrance and a soft
light as cozy as that from an antique Tiffany lamp.
The close walls of the packing crate were comforting
rather than claustrophobic. The ceaseless chorus of the
rain was lulling. But for the candles, perhaps it had
been something like this in the sac of fetal membranes:
snugly housed, suspended weightless in amniotic fluid,
surrounded by the soft liquid roar of Mother's blood
rushing through her veins and arteries, not merely
unconcerned about the future but unaware of it.

Even when the ratman pulled aside the hanging rug
that served as a door over the only opening in the crate,
Sammy was not delivered from his imitation prenatal
bliss. Deep down, he knew that he was in trouble, but
he was too whacked to be afraid.

The crate was eight feet by six, as large as many
walk-in closets. Bearish as he was, the ratman still
could have squeezed in across from Sammy without
knocking over the candles, but he remained crouched
in the doorway, holding back the rug with one arm.

His eyes were different from what they had always
been before. Shiny black. Without any whites at all.
Pinpoint yellow pupils in the center, glowing. Like
distant headlights on the night highway to Hell.

'How're you doing, Sammy?' the ratman asked in a
tone of voice that was uncharacteristically solicitous.
'You getting along okay, hmmmmm?'

133

Though a surfeit of wine had so numbed Sammy Shamroe's survival instinct that he couldn't get back in touch with his fear, he knew that he *should* be afraid. Therefore he remained motionless and watchful, as he might have done if a rattlesnake had slithered into his crate and blocked the only way out.

The ratman said, 'Just wanted you to know, I won't be stopping around for a while. Got new business. Overworked. Got to deal with more urgent matters first. When it's over, I'll be exhausted, sleep for a whole day, around the clock.'

Being temporarily fearless did not mean that Sammy had become courageous. He dared not speak.

'Did you know how much this exhausts me, Sammy? No? Thinning out the herd, disposing of the lame and the diseased – it's no piece of cake, let me tell you.'

When the ratman smiled and shook his head, shining beads of rainwater were flung off his beard. They spattered Sammy.

Even in the comforting womb of his wine haze, Sammy retained enough awareness to be amazed by the ratman's sudden garrulousness. Yet, as amazing as it was, the huge man's monologue was curiously reminiscent of something he had heard before, a long time ago in another place, though he could not recall where or when or from whom. It wasn't the gravelly voice or the words themselves that brought Sammy to the edge of déja vu, but the tonal quality of the ratman's revelations, the eerie earnestness, the cadences of his speech.

'Dealing with vermin like you,' the ratman said, 'is

draining. Believe me. Draining. It'd be so much easier if I could waste each of you the first time we meet, make you spontaneously combust or make your head explode. Wouldn't that be nice?'

No. Colorful, exciting, interesting for sure, but not nice, Sammy thought, although his fear remained in abeyance.

'But to fulfill my destiny,' the ratman said, 'to become what I am required to become, I have to show you my wrath, make you quiver and be humbled before me, make you understand the meaning of your damnation.'

Sammy remembered where he had heard this sort of thing before. Another street person. Maybe eighteen months ago, two years ago, up in Los Angeles. A guy named Mike, had a messiah complex, thought he was chosen by God to make the world pay for its sins, finally went over the top with the concept, knifed three or four people who were lined up outside an art-house theater that was showing a re-released director's cut of *Bill and Ted's Excellent Adventure* with twenty minutes of material never seen in the original version.

'Do you know what I am becoming, Sammy?'

Sammy just clutched his remaining two-liter jug.

'I am becoming the new god,' said the ratman. 'A new god is needed. I have been chosen. The old god was too merciful. Things have gotten out of hand. It's my duty to Become, and having Become, to rule more sternly.'

In the candlelight, the raindrops remaining in the ratman's hair and eyebrows and beard glimmered as if a woefully misguided artisan had decorated him with jewels in the manner of a Fabergé egg.

135

'When I deal out these more urgent judgments, and when I've had a chance to rest, I'll be back to see you,' the ratman promised. 'I just didn't want you to think you'd been forgotten. Wouldn't want you to feel neglected, unappreciated. Poor, poor Sammy. I won't forget you. That's not just a promise – it's the sacred word of the new god.'

Then the ratman worked a malevolent miracle to insure that *he* was not forgotten even in the thousand-fathom oblivion of a deep wine sea. He blinked, and when his lids popped up again, his eyes were no longer ebony and yellow, were not eyes at all any longer, but were balls of greasy white worms writhing in his sockets. When he opened his mouth, his teeth had become razor-sharp fangs. Venom dripped, a glossy black tongue fluttered like that of a questing serpent, and a violent exhalation erupted from him, reeking of putrefied flesh. His head and body swelled, burst, but didn't deconstruct into a horde of rats this time. Instead, ratman and clothes were transformed into tens of thousands of black flies that swarmed through the packing crate, buzzing fiercely, batting against Sammy's face. The thrumming of their wings was so loud that it drowned out even the drone of the pouring rain, and then—

They were gone.

Vanished.

The rug hung heavy and wet over the open section of the crate.

Candleglow flickered and pulsed across the wooden walls.

The air smelled of blueberry-scented wax.

Sammy chugged a couple of long swallows of wine directly from the mouth of the jug, instead of pouring it first into the dirty jelly jar that he had been using. A little of it spilled over his whisker-stubbled chin, but he didn't care.

He was eager to remain numb, detached. If he had been in touch with his fear during the past few minutes, he would no doubt have peed his pants.

He felt it was also important to remain detached in order to think less emotionally about what the ratman had said. Previously, the creature had spoken little and had never revealed anything of its own motivations or intentions. Now it was spouting all this babble about thinning the herd, judgment, godhood.

It was valuable to know the ratman's mind was filled with the same crazy stuff that had cluttered up the head of old Mike, stabber of moviegoers. Regardless of his ability to appear out of nowhere and disappear into thin air, in spite of his inhuman eyes and ability to change shapes, all of that god blather made him seem hardly more special than any of the countless heirs of Charles Manson and Richard Ramirez who roamed the world, heeding inner voices, killing for pleasure, and keeping refrigerators filled with the severed heads of their victims. If in some fundamental way he was like the other psychos out there, then even with his special talents he was as vulnerable as they were.

Though functioning in a wine fog, Sammy could see that this new insight might be a useful survival tool. The problem was, he had never been good at survival.

Thinking about the ratman made his head hurt. Hell, the mere prospect of *surviving* gave him a migraine. Who wanted to survive? And why? Death would only come later if not sooner. Each survival was merely a short-term triumph. In the end, oblivion for everyone. And in the meantime, nothing but pain. To Sammy, it seemed that the only terrible thing about the ratman was not that he killed people but that he apparently liked to make them suffer first, cranked up the terror, poured on the pain, did not remove his victims from this world with kindly despatch.

Sammy tipped the jug and poured wine into the jelly jar that was on the floor, braced between his splayed legs. He raised the glass to his lips. In the glimmering ruby liquid, he sought a glimmerless, peaceful, perfect darkness.

·9·

Mickey Chan was sitting alone in a back booth, concentrating on his soup.

Connie saw him as soon as she pushed through the front door of the small Chinese restaurant in Newport Beach, and she made her way toward him between black-lacquered chairs and tables with silver-gray tablecloths. A red and gold painted dragon coiled across the ceiling, serpentined around the light fixtures.

If Mickey saw her coming, he pretended to be

unaware. He sucked soup from the spoon, then spooned up more, never taking his gaze off the contents of his bowl.

He was small but sinewy, in his late forties, and wore his hair closely cropped. His skin was the shade of antique parchment.

Although he allowed his Caucasian clients to think that he was Chinese, he was actually a Vietnamese refugee who had fled to the States after the fall of Saigon. Rumor had it, he'd been a Saigon homicide detective or an officer in the South Vietnamese Internal Security Agency, which was probably true.

Some said that he'd had a reputation as a real terror in the interrogation room, a man who would resort to any tool or technique to break the will of a suspected criminal or Communist, but Connie doubted those stories. She liked Mickey. He was tough, but he had about him the air of a man who had known great loss and was capable of profound compassion.

As she reached his table, he spoke to her without shifting his attention from the soup: 'Good evening, Connie.'

She slid into the other side of the booth. 'You're fixated on that bowl as if the meaning of life is in it.'

'It is,' he said, still spooning.

'It is? Looks like soup to me.'

'The meaning of life can be found in a bowl of soup. Soup always begins with a broth of some kind, which is like the liquid flow of days that makes up our lives.'

'Broth?'

'Sometimes in the broth are noodles, sometimes vegetables, bits of egg white, slivers of chicken or shrimp, mushrooms, perhaps rice.'

Because Mickey would not look at her, Connie found herself staring across the table at his soup almost as intensely as he was.

He said, 'Sometimes it is hot, sometimes cool. Sometimes it is meant to be cool, and then it is good even if there's no slightest warmth in it. But if it's not meant to be cool, then it will taste bitter, or curdle in the stomach, or both.'

His strong but gentle voice had a hypnotic effect. Enthralled, Connie stared at the placid surface of the soup, oblivious now to everyone else in the restaurant.

'Consider. Before the soup is eaten,' Mickey said, 'it has value and purpose. After it is eaten, it is valueless to everyone except to whomever has consumed it. And in fulfilling its purpose, it ceases to exist. Left behind will be only the empty bowl. Which can symbolize either want and need – or the pleasant expectation of other soups to come.'

She waited for him to continue, and only shifted her gaze from his soup when she realized that he was now staring at her. She met his eyes and said, 'That's it?'

'Yes.'

'The meaning of life?'

'All of it.'

She frowned. 'I don't get it.'

He shrugged. 'Me neither. I make up this crap as I go along.'

She blinked at him. 'You what?'

Grinning, Mickey said, 'Well, it's sort of expected of a Chinese private detective, you see. Pithy sayings, impenetrable philosophical observations, inscrutable proverbs.'

He was not Chinese, nor was his real name Mickey Chan. When he arrived in the US and decided to put his police background to use by becoming a private detective, he had felt that Vietnamese names were too exotic to inspire confidence and too difficult for Westerners to pronounce. And he'd known he couldn't make a good living solely from clients of Vietnamese heritage. Two of his favorite American things were Mickey Mouse cartoons and Charlie Chan movies, and it made sense to him to have his name legally changed. Because of Disney and Rooney and Mantle and Spillane, Americans liked people named Mickey; and thanks to a lot of old movies, the name Chan was subconsciously associated with investigative genius. Evidently, Mickey had known what he was doing, because he had built a thriving business with a sterling reputation, and now had ten employees.

'You suckered me,' she said, indicating the soup.

'You're not the first.'

Amused, she said, 'If I could pull the right strings, I'd have the courts change your name to Charlie Mouse. See how that works.'

'I'm glad you can still smile,' Mickey said.

A beautiful young waitress with jet-black hair and almond eyes appeared at the table and asked if Connie would like to order dinner.

'Just a bottle of Tsing Tao please,' Connie said. And

to Mickey: 'I don't *feel* much like smiling, if you want to know the truth. You sure as hell ruined my day with that call this morning.'

'Ruined your day? *Me?*'

'Who else?'

'Maybe a certain gentleman with a Browning and a few grenades?'

'So you heard about that.'

'Who hasn't? Even in southern California it's the kind of story that gets on the news ahead of the sports report.'

'On a slow day maybe.'

He finished his soup.

The waitress returned with the beer.

Connie poured the Tsing Tao down the side of the chilled pilsner glass to minimize the head, took a sip, and sighed.

'I'm sorry,' Mickey said sincerely. 'I know how much you wanted to believe you had a family.'

'I *did* have a family,' she said. 'They're just all gone.'

* * *

Between the ages of three and eighteen, Connie had been raised in a series of state institutions and temporary foster homes, each more abysmal than the one before it, requiring her to be tough and to fight back. Because of her personality, she had not appealed to adoptive parents and could not escape by that route. Certain of her character traits, which she saw as strengths, were considered attitude problems by other people. From the youngest age, she had been independent-minded, solemn beyond her years, virtually unable to *be* a child. To act her age, she literally would have had to *act*, for she had been an adult in a child's body.

Until seven months ago, she had not given much thought to the identity of her parents. There seemed to be no percentage in caring. For whatever reason, they had abandoned her as a child, and she had no memory whatsoever of them.

Then one sunny Sunday afternoon, when she went sky-diving out of the airfield at Perris, her ripcord jammed. She fell four thousand feet toward brown desert scrub as arid as Hell, with the conviction that she was dead except for the actual dying. Her chute deployed at the last possible moment to allow survival. Although her landing was rough, she was lucky; it resulted in only a sprained ankle, abraded left hand, bruises – and a sudden need to know where she'd come from.

Everyone had to exit this life without a clue as to where they were going, so it seemed essential to know at least something about the entrance.

During off-duty hours, she could have used official channels, contacts, and computers to investigate her past, but she preferred Mickey Chan. She didn't want her colleagues getting involved with her search, pulling for her and curious – in case she found something she didn't want to share with them.

As it turned out, what Mickey had learned after six months of prying into official files was not pretty.

When he handed her the report in his stylish Fashion Island office with its nineteenth-century French art and Biedermeier furniture, he said, 'I'll be in the next room, dictating some letters. Let me know when you're finished.'

His Asian reticence, the implication that she might need to be alone, alerted her to just how bad the truth was.

According to Mickey's report, a court had removed her from the care of her parents because she had suffered repeated severe physical abuse. As punishment for unknown transgressions – perhaps merely for being alive – they beat her, shaved off all of her hair, blindfolded her and tied her and left her in a closet for eighteen hours at a stretch, and broke three of her fingers.

When remanded to the care of the court, she had not yet learned to speak, for her parents had never taught or permitted her to talk. But speech had come quickly to her, as if she relished the rebellion that the mere act of speaking represented.

However, she never had the opportunity to accuse her mother and father. While fleeing the state to avoid prosecution, they had died in a fiery head-on collision near the California-Arizona border.

Connie read Mickey's first report with grim fascination, less shaken by its contents than most people would have been because she had been a cop long enough to have seen the likes of it many times – and worse. She did not feel that the hatred directed against her had been earned by her shortcomings or because she had been less lovable than other kids. It was just how the world worked sometimes. Too often. At least she finally understood why, even at the tender age of three, she had been too solemn, too wise beyond her years, too independent-minded, just too damned *tough* to be the cute and cuddly girl that adoptive parents were seeking.

The abuse must have been worse than the dry language of the report made it sound. For one thing, courts usually tolerated a lot of parental brutality before taking such drastic action. For another – she had blocked all memories of it and of her sister, which was an act of some desperation.

Most children who survived such experiences grew up deeply troubled by their repressed memories and feelings of worthlessness – or even utterly dysfunctional. She was fortunate to be one of the strong ones. She had no doubts about her value as a human being or her specialness as an individual. Though she might have enjoyed being a gentler person, more relaxed, less cynical, quicker to laugh, she nevertheless liked herself and was content in her own way.

Mickey's report hadn't contained entirely bad news. Connie learned that she had a sister of whom she'd been unaware. Colleen. Constance Mary and Colleen Marie Gulliver, the former born three minutes before the latter. Identical twins. Both abused, both permanently removed from parental care, eventually sent to different institutions, they had gone on to lead separate lives.

As she sat in the client chair that day a month ago, in front of Mickey's desk, a shiver of delight had swept along Connie's spine at the realization that someone existed with whom she shared such a singularly intimate bond. Identical twins. She abruptly understood why she sometimes dreamed of being two people at once and appeared in duplicate in those sleeping fantasies. Though Mickey was still seeking leads on Colleen, Connie dared to hope she was not alone.

* * *

But now, a few weeks later, Colleen's fate was known. She had been adopted, raised in Santa Barbara – and died five years ago at the age of twenty-eight.

That morning, when Connie learned she had lost her sister again, and forever this time, she had known a more intense grief than at any time in her life.

She had not wept.

She seldom did.

Instead, she had dealt with that grief as she dealt with all disappointments, setbacks, and losses: she kept busy, obsessively busy – and she got angry. Poor Harry. He had taken the brunt of her anger all morning without having a clue as to the cause of it. Polite, reasonable, peace-loving, long-suffering Harry. He would never know just how perversely *grateful* she had been for the chance to chase down the moon-faced perp, James Ordegard. She had been able to direct her rage at someone more deserving of it, and work off the pent-up energy of the grief that she could not release through tears.

Now she drank Tsing Tao and said, 'This morning, you mentioned photographs.'

The busboy removed the empty soup bowl.

Mickey put a manila envelope on the table. 'Are you sure you want to look at them?'

'Why wouldn't I?'

'You can never know her. The pictures might bring that home.'

'I've already accepted it.'

She opened the envelope. Eight or ten snapshots slid out.

The photos showed Colleen as young as five or six, as old as her mid-twenties, which was nearly as old as she had ever gotten. She wore different clothes from those that Connie had ever worn, styled her hair differently, and was photographed in living rooms and kitchens, on lawns and beaches, that Connie had never seen. But in every fundamental way – height, weight, coloration, facial features, even expressions and unconscious body attitudes – she was Connie's perfect double.

Connie had the uncanny feeling that she was seeing photos of herself in a life that she could not remember having lived.

'Where did you get these?' she asked Mickey Chan.

'From the Ladbrooks. Dennis and Lorraine Ladbrook, the couple that adopted Colleen.'

Examining the photographs again, Connie was struck by the fact that Colleen was smiling or laughing in every one of them. The few pictures that had ever been taken of Connie as a child were usually institutional group shots with a crowd of other kids. She didn't have a single photograph of herself in which she was smiling.

'What are the Ladbrooks like?' she asked.

'They're in business. They work together, own an office-supply store in Santa Barbara. Nice people, I think, quiet and unassuming. They weren't able to have any children of their own, and they adored Colleen.'

Envy darkened Connie's heart. She coveted the love and years of normality that Colleen had known. Irrational, to envy a dead sister. And shameful. But she could not help herself.

Mickey said, 'The Ladbrooks haven't gotten over her death, not even after five years. They didn't know she was a twin. They never were given that information by the child welfare agencies.'

Connie returned the photographs to the manila envelope, unable to look at them any longer. Self-pity was an indulgence that she loathed, but that's what her envy was swiftly becoming. A heaviness, like piled stones, pressed upon her breast. Later, in the privacy of her apartment, maybe she would feel like spending more time with her sister's lovely smile.

The waitress arrived with moo goo gai pan and rice for Mickey.

Ignoring the chopsticks that were provided with a regular complement of flatware, Mickey picked up his fork. 'Connie, the Ladbrooks would like to meet you.'

'Why?'

'Like I said, they never knew Colleen had a twin.'

'I'm not sure it's a good idea. I can't be Colleen for them. I'm someone different.'

'I don't think it would be like that.'

After she drank some beer, she said, 'I'll think about it.'

Mickey dug into his moo goo gai pan as if nothing tastier had ever come out of any kitchen in the Western hemisphere.

The look and smell of the food made Connie half ill. She knew that nothing was wrong with the dinner, only with her reaction to it. She had more than one reason to be queasy. It had been a hard day.

Finally she asked the dreadful question that remained. 'How did Colleen die?'

Mickey studied her for a moment before answering. 'I was ready to tell you this morning.'

'I wasn't ready to hear, I guess.'

'Childbirth.'

Connie had been prepared for any of the stupid and pointless ways that death could come suddenly to an attractive twenty-eight-year-old woman in these dark terminal years of the millennium. She had not been prepared for this, however, and it jolted her.

'She had a husband?'

Mickey shook his head. 'No. Unwed mother. I don't know the circumstances, who the father was, but it doesn't seem to be a sore point with the Ladbrooks, nothing they consider a stain on her memory. She was a saint in their eyes.'

'What about the baby?'

'A girl.'

'She lived?'

'Yes,' Mickey said. He put down his fork, drank some

water, blotted his mouth with a red napkin, watching Connie all the while. 'Her name is Eleanor. Eleanor Ladbrook. They call her Ellie.'

'Ellie,' Connie said numbly.

'She looks a great deal like you.'

'Why didn't you tell me this morning?'

'You didn't give me a chance. Hung up on me.'

'I didn't.'

'Just about. Very brusque, you were. Tell me the rest this evening, you said.'

'Sorry. When I heard Colleen was dead, I thought it was over.'

'Now you have a family. You're someone's aunt.'

She accepted the reality of Ellie's existence, but she could not yet begin to get a handle on what Ellie might mean to her own life, her future. After having been alone for so long, she was stunned to learn for certain that someone of her own flesh and blood was also alive in this vast and troubled world.

'Having family somewhere, even one, must make a difference,' Mickey said.

She suspected it would make a huge difference. Ironically, earlier in the day, she had nearly been killed before learning that she had one very important new reason to live.

Putting another manila envelope on the table, Mickey said, 'The final report. The Ladbrooks' address and phone number's in there when you decide you need them.'

'Thank you, Mickey.'

'And the bill. It's in there too.'

She smiled. 'Thank you anyway.'

As Connie slid out of the booth and stood, Mickey said, 'Life's funny. So many connections with other people that we don't even know about, invisible threads linking us to some we've long forgotten and some we won't meet for years – if ever.'

'Yeah. Funny.'

'One more thing, Connie.'

'What's that?'

'There's a Chinese saying that goes . . . Sometimes life can be as bitter as dragon tears— '

'This more of your crap?'

'Oh, no. It's a real saying.' Sitting there, a small man in a large booth, with his gentle face and crinkled eyes full of good humor, Mickey Chan seemed like a thin Buddha. 'But that's only part of the saying – the part you already understand. The whole thing goes . . . Sometimes life can be as bitter as dragon tears. But whether dragon tears are bitter or sweet depends entirely on how each man perceives the taste.'

'In other words, life is hard, even cruel – but it's also what you make of it.'

Putting his slender hands flat together without interleaving his fingers, in the position of oriental prayer, Mickey bowed his head in her direction with mock solemnity. 'Perhaps wisdom may yet enter through the thick bone of your Yankee head.'

'Anything's possible,' she admitted.

She left with the two manila envelopes. Her sister's captured smile. The promise of her niece.

Outside, rain was still coming down at a rate that made her wonder if a new Noah was at work somewhere

151

world, even now marching pairs of animals up a boarding gangway.

The restaurant was in a new strip shopping center, and a deep overhang kept the pedestrian walkway dry. A man was standing to the left of the door. Peripheral vision gave Connie the impression that he was tall and husky, but she didn't actually look at him until he spoke to her.

'Have mercy on a poor man, will you, please? Mercy for a poor man, lady?'

She was about to step off the curb, out from under the overhang, but his voice was arresting. Soft, gentle, even musical, it seemed radically out of sync with the size of the person she had seen from the corner of her eye.

Turning, she was surprised by the formidable ugliness of the man, and wondered how he could possibly earn even a meager living as a beggar. His unusual size, knotted hair, and unkempt beard gave him the mad aspect of Rasputin, though that crazed Russian priest had been a pretty-boy by comparison. Terrible bands of scar tissue disfigured his face, and his beak nose was dark with broken blood vessels. His lips were marked by oozing blisters. One glimpse of his diseased teeth and gums reminded her of those in a corpse she had once seen after it had been exhumed for poison tests nine years after burial. And the eyes. Cataracts. Thick, milky membranes. She could barely see the dark circles of the irises underneath. His appearance was so threatening that Connie imagined most people, upon being panhandled by him, turned and fled rather than approached to press money into his extended hand.

'Mercy on a poor man? Mercy on the blind? Spare change for one less fortunate than you?'

The voice was extraordinary in its own right, but doubly so considering the source. Clear, melodious, it was the instrument of a born singer who would deliver every lyric sweetly. It must be the voice alone that, in spite of his appearance, made it possible for him to live as a mendicant.

Ordinarily, in spite of his voice, Connie would have told him to buzz off – though not so politely. Some beggars became homeless by no fault of their own; and having experienced homelessness of a kind when she'd been an institutionalized child, she had compassion for the genuinely victimized. But her job required daily contact with too many street people for her to be able to romanticize them as a class; in her experience, many were gravely demented and for their own sakes belonged in the mental institutions from which do-gooders had 'mainstreamed' them, while others had earned their perdition through alcohol, drugs, or gambling.

She suspected that in *every* strata of society, from the mansion to the gutter, the genuinely innocent were a distinct minority.

For some reason, however, although this guy looked as if he had made every bad decision and self-destructive choice it was within his power to make, she fished in her jacket pockets until she found a couple of quarters and a ten-dollar bill worn soft with age. To her greater surprise, she kept the quarters and gave him the ten bucks.

'Bless you, lady. God bless you and keep you and make His face to shine upon you.'

Astonished at herself, she turned away from him. She hurried out into the rain, toward her car.

As she ran, she wondered what had possessed her. But it really wasn't hard to figure. She had been given more than one gift during the course of the day. Her life had been spared in the pursuit of Ordegard. And they had nailed the creep. And then there was five-year-old Eleanor Ladbrook. Ellie. A niece. Connie could not recall many days as fine as this, and she supposed her good fortune had put her in the mood to give something back when an opportunity arose.

Her life, one wasted perp, and a new direction for her future – not a bad trade for ten dollars.

She got in the car, slammed the door. She already had the keys in her right hand. She switched on the engine and gunned it because it chugged a little as if protesting the weather.

Suddenly she was aware that her left hand was clenched in a tight fist. She wasn't conscious of having made the fist. It was as if her hand had closed in a lightning-quick spasm.

Something was in her hand.

She uncurled her fingers to look at what she held.

The parking-lot lamps shed enough light through the rain-smeared windshield for her to see the crumpled item.

A ten-dollar bill. Worn soft with age.

She stared at it in confusion, then with growing disbelief. It must be the same ten bucks she thought she had given to the beggar.

But she *had* given the money to the tramp, had seen his grimy mitt close around it as he babbled his gratitude.

Bewildered, she looked through the side window of the

car toward the Chinese restaurant. The beggar was no longer there.

She scanned the entire pedestrian walkway. He was nowhere in front of the strip shopping center.

She stared at the crumpled money.

Gradually her good mood faded. She was overcome by dread.

She had no idea why she should be afraid. And then she did. Cop instinct.

·10·

Harry took longer than he expected to get home from Special Projects. Traffic moved sluggishly, repeatedly clogging up at flooded intersections.

He lost more time when he stopped at a 7-Eleven to get a couple of things he needed for dinner. A loaf of bread. Mustard.

Every time he went into a convenience store, Harry thought of Ricky Estefan stopping after work that day for a quart of milk – and buying a drastic life change instead. But nothing bad happened in the 7-Eleven, except that he heard the story about the baby and the birthday party.

A small television on the check-out counter kept the clerk entertained when business was slow, and it was turned to the news while Harry was paying for his purchases. A young mother in Chicago had been charged with murdering her own infant child. Her relatives had planned a big birthday party for her, but

155

when her baby-sitter failed to show up, it had looked as if she wouldn't be able to go and enjoy herself. So she dumped her two-month-old infant down the chute of her apartment-building trash incinerator, went to the party, and danced up a storm. Her lawyer had already said her defense would be postpartum depression.

Yet another example of the continuing crisis for Connie's collection of outrages and atrocities.

The clerk was a slender young man with dark, sorrowful eyes. In Iranian-accented English, he said, 'What's this country coming to?'

'Sometimes I wonder,' Harry said. 'But then again, in your former country, they don't just let the lunatics run around free, they actually put them in charge.'

'True,' the clerk said. 'But here, too, sometimes.'

'Can't argue that.'

As he was pushing through one of the two glass doors on his way out of the store, with the bread and mustard in a plastic bag, Harry suddenly realized he was carrying a folded newspaper under his right arm. He stopped with the door half open, took the paper from under his arm, and stared at it uncomprehendingly. He was sure he had not picked up a paper, let alone folded one and put it under his arm.

He returned to the cash register. When he put the paper on the counter, it unfolded.

'Did I pay for this?' Harry asked.

Puzzled, the clerk said, 'No, sir. I didn't even see you pick it up.'

'I don't *remember* picking it up.'

'Did you want it?'

'No, not really.'

Then he noticed the headline at the top of the front page: SHOOTOUT AT LAGUNA BEACH RESTAURANT. And the subhead: TWO DEAD, TEN WOUNDED. It was the late edition with the first story about Ordegard's bloody rampage.

'Wait,' Harry said. 'Yes. Yes, I guess I'll take it.'

On those occasions when one of his cases became newsworthy, Harry never read about himself in the papers. He was a cop, not a celebrity.

He gave the clerk a quarter and took the evening edition.

He still didn't understand how the paper had gotten folded and tucked under his arm. Blackout? Or something stranger, more directly related to the other inexplicable events of the day?

*   *   *

When Harry opened the front door and, dripping, stepped into the foyer of his condominium, home had never seemed so inviting. It was a neat and ordered haven, into which the chaos of the outside world could not intrude.

He took off his shoes. They were saturated, probably ruined. He should have worn galoshes, but the weather report had not called for rain until after nightfall.

His socks were wet, too, but he left them on. He would mop the foyer tile after he changed into clean, dry clothes.

He stopped in the kitchen to put the bread and mustard on the counter beside the cutting board. Later he would make sandwiches with some cold poached chicken. He was starved.

The kitchen sparkled. He was so pleased that he had taken the time to clean up the breakfast mess before going to work. He would have been depressed to see it now.

From the kitchen he went through the dining room, down the short hall to the master bedroom, carrying the evening newspaper. As he crossed the threshold, he snapped on the lights – and discovered the hobo on his bed.

Alice never fell down any rabbit hole deeper than the one into which Harry dropped at the sight of the vagrant.

The man seemed even bigger than he had been out of doors or from a distance in the Special Projects corridor. Dirtier. More hideous. He did not have the semi-transparency of an apparition; in fact, with his masses of tangled hair and intricately layered varieties of grime and webwork of scars, with his dark clothes so wrinkled and tattered that they recalled the interment wrappings of an ancient Egyptian mummy, he was more real than the room itself, like a painstakingly detailed figure painted by a photorealist and then inserted into a minimalist's line-drawing of a room.

The tramp's eyes opened. Like pools of blood.

He sat up and said, 'You think you're so special. But you're just one more animal, walking meat like all the rest of them.'

Dropping the newspaper, pulling his revolver from his shoulder holster, Harry said, 'Don't move.'

Ignoring the warning, the intruder swung his legs over the side of the bed, got up.

The impression of the vagrant's head and body remained in the spread, pillows, and mattress. A ghost could walk through snow, leaving no footprints, and hallucinations had no weight.

'Just another diseased animal.' If anything, the vagrant's voice was deeper and raspier than it had been on the street in Laguna Beach, the guttural voice of a beast that had laboriously learned to talk. 'Think you're a hero, don't you? Big man. Big hero. Well, you're nothing, less than a pissant, that's what you are. *Nothing!*'

Harry couldn't believe it was going to happen again, not twice in one day, and for God's sake not in his own home.

Backing up one step into the doorway, he said, 'You don't lie down on the floor right now, on your face, hands behind your back, *right now*, so help me God I'll blow your head off.'

Starting around the bed toward Harry, the vagrant said, 'You think you can shoot anyone you like, push anyone around if you want to, and that's the end of it, but that's not the end of it with me, shooting *me* is never the end of it.'

'Stop, right now, I mean it!'

The intruder didn't stop. His moving shadow was huge on the wall. 'Rip your guts out, hold them in your face, make you smell them while you die.'

Harry had the revolver in both hands. A shooter's

stance. He knew what he was doing. He was a good marksman. He could have hit a flitting hummingbird at such close range, let alone this great looming hulk, so there was only one way it could end, the intruder as cold as a side of beef, blood all over the walls, only one plausible scenario – yet he felt in greater danger than ever before in his life, infinitely more vulnerable than he had been among the mannequins in the box-maze attic.

'You people,' the vagrant said, rounding the foot of the bed, 'are so much fun to play with.'

One last time, Harry ordered him to stop.

But he kept coming, maybe ten feet away, eight, six.

Harry opened fire, squeezing shots off nice and smooth, not letting the hard recoil of the handgun pull the muzzle off target, once, twice, three times, four, and the explosions were deafening in the small bedroom. He knew every round did damage, three in the torso, the fourth in the base of the throat from only inches more than arm's length, causing the head to snap around as if doing a comic doubletake.

The hobo didn't go down, didn't stagger backward, only jerked with each hit he took. Inflicted pointblank, the throat wound was ghastly. The bullet must have punched all the way through, leaving an even worse exit wound in the back of the neck, fracturing or severing the spine, but there was no blood, no spray or spout or smallest spurt, as if the man's heart had stopped beating long ago and all the blood had dried and hardened in his vessels. He kept coming, no more stoppable than an express train, rammed into Harry, knocking the wind out of him, lifting him, carrying him backward through the doorway, slamming him so hard against the far hallway wall that Harry's teeth snapped together with an audible *clack* and the revolver flipped out of his hand.

Pain spread like a Japanese accordion fan from the small of Harry's back across both shoulders. For a moment he thought he was going to black out, but terror kept him conscious. Pinned to the wall, feet dangling off the floor, stunned by the plaster-cracking force with which he'd been hammered, he was as helpless as a child in the iron grip of his assailant. But if he could remain conscious, his strength might flood back into him, or maybe he would think of something to save himself, anything, a move, a trick, a distraction.

The hobo leaned against Harry, crushing him. The nightmarish face loomed closer. The livid scars were encircled by enlarged pores the size of match heads, packed with filth. Tufts of wiry black hair bristled from his flared nostrils.

When the man exhaled, it was like a mass grave venting the gases of decomposition, and Harry choked in revulsion.

'Scared, little man?' the vagrant asked, and his ability to speak seemed unaffected by the hole in his throat and the fact that his vocal chords had been pulverized and blown out through the back of his neck. 'Scared?'

Harry was scared, yes, he would have been an idiot if he hadn't been scared. No amount of weapons training or police work prepared you for going face to face with the boogeyman, and he didn't mind admitting it, was prepared to shout it from a rooftop if that's what the vagrant wanted, but he couldn't get his breath to speak.

'Sunrise in eleven hours,' the hobo said. 'Ticktock.'

Things were moving in the depths of the tramp's bushy beard. Crawling. Maybe bugs.

He shook Harry fiercely, rattling him against the wall.

Harry tried to bring his arms up between them, break the big man's hold. It was like trying to force concrete to yield.

'First everything and everyone you love,' the vagrant snarled.

Then he turned, still holding Harry, and threw him back through the bedroom doorway.

Harry hit the floor hard and rolled into the side of the bed.

'*Then you!*'

Gasping and dazed, Harry looked up and saw the hobo filling the doorway, watching him. The revolver was at the big man's feet. He kicked it into the room, toward Harry, and it spun to a stop on the carpet, just out of reach.

Harry wondered if he could get to the gun before the bastard came down on him. Wondered if there was any point trying. Four shots, four hits, no blood.

'Did you hear me?' the vagrant demanded. 'Did you hear me? Did you hear me, hero? Did you hear me?' He didn't pause for an answer, kept repeating the question in an increasingly angry and curiously mocking tone of voice, louder, louder still, 'Did you hear me, hero? Did you hear me, did you hear me, did you hear me, hear me, hear me? *Did you hear me? DID YOU HEAR ME, DID YOU, DID YOU, DID YOU, HERO, DID YOU, DID YOU?*'

The hobo was trembling violently, and his face was dark with rage and hatred. He wasn't even looking at Harry any longer, but at the ceiling, howling the words – *'DID YOU HEAR ME, DID YOU HEAR ME?'* – as if his fury had become so enormous that one man could no longer be a satisfactory target for it, screaming at the whole world or even worlds beyond, voice oscillating between bass thunder and a piercing shriek.

Harry tried to get to his feet by supporting himself against the bed.

The vagrant raised his right hand, and green static electricity crackled between his fingers. Light shimmered in the air above his palm, and suddenly his hand was on fire.

He snapped his wrist and flung a fireball across the room. It hit the drapes, and they exploded into flames.

His eyes were not red liquid pools any longer. Instead, fire licked out of the sockets, lapping up over his eyebrows, as though he was just the hollow figure of a man, made of wicker, burning from the inside out.

Harry was on his feet. His legs were shaky.

All he wanted was to get out of there. Burning drapes covered the window. The hobo was in the doorway. No exit.

The vagrant turned and snapped his wrist in the manner of a magician revealing a dove, and another white-hot churning sphere spun across the room, smashed into the dresser, burst like a Molotov cocktail, showering flames. The dresser mirror shattered. Wood split, drawers popped open, and the conflagration spread.

Smoke curled out of his beard, and fire spat from his nostrils. His hooked nose blistered and began to melt. His mouth was open in a shout, but the only sounds he made were the hiss, pop, and crackle of combustion. He exhaled a pyrotechnic cascade, sparks in all the colors of the rainbow, and then flames shot from his mouth. His lips curled up as crisp as deep-fried pork rinds, turned black, and peeled back from smouldering teeth.

Harry saw snakes of flame wriggle up the wall from the dresser and onto the ceiling. In places the carpet was burning.

Already the heat was tremendous. Soon the air would be full of acrid smoke.

Bright flares squirted out of the three bullet holes in the vagrant's chest, red and gold fire instead of blood. He flicked his wrist once more, and a third bright sputtering globe erupted from his hand.

The hissing mass streaked at Harry. He dropped into a crouch. It passed over his head, so close that he protected his face with one arm and cried out when the wake of searing heat washed over him. The bedclothes erupted into flames as if they had been soaked in gasoline.

When Harry looked up, the doorway was empty. The vagrant was gone.

He scooped the revolver off the floor and rushed into the hall, with the carpet sprouting flames around his stockinged feet. He was glad his socks were sopping wet.

The hallway was deserted, which was good, because he didn't want another confrontation with . . . with whatever the hell he'd just *had* a confrontation with, not if bullets didn't work. The kitchen to his left. He hesitated, then stepped in front of the doorway, gun at the ready. Fire eating the cabinets, curtains flapping like the skirts of dancers in Hell, smoke rolling toward him. He kept moving. The foyer ahead, living room to the right, where the thing must have gone, *thing* not hobo. He was reluctant to pass the archway, afraid the thing would plunge out at him, seize him in its incandescent hands, but he had to get out fast, the place was filling with smoke, and he was coughing, unable to draw enough clean air.

Edging to the foyer with his back against the hallway wall, facing the arch, Harry kept the gun in front of him, more because of training and habit than because he had any faith in its efficacy. Anyway, only one round remained in the cylinder.

The living room was burning, too, and in the middle stood the fiery figure, fully engulfed, arms spread wide to embrace the torrid tempest, consumed by it yet obviously in no pain, perhaps even in a state of rapture. Each lambent caress of flame seemed to be a source of perverse pleasure to the thing.

Harry was sure that it was watching him from within its shrouds of fire. He was afraid it might suddenly approach, arms still in a cruciform posture, to pin him against the wall again.

He crabbed sideways past the archway into the small foyer, as a black tide of smothering, blinding smoke rolled down the hall from the bedroom and submerged him. The last thing Harry saw was his soggy shoes, and he snatched them up in the same hand with which he held the gun. The smoke was so dense that no light penetrated to the foyer even from the leaping flames behind him. Anyway, his eyes stung and flooded with tears; he was forced to squeeze them tight shut. In the tarry blackness, there was a danger of becoming disoriented, even in such a small space.

He held his breath. One inhalation would be toxic enough to bring him to his knees, choking, dizzy. But he hadn't been getting clean air since the master bedroom, so he wasn't going to be able to hold out long, a few seconds. Even as he scooped up the shoes, he grabbed for the doorknob, couldn't find it in the darkness, fumbled, began to panic, but closed his left hand around it. Locked. Dead-bolt latch. His lungs were hot, as if fire had gotten into them. Chest ached. Where was the dead-bolt? Should be above the knob. He wanted to breathe, found the dead-bolt, *had* to breathe, couldn't, disengaged the lock, was aware of a growing inner darkness more dangerous than the outer one, grasped the knob, tore the door open, plunged outside. The smoke was still around him, sucked out by the cool night, and he had to weave to the right to find clean air, the first breath of which was painfully icy in his lungs.

In the garden courtyard, where walkways wound among azaleas and plum-thorn hedges and lush beds of English primrose, with the U-shaped building around him, Harry blinked furiously, clearing his vision. He saw a few neighbors coming out of their apartments onto the lower promenade, and above were two people on the second-story promenade by which all of the upper apartments were accessed. They'd probably been drawn by the gunfire, because it was not a neighborhood where that sound was common. They were staring in shock at him and at the plumes of oily smoke churning out of his front door, but he didn't think he'd heard anybody yelling 'fire,' so he began to shout it, and then the others picked up the cry.

Harry sprinted to one of the two alarm boxes along the ground-floor promenade. He dropped his gun and shoes, and yanked down the lever that broke the fogged glass. Bells clanged stridently.

To his right the living-room window of his own condo, which faced the courtyard, blew out and showered glass onto the concrete deck of the promenade. Smoke followed, and whipping pennants of fire, and Harry expected to see the burning man climb out through the broken window and continue the pursuit.

Crazily, a line from a movie theme song flashed through his mind: *Who you gonna call? GHOSTBUSTERS!*

He was living in a Dan Ackroyd movie. He might have found it funny if he hadn't been so scared that his thudding heart was halfway up his throat.

Sirens rose in the distance, fast approaching.

He ran from door to door, pounding with his fists on

each. More soft explosions. A strange metallic screech. Ceaselessly clanging alarm bells. Sequenced bursts of shattering glass rang like hundreds of windchimes hammered by an erratically gusting storm. Harry didn't look back for the source of any of the sounds, kept moving from door to door.

When the sirens grew to dominate all other sounds and seemed to be only a couple of blocks away, he was finally confident that everyone in the building had been alerted and gotten out. People were scattered across the courtyard garden, staring up at the roof or watching the street for the fire engines, horrified and scared, stunned silent or weeping.

He raced back to the first alarm box and pulled on his shoes, which he'd left there. He snatched up his revolver, stepped over a border of azaleas, waded through bloom-laden primrose, and splashed through a couple of puddles on a concrete walkway.

Only then did he realize the rain had stopped falling during the few minutes he had been in his apartment. The ficus and palm trees were still dripping, as was the shrubbery. The wet fronds and leaves were bejeweled with thousands of tiny ruby reflections of the growing fire.

He turned and, like his neighbors, looked back at the building, startled to see how fast the blaze was spreading. The apartment above his was engulfed. At broken windows, bloody tongues of flame licked across the remaining teeth of glass that bristled from the frames. Smoke billowed, and dreadful light pulsed and sputtered against the night.

Looking toward the street, Harry was relieved to see that fire trucks had entered the sprawling Los Cabos complex. Less than a block away, the sirens began to die, but the beacons kept flashing.

People had rushed into the street from other buildings, but they quickly got out of the way of the emergency vehicles.

An intense wave of heat drew Harry's attention to his own building again. The blaze had broken through to the roof.

As in a fairy tale, high upon the shingled peak, fire like a dragon was silhouetted against the dark sky, lashing its yellow and orange and vermillion tail, spreading huge carnelian wings, scales scintillant, scarlet eyes flashing, roaring a challenge to all knights and would-be slayers.

·11·

Connie stopped for a pepperoni and mushroom pizza on the way home. She ate at the kitchen table, washing the food down with a can of Coors.

For the past seven years, she had rented a small apartment in Costa Mesa. The bedroom contained only a bed, a nightstand, and a lamp, no dresser; her wardrobe was so simple that she was easily able to store all of her clothes and shoes in the single closet. The living room contained a black leather recliner, a floor lamp on one side of the big chair for when she wanted to read, and an end table on the other side; the recliner faced a television set and VCR on a wheeled stand. The dining area in the kitchen was furnished with a card table and four folding chairs with padded seats. The cabinets were mostly empty, containing only the minimum pots and utensils for cooking quick meals, a few bowls, four dinner plates, four salad plates, four cups and saucers, four glasses – always four because that was the number in the smallest set she could find to buy – and canned goods. She never entertained.

Possessions did not interest her. She had grown up without them, drifting from one foster home and institution to another with only a battered cloth suitcase.

In fact she felt encumbered by possessions, tied down, trapped. She owned not a single knick-knack. The only artwork or decoration on the walls was a poster in the kitchen, a photograph taken by a sky-diver from five thousand feet – green fields, rolling hills, a dry riverbed, scattered trees, two blacktop and two dirt roads narrow as threads, intersecting in the manner of lines on an abstract painting. She read voraciously, but all her books were from the library. All videotapes that she watched were rented.

She owned her car, but that was as much a machine of freedom as it was a steel albatross.

Freedom was the thing she sought and cherished, in place of jewelry and clothes and antiques and art, but it was sometimes more difficult to acquire than an original Rembrandt. In the long, sweet freefall before the parachute had to be deployed, there was freedom. Astride a powerful motorcycle on a lonely highway, she could find a measure of freedom, but a dirt bike in the desert vastness was even better, with only vistas of sand and rocky outcroppings and withered scrub brush rolling toward the blue sky in all directions.

While she ate pizza and drank beer, she took the snapshots out of the manila envelope and studied them. Her dead sister, so like herself.

She thought about Ellie, her sister's child, living up in Santa Barbara with the Ladbrooks, no image of her face among the pictures but perhaps as much like Connie as Colleen had been. She tried to decide how she felt about having a niece. As Mickey Chan suggested, it was a wonderful thing to have family, not to be alone in the world after having been alone for as long as she could remember. A pleasant thrill shivered through her when she thought about Ellie, but it was tempered by the concern that a niece might be an encumbrance far heavier than all the material possessions in the world.

What if she met Ellie and developed an affection for her?

No. She wasn't concerned about affection. She had given and received that before. Love. That was the worry.

She suspected that love, though a blessing, could also be a confining chain. What freedom might be lost by loving someone – or by being loved? She didn't know because she had never given or received any emotion as powerful and profound as love – or as what she thought love must be like, having read of it in so many great novels. She had read that love could be a trap, a cruel prison, and she had seen people's hearts broken by the weight of it.

She had been alone so long.

But she was comfortable in her solitude.

Change involved a terrible risk.

She studied her sister's smiling face in the almost-real colors of Kodachrome, separated from her by the thin glossy veneer of the photographic finish – and by five long years of death.

Of all sad words of tongue or pen, the saddest are these: '*It might have been.*'

She could never know her sister. However, she could still know her niece. All she needed was the courage.

She got another beer from the refrigerator, returned to the table, sat down to study Colleen's face for a while longer – and found a newspaper obscuring the photographs. The *Register*. A headline caught her eye: SHOOTOUT AT LAGUNA BEACH RESTAU-RANT . . . TWO DEAD, TEN WOUNDED.

For a long uneasy moment she stared at the headline. The paper hadn't been there a minute ago, hadn't been anywhere in the house, in fact, because she had never bought it.

When she'd gone to get a fresh beer from the refrigerator, her back had never been turned to the table. She knew beyond doubt that no one else was in the apartment. But even if an intruder had gotten in, she could not possibly have missed seeing him enter the kitchen.

Connie touched the paper. It was real, but the contact chilled her as deeply as if she had touched ice.

She picked it up.

It stank of smoke. Its pages were brown along the cut

edges, feathering to yellow and then to white toward the center, as if it had been salvaged from a fire just before it burned.

·12·

The crowns of the tallest palm trees disappeared into roiling clouds of smoke.

Stunned and weeping residents moved back as firemen in yellow and black slickers and high rubber boots unrolled hoses from the trucks and pulled them across walkways, flowerbeds. Other firemen appeared at a trot, carrying axes. Some were wearing breathing apparatus so they could enter the smoke-filled condominiums. Their swift arrival virtually insured that most of the apartments would be saved.

Harry Lyon glanced toward his own unit, at the south end of the building, and a sharp pang of loss stabbed through him. Gone. His alphabetically shelved collection of books, his CDs neatly arranged in drawers according to type of music and then by the artist's name, his clean white kitchen, carefully nurtured houseplants, the twenty-nine volumes of his daily diary which he had been keeping since he was nine (a separate journal for each year) – all gone. When he thought of the ravenous fire eating its way through his rooms, soot sifting over what little the fire didn't consume, everything glossy turning mottled and dull, he felt nauseous.

He remembered his Honda in the attached garage behind the building, started in that direction, then halted because it seemed foolish to jeopardize his own life to save a car. Besides, he was the president of the homeowner's association. At a time like this he ought to stay with his neighbors, offer them reassurance, comfort, advice about insurance and other issues.

As he holstered his revolver to avoid alarming the firemen, he remembered something the vagrant had said to him when he was pinned against the wall, the breath knocked out of him: *First everything and everyone you love . . . then you!*

When he thought about those words, considered the ramifications of them, profound fear crept spider-quick through him, worse than any fright he'd known so far, as dark as the fire was bright.

He headed for the garages, after all. Suddenly he desperately needed the car.

As Harry dodged firemen and rounded the side of the building, the air was filled with thousands of glowing embers like luminescent moths, swooping and fluttering, adance upon the spiraling thermal currents. High on the roof a cataclysmic crack was followed by a crash that jarred the night. A hail of burning shingles clattered down on the sidewalk and flanking shrubs.

Harry crossed his arms over his head, afraid the flaming cedar shakes would set his hair on fire, hoping that his clothes were still too damp to ignite. Slipping out of the firefall unharmed, he pushed through a wet iron gate still cold from the rain.

Behind the building, the wet blacktop was sequined with glass from exploded rear windows, spangled with puddles. Every mirrored surface swarmed with copper and claret images of the bright tempest raging on the roof of the main building. Glowing serpents slithered around Harry's feet as he ran.

The back driveway was still deserted when he reached his garage door and yanked it up. But even as it was swinging out of the way, a fireman appeared and shouted at him to get out of there.

'Police!' Harry replied. He hoped that would buy him the few seconds he needed, though he didn't pause to flash his badge.

Falling embers had seeded a few flames on the long garage roof. Thin smoke filled his double-wide stall, trickling down from the smouldering tar paper between the rafters and the shingles.

Keys. Harry was suddenly afraid he had left them on the foyer table or in the kitchen. Approaching the car, coughing because of the wispy but bitter smoke, he frantically patted his pockets and was relieved to hear the keys jingle in his sport coat.

First everything and everyone you love . . .

He reversed out of the garage, shifted gears, drove past the fireman who had shouted, and escaped the far end of the driveway two seconds before an approaching fire truck would have turned in and blocked it. They nearly kissed bumpers as Harry swung the Honda into the street.

When he had driven three or four blocks with uncharacteristic recklessness, weaving through traffic and running red lights, the radio snapped on of its own accord. The vagrant's deep, raspy voice echoed from the stereo speakers, startling him.

'*Gotta rest now, hero. Gotta rest.*'

'What the hell?'

Only a static hiss answered him.

Harry eased up on the accelerator. He reached toward the radio to switch it off, but hesitated.

'*Very tired . . . a little nap . . .*'

Hissing static.

'*. . . so you have an hour . . .*'

Hissing.

'*. . . but I'll be back . . .*'

Hissing.

Harry kept glancing away from the busy street ahead, at the lighted dial of the radio. It glowed a soft green but recalled to him the radiant red eyes – first blood, then fire – of the vagrant.

'*. . . big hero . . . just walking meat . . .*'

Hissing.

'*. . . shoot anyone you like . . . big man . . . but shooting me . . . never the end of it . . . not me . . . not me . . .*'

Hissing. Hissing. Hissing.

The car passed through a flooded depression in the pavement. Phosphorescent white water plumed like angels' wings on both sides.

Harry touched the radio controls, half expecting an electric shock or worse, but nothing happened. He punched the OFF button, and the hissing stopped.

He didn't try to run the next red traffic light. He eased to a stop behind a line of cars, struggling to sort through the events of the past several hours and make sense of them.

Who you gonna call?

He didn't believe in ghosts or ghostbusters.

Nevertheless he was shivering, and not merely because his clothes were still damp. He switched on the heater.

Who you gonna call?

Ghost or not, at least the vagrant had not been hallucinated. He wasn't a sign of mental breakdown. He was real. Not human, perhaps, but real.

That understanding was strangely calming. The thing Harry feared the most was not the supernatural or the unknown – but the internal disorder of madness, a threat that now seemed to have been replaced by an external adversary, bizarre beyond reckoning and terrifyingly powerful but, at least, external.

As the light changed to green and the traffic started moving again, he looked around at the streets of Newport Beach. He saw that he had headed west toward the coast and north from Irvine, and for the first time became consciously aware of where he was going. Costa Mesa. Connie Gulliver's apartment.

He was surprised. The burning apparition had promised to destroy everyone and everything he loved before destroying him, and all by the break of dawn. Yet Harry had chosen to go to Connie before checking in with his own parents in Carmel Valley. Earlier he had admitted to a keener interest in her than he had previously been willing to acknowledge, but perhaps that admission had not exposed the true complexity of his feelings even to himself. He knew that he cared for her, though the *why* of his caring was still in part a mystery to him, considering how utterly different from one another they were and how tightly closed upon herself she was. Neither was he sure of the depth of his caring, except that it was deep, more than deep enough to be the biggest revelation in a day filled with revelations.

As he passed Newport Harbor, through the gaps between the commercial buildings on his left, he saw the tall masts of yachts thrusting into the night, sails furled. Like a forest of church steeples. They were reminders that, like many of his generation, he had been raised without any specific faith and, as an adult, had never managed to discover a faith of his own. It wasn't that he denied the existence of God, only that he could not find a way to believe.

When you encounter the supernatural, who you gonna call? If not ghostbusters, then God. If not God . . . who you gonna call?

For most of his life Harry had placed his faith in order, but order was merely a condition, not a force he could call upon for help. In spite of the brutalities with which his job brought him into contact, he continued to believe, as well, in the decency and courage of human beings. That was what sustained him now. He was going to Connie Gulliver not merely to warn her but to seek her counsel, to ask her to help him find his way out of the darkness that had descended upon him.

Who you gonna call? Your partner.

When he stopped at the next red traffic light, he was surprised again, but this time not by what he found within himself. The heater had warmed the car and chased away the worst of his shivers. But he still felt a hard coldness over his heart. This newest surprise was in his shirt pocket, against his breast, not emotions but something tangible that he could fish out and hold and see. Four shapeless dark lumps. Metal. Lead. Though he could not begin to grasp how they had wound up in his pocket, he knew what the objects were: the shots that he had pumped into the vagrant, four lead slugs misshapen by high-velocity impacts with flesh, bone, and cartilage.

·13·

Harry took off his jacket, tie, and shirt to clean up as best he could in Connie's bathroom. His hands were so grimy they reminded him of the vagrant's hands, and required vigorous lathering to come clean. He washed his hair, face, chest, and arms in the sink, sluicing away some of his weariness with the soot and ashes, then slicked his hair back with her comb.

He could not do much with his clothes. He wiped them with a dry washcloth to remove the surface grit, but they remained somewhat spotted and heavily wrinkled. His white shirt was gray now, fouled by a vague perspiration odor and the heavier stench of smoke, but he had to put it on again because he had no other clothes into which he could change. In memory, he had never allowed himself to be seen in such a disheveled state.

He attempted to rescue his dignity by securing the top button on his shirt and knotting his tie.

More than the dismaying condition of his clothes, the condition of his body worried him. His abdomen was sore where the hand of the mannequin had rammed into him. A dull ache throbbed in the small of his back and did not fade altogether until it reached halfway up his spine, a reminder of the force with which the hobo had slammed him into the wall. The back of his left arm, all along the triceps, was tender, as well, because he had landed on it when the hobo had thrown him out of the hallway into the bedroom.

While he had been on the move, running for his life, pumped up with adrenalin, he hadn't been aware of his various pains, but inactivity revealed them. He was concerned that his muscles and joints might begin to stiffen. He was pretty sure, before the night was out, he would need to be quick and agile more than once if he hoped to save his butt.

In the medicine cabinet he found a bottle of Anacin. He shook four into the palm of his right hand, then capped the bottle and put it in a jacket pocket.

When he returned to the kitchen and asked for a glass of water with which to take the pills, Connie handed him a can of Coors.

He declined. 'I've got to keep a clear head.'

'One beer won't hurt. Might even help.'

'I don't drink much.'

'I'm not asking you to mainline vodka with a needle.'

'I'd prefer water.'

'Don't be a prig, for Christ's sake.'

He nodded, accepted the beer, popped the tab, and chased the four aspirin with a long cold swallow. It tasted wonderful. Maybe it was just what he needed.

Starved, he took a slice of cold pizza from the open

box on the counter. He tore off a mouthful and chewed enthusiastically, with none of his usual concern for manners.

He had never been to her place before, and he had noticed how Spartan it was. 'What do they call this style of decor Early Monk?'

'Who cares about decor? I'm just showing my landlord a little courtesy. If I croak in the line of duty, he can hose the place out in an hour and have it rented tomorrow.'

She returned to the card table and stared at the six objects she had lined up on it. A ten-dollar bill worn soft with age. One heat-discolored newspaper with pages slightly burnt along one edge. Four misshapen lead slugs.

Joining her, Harry said, 'Well?'

'I don't believe in ghosts, spirits, demons, that crap.'

'Me neither.'

'I saw this guy. He was just a bum.'

'I still can't believe you gave him ten bucks,' Harry said.

She actually blushed. He had never seen her blush before. The first thing ever to embarrass her in his company was this indication that she possessed some compassion.

She said, 'He was . . . compelling somehow.'

'So he wasn't "just a bum."'

'Maybe not, if he could get ten bucks out of me.'

'I'll tell you one thing.' He stuffed the last bite of pizza in his mouth.

'So tell me.'

Around the pizza, Harry said, 'I saw him burn up alive in my living room, but I don't think they'll find any charred bones in the ashes. And even if he hadn't spoken out of the car radio, I'd expect to see him again, as big and dirty and weird and unburnt as ever.'

As Harry got a second piece of pizza, Connie said, 'Thought you just told me you don't believe in ghosts either.'

'Don't.'

'Then what?'

Chewing, he regarded her thoughtfully. 'You believe me, then?'

'Part of it happened to me, too, didn't it?'

'Yeah. I guess enough to make you believe me.'

'Then what?' she repeated.

He wanted to sit down at the table, take a load off his feet, but he figured he was more likely to stiffen up if he settled in a chair. He leaned against the counter by the sink.

'I've been thinking . . . Every day, working an investigation, out on the street, we meet people who aren't like us, who think the law is just a sham to gull the ignorant masses into obedience. These people care about nothing but themselves, satisfying their own desires, regardless of the cost to others.'

'Hairballs, scumbags – they're our business,' she said.

'Criminal types, sociopaths. They have lots of names. Like the pod people from *Invasion of the Body Snatchers*, they walk among us and pass for civilized, ordinary human beings. But even though there's a lot of them, they're still a small minority and anything *but* ordinary. Their civilization is a veneer, stage makeup concealing the scaly, crawling savage thing we evolved from, the ancient reptile consciousness.'

'So? This isn't news,' she said impatiently. 'We're the thin line between order and chaos. We look into that abyss every day. Teetering on that edge, testing myself, proving I'm not one of them, won't fall into that chaos, won't become, *can't* become, like them – that's what makes this work so exciting. It's why I'm a cop.'

'Really?' he said, surprised.

That was not at all why he was a cop. Protecting the genuinely civilized, guarding them from the pod people among them, preserving peace and the beauty of order, providing for continuity and progress – that was why he had become a police officer, at least part of the reason, and certainly not to prove to himself that he was not one of the reptilian throwbacks.

While Connie spoke, she turned her eyes from Harry and stared at a nine-by-twelve manila envelope lying on one of the chairs at the table. He wondered what it contained.

'When you don't know where you come from, when you don't know if you can love,' she said quietly, almost as if talking to herself, 'when all you want is freedom, you have to force yourself to take on responsibility, a lot of it. Freedom without responsibility is pure savagery.' Her voice was not merely quiet. It was haunted. 'Maybe you come from savagery, you can't be sure, but what you *do* know about yourself is you can hate real well even if you can't love, and that scares you, means maybe you could slide into that abyss yourself . . .'

Harry stopped chewing halfway through a mouthful of pizza, riveted by her.

He knew she was revealing herself as she had never done before. He just didn't fully understand *what* she was revealing.

As if she had broken out of a trance, her gaze clicked up from the envelope to Harry, and her soft voice hardened. 'So, all right, the world is full of these shitheads, scumbags, sociopaths, whatever you want to call them. What's your point?'

He swallowed the pizza. 'So suppose an ordinary cop, going about his business, runs into a sociopath who's worse than the usual scumbags, infinitely worse.'

She had gone to the refrigerator while he was talking. She took another beer from it. 'Worse? In what way?'

'This guy has . . .'

'What?'

'He has a . . . gift.'

'What gift? Is this riddle hour? Spit it out, Harry.'

He stepped to the table, stirred one finger through the four lead slugs lying there. They rattled against the Formica surface with a sound that seemed to echo down eternity.

'Harry?'

Though he needed to tell her his theory, he was reluctant to begin. What he had to say would no doubt forever blow his image as Mr Equanimity.

He took a pull on his beer, followed it with a deep breath, and plunged: 'Suppose you had to deal with a sociopath, maybe even a psychotic sociopath, with paranormal powers that made going up against him like duking it out with an apprentice God. Psychic powers.'

She was gaping at him. The ring-pull on the beer can encircled her index finger, but she wasn't popping it open. She appeared to be holding a pose for a painter.

Before she could interrupt, he said, 'I don't mean he can just predict the suit of a playing card chosen randomly from a deck, tell you who's going to win the next World Series, or levitate a pencil. Nothing as smalltime as that. Maybe this guy has the power to manifest himself out of thin air – and vanish into it. The power to start fires, to burn without being consumed, to take bullets without really being killed. Maybe he can pin a psychic tag on you the way a game warden might tag a deer with an electronic transmitter, then keep track of you when you're out of his sight, no matter where you go or how far you run. I know, I know, it's absurd, it's crazy, it's like stumbling into a Spielberg movie, only darker, something by James Cameron out of David Lynch, but maybe it's true.'

Connie shook her head, incredulous. Opening the refrigerator door and putting the unpopped beer can back on the shelf, she said, 'Maybe two should be my limit tonight.'

He urgently needed to convince her. He was aware of how quickly the night was slipping away, how fast dawn was coming.

Turning from the refrigerator, she said, 'Where'd he get these amazing powers?'

'Who knows? Maybe he lived too long under high-power electric lines, the magnetic fields caused changes in his brain. Maybe there was too much dioxin in his milk when he was a baby, or he ate too many apples contaminated with some bizarre toxic chemical, his house is right under a hole in the ozone layer, aliens are experimenting on him to give the *National Enquirer* a good story, he ate too damn many Twinkies, he listened to way too much rap music! How the fuck do I know?'

She stared at him. At least she was no longer gaping. 'You're serious about this.'

'Yeah.'

'I know, because in the six months we've worked together, that's the first time you've ever used the F word.'

'Oh. I'm sorry.'

'Of course you are,' she said, managing a trace of sarcasm even under these circumstances. 'But this guy . . . he's just a bum.'

'I don't think that's his real appearance. I think he can be anything he wants to be, manifest himself in any form he chooses, because the manifestation isn't really him . . . it's a projection, a thing he wants us to see.'

'Isn't this the next thing to a ghost?' she asked. 'And didn't we agree that neither of us believes in ghosts?'

He snatched the ten-dollar bill off the table. 'If I'm so completely wrong, then how do you explain this?'

'Even if you're right . . . how do *you* explain it?'

'Telekinesis.'

'What's that?'

'The power to move an object through time and space with only the power of the mind.'

'Then why didn't I see the bill floating through the air into my hand?' she asked.

'That's not how it works. More like teleportation. It goes from one place to another, poof, without physically travelling the distance inbetween.'

She threw her hands up in exasperation. 'Beam me up, Scotty!'

He glanced at his wristwatch. 8:38. Ticktock . . . ticktock . . .

He knew he sounded like a lunatic, better suited to the afternoon television talkshow circuit or late-night radio call-in programs than to police work. But he also knew he was right, or at least that he was circling the periphery of the truth if not yet at the heart of it.

'Look,' he said, picking up the fire-browned newspaper and shaking it at her, 'I haven't read it yet, but if you comb through this paper, I know you'll find a few stories to add to that damn collection of yours, evidence of the new dark ages.' He dropped the paper, and the odor of smoke puffed from it. 'Let me see, what are some of the stories you've told me lately, things you picked up from other papers, television? I'm sure I can remember some of them.'

'Harry— '

'Not that I want to remember. I'd rather forget, God knows.' He started to pace more or less in a circle. 'Wasn't there one about a judge in Texas sentencing a guy to thirty-five years in jail for stealing a twelve-ounce can of Spam? And at the same time, up in Los Angeles, some rioters beat a guy to death in the street, all of it recorded by newsmen on videotape, but no one really wants to further disturb the community by tracking down the killers, not when the beating was a protest against injustice?'

She went to the table, pulled out a chair, turned it backward, and sat down. She stared at the burnt newspaper and other objects.

He kept pacing, speaking with increasing urgency: 'And wasn't there one about a woman who got her boyfriend to rape her eleven-year-old daughter, because she wanted a fourth child but wasn't able to have any more, so she figured she could be a mother to her little girl's bastard? Where was that? Wisconsin, was it? Ohio?'

'Michigan,' Connie said somberly.

'And wasn't there one about a guy beheading his six-year-old stepson with a machete— '

'Five. He was five.'

'—and a bunch of teenage boys somewhere stabbed a woman a hundred and thirty times to steal a lousy dollar— '

'Boston,' she whispered.

'—oh, yes, and there was that little jewel about the father who beat his preschooler to death because the boy couldn't remember the alphabet past G. And some woman in Arkansas or Louisiana or Oklahoma laced her baby's cereal with crushed glass, hoping to make her sick enough so the father would get a leave from the Navy and be able to spend some time at home.'

'Not Arkansas,' Connie said. 'Mississippi.'

Harry stopped pacing, crouched beside her chair, face to face with her.

'See, you accept all these incredible things, incredible as they are. You know they happened. These are the '90s, Connie. The pre-millennium cotillion, the new dark ages, when anything can happen and usually does, when the unthinkable isn't only thinkable but accepted, when every miracle of science is matched by an act of human barbarity that hardly raises anyone's eyebrow. Every brilliant technological achievement is countered by a thousand atrocities of human hatred and stupidity. For every scientist seeking a cure for cancer there are five thousand thugs willing to hammer an old lady's skull to applesauce just for the change in her purse.'

Troubled, Connie looked away from him. She picked up one of the misshapen slugs. Frowning, she turned it over and over between her thumb and forefinger.

Spooked by the uncanny speed with which the minutes changed on the liquid-crystal display of his wrist-watch, Harry would not relent.

'So who's to say there couldn't be some guy in a lab somewhere who discovered something to enhance the power of the human brain, to magnify and tap the powers we've always suspected are within us but could never use? Maybe this guy injected himself with this stuff. Or maybe the guy we're after, he's the subject of the experiment, and when he realized what he'd become, he killed everyone at the lab, everyone who knew. Maybe he walks the world among us now, the scariest damn pod person of them all.'

She put down the deformed slug. She turned to him again. She had beautiful eyes. 'The experiment thing makes sense to me.'

'But it's probably not anything like that, not anything we could figure, something different.'

'If such a man exists, can he be stopped?'

'He's not God. No matter what powers he has, he's still a man – and a deeply disturbed one at that. He'll have weaknesses, points of vulnerability.'

He still crouched beside her chair, and she put one hand against the side of his face. The tender gesture surprised him. She smiled. 'You've got one hell of a wild imagination, Harry Lyon.'

'Yeah, well, I've always liked fairy tales.'

Frowning again, she took her hand away as if chagrinned to have been caught in a moment of tenderness. 'Even if he's vulnerable, he can't be dealt with if he can't be found. How will we track down this Ticktock?'

'Ticktock?'

'We don't know his real name,' she said, 'so Ticktock seems as good as any for the time being.'

Ticktock. It was a fairy-tale villain's name if he had ever heard one. Rumpelstiltskin, Mother Gothel, Knucklebone – and Ticktock.

'All right.' Harry stood. He paced again. 'Ticktock.'

'How do we find him?'

'I don't know for sure. But I know where I want to start. The Laguna Beach city morgue.'

She twitched at that. 'Ordegard?'

'Yeah. I want to see the autopsy report if they've done

one yet, talk to the coroner if possible. I want to know if they found anything strange.'

'Strange? Like what?'

'Damned if I know. Anything out of the ordinary.'

'But Ordegard's dead. He wasn't just a . . . a projection. He was real, and now he's dead. He can't be Ticktock.'

Countless fairy tales, legends, myths, and fantasy novels gave Harry a vast store of incredible concepts from which to draw. 'So maybe Ticktock has the power to take over other people, slip into their minds, control their bodies, use them as if they were puppets, then dispose of them when he wants, or slip out again when they die. Maybe he was controlling Ordegard, then he moved on to the hobo, and now maybe the hobo is dead, really dead, his bones in my burned-out living room, and Ticktock will turn up in some other body next time.'

'Possession?'

'Something like it.'

'You're beginning to scare me,' she said.

'Beginning? You *are* a tough broad. Listen, Connie, just before he trashed my condo, Ticktock said something like . . . "You think you can shoot anyone you like, and that's the end of it, but not with me, shooting *me* isn't the end of it."' Harry tapped the butt of the gun in his shoulder holster. 'So who'd I shoot today? Ordegard. And this Ticktock is telling me that's not the end of it. So I want to find out if there's anything odd about Ordegard's corpse.'

She was amazed but not disbelieving. She was getting

in the swing of it. 'You want to know if there were signs of possession.'

'Yeah.'

'Exactly what *are* the signs of possession?'

'Anything odd.'

'Like the corpse's skull is empty, no brain, just ashes in there? Or maybe the number 666 burnt into the back of his neck?'

'I wish it would be something that obvious, but I doubt it.'

Connie laughed. A nervous laugh. Shaky. Brief.

She got up from the chair. 'Okay, let's go to the morgue.'

Harry hoped that a talk with the coroner or a quick reading of the autopsy report would tell him what he needed to know, and that it would not be necessary to view the corpse. He didn't want to have to look at that moon face again.

·14·

The large institutional kitchen at Pacific View Care Home in Laguna Beach was all white tile and stainless steel, as clean as a hospital.

Any rats or roaches creep in here, Janet Marco thought, they better be able to live on scouring powder, ammonia water, and wax.

Though antiseptic, the kitchen did not *smell* like a hospital. Lingering aromas of ham, roast turkey, herb stuffing, and scalloped potatoes were overlaid by the yeasty, cinnamon fragrance of the sweetrolls that they were baking for breakfast in the morning. It was a warm place, too, and the warmth was welcome after the chill that the recent storm had brought to the March air.

Janet and Danny were having dinner at one end of a long table in the southeast corner of the kitchen. They were in no one's way but enjoyed a vantage point from which they could watch the busy staff.

Janet was fascinated by the operation of the big kitchen, which ticked along like clockwork. The workers were industrious and seemed happy in their busyness. She envied them. She wished she could get a job at Pacific View, in the kitchen or any other department. But she didn't know what skills were required. And she doubted that even the owner – Mr Ishigura – good man that he was, would hire anyone who lived in a car, washed in public lavatories, and had no permanent address.

Though she liked watching the kitchen staff, the sight of them sometimes frustrated the devil out of her.

But she couldn't blame Mr Ishigura, the owner and operator of Pacific View, because he was a godsend on nights like this. Both thrifty and kind, he was dismayed by waste and by the thought of anyone going hungry in such a prosperous country. Invariably, after almost a hundred patients and the staff had eaten dinner, enough food remained to provide for ten or twelve people, because recipes could not be refined to produce precisely the number of portions needed. Mr Ishigura provided these meals free to certain of the homeless.

The food was good, too, really good. Pacific View

was not an ordinary nursing home. It was classy. The patients were rich, or had relatives who were rich.

Mr Ishigura did not advertise his generosity, and his door was not open to everyone. When he saw street people who seemed, to him, to have fallen to their fate not entirely by their own doing, he approached them about the free lunches and dinners at Pacific View. Because he was selective, it was possible to eat there without having to share the table with some of the moody and dangerous alcoholics and addicts who made many of the church and mission kitchens so unappealing.

Janet didn't take advantage of Mr Ishigura's hospitality nearly as often as it was available. Of the seven lunches and seven dinners she might have eaten at Pacific View each week, she limited herself to no more than two of each. Otherwise, she was able to provide for herself and Danny, and she took pride in every meal that was bought with her own earnings.

That Tuesday night, she and Danny shared the facilities with three elderly men, one aged woman whose face was as wrinkled as a crumpled paper bag but who wore a gaily colored scarf and bright red beret, and an unfortunately ugly young man with a deformed face. They were all ragged but not filthy, unbarbered but clean-smelling enough.

She didn't speak to any of them, although she would have enjoyed conversation. It had been so long since she had spoken at any length to anyone but Danny that she was not confident of making chit-chat with another adult.

Besides, she was leery of encountering someone with a keen curiosity. She did not want to have to answer questions about herself, her past. She was, after all, a murderer. And if Vince's body had been found in the Arizona desert, she might also be wanted by the police.

She didn't even speak to Danny, who needed no encouragement either to eat or to mind his manners. Though he was only five, the boy was well behaved and knew how to conduct himself at the table.

Janet was fiercely proud of him. From time to time, as they ate, she smoothed his hair or touched the back of his neck or patted his shoulder, so he would know that she was proud.

God, she loved him. So little, so innocent, so patiently enduring of one hardship after another. Nothing must happen to him. He must have his chance to grow up, become something in this world.

She could enjoy dinner only as long as she kept thoughts of the policeman to a minimum. The policeman who could change shape. Who had almost become a werewolf like out of a movie. Who *had* become Vince, while thunder rolled and lightning flashed, and who had halted Woofer in mid-air.

After the encounter in that alleyway earlier in the day, Janet had driven north in the pouring rain, out of Laguna Beach, heading for Los Angeles, desperate to put a lot of miles between them and the mysterious creature who wanted to kill them. It had said that it could find them no matter where they ran, and she had believed it. But just waiting to be killed was intolerable.

She got only as far as Corona Del Mar, the next town up the coast, before realizing that she must go back. In Los Angeles, she would have to learn what neighborhoods were best for scavenging, when the garbage pickups were scheduled so she could search the cans just ahead of the sanitation trucks, which communities had the most tolerant police, where cans and bottles could be redeemed, where to find another humanitarian like Mr Ishigura, and so much more. Her cash on hand was low at the moment, and she could not afford to live on their meager savings long enough to learn the ropes in a new place. It was Laguna Beach or nowhere.

Maybe the worst thing about being dirt poor was not having any choices.

She'd driven back to Laguna Beach, mentally chastising herself for the gasoline she'd wasted.

They parked on a side street and stayed in the car during all the rainy afternoon. By the gray storm light, with Woofer dozing in the back seat, she read to Danny from a thick storybook rescued from a trash bin. He loved being read to. He sat enthralled, while pearl and silver water shadows played across his face in patterns that matched the streams of rain shimmering down the windshield.

Now the rain was gone, the day was ended, dinner was finished, and it was time to return to the old Dodge for the night. Janet was exhausted, and she knew Danny would drop quickly into sleep like a stone sinking in a pond. But she dreaded closing her eyes, for she was afraid that the policeman thing would find them while they slept.

When they gathered up their dirty dishes and carried them to the sink where they always left them, Janet and Danny were approached by a cook whose first name was Loretta and whose last name was unknown to Janet. Loretta was a heavy-set woman of about fifty, with skin as smooth as porcelain and a brow so free of lines that she must never have had a worry in her entire life. Her hands were strong, and red from kitchen work. She was carrying a disposable pie tin full of meat scraps.

'That dog still hanging around?' Loretta asked. 'The cute fella who's been trailing after you the last few times?'

'Woofer,' Danny said.

'He's taken a shine to my boy,' Janet said. 'He's out in the alley now, waiting for us.'

'Well, I've got a treat for the cutie,' Loretta said, indicating the meat scraps.

A pretty blond nurse, standing at a nearby butcher's block and drinking a glass of milk, overheard their conversation. 'Is he really cute?'

'Just a mutt,' Loretta said, 'no fancy breed, but he oughta be in pictures, this one.'

'I'm a dog nut,' the nurse said. 'I have three. I love dogs. Can I see him?'

'Sure, sure, come on,' Loretta said. Then she checked herself and smiled at Janet. 'You mind if Angelina sees him?'

Angelina was evidently the nurse.

197

'Heavens no, why would I mind?' Janet said.

Loretta led the way to the alley door. The scraps in the pie tin were not fat and gristle, but choice bits of ham and turkey.

Outside the door in a cone of yellow light from a security lamp, Woofer sat in patient anticipation, his head cocked to the right, one ear pricked up and one ear floppy as usual, a quizzical look on his face. A cool breeze, the first stirring of the air since the storm had passed, ruffled his fur.

Angelina was instantly captivated. 'He's *wonderful*!'

'He's mine,' Danny said so softly that it was doubtful anyone but Janet had heard him.

As if he understood the nurse's praise, Woofer grinned, and his bushy tail vigorously swept the blacktop.

Maybe he *did* understand. Within a day of encountering Woofer, Janet had decided that he was a smart mutt.

Taking the pie tin full of scraps from the cook, Angelina moved in front of everyone and squatted down before the dog. 'You *are* a cutie. Look at this, fella. Does this look good? Bet you'll like this.'

Woofer glanced at Janet, as if seeking permission to feast on the scraps. He was just a collarless street dog now, but evidently he had been someone's house pet at one time. He had the restraint that came from training and the capacity for reciprocal affection that in animals – perhaps in people as well – grew from being loved.

Janet nodded.

Only then did the pooch take his dinner, snatching hungrily at the chunks and slivers of meat.

Unexpectedly, Janet Marco perceived a kinship with the dog that unnerved her. Her parents had treated her with the cruelty that some sick people directed against animals; indeed, they would have dealt with any cat or dog more humanely than they'd dealt with her. Vince had been no kinder. And though there were no indications that the dog had been beaten or starved, he had surely been abandoned. Though he was without a collar, he clearly had not been raised wild; for he was too eager to please and too needful of affection. Abandonment was just another form of abuse, which meant that Janet and the dog had shared a host of hardships, fears, and experiences.

She decided to keep the dog regardless of the trouble and expense he might pose. There was a bond between them, worthy of respect: they were both living creatures capable of courage and commitment – and both in need.

While Woofer ate with canine enthusiasm, the young blond nurse petted him, scratched behind his ears, and cooed to him.

'Told you he was a cutie,' said the cook, Loretta, folding her arms across her immense bosom and beaming at Woofer. 'Oughta be in movies, he should. A regular little charmer.'

'He's mine,' Danny said worriedly, and again in such a low voice that only Janet could have heard him. He was standing at her side, holding fast to her, and she put a hand on his shoulder reassuringly.

Halfway through his meal, Woofer suddenly looked up from the pie tin and regarded Angelina curiously. His good ear pricked again. He sniffed at her starched white uniform, her slender hands, then pushed his head under her knees to get a good whiff of her white shoes. He sniffed her hands again, licked her fingers, chuffing and whining, prancing in place, increasingly excited.

The nurse and cook laughed, thinking that Woofer was reacting only to the good food and all of the attention, but Janet knew he was responding to something else. Mixed up with all the chuffing and whining were brief low growls as he caught some scent that he didn't like. And his tail had stopped wagging.

Without warning and to Janet's great mortification, the dog slipped out of Angelina's cuddling hands, shot around her, streaked past Danny, between the cook's legs, and straight through the open door into the kitchen.

'Woofer, no!' Janet cried.

The dog didn't heed her, kept going, and everyone in the alleyway went after him.

The kitchen staff tried to capture Woofer, but he was too quick for them. He dodged and feinted, claws clicking on the tile floor. He scrambled under food preparation tables, rolled and leaped and abruptly changed directions again and again to elude grasping hands, exhibiting all the agility of an eel, panting and grinning and apparently having a good time.

However, it wasn't entirely fun and doggy games. At the same time, he was urgently searching for something, following an elusive scent, sniffing at the floor and at

200

the air. He appeared to be disinterested in the ovens filled with baking sweetrolls from which flowed a virtual flood of mouth-watering aromas, and he didn't leap up toward any of the counters on which food was exposed. Something else interested him, whatever he had first detected on the young blond nurse named Angelina.

'Bad dog,' Janet kept repeating as she joined the chase, 'bad dog, bad dog!'

Woofer cast a couple of hurt looks her way but didn't settle down.

A nurse's aide, unaware of what was happening in the kitchen, pushed through a pair of swinging doors with a cart of supplies, and the dog instantly took advantage of the opening. He shot past the aide, through the doors, into another part of the care home.

*   *   *

Bad Dog. Not true. Good dog. Good.

The food place is full of so many tasty odors, he can't track the other scent, the strange scent, quick as he wants to. But on the other side of the swinging doors is a long, long narrow place with other places opening off both sides. Here the hungry-making smells aren't as heavy.

Lots of other smells, though, mostly people smells, mostly not wonderful. Sharp odors, salty odors, sick-making sweet odors, sour.

Pine. A bucket of pine in the long, long narrow place. He real quick sticks his nose in the bucket of pine, wondering how the whole tree got in there, but it

201

isn't a tree, only water, dirty-looking water that smells like a whole pine tree, a bunch of them, all in a bucket. Interesting.

Hurry on.

Pee. He can smell pee. People pee. Different kinds of people pee. Interesting. Ten, twenty, thirty different pee smells, none of them real strong but *there*, lots more people pee than he had ever smelled inside anyplace anytime. He can tell a lot from the smell of people's pee, what they ate, what they drank, where they've been today, whether they've rutted lately, whether they're healthy or sick, angry or happy, good or bad. Most of these people haven't rutted in a long time, and are sick one way or another, some of them bad sick. None of the pee is the kind of pee that's fun to smell.

He smells shoe leather, floor wax, wood polish, starch, roses, daisies, tulips, carnations, lemons, ten-twenty-lots of kinds of sweat, chocolate good, poop bad, dust, damp earth from a plant pot, soap, hair spray, peppermint, pepper, salt, onions, the sneeze-making bitterness of termites in one wall, coffee, hot brass, rubber, paper, pencil shavings, butterscotch, more pine trees in a bucket, another dog. Interesting. Another dog. Somebody has a dog and brings its scent in on their shoes, interesting dog, female, and they track the scent around the long narrow place. Interesting. There are countless other odors – his world is odors more than anything – including that strange scent, strange and bad, bare-your-teeth bad, enemy, hateful thing, smelled before, policeman smell, wolf smell, policeman-wolf-thing smell, there, got it again, this way, this way, follow.

People are chasing him because he doesn't belong here. All sorts of places people think you don't belong, though you never smell as bad as most people, even the clean ones, and though you aren't as big or crashing around with so much noise and taking up so much space as people do.

Bad dog, the woman says, and that hurts him because he likes the woman, the boy, is doing this for them, finding out about the bad policeman-wolf-thing with the strange smell.

Bad dog. Not true. Good dog. Good.

Woman in white, coming through a door, looking surprised, smelling surprised, trying to stop him. Quick snarl. She jumps back. So easy to scare, people. So easy to fool.

The long narrow place meets another long narrow place. More doors, more odors, ammonia and sulphur and more kinds of sick smells, more kinds of pee. People live here but also pee here. So strange. Interesting. Dogs don't pee where they live.

Woman in the narrow place, carrying something, looks surprised, smells surprised, says, *Oh, look, how cute.*

Give her a wag of the tail. Why not? But keep going.

That scent. Strange. Hateful. Strong, getting stronger.

An open door, soft light, a space with a sick woman lying on a bed. He goes in, suddenly wary, looking left and right, because this place reeks of the strange odor, the bad thing, the floor, the walls, and especially a chair, where the bad thing sat. It was here for a long time, more than once, lots of times.

The woman says, *Who's there?*

She stinks. Faint sour sweat. Sickness but more than that. Sadness. Deep, low, terrible unhappiness. And fear. More than anything else, the sharp, lightning-storm, iron smell of fear.

Who's there? Who is it?

Running feet in the long narrow space outside, people coming.

Fear so heavy that the strange-bad odor is almost blotted out by the fear, fear, fear, fear.

Angelina? Is that you? Angelina?

The bad scent, thing scent, is all around the bed, up on the bed. The thing stood here and talked to the woman, not long ago, today, touching her, touching the white cloth draped over her, its vile residue there, up there in the bed, rich and ripe up there in the bed with the woman, and interesting, oh-so-very interesting.

He races back to the door, turns, runs at the bed, leaps, sails, one paw catching the railing but otherwise clearing all obstacles, up with the sick and fear-soaked woman, plop.

* * *

A woman screamed.

Janet had never been afraid that Woofer would bite anyone. He was a gentle and friendly dog, and seemed incapable of harming a soul except, perhaps, the thing that had confronted them in the alleyway earlier in the day.

But when she burst into the softly lighted hospital room behind Angelina, and saw the dog on the patient's bed, for an instant Janet thought it was attacking the woman. She pulled Danny against her to shield him from the savage sight, before she realized Woofer was only straddling the patient and sniffing her, *vigorously* sniffing but nothing worse.

'No,' the invalid cried, 'no, no,' as if not merely a dog but something out of the deeper pits of Hell had leapt upon her.

Janet was ashamed of the commotion, felt responsible, and was afraid of the consequence. She doubted that she and Danny would be welcome to take meals in the Pacific View kitchen any longer.

The woman in the bed was thin – beyond thin, wasted – and so pale, as softly radiant as a ghost in the lamplight. Her hair was white and lusterless. She seemed ancient, a shriveled crone, but some indefinable aspect of her made Janet think the poor soul might be much younger than she appeared.

Obviously weak, she was struggling to rise slightly from her pillows and ward off the dog with her right arm. When she became aware of the arrival of those pursuing Woofer, she turned her head toward the door. Her gaunt face might once have been beautiful but was now cadaverous and, in one respect at least, nightmarish.

Her eyes.

She had none.

205

Janet shuddered involuntarily – and was glad she had shielded Danny, after all.

'Get it off me!' the woman shrieked in terror out of proportion to any threat that Woofer posed. 'Get it off me!'

At first, glimpsed in the gray and purple shadows, the invalid's eyelids merely appeared to be closed. But as the lamplight fell more directly across her drawn face, the true horror of her condition became apparent. Her lids were sewn shut like those of a corpse. The surgical thread had no doubt long ago dissolved, but upper and lower lids had grown together. Nothing existed immediately beneath the flaps of skin to support them, so they sagged inward, leaving shallow concavities.

Janet felt sure the woman had not been born without eyes. Some terrible experience, not nature, had stolen her vision. How severe must the injuries have been, if physicians had concluded it wasn't possible to install glass eyes even for cosmetic reasons? Dire intuition told Janet that this blind and shriveled patient had encountered someone worse than Vince, and more cold-blooded than Janet's own reptilian parents.

As Angelina and a male orderly closed in on the bed, calling the blind woman 'Jennifer' and assuring her everything was going to be all right, Woofer leaped to the floor again and foiled them with another unanticipated move. Instead of making directly for the door to the corridor, he streaked into the adjoining bathroom, which was shared with the room next door, and from there scrambled into the hall.

Holding Danny's hand in hers, Janet led the chase

this time, not solely because she felt responsible for what had happened and was afraid that their dining privileges at Pacific View were on the verge of being canceled forever, but because she was eager to leave the shadowed, stuffy room and its mealy-skinned, eyeless resident. This time the chase led into the main hall and from there into the public lounge.

Janet damned herself for ever letting the mutt into their lives. The worst thing wasn't even the humiliation he'd brought them with this prank, but all of the attention he was drawing. She feared attention. Huddling down, keeping quiet, staying in the corners and shadows of life was the only way to reduce the amount of abuse you had to take. Besides, she wanted to remain virtually transparent to others at least until her dead husband had rested under Arizona sands for another year or two.

Woofer was too fast for them even though he kept his snout to the floor, sniffing every step of the way.

The evening receptionist in the lounge was a young Hispanic woman in a white uniform, hair in a ponytail secured by a red ribbon. Having risen from her desk to check out the source of the oncoming tumult, she assessed the situation and acted quickly. She stepped to the front door as Woofer flew into the lounge. She opened it, and let him shoot past her into the street.

Outside, breathless, Janet halted at the bottom of the front steps. The care home was east of the coast highway, on a sloped street lined with Indian laurels and bottle-brush trees. The mercury-vapor streetlamps shed a vaguely blue light. When a fluctuant breeze shivered branches, the pavement crawled with jittering leaf shadows.

Woofer was about forty feet away, dappled by the blue light, sniffing continuously at the sidewalk, shrubs, tree trunks, curb. He tested the night air most of all, apparently seeking an elusive scent. From the bottle-brush trees, the storm had knocked down scores of bristly red blooms which littered the pavement, like colonies of mutant sea anemones washed up by an apocalyptic tide. When the dog sniffed at these, he sneezed. His progress was halting and uncertain but steadily southward.

'Woofer!' Danny shouted.

The mutt turned and looked at them.

'Come back!' Danny pleaded.

Woofer hesitated. Then he twitched his head, snapped at the air, and continued after whatever phantom he was pursuing.

Fighting back tears, Danny said, 'I thought he liked me.'

The boy's words made Janet regret the unvoiced curses she had heaped upon the dog during the chase. She called after him, as well.

'He'll come back,' she assured Danny.

'He's not.'

'Maybe not now but later, maybe tomorrow or the day after, he'll come home.'

The boy's voice trembled with loss: 'How can he come home when there's no home to find us at?'

'There's the car,' she said lamely.

She was more acutely aware than ever that a rusted

old Dodge was a grievously inadequate home. Being able to provide no better for her son suddenly made her heart so heavy that it ached. She was troubled by fear, anger, frustration, and a desperation so intense that it made her nauseous.

'Dogs have sharper senses than we do,' she said. 'He'll track us down. He'll track us down, all right.'

Black tree shadows stirred on the pavement, a vision of the dead leaves of autumns to come.

The dog reached the end of the block and turned the corner, moving out of sight.

'He'll track us down,' she said, but did not believe.

* * *

Stink beetles. Wet tree bark. The lime odor of damp concrete. Roasting chicken in a people place nearby. Geraniums, jasmine, dead leaves. The moldy-sour scent of earthworms rutting in the rain-soaked dirt of flower beds. Interesting.

Most smells now are after-the-rain smells because rain cleans up the world and leaves its own tang afterwards. But even the hardest rain can't wash away *all* of the old smells, layers and layers, days and weeks of odors cast off by birds and bugs, dogs and plants, lizards and people and worms and cats—

He catches a whiff of cat fur, and freezes. He clenches his teeth at the scent, flares his nostrils. He tenses.

Funny about cats. He doesn't hate them, really, but they're so chaseable, so hard to resist. Nothing's more fun than a cat at its best, unless maybe a boy with a ball to throw and then something good to eat.

He's almost ready to go after the cat, track it down, but then his snout burns with an old memory of claw scratches and a sore nose for days. He remembers the bad things about cats, how they can move so fast, slash you, then go straight up a wall or tree where you can't go after them, and you sit below barking at them, your nose stinging and bleeding, feeling stupid, and the cat licks its fur and looks at you and then settles down to sleep, until finally you just have to go somewhere and bite on an old stick or snap a few lizards in two until you feel better.

Car fumes. Wet newspaper. Old shoe full of people foot smell.

Dead mouse. Interesting. Dead mouse rotting in the gutter. Eyes open. Tiny teeth bared. Interesting. Funny how dead things don't move. Unless they're dead long enough, and then they're full of movement, but it's still not them moving but things in them. Dead mouse, stiff tail sticking straight up in the air. Interesting.

Policeman-wolf-thing.

He snaps his head up and seeks the faint scent. Mostly this thing has a scent unlike any creature he's ever met up with before, which is what makes it interesting. Partly it's a human odor but only partly. It's also a thing-that-will-kill-you odor, which you sometimes smell on people and on certain crazy-mean dogs bigger than you and on coyotes and on snakes that rattle. In fact it has more of a thing-that-will-kill-you stink than anything he's ever run across before, which means he's got to be careful. Mostly it has its own scent: like yet not like the sea on a cold night; like yet not like an iron fence on a hot day; like yet not like the dead and rotting mouse; like yet not like lightning, thunder, spiders, blood, and dark holes in the ground that are interesting but scary. Its faint scent is one fragile thread in the rich tapestry of night aromas, but he follows it.

Part Two

POLICE WORK AND THE DOG'S LIFE

Living in the modern age,
death for virtue is the wage.
So it seems in darker hours.
Evil wins, kindness cowers.

Ruled by violence and vice
We all stand upon thin ice.
Are we brave or are we mice,
here upon such thin, thin ice?

Dare we linger, dare we skate?
Dare we laugh or celebrate,
knowing we may strain the ice?
Preserve the ice at any price?

—The Book of Counted Sorrows

When tempest-tossed,
embrace chaos.

—The Book of Counted Sorrows

THREE

·1·

They took the coast highway because a tanker truck loaded with liquid nitrogen had overturned at the junction of the Costa Mesa and San Diego Freeways, transforming them into parking lots. Harry cranked the Honda, weaving from lane to lane, speeding through yellow traffic lights, running the reds if no cars were approaching on the cross streets, driving more like Connie in a mood than like himself.

As relentless as a circling vulture, doom shadowed his every thought. In Connie's kitchen, he'd spoken confidently of Ticktock's vulnerability. But how vulnerable could the guy be if he could laugh off bullets and bonfires?

He said, 'Thanks for not being like the people in one of those movies, they see huge bats against the full moon, victims with all the blood drained out, but they keep arguing it can't be happening, vampires aren't real.'

'Or like the priest sees the little girl's head spin three-hundred-sixty-degrees, her bed levitates – but he still can't believe there's a devil, so he consults psychology books to diagnose her.'

215

'What listing you think he looks up in the index?'

Connie said, 'Under W for Weird shit.'

They crossed a bridge over a back channel of Newport Harbor. House and boat lights glimmered on the black water.

'Funny,' Harry said. 'You go through life think-ing people who believe this stuff are as dumb as lobotomized newts – then something like this happens, and you're instantly able to accept all kinds of fantastic ideas. At heart we're all moon-worshipping savages who *know* the world's a lot stranger than we want to believe.'

'Not that I've accepted your theory yet, your psycho superman.'

He looked at her. In the instrument-panel light, her face resembled a sculpture of some goddess from Greek mythology, rendered in hard bronze with verdigris patina. 'If not my theory, then what?'

Instead of answering him, she said, 'If you're gonna drive like me, keep your eyes on the road.'

That was good advice, and he took it in time to avoid making a ton and a half of Honda jelly against the back of a lumbering old Mercedes driven by Methuselah's grandmother and sporting a bumper sticker that said LICENSED TO KILL. Tires squealing, he whipped around the sedan. As they passed it, the venerable lady behind the wheel scowled and gave them the finger.

'Even grandmothers aren't grandmothers any more,' Connie said.

'If not my theory, then what?' he persisted.

'I don't know. I'm just saying – if you're going to surf

216

on the chaos, better never think you've got the pattern of the currents all figured out, 'cause that's when a big wave will dump you.'

He thought about that, driving in silence for a while.

To their left, the Newport Center hotels and office towers drifted by as if they were moving instead of the car, great lighted ships sailing the night on mysterious missions. The bordering lawns and rows of palms were unnaturally green and too perfect to be real, like a gargantuan stage setting. The recent storm seemed to have swept across California from out of another dimension, washing the world with strangeness, leaving behind a residue of dark magic.

'What about your mom and dad?' Connie asked. 'This guy said he'd destroy everyone you love, *then* you.'

'They're a few hundred miles up the coast. They're out of this.'

'We don't know how far he can reach.'

'If he can reach that far, he *is* God. Anyway, remember what I said, how maybe this guy pins a psychic tag on you? Like game wardens tag a deer or bear with an electronic gizmo to learn its migratory habits. That *feels* right. Which means it's possible he can't find my mom and dad unless I lead him to them. Maybe all he knows about me is what I've shown him since he tagged me this afternoon.'

'So you came to me first because . . .'

Because I love you? he wondered. But he said nothing.

He was relieved when she let him off that hook:

217

'. . . because we brought Ordegard down together. And if this guy was controlling Ordegard, he's almost as angry with me as with you.'

'I had to warn you,' Harry said. 'We're in this together.'

Though he was aware of her studying him with keen interest, she said nothing. He pretended to be oblivious of her analytic stare.

After a while she said, 'You think this Ticktock can tune in and hear us, see us, any time he wants? Like now?'

'I don't know.'

'He can't know everything, like God,' Connie said. 'So maybe we're just a blinking light on his mental tracking board, and he can only see or hear us when we can see and hear *him*.'

'Maybe. Probably. Who knows?'

'We better hope that's how it is. Because if he's listening and watching all the time, we don't have a snowball's chance in Hell of nailing the son of a bitch. The moment we start getting close, he'll burn us to the ground as sure as he burned down your condo.'

On the shop-lined main street of Corona Del Mar, and along the dark Newport Coast where land was being graded for a new community on the ocean-facing hills and where enormous earth-moving machines stood like prehistoric beasts asleep on their feet, Harry had a crawling sensation along the back of his neck. Descending the coast highway into Laguna Beach, it got worse. He felt as if he were being watched in the same way that a mouse is watched by a stalking cat.

Laguna was an arts colony and tourist mecca, still

renowned for its beauty even though it had seen better days. Speckled with golden lights and adorned with a softening mantle of greenery, serried hills sloped down from the east to the shores of the Pacific, as graceful as a lovely woman descending a stairway to the surf. But tonight the lady seemed less lovely than dangerous.

·2·

The house stood on a bluff above the sea. The west wall of tinted glass encompassed a primal view of sky, water, and crashing surf.

When Bryan wished to sleep during the day, electrically operated Rolladen shutters motored down to banish the sun. It was night, however, and, while Bryan slept, the huge windows revealed a black sky, blacker sea, and phosphorescent incoming breakers like marching ranks of soldier ghosts.

When Bryan slept, he always dreamed.

Though most people's dreams were in black and white, his were in full color. In fact the spectrum of colors in his dreams was greater than in real life, a fabulous variety of hues and shadings that made each vision enthrallingly intricate.

Rooms in his dreams were not simply vague suggestions of places, and landscapes were not impressionistic smears. Every locale in his sleep was vividly – even excruciatingly – detailed. If he dreamed of a forest, every leaf was rendered with veining, individually mottled and shaded. If snow, every flake was unique.

After all, he was not a dreamer like every other. He was a slumbering god. Creative.

That Tuesday evening Bryan's dreams were, as always, filled with violence and death. His creativity was best expressed in imaginative forms of destruction.

He walked the streets of a fantasy city more labyrinthine than any that existed in the real world, a metropolis of crowding spires. When children looked upon him, they were stricken by a plague of such exquisite virulence that their small faces instantly erupted in masses of oozing pustules; bleeding lesions split their skin. When he touched strong men, they burst into flame and their eyes melted from their sockets. Young women aged before his eyes, withered and died in seconds, transformed from objects of desire into piles of worm-riddled refuse. When Bryan smiled at a shopkeeper standing in front of a corner grocery, the man fell to the pavement, writhing in agony, and swarms of cockroaches erupted from his ears, nostrils, and mouth.

For Bryan, this was not a nightmare. He enjoyed his dreams and always woke from them refreshed and excited.

The city streets faded into the uncountable rooms of an infinite bordello, with a different beautiful woman waiting to please him in every richly decorated chamber. Naked, they prostrated themselves before him, pleaded to be allowed to provide him with relief, but he would lie with none of them. Instead, he slaughtered each woman in a different fashion, endlessly inventive in his brutalities, until he was drenched with their blood.

He was not interested in sex. Power was more satisfying than sex could ever be, and by far the most satisfying power was the power to kill.

He never tired of their cries for mercy. Their voices were very much like the squeals of the small animals that had learned to fear him when he'd been a child and had just begun to Become. He had been born to rule both in the dream world and the real, to help humankind relearn the humility that it had lost.

He woke.

For long delicious minutes, Bryan lay in a tangle of black sheets, as pale upon that rumpled silk as the luminescent foam was pale upon the crest of each wave that broke on the shore below his windows. The euphoria of the bloody dream stayed with him for a while and was immeasurably better than a post-orgasmic glow.

He longed for the day when he could brutalize the real world as he did the world in his dreams. They deserved punishment, these swarming multitudes. In their self-absorption, they had pridefully assumed that the world had been made for them, for their pleasure, and they had overrun it. But *he* was the apex of creation, not them. They must be profoundly humbled, and their numbers reduced.

However, he was still young, not in full control of his power, still Becoming. He didn't yet dare to begin the cleansing of the earth that was his destiny.

Naked, he got out of bed. The slightly cool air felt good against his bare skin.

In addition to the sleek, ultra-modern, black lacquered bed with its silk sheets, the large room contained no other furniture except two matching black nightstands and black marble lamps with black shades. No stereo, television, or radio. There was no chair in which to relax and read; books were of no interest to him, for they contained no knowledge he needed to acquire and no entertainment equal to that he could provide himself. When he was creating and manipulating the phantom bodies in which he patrolled the outer world, he preferred to lie in bed, staring at the ceiling.

He had no clock. Didn't need one. He was so attuned to the mechanics of the universe that he always knew the hour, minute, and second. It was part of his gift.

The entire wall opposite the bed was mirrored floor to ceiling. He had mirrors throughout the house; he liked what they showed him of himself, the image of godhood Becoming in all its grace, beauty, and power.

Except for the mirrors, the walls were painted black. The ceiling was black as well.

The black lacquered shelves of a large bookcase contained scores of one-pint Mason jars filled with formaldehyde. Floating therein were pairs of eyes, visible to Bryan even in deep gloom. Some were the eyes of human beings: men, women, and children who had received his judgment; various shades of blue, brown, black, gray, green. Others were the eyes of the animals on which he'd first experimented with his power years ago: mice, gerbils, lizards, snakes, turtles, cats, dogs, birds, squirrels, rabbits; some were softly luminescent even in death, glowing pale red or yellow or green.

Votive eyes. Offered by his subjects. Symbols acknowledging his power, his superiority, his Becoming. At every hour of the day and night, the eyes were there, acknowledging, admiring, adoring him.

Look upon me and tremble, sayeth the Lord. For I am mercy but also am I wrath. I am forgiveness but also am I vengeance. And whatever floweth to thee shall flow from me.

·3·

In spite of the humming vent fans, the room was redolent of blood, bile, intestinal gases, and an astringent disinfectant that made Connie squint.

Harry sprayed his left hand with some Binaca breath-freshener. He cupped his moistened palm over his nose, so the minty fragrance would block out at least some of the smell of death.

He offered Connie the Binaca. She hesitated, then accepted it.

The dead woman lay naked and staring on the tilted, stainless-steel table. The coroner had made a large Y incision in her abdomen, and most of her organs had been carefully removed.

She was one of Ordegard's victims from the restaurant. Her name was Laura Kincade. Thirty years old. She had been pretty when she'd gotten out of bed that morning. Now she was a fright figure from a grisly carnival funhouse.

The fluorescent lights imparted a milky sheen to her eyes, on which were reflected twin images of the overhead microphone and the flexible, segmented-metal cable on which it hung. Her lips were parted, as if she were about to sit up, speak into the mike, and add a few comments to the official record of her autopsy.

The coroner and two assistants were working late, finishing the final of three examinations of Ordegard and his two victims. The men looked weary, both physically and spiritually.

In all her years of police work, Connie had never encountered one of those hardened forensic pathologists who appeared so frequently in the movies and on television, carving up corpses while they made crude jokes and ate pizza, untouched by the tragedies of others. On the contrary, although it was necessary to approach such a job with professional detachment, regular intimate contact with the victims of violent crime always took its toll one way or another.

Teel Bonner, the chief medical examiner, was fifty but seemed older. In the harsh fluorescent light, his face looked less tanned than sallow, and the bags under his eyes were large enough to pack for a weekend getaway.

Bonner paused in his cutting to tell them that the tape of the Ordegard autopsy had already been transcribed by a typist. The transcription was in a folder on his desk, in the glass-walled office adjacent to the dissection room. 'I haven't written the summary yet, but the facts are all there.'

Connie was relieved to get into the office and close the door. The small room had a vent fan of its own, and the air was relatively fresh.

The brown vinyl upholstery on the chair was scarred, creased, and mottled with age. The standard-issue metal desk was scratched and dented.

This was no big-city morgue with several dissection rooms and a professionally decorated office for receptions with reporters and politicians. In smaller towns, violent death was still generally viewed as less glamorous than in larger metropolises.

Harry sat and read from the autopsy transcript while Connie stood at the glass wall and watched the three men gathered around the corpse in the outer room.

The cause of James Ordegard's death had been three gunshot wounds to the chest which Connie and Harry already knew because all three rounds had come from Harry's gun. The effects of the gunshots included puncture and collapse of the left lung, major damage to the large intestine, nicks to the common iliac and the celiac arteries, the complete severing of the renal artery, deep laceration of the stomach and liver by fragments of bone and lead, and a tear in the heart muscle sufficient to cause sudden cardiac arrest.

'Anything odd?' she asked, her back to him.

'Like what?'

'Like what? Don't ask *me*. You're the guy who thinks possession ought to leave its mark.'

In the dissection room, the three pathologists working over Laura Kincade were uncannily like doctors attending to a patient whose life they were struggling to preserve. The postures were the same; only the pace was different. But the sole thing that these men could preserve was a record of precisely the means by which one bullet had fatally damaged one fragile human body, the *how* of Laura's death. They couldn't begin to answer the bigger question: *Why?* Even James Ordegard and his twisted motivations could not explain the *why* of it; he was only another part of the *how*. Explaining why was a task for priests and philosophers, who floundered helplessly for meaning every day.

'They did a craniotomy,' Harry said from the coroner's creaking chair.

'And?'

'No visible surface hematoma. No unusual quantity of cerebrospinal fluid, no indications of excess pressure.'

'They do a cerebrotomy?' she asked.

'I'm sure.' He rustled through the pages of the transcript. 'Yeah, here.'

'Cerebral tumor? Abscess? Lesions?'

He was silent for a long moment, scanning the report. Then: 'No, nothing like that.'

'Hemorrhage?'

'None noted.'

'Embolism?'

'None found.'

'Pineal gland?'

Sometimes the pineal gland could shift out of position and come under pressure from surrounding brain tissues, resulting in extremely vivid hallucinations, sometimes paranoia and violent behavior. But that was not the case with Ordegard.

Watching the autopsy from a distance, Connie thought of her sister, Colleen, dead these five years, killed by childbirth. It seemed to her that Colleen's death made no more sense than that of poor Laura Kincade who had made the mistake of stopping at the wrong restaurant for lunch.

Then again, no death made sense. Madness and chaos were the engines of this universe. Everything was born only to die. Where was the logic and reason in that?

'Nothing,' Harry said, dropping the report back onto the desk. The chair springs squeaked and twanged as he got up. 'No unexplained marks on the body, no peculiar physiological conditions. If Ticktock was in possession of Ordegard, there's no clue of it in the corpse.'

Connie turned away from the glass wall. 'Now what?'

* * *

Teel Bonner pulled open the morgue drawer.

The naked body of James Ordegard lay within. His white skin had a bluish cast in some places. Black-thread stitches had been used to close the extensive incisions from the autopsy.

The moon face. Rigor mortis had pulled his lips into a lopsided smile. At least his eyes were closed.

'What did you want to see?' Bonner asked.

'If he was still here,' Harry said.

The coroner glanced at Connie. 'Where else would he be?'

227

·4·

The bedroom floor was covered with black ceramic tile. Like purling water, it glistened in places with dim reflections of the ambient light from the night beyond the windows. It was cool beneath Bryan's feet.

As he walked to the glass wall that faced the ocean, the huge mirrors reflected black on black, and his naked form drifted like a wraith of smoke through the layered shadows.

He stood at the window, staring at the sable sea and tarry sky. The smooth ebony vista was relieved only by the crests of the combers and by frostlike patches on the bellies of the clouds. That frost was a reflection of the lights of Laguna Beach behind him; his home was on one of the western-most points of the city.

The view was perfect and serene because it lacked the human element. No man or woman or child, no structure or machine or artifact intruded. So quiet, dark. So clean.

He longed to eradicate humanity and all its works from large portions of the earth, restrict people to selected preserves. But he was not yet fully in control of his power, still Becoming.

He lowered his gaze from the sky and sea to the pallid beach at the foot of the bluff.

Leaning his forehead against the glass, he imagined life – and by imagining, created it. On the sward just above the tide line, the sand began to stir. It rose, forming a cone as big as a man – and then *became* a man. The hobo. The scarred face. Reptile eyes.

No such person had ever existed. The vagrant was strictly a creature of Bryan's imagination. Through this construct and others, Bryan could walk the world without being in danger from it.

Though his phantom bodies could be shot and burned and crushed without causing harm to him, his own body was dismayingly vulnerable. When cut, he bled. When struck, he bruised. He assumed that when he had Become, then invulnerability and immortality would be the final gifts bestowed on him, signaling his Ascension to godhood – which made him eager to fulfill his mission.

Now, leaving only a portion of his consciousness in his real body, he moved into the hobo on the night beach. From within that hulking figure, he gazed up at his house on the bluff. He saw his own naked body at the window, staring down.

In Jewish folklore there was a creature called a golem. Made of mud in the shape of a man, endowed with a form of life, it was most often an instrument of vengeance.

Bryan could create an infinite variety of golems and through them stalk his prey, thin the herd, police the world. But he could not enter the bodies of real people and control their minds, which he would very much have enjoyed. Perhaps that power would be his, as well, when at last he had Become.

He withdrew his consciousness from the golem on the beach and, regarding it from his high window, caused it to change shape. It tripled in size, assumed a reptilian form, and developed immense membranous wings.

Sometimes an effect could spiral beyond what he intended, acquire a life of its own, and resist his efforts at containment. For that reason, he was always practicing, refining his techniques and exercising his power in order to strengthen it.

He had once created a golem inspired by the movie *Alien*, and used it to savage the vagrants in an encampment of ten homeless people under a Los Angeles freeway overpass. His intention had been to slaughter two of them, lightning quick, and leave the others with the memory of his power and merciless judgment. But then he became excited by their abject terror at the inexplicable manifestation of that movie monster. He thrilled to the feel of his claws ripping through their flesh, the heat of spurting blood, the rank steaming gush of disembowelment, the crack of bones as fragile as chalk sticks in his monstrous hands. The screams of the dying were piercingly shrill at first but became weak, tremulous, erotic; they surrendered their lives to him as lovers might have surrendered, so exhausted by the intensity of their passion that they succumbed only with sighs, whispers, shudders. For a few minutes he *was* the creature that he had created, all razored teeth and talons, spiked spine and lashing tail, having forgotten about his real body in which his mind actually reposed. When he regained his senses, he discovered he had killed all ten men beneath the overpass and stood in a charnel house of blood, eviscerated torsos, severed heads and limbs.

He hadn't been shocked or daunted by the degree of violence he'd wrought – only that he'd killed them all in a mindless frenzy. Learning control was vital if he were to accomplish his mission and Become.

He had used the power of pyrokinesis to set the bodies afire, searing them with flames so intense that even bones were vaporized. He always disposed of those on whom he practiced because he didn't want ordinary people to know that he walked among them, at least not until his power had been perfected and his vulnerability was nil.

That was also why for the time being he focused his attentions primarily on street people. If they were to report being tormented by a demon who could change shape at will, their complaints would be dismissed as the ravings of mentally deranged losers with drug and alcohol addictions. And when they vanished from the face of the earth, no one would care or attempt to discover what had happened to them. Someday soon, however, he would be able to bring holy terror and divine judgment to people in all strata of society.

So he practiced.

Like a magician improving his dexterity.

Control. Control.

On the beach, the winged form leapt off the sand from which it had been born. It flapped into the night, like a truant gargoyle returning to a cathedral parapet. It hovered before his window, peering in with luminous yellow eyes.

Although it was a brainless thing until he projected part of himself into it, the pterodactyl was nevertheless an impressive creation. Its immense leathery wings fluidly fanned the air, and it easily remained aloft on the updrafts along the bluff.

Bryan was aware of the eyes in the jars behind him. Staring. Watching him, astonished, admiring, adoring.

'Be gone,' he said to the pterodactyl, indulging in theatrics for his audience.

The winged reptile turned to sand and rained on the beach below.

Enough play. He had work to do.

·5·

Harry's Honda was parked near the municipal building, under a street lamp.

Early spring moths, having come out in the wake of the rain, swooped close to the light. Their enormous, distorted shadows played over the car.

As she and Harry crossed the sidewalk toward the Honda, Connie said, 'Same question. Now what?'

'I want to get into Ordegard's house and have a look around.'

'What for?'

'I don't have a clue. But it's the only other thing I can think to do. Unless you've got an idea.'

'Wish I did.'

As they approached the car, she saw something dangling from the rearview mirror, rectangular and softly gleaming beyond the moth shadows that swarmed over the windshield. As far as she could recall, there had been no air-freshener or ornament of any kind tied to the mirror.

She was the first into the car and got a close look at the silvery rectangle before Harry did. It was dangling on a red ribbon from the mirror shank. Initially she didn't realize what it was. She took hold of it, turned it so the light struck it more clearly, and saw that it was a handcrafted belt buckle worked with Southwest motifs.

Harry got in behind the wheel, slammed his door, and saw what she held in her hand.

'Oh, Jesus,' Harry said, 'Oh, Jesus, Ricky Estefan.'

· 6 ·

Most of the roses had taken a beating from the rain, but a few blooms had come through the storm untouched. They bobbed gently in the night breeze. The petals caught the light spilling from the kitchen windows and seemed to magnify it, glowing as if radioactive.

Ricky sat at the kitchen table, from which his tools and current projects had been removed. He had finished dinner more than an hour ago and had been sipping port wine ever since. He wanted to get a buzz on.

Before being gutshot, he'd not been much of a drinker, but when he *had* wanted a drink, he'd been a Tequila and beer man. A shot of Sauza and a bottle of Tecate were as sophisticated as he got. After all the abdominal surgeries he endured, however, a single jigger of Sauza – or any other hard liquor – gave him intense heartburn and a sour stomach that lasted the better part of a day. The same was true of beer.

He learned that he could handle liqueurs well enough, but getting drunk on Bailey's Irish Cream or Crème de Menthe or Midori required the ingestion of so much sugar that his teeth would rot long before he did any damage to his liver. Regular wines did not go down well, either, but port proved to be just the thing, sweet enough to soothe his delicate gut but not so sweet as to induce diabetes.

Good port was his only indulgence. Well, good port and a little self-pity now and then.

Watching the roses nodding in the night, he sometimes pulled his gaze back to a closer point of focus and stared at his reflection in the window. It was an imperfect mirror, revealing to him a colorless transparent countenance like that of a haunting spirit; but perhaps it was an accurate reflection, after all, because he was a ghost of his former self and in some ways dead already.

A bottle of Taylor's stood on the table. He refilled his port glass and took a sip.

Sometimes, like now, it was difficult to believe that the face in the window was actually his. Before he'd been shot, he had been a happy man, seldom given to troubled introspection, never a brooder. Even during recuperation and rehabilitation, he had retained a sense of humor, an optimism about the future that no amount of pain could entirely darken.

His face had become the face in the window only

after Anita left. More than two years later, he still had difficulty believing that she was gone – or figuring out what to do about the loneliness that was destroying him more surely than bullets could have done.

Raising his drink, Ricky sensed something wrong just as he brought it to his mouth. Perhaps he subconsciously registered the lack of a port-wine aroma – or the faint, foul smell of what had replaced it. He stopped as he was about to tilt the glass to his lips, and saw what it contained: two or three fat, moist, entwined earthworms, alive and oozing languorously around one another.

Startled, he cried out, and the glass slipped from his fingers. Because it dropped only a couple of inches onto the table, it didn't shatter. But when it tipped over, the worms slithered onto the polished pine.

Ricky pushed his chair back, blinking furiously—

—and the worms were gone.

Spilled wine shimmered on the table.

He halted halfway to his feet, his hands on the arms of his chair, staring in disbelief at the puddle of ruby-red port.

He was sure he had seen the worms. He wasn't imagining things. Wasn't drunk. Hell, he hadn't even *begun* to feel the port.

Easing back into his chair, he closed his eyes. Waited a second, two. Looked. The wine still glistened on the table.

Hesitantly he touched one index finger to the puddle. It was wet, real. He rubbed his finger and thumb together, spreading the drop of wine over his skin.

He checked the Taylor's to be sure that he hadn't drunk more than he'd realized. The bottle was dark, so he had to hold it up to the light to see the level of the liquid within. It was a new liter, and the line of the port was just below the neck. He had poured only the two glasses.

Rattled as much by his inability to come up with an explanation as by what had happened, Ricky went to the sink, opened the cabinet below it, and got the damp dishcloth from the rack on the back of the door. At the table again, he wiped up the spilled wine.

His hands were shaking.

He was angry at himself for being afraid, even though the source of the fear was understandable. He worried that he had suffered what the doctors would call a 'small cerebral incident,' a minor stroke of which the flickering hallucination of earthworms was the only sign. More than anything else during his long hospitalization, he had dreaded a stroke.

The development of blood clots in the legs and around the sutures in repaired veins and arteries was one especially dangerous potential side-effect of major abdominal surgery of the extent that he had undergone and of the protracted bed rest that followed it. If one broke free and traveled to the heart, sudden death might ensue. If it traveled instead to the brain, obstructing circulation, the result could be total or partial paralysis, blindness, loss of speech, and the horrifying destruction of intellectual capacity. His doctors had medicated him to inhibit clotting, and the nurses had put him through a program of passive exercise even when he had been required to remain flat on his back, but there hadn't been one day during his long recovery that he hadn't worried about suddenly finding himself unable to move or talk, unsure of where he was, unable to recognize his wife or his own name.

At least then he'd had the comfort of knowing, whatever happened, Anita would be there to take care of him. Now he had no one. From now on, he would have to face adversity alone. If silenced and badly crippled by a stroke, he would be at the mercy of strangers.

Although his fear was understandable, he also realized that it was to some extent irrational. He was healed. He had his scars, sure. And his ordeal had left him diminished. But he was no more ill than the average man on the street and probably healthier than a lot of them. More than two years had passed since his most recent surgery. His chances of suffering a cerebral embolism were now only average for a man his age. Thirty-six. Men that young rarely had debilitating strokes. Statistically, he was more likely to die in a traffic accident, from a heart attack, as the victim of violent crime, or perhaps even from being struck by lightning.

What he feared was not so much paralysis, aphasia, blindness or any other physical ailment. What frightened him, really, was being alone, and the weirdness with the earthworms had impressed upon him just how alone he would be if anything untoward happened.

Determined not to be ruled by fear, Ricky put the port-stained dishcloth aside and righted the overturned glass. He would sit down with another drink and think it through. The answer would be obvious when he thought about it. There was an explanation for the worms, maybe a trick of light that could be duplicated by holding the glass just so, turning it just so, re-creating the precise circumstances of the illusion.

He picked up the bottle of Taylor's and tipped it toward the glass. For an instant, though he had held it up to the light only a couple of minutes ago to check the level of the wine, he expected the bottle to disgorge oily knots of writhing earthworms. Only port poured forth.

He put down the bottle and raised the glass. As he brought it to his lips, he hesitated, repulsed by the thought of drinking out of a glass that had contained earthworms slick with whatever cold mucus they exuded.

His hand was shaking again, his brow was suddenly damp with perspiration, and he was furious with himself for being so damned silly about this. The wine slopped against the sides of the glass, glimmering like a liquid jewel.

He brought it to his lips, took a short sip. It tasted sweet and clean. He took another sip. Delicious.

A soft and tremulous laugh escaped him. 'Asshole,' he said, and felt better for making fun of himself.

Deciding that some nuts or crackers would go well with the port, he put his glass down and went to the kitchen cabinet where he kept cans of roasted almonds, mixed nuts, and packages of Che-Cri Cheese Crispies. When he pulled the door open, the cabinet was alive with tarantulas.

Faster and more agile than he'd been in years, he backed away from the open cabinet, slamming into the counter behind him.

Six or eight of the huge spiders were climbing over cans of Blue Diamond Almonds and Planter's Party Mix, exploring the boxes of Che-Cri. They were bigger even than tarantulas should have been, larger than halved cantaloupes, jittering denizens of some arachnophobe's worst nightmare.

Ricky squeezed his eyes shut. Opened them. The spiders were still there.

Above the drumming of his own heart and his shallow noisy breathing, he could actually hear the hairy legs of the tarantulas brushing against the cellophane on the packages of cheese crackers. The chitinous *tick-tick-tick* of their feet or mandibles against the stacks of cans. Low, evil hissing.

But then he realized he was misinterpreting the source of the sounds. The noises were not coming from the open cabinet across the room but from the cabinets immediately above and behind him.

He looked over his shoulder, up at the pine doors, on the other side of which should have been nothing but plates and bowls, cups and saucers. They were being forced outward by some expanding bulk, just a quarter of an inch ajar, then half an inch. Before Ricky could move, the cabinet doors flew open. An avalanche of snakes cascaded over his head and shoulders.

Screaming, he tried to run. He slipped on the wriggling carpet of serpents and fell among them.

Snakes thin as whips, snakes thick and muscular,

black snakes and green, yellow and brown, plain and patterned, red-eyed, yellow-eyed, some hooded like cobras, watchful and grinning, supple tongues fluttering, hissing, hissing. Had to be dreaming. Hallucinating. A big blacksnake, at least four feet long, bit him, oh Jesus, struck at the back of his left hand, sinking its fangs deep, blood brimming, and still it might have been a dream, nightmare, except for the pain.

He had never felt pain in a dream, and certainly not like this. A sharp stinging filled his left hand, and then a sharper stabbing agony shot like an electrical charge through his wrist and all the way along his forearm to his elbow.

Not a dream. This was happening. Somehow. But where had they come from? *Where?*

They were all over him, sixty or eighty of them, slithering. Another one struck at him, sank fangs through his shirt sleeve and pierced his left forearm, tripling the pain in it. Another bit through his sock, raked teeth down his ankle.

He scrambled to his feet, and the snake that had bitten his arm fell away, as did the one at his ankle, but the one with its fangs through his left hand hung fast, as if it had stapled itself to him. He grabbed it, tried to jerk it loose. The flash of pain was so intense, white hot, that he almost passed out, and still the snake was clamped tight to his bleeding hand.

A turmoil of snakes hissed and coiled around him. He didn't see any rattlers at a glance, or hear them. He had too little knowledge to identify the other species, wasn't sure which were poisonous, or even if *any* of them were, including the ones that had already bitten him. Poisonous or not, more of them were going to bite if he didn't move fast.

He snatched a meat cleaver from a wall rack of knives. When he slammed his left arm down on the nearest counter, the relentless blacksnake flopped full-length across the tile counter top. Ricky swung the cleaver high, brought it down, chopped through the snake, and the steel blade rang off the ceramic surface underneath.

The hateful-looking head still held fast to his hand, trailing only a few inches of the black body, and the glittering eyes seemed to be watching him, alive. Ricky dropped the cleaver and attempted to pry open the serpent's mouth, spring its long curved teeth out of his flesh. He shouted and cursed, furious with pain, kept prying, but it was no use.

The snakes on the floor were agitated by his shouting.

He plunged toward the archway between the kitchen and the hall, kicking snakes out of his way before they could coil and spring at him. Some were already coiled, and they struck, but his heavy, loose-fitting khaki pants foiled them.

He was afraid they would slither over his shoes, under a pants cuff, up and under one of the legs of his khakis. But he reached the hall safely.

The snakes were behind him and not pursuing. Two tarantulas had fallen out of the snack cabinet into the herpetological nightmare on the floor, and the snakes were fighting over them. Frantically kicking arachnid legs vanished under rippling scales.

Thump!

Ricky jumped in surprise.

Thump!

Until now he hadn't associated the strange noise, which had plagued him earlier in the evening, with the spiders and snakes.

Thump!

Thump!

Someone had been playing games with him then, but this was not a game any more. This was deadly serious. Impossible, as fantastic as anything in a dream, but serious.

Thump!

Ricky couldn't pinpoint the source of the pounding or even tell for sure if it came from above or below him. Windows reverberated, and echoes of each blow vibrated hollowly in the walls. He sensed that something was coming, worse than spiders or snakes, something he did not want to encounter.

Gasping, with the head of the blacksnake still dangling from his left hand, Ricky turned away from the kitchen toward the front door at the end of the hall.

His twice-bitten arm throbbed horribly with each beat of his trip-hammering heart. No good, dear Jesus, a racing heart spread the poison faster, if there was any poison. What he had to do was calm down, take deep slow breaths, walk instead of run, go to a neighbor's house, call 911, and get emergency medical attention.

THUMP!

He could have used the telephone in his bedroom, but he didn't want to go in there. He didn't trust his own house any more, which was nuts, yes, crazy, but he felt the place had come alive and turned against him.

THUMP, THUMP, THUMP!

The house shook as if riding the back of a bucking earthquake, almost knocking him down. He staggered sideways, bounced against the wall.

The ceramic statue of the Holy Virgin toppled off the hall table that he had set up as a shrine like all of the shrines his mother had kept in her home. Since being gutshot, he had been reduced by fear to his mother's choice of armor against the cruelties of the world. The statue crashed to the floor, shattered at his feet.

The heavy red-glass container with the votive candle bounced on the table, causing goblin shadows to dance across the wall and ceiling.

THUMPTHUMPTHUMPTHUMP!

Ricky was two steps from the front door when the oak flooring creaked ominously, pushed upward, and cracked almost as loudly as a thunderclap. He stumbled backward.

Something smashed out of the crawlspace under the bungalow, shattering the floor as if it were an eggshell. For a moment the blizzard of dust and splinters and jagged boards made it impossible to glimpse what had been born into the hallway.

Then Ricky saw a man in the hole, feet planted in the earth about eighteen inches under the floor of the house. In spite of standing below Ricky, the guy *loomed*, immense and threatening. His untamed hair and beard were tangled and dirty, and the visible portions of his face were grossly scarred. His black raincoat billowed like a cape around him as a draft whistled out of the crawlspace and up through the broken boards.

Ricky knew he was looking at the vagrant who had appeared to Harry out of a whirlwind. Everything about him fit the description – except his eyes.

When he glimpsed those grotesque eyes, Ricky froze midst the fragments of the Holy Virgin, paralyzed by fear and by the certainty that he had gone mad. Even if he had kept backing away or had turned and tried to run for the rear door, he would not have escaped, for the vagrant clambered out of the hole and into the hall as lightning-quick as any striking serpent. He seized Ricky, swept him off the floor with such unhuman power that any resistance was pointless, and slammed him against the wall hard enough to crack the plaster and his spine.

Face to face, washed by the vagrant's foul breath, Ricky gazed into those eyes and was too terrified to scream. They were not the pools of blood that Harry had described. They were not really eyes at all. Nestled in the deep sockets were two snake heads, two small yellow eyes in each, forked tongues fluttering.

Why me? Ricky wondered.

As if they were a pair of jack-in-the-box fright figures, the snakes sprang from the vagrant's sockets and bit Ricky's face.

·7·

Between Laguna Beach and Dana Point, Harry drove so fast that even Connie, lover of speed and risk-taking, braced herself and made wordless noises of dismay when he took some of the turns too sharply. They were in his own car, not a department sedan, so he didn't have a detachable emergency beacon to stick on the roof. He didn't have a siren either; however, the coast highway was not heavily used at ten-thirty on a Tuesday night, and by pounding the horn and flashing the headlights, he was able to clear a way through what little obstructive traffic he encountered.

'Maybe we should call Ricky, warn him,' she said, when they were still in south Laguna.

'Don't have a car phone.'

'Stop at a service station, convenience store, somewhere.'

'Can't waste the time. I figure his phone won't work anyway.'

'Why won't it?'

'Not unless Ticktock wants it to work.'

They shot up a hill, rounded a curve too fast. The rear tires dug up gravel from the shoulder of the highway, sprayed it against the undercarriage and fuel tank. The right rear bumper kissed a metal guardrail, and then they were back on the pavement, rocketing onward without having braked.

'So let's call Dana Point police,' she said.

'The way we're moving, if we don't stop to call, we'll be there before they could make it.'

'We might be able to use the backup.'

'Won't need backup if we're too damned late and Ricky's dead when we get there.'

Harry was sick with apprehension and furious with

himself. He had endangered Ricky by going to him earlier in the day. He couldn't have known the heap of trouble he was bringing down on his old friend at the time, but later he should have realized Ricky was a target when Ticktock had promised *first everything and everyone you love*.

Sometimes it was hard for a man to admit he loved another man, even in a brotherly way. He and Ricky Estefan had been partners, through some tight scrapes together. They were still friends, and Harry loved him. It was that simple. But the American tradition of macho self-reliance mitigated against admitting as much.

Bullshit, Harry thought angrily.

The truth was, he found it difficult to admit he loved anyone, male or female, even his parents, because love was so damned messy. It entailed obligations, commitments, entanglements, the sharing of emotions. When you admitted to loving people, you had to let them into your life in a more major way, and they brought with them all of their untidy habits, indiscriminate tastes, muddled opinions, and disorganized attitudes.

As they roared across the Dana point city line, the muffler clanging against a bump in the road, Harry said, 'Jesus, sometimes I'm an idiot.'

'Tell me something I don't know,' Connie said.

'A really screwed-up specimen.'

'We're still in familiar territory.'

He had only one excuse for not realizing that Ricky would become a target: Since the fire at his condo less than three hours ago, he had been reacting instead of acting. He'd had no other option. Events had moved so fast, and were so weird, one piece of strangeness piled atop another, that he hadn't time to *think*. A poor excuse, but he clung to it.

He didn't even know *how* to think about bizarre crap like this. Deductive reasoning, every detective's most useful tool, was not adequate to deal with the supernatural. He'd been trying inductive reasoning, which was how he'd come up with the theory of a sociopath with paranormal powers. But he wasn't good at it because inductive reasoning seemed, to him, the next thing to intuition, and intuition was so illogical. He liked hard evidence, sound premises, logical deductions, and neat conclusions tied up in ribbons and bows.

As they turned the corner into Ricky's street, Connie said, 'What the hell?'

Harry glanced at her.

She was staring into her cupped hand.

'What?' he asked.

Something was cradled in her palm. Voice quavering, she said, 'I didn't have this a second ago, where the hell did it come from?'

'What is it?'

She held it up for him to see as he pulled under the street lamp in front of Ricky's house. The head of a ceramic figurine. Broken off at the neck.

Scraping the tires against the curb, he braked to a hard stop, and his safety harness jerked tight across his chest.

She said, 'It was like my hand snapped shut, spasmed shut, and this was in it, out of nowhere, for God's sake.'

247

Harry recognized it. The head of the Virgin Mary that had been at the center of the shrine on Ricky Estefan's hall table.

Overcome by dark expectations, Harry threw open the door and got out of the car. He pulled his gun.

The street was peaceful. Lights glowed warmly in most of the houses, including Ricky's. Music from a neighbor's stereo drifted on the cool air, so faint he could not quite identify the tune. The breeze whispered and softly clattered in the fronds of the big date palms in Ricky's front yard.

Nothing to worry about, the breeze seemed to say, all is calm here, all is right with this place.

Nevertheless, he kept his revolver in hand.

He hurried up the front walk, through the night shadows of the palm trees, onto the bougainvillea-draped porch. He was aware that Connie was right behind him and that she also had drawn her weapon.

Let Ricky be alive, he thought fervently, please let him be alive.

That was as close to prayer as he had gotten in many years.

Behind the screen door, the front door was ajar. A narrow wedge of light projected the pattern of the screen onto the porch floor.

Although he thought no one noticed and would have been mortified to know that his fear was obvious, Ricky had been obsessive about security ever since he'd been shot. He kept everything locked tight. A door standing open even an inch or two was a bad sign.

Harry tried to survey the foyer through the gap

between the door and the jamb. With the screen door in the way, he couldn't get close enough to the crack to see anything.

Drapes blocked the windows flanking the door. They were tightly drawn, overlapping at the center.

Harry glanced at Connie.

With her revolver she indicated the front entrance.

Ordinarily they might have split up, Connie going around to cover the back while Harry took the front. But they weren't trying to keep the perp from getting away, because this was one bastard who couldn't be cornered, subdued, and cuffed. They were just trying to stay alive, and to keep Ricky alive if it was not already too late for him.

Harry nodded and cautiously eased open the screen door. Hinges squeaked. The closure spring sang a long, low swamp-insect note.

He hoped to be silent, but when the outer door defeated him, he put one hand on the inner door and pushed it, intending to go in low and fast. It swung to the right, and he shouldered through the widening gap. The door bumped against something and stopped before there was enough of an opening. He shoved it. Cracking. Scraping. A hard clatter. The door swung all the way open, pushing debris of some nature out of the way, and Harry burst inside so aggressively that he almost plunged through the hole in the hallway floor.

He was reminded of the shattered corridor in the building in Laguna, above the restaurant. If a grenade had done this damage, however, it had exploded in the crawlspace *under* the bungalow. The blast had driven joists, insulation, and floorboards upward into the hallway. But he could detect none of the charred, chemical odor of a bomb.

The overhead foyer light shone down onto the bare earth below the smashed oak flooring and sub-flooring. Standing perilously near the edge of the shrine table, the votive candle in the squat red glass threw off fluttering pennants of light and shadow.

Halfway back the hall, the left-hand wall was spattered with blood, not buckets of it but enough to signify mortal combat. On the floor under the bloodstains, close against the wall, lay the body of a man, twisted into such an unnatural posture that the fact of death was grimly obvious at a glance.

Harry could see just enough of the corpse to know beyond a doubt that it was Ricky. Never had he felt so sick at heart. A coldness rose in the pit of his stomach, and his legs grew weak.

As Harry moved around the hole in the floor, Connie entered the house after him. She saw the body, said nothing, but gestured toward the living-room arch.

Habitual police procedure had tremendous appeal for Harry at the moment, even if it was pointless to search for the killer in this instance. Ticktock, whatever manner of creature he was, would not be cowering in a corner or clambering out a back window, not when he could vanish in a whirlwind or a pillar of fire. And what good were guns against him, even if he could be found? Nonetheless, it was calming to proceed as if they were the first to arrive at an ordinary crime scene; order was imposed on chaos through policy, method, custom, and ritual.

Just inside the living-room archway and to the left lay a pile of dark mud, an eighth of a ton if there was an ounce. He would have thought that it had come from under the house, geysering up with the explosion, except that no mud was splattered in the foyer or hallway. It was as if someone had carefully carried the mud into the house in buckets and heaped it on the living-room carpet.

Curious as it was, Harry gave the mud only a cursory glance before continuing across the living room. Later there would be time to ponder it at length.

They searched the two baths and bedrooms, but found only a fat tarantula. Harry was so startled by the spider, he almost squeezed off a shot. If it had run toward him instead of out of sight under a dresser, he might have blown it to bits before realizing what it was.

Southern California, a desert before man had brought in water and made larger areas of it habitable, was a perfect breeding ground for tarantulas, but they kept to undeveloped canyons and scrublands. Though fearsome in appearance, they were shy creatures, living most of their lives underground, rarely surfacing outside of the mating season. Dana Point, or this part of it at least, was too civilized to be of interest to tarantulas, and Harry wondered how one had found its way into the heart of the town, where it was as out of place as a tiger would have been.

Silently they retraced their route through the house, into the foyer, the hall, then moved past the body.

A quick glance confirmed that Ricky was far beyond help. Fragments of the ceramic religious statue clinked underfoot.

The kitchen was full of snakes.

'Oh shit,' Connie said.

One snake was just inside the archway. Two more were questing among the chair and table legs. Most were at the far side of the room, a tangled mass of squirming, serpentine coils, no fewer than thirty or forty, perhaps half again as many. Several seemed to be feeding on something.

Two more tarantulas were scuttling along a white tile counter, near the edge, keeping a watch on the teeming serpents below.

'What the hell happened here?' Harry wondered, and was not surprised to hear a tremor in his voice.

The snakes began to notice Harry and Connie. Most of them were disinterested, but a few slithered forth from the churning mass to investigate.

A pocket door separated the kitchen from the hall. Harry quickly slid it shut.

They checked the garage. Ricky's car. A damp spot on the concrete where the roof had leaked earlier in the day, and a puddle that had not entirely evaporated. Nothing else.

Back in the hallway, Harry finally knelt beside the body of his friend. He had delayed the dreaded examination as long as possible.

Connie said, 'I'll see if there's a bedroom phone.'

Alarmed, he looked up at her. 'Phone? No, for God's sake, don't even think about it.'

252

'We've gotta put in a homicide call.'

'Listen,' he said, checking his wristwatch, 'it's going on eleven o'clock already. If we report this, we're going to be tied up here for hours.'

'But— '

'We don't have the time to waste. I don't see how we're ever going to find this Ticktock before sunrise. We don't seem to have a chance in hell. Even if we find him, I don't know how we could deal with him. But we'd be foolish not to try, don't you think?'

'Yeah, you're right. I don't just want to sit around waiting to be whacked.'

'Okay then,' he said. 'Forget the phone.'

'I'll just . . . I'll wait for you.'

'Watch out for snakes,' he said as she moved up the hall.

He turned his attention to Ricky.

The condition of the corpse was even worse than he anticipated. He saw the snake head fixed by deep-sunk fangs to Ricky's left hand, and he shivered. Pairs of small holes on the face might have been bite marks. Both arms were bent backward at the elbows; the bones were not just broken but pulverized. Ricky Estefan was so battered that it was difficult to specify one injury as the cause of death; however, if he had not been dead when his head had been wrenched a hundred and eighty degrees around on his shoulders, he had surely died in that savage moment. His neck was torn and bruised, his head lolled loosely, and his chin rested between his shoulder blades.

His eyes were gone.

'Harry?' Connie called.

Staring into the dead man's empty eye sockets, Harry was unable to answer her. His mouth was dry, and his voice caught like a burr in his throat.

'Harry, you better look at this.'

He had seen enough of what had been done to Ricky, too much. His anger at Ticktock was exceeded only by his fury with himself.

He rose from the body, turned, and caught sight of himself in the silver-leafed mirror above the shrine table. He was ashen. He looked as dead as the man on the floor. A part of him *had* died when he'd seen the body; he felt diminished.

When he met his own eyes, he had to look away from the terror, confusion, and primitive rage that he saw in them. The man in the mirror was not the Harry Lyon he knew – or wanted to be.

'Harry?' she said again.

In the living room, he found Connie crouching beside the pile of mud. It was not sloppy enough to be mud, actually, just two or three hundred pounds of moist, compacted earth.

'Look at this, Harry.'

She pointed to an inexplicable feature that he had not noticed during the search of the house. For the most part, the pile was shapeless, but sprouting from the formless heap was one human hand, not real but shaped from moist earth. It was large, strong, with blunt spatulate fingers, as exquisitely detailed as if it had been carved by a great sculptor.

The hand extended from the cuff of a coat sleeve that

was also molded from the dirt, complete with sleeve strap, vent, and three mud buttons. Even the texture of the fabric was well realized.

'What do you make of it?' Connie asked.

'Damned if I know.'

He put one finger to the hand and poked at it, half expecting to discover that it was a real hand coated thinly with mud. But it was dirt all the way through, and it crumbled at his touch, more fragile than it appeared, leaving only the coat cuff and two fingers.

A pertinent memory swam into Harry's mind and out again before he could catch it, as elusive as a half-glimpsed fish quickening with a flash of color into the murky depths of a koi pond. Staring at what remained of the dirt hand, he felt that he was close to learning something of tremendous importance about Ticktock. But the harder he seined for the memory, the emptier his net.

'Let's get out of here,' he said.

Following Connie into the hallway, Harry didn't look toward the body.

He was walking a thin line between control and derangement, filled with a rage so intense that he could barely contain it, like nothing he had ever felt before. New feelings always troubled him because he could not be sure where they might lead; he preferred to keep his emotional life as ordered as his homicide files and his CD collection. If he looked at Ricky just once more, his anger might grow beyond containment, and hysteria of a sort might grip him. He felt the urge to shout at someone, anyone at all, scream until his throat ached, and he needed to punch someone, too, punch and gouge and kick. Lacking a deserving target, he wanted to turn his wrath on inanimate objects, break and smash anything within reach, stupid and pointless as that would be, even if it drew the desperately unwanted attention of neighbors. The only thing that restrained him from venting his rage was a mental image of himself in the throes of such a frenzy, wild-eyed and bestial; he could not tolerate the thought of being seen that far out of control, especially if the one who saw him was Connie Gulliver.

Outside, she closed the front door all the way. Together, they walked to the street.

Just as they reached the car, Harry stopped and surveyed the neighborhood. 'Listen.'

Connie frowned. 'What?'

'Peaceful.'

'So?'

'It would've made one hell of a lot of noise,' he said.

She was with him: 'The explosion that tore up the hall floor. And he would have screamed, maybe called for help.'

'So why didn't any curious neighbors come out to see what was happening? This isn't the big city, this is a fairly tight little community. People don't pretend to be deaf when they hear trouble next door. They come to help.'

'Which means they didn't hear anything,' Connie said.

'How's that possible?'

A night bird sang in a tree nearby.

Faint music still came from one of the houses. He could identify the tune this time. *A String of Pearls*.

Perhaps a block away, a dog let out a lonely sound between a moan and a howl.

'Didn't hear anything . . . How's that possible?' Harry repeated.

Farther away still, a big truck started up a steep grade on a distant highway. Its engine made a sound like the low bellow of a brontosaurus displaced in time.

·8·

His kitchen was all white – white paint, white floor tile, white marble counters, white appliances. The only relief from white was polished chrome and stainless steel where metal frames or panels were required, which reflected other white surfaces.

Bedrooms should be black. Sleep was black except when dreams were unreeling in the theater of the mind. And although his dreams always seethed with color, they were also somehow dark; the skies in them were always black or churning with contusive storm clouds. Sleep was like a brief death. Death was black.

However, kitchens must be white because kitchens were about food, and food was about cleanliness and energy. Energy was white: electricity, lightning.

In a red silk robe, Bryan sat in a shell-white chair with white leather upholstery in front of a white-lacquered table with a thick glass top. He liked the robe. He had five more of the same. The fine silk felt good against his skin, slippery and cool. Red was the color of power and authority: the red of a cardinal's cassock; the gold- and ermine-trimmed red of a king's imperial mantle; the red of a Mandarin emperor's dragon robe.

At home, when he chose not to be naked, he dressed only in red. He was a king in hiding, a secret god.

When he went out into the world, he wore drab clothing because he did not wish to call attention to himself. Until he had Become, he was at least marginally vulnerable, so anonymity was wise. When his power had fully developed and he had learned total control of it, he would at last be able to venture out in costumes that befitted his true station, and everyone would kneel before him or turn away in awe or flee in terror.

The prospect was exciting. To be acknowledged. To be known and venerated. Soon.

At his white kitchen table, he ate chocolate ice cream in fudge sauce, smothered in maraschino cherries, sprinkled with coconut and crumbled sugar cookies. He loved sweets. Salties too. Potato chips, cheese twirls, pretzels, peanuts, corn chips, deep-fried pork rinds. He ate sweets and salties, nothing else, because no one could tell him what to eat any more.

Grandmother Drackman would have a stroke if she could see what his diet consisted of these days. She had raised him virtually from birth until he was eighteen, and she had been uncompromisingly strict about diet. Three meals a day, no snacks. Vegetables, fruits, whole grains, breads, pasta, fish, chicken, no red meat, skim milk, frozen yogurt instead of ice cream, minimal salt, minimal sugar, minimal fat, minimal fun.

Even her hateful dog, a nervous poodle named Pierre, was forced to eat according to Grandma's rules, which in his case required a vegetarian regimen. She believed that dogs ate meat only because they were expected to eat it, that the word 'carnivore' was a meaningless label applied by know-nothing scientists, and that every species – especially dogs, for some reason – had the power to rise above their natural urges and live more peaceful lives than they usually did. The stuff in Pierre's bowl sometimes looked like granola, sometimes like tofu cubes, sometimes like charcoal, and the closest he ever came to the taste of flesh was the imitation-beef soy gravy spiked with protein powder that drenched most of what he was served. A lot of the time, Pierre had a strained and desperate look, as if maddened by a craving for something that he could not identify and therefore could not satisfy. Which was probably why he'd been so hateful, sneaky, and so given to nervous peeing in inconvenient places like Bryan's closet, all over his shoes.

She was a demon rulemaker, Grandma Drackman. She had rules for grooming, dressing, studying, and deportment in every conceivable social situation. A ten megabyte computer would offer insufficient capacity for the cataloguing of her rules.

Pierre the dog had his own rules to learn. Which chairs he could sit on, which he could not. No barking. No whining. Meals on a strict schedule, no table scraps.

Semi-weekly brushing, be still, don't fuss. Sit, roll over, play dead, don't claw the furniture . . .

Even as a child of four or five, Bryan had understood in his own terms that his grandmother was something of an obsessive-compulsive personality, an anal-retentive wreck, and he had been cautious with her, polite and obedient, pretending love but never letting her into his true inner world. When, at that young age, his specialness initially manifested itself in small ways, he was canny enough to conceal his budding talents from her, aware that her reaction might be . . . dangerous to him. Puberty brought with it a surge of growth not merely in his body but in his secret abilities, yet still he kept his own counsel, exploring his power with the help of a host of small animals that perished in a wide variety of satisfying torments.

Two years ago, only a few weeks after his eighteenth birthday, the strange and dynamic force within him surged again, as it did periodically, and though he still didn't feel strong enough to deal with the entire world, he knew that he was ready to deal with Grandma Drackman. She was sitting in her favorite armchair with her feet on an ottoman, eating carrot sticks, sipping at a glass of sparkling water, reading an article about capital punishment in the *Los Angeles Times*, adding her heartfelt comments about the need for extending compassion even to the worst of criminals, when Bryan used his newly refined power of pyrokinesis to set her on fire. Jeez, did she burn! In spite of the fact that she had less fat on her bones than did the average praying mantis, she went up like a tallow candle. Although one of her rules was never to raise one's voice in the house, she screamed nearly loud enough to shatter windows – though not for long. It was a controlled burn, focused on grandmother and her clothes, only singeing the armchair and ottoman, but she herself blazed so white-hot that Bryan had to squint when he looked at her. Like a caterpillar dipped in alcohol and lit with a match, she sizzled and popped and flared even brighter, then blackened to a crisp and curled up on herself. Still, he kept her burning until the charcoal residue of her bones became ashes and until the ashes became soot and until the soot just disappeared in a final puff of green sparks.

Then he dragged Pierre out of hiding and fried him too.

It was a lovely day.

That was the end of Grandma Drackman *and* her rules. From then on Bryan lived according to his own rules. Soon the whole world would live according to them as well.

He got up and went to the refrigerator. It was filled with candies and dessert toppings. Not a mushroom or piece of chopped jicama to be found. He took a jar of butterscotch topping back to the table and added some of it to the sundae.

'Dingdong, the witch is dead, the wicked old witch, the witch is dead,' he sang happily.

By tampering with public records, he had given Grandma an official death certificate, altered his official age to twenty-one (so no court would appoint a trustee), and had made himself the sole heir in her will. This was child's play, since no locked office or vault was proof against him; by the exercise of his Greatest and Most Secret Power, he could go where he wanted, do anything he wanted, and no one would know he had ever been there. After taking possession of the house, he had arranged for it to be gutted and remodeled to his own taste, eliminating every trace of the carrot-eating bitch.

Although he had spent more in the past two years than he had inherited, extravagance was no problem. He could get any amount of money any time he needed it. He didn't need it often because, thanks to his Greatest and Most Secret Power, he could also take virtually anything else he wanted and never be caught.

'Here's to you, Grandma,' he said, raising a heaping spoonful of ice cream and fudge sauce.

Although he was unable – quite yet – to heal his own injuries or even fade a bruise, he seemed able to maintain his proper weight and excellent body tone simply by concentrating on it for a few minutes every day, setting his metabolism as he might an ordinary thermostat. Because of this ability, he was confident that, after another growth surge or two, his power would extend to rapid self-healing and eventually to invulnerability.

Meanwhile, in spite of all the sweets and salties, he had a trim body. He was proud of his lean muscularity, which was one reason he sometimes liked to be naked around the house and enjoyed catching unexpected glimpses of himself in the many mirrors.

He knew that women would like his body. If he had

cared for women, he could have had any of them he wanted, maybe even without using any of his powers.

But sex was of no interest to him. For one thing, sex was the old god's biggest mistake. People had become obsessed with it, and all of their endless frantic breeding had ruined the world. Because of sex, the new god must thin the herd and clean up the planet. Besides, for him, orgasm was triggered not by sex but by the violent termination of a human life. After using one of his golems to kill someone, when he brought his entire consciousness back into his real body, he often found the black silk sheets wet with glistening streams of semen.

What would Grandma think of *that*!

He laughed.

He could do what he wanted and eat what he wanted, and where was his nagging grandmother? Burned, dead, gone forever – that's where.

He was twenty years old, and he might live to be a thousand, two thousand, possibly forever. When he had lived long enough, he would most likely forget about his grandmother altogether, and that would be good.

'Stupid old cow,' he said, and giggled. It tickled him to be able to talk about her any way he wanted, in what had been her house.

Though he had made the sundae in a large serving dish, he ate every bite of it. Exercising his powers was extremely taxing, and he required both more than the usual amount of sleep and far more calories per day than other people. He napped and snacked a lot of the time, but he assumed the need for food and sleep might entirely vanish when he had finished Becoming and was, at last, the new god. When his Becoming was complete, he might never sleep, and take food not out of necessity but only for the pleasure of it.

After he had scooped up the last spoonful, he licked out the dish.

Grandma Drackman *hated* that.

He licked it thoroughly. When he was finished, it looked as clean as if it had been washed.

'I can do anything I want,' he said. 'Anything.'

On the table, in a Mason jar, floating in preservative fluid, the eyes of Enrique Estefan watched him adoringly.

·9·

Driving north along the night coast with Ricky lying dead in the snake-infested house in Dana Point, Harry said, 'It's my fault, what happened to him.'

From the passenger seat, Connie said, 'The hell it is.'

'The hell it isn't.'

'I suppose it's your fault he walked into that convenience store after he got off duty three years ago.'

'Thanks for trying to make me feel better, but no thanks.'

'Should I try to make you feel worse? Look, this thing we're up against, this Ticktock – there's no way you can figure what he's going to do next.'

'But maybe I can. I'm getting a handle on him, sort

of. I'm starting to know what to expect. It's just that I'm running one step behind the sonofabitch. As soon as I saw that belt buckle, I knew it was natural for him to go after Ricky. That's part of what his threat meant. I just saw it too late.'

'My point exactly. Maybe there's no way to get ahead of this guy. He's something new, damn new, and he thinks a lot different from the way you and I think, from the way the average sleazebag thinks, doesn't fit any psychological profile, so there's no way you or anyone can be expected to out-think the bastard. Look, Harry, this is just not your responsibility.'

He snapped at her, not meaning to, not in the least blaming her for anything, but unable to contain his anger any longer. 'That's what's wrong with the world these days, Jesus, that's *exactly* what's wrong! Nobody wants to be responsible for anything. Everybody wants a license to be and do any damn thing, nobody wants to pay the bill.'

'You're right.'

She obviously meant what she said, agreed with him, wasn't just humoring him, but he would not be defused that easily.

'These days, if your life is screwed up, if you've failed your family and friends, it's never your fault. You're a drunkard? Why, maybe it's a genetic predisposition. You're a compulsive adulterer, have a hundred sex partners a year? Well, maybe you just never felt loved as a child, maybe your parents never gave you all the cuddling you needed. It's crap, all of it.'

'Exactly,' she said.

'You just blew some shopkeeper's head off or beat some old lady to death for twenty bucks? Why, you're not a bad guy, no, you're not to blame! Your parents are to blame, your teachers are to blame, society is to blame, all of Western culture is to blame, but not you, never you, how crass to suggest such a thing, how insensitive, how hopelessly old-fashioned.'

'You had a radio show, I'd listen to it every day,' she said.

He was passing slow traffic even when he had to cross a double yellow line. He had never done that before in his life, not even when he'd been in a car with a siren and emergency beacons flashing.

He wondered what had gotten into him. He wondered how he could wonder about it but keep doing it anyway, now swinging around a van with a Rocky Mountain mural on the side, into the oncoming-traffic lane in what was essentially a blind turn, even though the van was doing five miles an hour over the speed limit in the first place.

He raged on: 'You can walk out on your wife and kids without paying child support, bilk your investors out of millions, beat some guy's brains to jelly because he's gay or he showed you disrespect— '

Connie joined in: '—drop your baby in a garbage dumpster because you had second thoughts about the joys of motherhood— '

'—cheat on your taxes, defraud the welfare— '

'—sell drugs to grade-school kids— '

'—abuse your own daughter, and still claim *you're* the victim. Everyone's a victim these days. No one's a victimizer. No matter what atrocity you commit, you can stake a claim for sympathy, moan about being a victim of racism, reverse racism, sexism, ageism, classism, prejudice against fat people, ugly people, dumb people, smart people. That's why you robbed the bank or blew away that cop, because you're a victim, there're a million ways to be a victim. Yeah, sure, you devalue the honest complaints of real victims, but what the hell, we only go around once, might as well get your piece of the action, and who cares about those real victims anyway, for God's sake, they're *losers*.'

He was coming up fast behind a slow-moving Cadillac.

A passing lane was provided. But an equally slow-moving Jeep station wagon with two bumperstickers on the rear window – I TRAVEL WITH JESUS and BEACHES, BIKINIS & BEER – was blocking the way.

He couldn't cross the double yellow line again because suddenly a stream of oncoming traffic appeared behind dazzling headlights.

He thought of blowing his horn, trying to make the Caddy or the Jeep speed up, but he didn't have the patience for that.

The shoulder of the highway was unusually wide at that point, and he took advantage of it, accelerating hard as he pulled off the pavement, passing the Cadillac on the right side. Even as he was doing it, he couldn't *believe* he was doing it. Neither could the driver of the Cadillac; Harry looked over to his left and saw the man staring at him in astonishment, a funny little guy with a pencil mustache and a bad toupee. A soft

267

bank of eroded earth, hung with ice plant and wild ivy, pressed close on the right side of the Honda. It was just inches away from the door even where the shoulder was broad . . . and then the shoulder began to narrow. The Cadillac dropped back, trying to get out of his way. Harry accelerated, and the shoulder shrank further. A California Highway Department NO STOPPING sign appeared directly ahead of him and was absolutely certain to stop him if he hit it. He swerved off the diminishing berm, onto the blacktop again, fishtailing in front of the Caddy, got control, and continued north with the Pacific vastness to his left, as black as his mood.

'*Way cool!*' Connie said.

He didn't know if she was being sarcastic or approving. With her love of speed and risk, it could be either.

'What I'm saying,' he told her, struggling to keep his anger white-hot, 'is that I don't want to be like that, always pointing the finger somewhere else. When I'm responsible, I want to *choke* on my responsibility.'

'I hear you.'

'I'm responsible for Ricky.'

'Whatever you say.'

'If I'd been smarter, he'd still be alive.'

'Whatever.'

'He's on my conscience.'

'Fine with me.'

'I'm responsible.'

'And I'm sure you'll rot in hell for it.'

He couldn't help it: he laughed. The laughter was dark, and for a moment he was afraid it was going to turn into tears for Ricky, but she was not about to let that happen.

She said, 'Sit for eternity in a pit of dog vomit, if that's what you think you deserve.'

Though Harry wanted to keep his rage at full blaze, it was dimming – as it should. He glanced at her and laughed harder.

She said, 'You're such a bad guy, you'll have to eat maggots and drink demon bile for, oh, maybe a thousand years— '

'I hate demon bile— '

She was laughing too: '—and for sure you'll have to let Satan give you a high colonic— '

'—and watch *Hudson Hawk* ten thousand times— '

'Oh, no, even Hell has its limits.'

They were both howling now, letting off steam, and the laughter didn't fade for a while.

When silence finally settled between them, Connie was the one to break it: 'You okay?'

'I feel rotten.'

'But better?'

'A little.'

'You'll be okay.'

He said, 'I will be, I guess.'

'Of course you will. When everything's said and done, maybe that's the *real* tragedy. Somehow we grow scabs over all the hurts and losses, even the worst ones, deepest ones. We go on, and nothing hurts forever, though sometimes it seems right that it should.'

They continued north. Sea to the left. Dark hills speckled with house lights to the right.

They were in Laguna Beach again, but he didn't know where they were going. What he wanted to do was keep driving toward the top of the compass, all the way up the coast, past Santa Barbara, along Big Sur, over the Golden Gate, into Oregon, Washington, Canada, maybe up into Alaska, far and away, see some snow and feel the bite of arctic wind, watch moonlight glimmer on glaciers, then keep right on going across the Bering Straits, the car handling water with all the magic ease of some fairy-tale conveyance, then down the frozen coast of what had once been the Soviet Union, thence into China, stopping for some good Szechwan cooking.

He said, 'Gulliver?'

'Yeah.'

'I like you.'

'Who doesn't?'

'I mean it.'

'Well, I like you too, Lyon.'

'Just thought I'd say it.'

'Glad you did.'

'Doesn't mean . . . we're going steady or anything.'

She smiled. 'Good. By the way, where *are* we going?'

He resisted suggesting spicy duck in Beijing. 'Ordegard's place. You wouldn't happen to know the address, I guess.'

'I don't just know it – I've been there.'

He was surprised. 'When?'

'Between leaving the restaurant and coming back to the office, while you were typing reports. Nothing special about the place, creepy, but I don't think we'll find anything helpful there.'

'When you were there before, you didn't know about Ticktock. Now you'll be looking at things with a different attitude.'

'Maybe. Two blocks ahead, turn right.'

He did, and they went up into the hills, along cramped and winding streets canopied by palms and overgrown eucalyptuses. A white owl with a three-foot wingspan swooped from the chimney of one house to the gabled roof of another, sailing through the night like a lost soul seeking heaven, and the starless sky pressed down so close that Harry could almost hear it grinding softly against the high points of the eastern ridges.

·10·

Bryan opened one of the pair of French doors and stepped onto the master-bedroom balcony.

The doors were unlocked, as were all others in the house. Though it was prudent to keep a low profile until he had Become, he feared no one, never had. Other boys were cowards, not him. His power made him confident to an extent that perhaps no one else in the history of the world had ever been. He knew that no one could prevent him from fulfilling his destiny; his journey to the ultimate throne was ordained, and all he needed was patience in order to finish Becoming.

The hour before midnight was cool and humid. The balcony deck was beaded with dew. A refreshing breeze swept in from the sea. His red robe was belted tightly at the waist, but around his legs the hem belled out like a spreading pool of blood.

The lights of Santa Catalina, twenty-six miles to the west, were hidden by a thick bank of fog lying more than twenty miles off shore and invisible itself. In the wake of the rain, the sky remained low, forbidding any relief from starlight, moonlight. He could not see his neighbors' bright windows, for his house sat farthest out on the point, with the bluff falling away on three sides of the rear yard.

He felt wrapped by a darkness as comforting as his fine silk robe. The rumble and splash and ceaseless susurration of the surf was soothing.

Like a sorcerer at a lonely altar high upon a pinnacle of rock, Bryan closed his eyes and got in touch with his power.

He ceased to feel the cool night air and the chilly dew on the balcony deck. He could no longer feel the robe billowing around his legs, either, or hear the waves breaking on the shore below.

First he reached out to find the five diseased cattle that were awaiting the axe. He had marked each of them with a loop of psionic energy for easy location. With eyes closed, he felt as if he were floating high above the earth, and gazing down he saw five special lights, auras different from all other sources of energy along the southern coast. The objects of his blood sport.

Employing clairvoyance – or 'far-seeing' – he could observe these cattle, one at a time, as well as their immediate surroundings. He couldn't hear them, which was occasionally frustrating. However, he assumed that he would develop full five-sense clairvoyance when at last he Became the new god.

Bryan looked in upon Sammy Shamroe, whose torments had been postponed due to the unanticipated need to deal with the smartass hero cop. The booze-soaked loser was not huddled in his crate under the drooping boughs of alleyway oleander, not sucking down his second double-liter jug of wine, as Bryan expected. Instead he was on the move in downtown Laguna, carrying what appeared to be a thermos bottle, stumbling drunkenly past shuttered shops, leaning for a moment against the trunk of a tree to catch his breath and orient himself. Then he staggered ten or twenty steps only to lean against a brick wall and hang his head, evidently considering whether to heave up his guts. Deciding against regurgitation, he staggered forth again, blinking furiously, squinting, head thrust forward, an uncharacteristic look of determination on his face, as if he had some meaningful destination in mind, although he was most likely on a random ramble, driven by irrational ox-stupid motivations that would be explicable only to someone whose brain, like his, was pickled in alcohol.

Leaving Sam the Sham, Bryan next looked in upon the bigshot hero jackass and, by association, his bitch-cop partner. They were in the hero's Honda, pulling into the driveway of a contemporary house with weathered-cedar siding and lots of big windows, high in the hills. They were talking. Couldn't hear what they were saying. Animated. Serious. The two cops got out of the car, unaware that they were being observed. Bryan looked around. He recognized the neighborhood because he had lived all his life in Laguna Beach, but he didn't know to whom the house belonged.

In a few minutes he would visit Lyon and Gulliver more directly.

Finally he tuned in on Janet Marco and her ragamuffin child, where they were huddled in their dilapidated Dodge in the parking lot beside the Methodist Church. The boy appeared to be asleep on the back seat. The mother was behind the steering wheel, slumped down in the seat and against the driver's door. She was wide awake, keeping a watch on the night around the car.

He had promised to kill them at dawn, and intended to meet his self-imposed deadline. Dealing with them *and* two cops, after recently expending so much energy to torment and waste Enrique Estefan, would be taxing. But with a nap or two between now and sunrise, with a couple of bags of potato chips and some cookies and possibly another sundae, he believed he would be able to crush all of them in ways that would be wonderfully satisfying.

Ordinarily he would manifest himself through a golem at least two or three times during the last six hours of the mother's and son's lives, harassing them to bring the sharpest possible edge to their terror. Killing was pure pleasure, intense and orgiastic. But the hours – and sometimes days – of torment that preceded most of his killings were almost as much fun as the moment when, at last, blood flowed. He was excited by the fear the cattle showed, by the horror and awe that he engendered in them; he was thrilled by their stunned disbelief and hysteria when they failed in their pathetic attempts to hide or run, as they all did sooner or later. But with Janet Marco and her boy, he would have to forgo the foreplay, visit them only once more, at dawn, when they would receive a bill of pain and blood for having polluted the world with their presence.

Bryan needed to conserve his energy for the bigshot cop. He wanted the great and mighty hero to suffer more torment than usual. Humble him. Break him. Reduce him to a begging, sniveling baby. There was a coward in the hotshot hero. Cowards hid in all of them. Bryan intended to make the coward crawl on his belly, reveal what a weakling he really was, a jellyfish, nothing but a fraidy-cat hiding behind his badge and gun. Before he killed the two cops, he was going to run them to exhaustion, take them apart piece by piece, and make them wish they had never been born.

He stopped far-seeing and withdrew from the Dodge in the church parking lot. He returned his full consciousness to his body on the master-bedroom balcony.

High waves tilted out of the lightless west and crashed onto the shore below, reminding Bryan Drackman of the gleaming highrises in the cities of his dreams, which toppled to the pull of his power and drowned millions of screaming people in tides of glass and splintered steel.

When he had completed his Becoming, he would never need to rest again or preserve energy. His power would be that of the universe, endlessly renewable and beyond measure.

He returned to the black bedroom and slid the balcony door shut behind him.

He slipped off his red robe.

Naked, he stretched out on the bed, head propped up on two goose-down pillows in black silk cases.

A few slow, deep breaths. Close the eyes. Make the body limp. Clear the mind. Relax.

In less than a minute he was ready to create. He projected a substantial measure of his consciousness to the side yard of the modern house with weathered-cedar siding and big windows, high in the hills, where the cop's Honda stood in the driveway.

The nearest street lamp was half a block away. Shadows were everywhere and deep.

In the deepest, a section of the lawn began to churn. The grass folded into the earth beneath it as if an invisible tilling machine was at work, and the dirt boiled up with only a soft, wet sound like thick cake batter being folded over a rubber spatula. All of it – grass, soil, stones, dead leaves, earthworms, beetles, a cigar box containing the feathers and crumbled bones of a pet parakeet buried by a child long ago – rose in a swarthy, seething column as tall and broad as a large man.

Out of that mass, the hulking figure took shape from the top down. The hair appeared first, tangled and greasy. Then the beard. A mouth cracked open. Crooked, discolored teeth sprouted. Lips with oozing sores.

One eye opened. Yellow. Malevolent. Inhuman.

·11·

He is in a dark alley, padding along, seeking the scent of the thing-that-will-kill-you, knowing he's lost it but sniffing for it anyway because of the woman, because of the boy, because he's a good dog, good.

Empty can, metal smell, rust. Puddle of rainwater, drops of oil shining on top. Dead bee floating in the water. Interesting. Not as interesting as a dead mouse but interesting.

Bees fly, bees buzz, bees hurt you like a cat can hurt you, but this bee is dead. First dead bee he's ever seen. Interesting, that bees can die. He can't remember ever seeing a dead cat, either, so now he wonders if cats can die like bees.

Funny to think maybe cats can die.

What could kill them?

They can go straight up trees and places nothing else can go, and slash your nose with their sharp claws so fast you don't see it coming, so if something is out there that kills cats, it can't be good for dogs either, not good at all, something quicker than cats and mean.

Interesting.

He moves along the alley.

Somewhere in a people place, meat is cooking. He licks his chops because he's still hungry.

Piece of paper. Candy wrapper. Smells good. He puts a paw on it to hold it down, and licks it. The wrapper tastes good. He licks, licks, licks, but that's all of it, not much, just a little sweet on the paper. That's the way it usually is, a few licks or bites and then it's all

277

gone, seldom as much as he wants, never *more* than he wants.

He sniffs the paper just to be sure, and it sticks to his nose, so he shakes his head, flinging the paper free. It swoops up into the air and then floats along the alley on the breeze, up and down, side to side, like a butterfly. Interesting. All of a sudden alive and flying. How can that be? Very interesting. He trots after it, and it floats up there, so he jumps, snaps at it, misses, and now he wants it, really wants it, *has* to have it, jumps, snaps, misses. What's going on here, what is this thing? Just a paper and now it's flying like a butterfly. He really really really *needs* it. He trots and jumps and snaps and gets it this time, chews on it, but it's only paper, so he spits it out. He stares at it, stares and stares at it, waiting, watching, ready to pounce, not going to be fooled, but it doesn't move any more, dead as the bee.

Policeman-wolf-thing! The thing-that-will-kill-you.

That strange and hateful scent suddenly comes to him on a breeze from the sea, and he twitches. He sniffs, seeking. The bad thing is out in the night, standing in the night, somewhere near the sea.

He follows the odor. At first it is faint, almost fading away at times, but then it grows stronger. He begins to get excited. He is getting closer, not yet really close, but a little closer all the time, moving from alley to street to park to alley to street again. The bad thing is the strangest, most interesting thing he has ever smelled, ever.

Bright lights. *Beep-beep-beeeeeeeeep*. Car. Close. Could've been dead in a puddle like a bee.

He chases after the bad thing's scent, moving faster, ears pricked, alert and watchful, but still relying on his nose.

Then he loses the trail.

He stops, turns, sniffs the air this way and that. The breeze hasn't changed direction, still coming off the sea. But the smell of the bad thing is no longer on it. He waits, sniffs, waits, turns, whines in frustration, and sniffs sniffs sniffs.

The bad thing isn't out in the night any more. It went in somewhere, maybe into a people place where the breeze doesn't wash across it. Like a cat going high up a tree, out of reach.

He stands around for a while, panting, not sure what to do, and then the most amazing man comes along the sidewalk, stumbling and weaving back and forth, carrying a funny bottle in one hand, mumbling to himself. The man is putting off more odors than the dog has ever smelled on one people before, most of them bad, like lots of stinky people in one body. Sour wine. Greasy hair, sour sweat, onions, garlic, candle smoke, blueberries. Newspaper ink, oleander. Damp khaki. Damp flannel. Dried blood, faint people pee, peppermint in one coat pocket, an old bit of dried ham and moldy bread forgotten in another pocket, dried mustard, mud, grass, just a little people vomit, stale beer, rotting canvas shoes, rotten teeth. Plus he keeps farting as he weaves along, farting and mumbling, leaning against a tree for a while, farting, then weaving farther and stopping to lean against the wall of a people place and fart some more.

All of this is interesting, very, but the most interesting thing of all is that, among the many other odors, the man is carrying a trace of the bad thing's smell. He is not the bad thing, no, no, but he knows the bad thing, is coming from a place where he met the bad thing not long ago, has the touch of the bad thing on him.

Without a doubt it is *that* scent, so strange and evil: like the smell of the sea on a cold night, an iron fence on a hot day, dead mice, lightning, thunder, spiders, blood, dark holes in the ground – like all of those things yet not really like any of them.

The man stumbles past him, and he backs off with his tail between his legs. But the man doesn't even seem to see him, just weaves on and turns the corner into an alley.

Interesting.

He watches.

He waits.

Finally he follows.

·12·

Harry was uneasy about being in Ordegard's house. A police notice on the front door had restricted entrance until the criminal investigation had been completed, but he and Connie had not followed proper procedure to get in. She carried a complete set of lock picks in a small leather pouch, and she was able to go through Ordegard's locks faster than a politician could go through a billion dollars.

Ordinarily, Harry was appalled by such methods, and this was the first time he'd allowed her to use her picks since she'd been his partner. But there just wasn't enough time to follow the rules; dawn was less than seven hours away, and they were no closer to finding Ticktock than they had been hours ago.

The three-bedroom house was not large, but the space was well designed. Like the exterior, the interior lacked sharp angles. All corners were soft radiuses, and many rooms had at least one curved wall. Radiused, extremely shiny white-lacquered moldings were used throughout. High-gloss white paint had been applied to most walls, too, which lent the rooms a pearly luster, though the dining room had been faux-finished to give the illusion that it was upholstered in plush beige leather.

The place felt like the interior of a cruise ship, and it should have been soothing if not cozy. But Harry was edgy, not just because the moon-faced killer had lived there or because they had entered illegally, but for other reasons that he could not pin down.

Maybe the furnishings had something to do with his apprehension. Every piece was Scandinavian modern, severe, unornamented, in flat-yellow maple veneers, as angular as the house was soft-edged and rounded. The extreme contrast with the architecture made the sharp edges of the chair arms and end tables and sofa frames seem as if they were bristling at him. The carpet was the thinnest Berber with minimal padding; if it gave at all underfoot, the resilience was too minor to be detected.

As they moved through the living room, dining room, den, and kitchen, Harry noted that no artwork adorned the walls. There were no decorative objects of any kind; tables were utterly bare except for plain ceramic lamps in white and black. No books or magazines were to be found anywhere.

The rooms had a monastic feel, as if the person living in them was doing long-term penance for his sins.

Ordegard seemed to be a man of two distinct characters. The organic lines and textures of the house itself described a resident who had a strong sensual nature, who was easy with himself and his emotions, relaxed and self-indulgent to some extent. On the other hand, the relentless sameness of the furniture and utter lack of ornamentation indicated that he was cold, hard on himself and others, introverted, and brooding.

'What do you think?' Connie asked as they entered the hall that served the bedrooms.

'Creepy.'

'I told you. But why exactly?'

'The contrasts are . . . too extreme.'

'Yeah. And it just doesn't look lived-in.'

Finally, in the master bedroom, there was a painting on the wall directly opposite the bed. Ordegard would have seen it first thing upon waking and last thing before falling asleep each night. It was a reproduction of a famous work of art with which Harry was familiar, though he had no idea what the title was. He thought the artist was Francisco de Goya; that much had stuck with him from Art Appreciation 101. The work was menacing, abrasive to the nerves, conveying a sense of horror and despair, not least of all because it included the figure of a giant, demonic ghoul in the act of devouring a bloody and headless human body.

Profoundly disturbing, brilliantly composed and executed, it was without doubt a major work of art – but more suited to the walls of a museum than to a private home. It needed to be dwarfed by a huge exhibition space with vaulted ceiling; here, in this room of ordinary dimensions, the painting was too overpowering, its dark energy almost paralyzing.

Connie said, 'Which do you think he identified with?'

'What do you mean?'

'The ghoul or the victim?'

He thought about it. 'Both.'

'Devouring himself.'

'Yeah. Being devoured by his own madness.'

'And unable to stop.'

'Maybe worse than unable. Unwilling. Sadist and masochist rolled up in one.'

Connie said, 'But how does any of this help us figure out what's been happening?'

Harry said, 'As far as I can see, it doesn't.'

'Ticktock,' said the hobo.

When they spun around in surprise at hearing the low gravelly voice, the vagrant was only inches away. He could not have crept so close without alerting them, yet there he was.

Ticktock's right arm slammed across Harry's chest with what seemed like as much force as the steel boom of a construction crane. He was hurled backward. He crashed into the wall hard enough to make the bedroom windows vibrate in their frames, his teeth snapping together so forcefully that he would have bitten his tongue off if it had been in the way. He collapsed on his face, sucking up dust and carpet fibers, struggling to recapture the breath that had been knocked out of him.

With tremendous effort, he raised his face from the Berber, and saw that Connie had been lifted off her feet. Ticktock pinned her against the wall and shook her furiously. The back of her head and the heels of her shoes drummed the Sheetrock.

Ricky, now Connie.

First everyone you love . . .

Harry got up as far as his hands and knees, choking on carpet fibers that were stuck to the back of his throat. Every cough sent a quiver of pain through his chest, and he felt as if his rib cage was a vise that had closed around his heart and lungs.

Ticktock was screaming in Connie's face, words Harry couldn't understand because his ears were ringing.

Gunfire.

She had managed to draw her revolver and empty it into her assailant's neck and face. The slugs jolted him slightly but didn't loosen his grip on her.

Grimacing at the pain in his chest, pawing at a stark Danish-modern dresser, Harry lurched to his feet. Dizzy, wheezing. He pulled his own gun, knowing it would be ineffective against this adversary.

Still shouting and holding Connie off the floor, Ticktock swung her away from the wall and threw her at the two sliding glass doors to the balcony. She exploded through one of them as if she had been shot from a cannon, and the pane of tempered glass dissolved into tens of thousands of gummy fragments.

No. It couldn't happen to Connie. He couldn't lose Connie. Unthinkable.

Harry fired twice. Two ragged holes appeared in the back of Ticktock's black raincoat.

The vagrant's spine should have been shattered. Bone and lead shrapnel should have skewered all of his vital organs. He should have gone down like King Kong taking the plunge off the Empire State Building.

Instead, he turned.

Didn't cry out in pain. Didn't even wobble.

He said, 'Bigshot hero.'

How he could still talk was a mystery, maybe a miracle. In his throat was a bullet wound the size of a silver dollar.

Connie had also blown away part of his face. Missing tissue left a large concavity on the left side, from jaw line to just under the eye socket, and his left ear was gone.

No blood flowed. No bone lay exposed. The meat of him was not red but brown-black and strange.

His smile was more terrible than ever because the disintegration of his left cheek had exposed his rotten teeth all the way back along the side of his face. Within that calcium cage, his tongue squirmed like a fat eel in a fisherman's trap.

'Think you're so cool, big hero cop, bigshot tough guy,' Ticktock said. In spite of his deep and raspy voice, he sounded curiously like a schoolboy issuing a challenge to a playground fight, and even his fearsome appearance could not entirely conceal that childish quality in his demeanor. 'But you're nothing, you're nobody, just a scared little man.'

Ticktock stepped toward him.

Harry pointed the revolver at the huge assailant and—

—was sitting on a chair in James Ordegard's kitchen. The gun was still in his hand, but the muzzle was pressed to the underside of his chin, as if he were about to commit suicide. The steel was cold against his skin, and the gunsight dug painfully at his chin bone. His finger was curled around the trigger.

Dropping the revolver as if he had discovered a poisonous snake in his hand, he bolted up from the chair.

He had no memory of going to the kitchen, pulling the chair out from the table, and sitting down. In the blink of an eye, he seemed to have been transported there and encouraged to the brink of self-destruction.

Ticktock was gone.

The house was silent. Unnaturally silent.

Harry moved toward the door—

—and was sitting on the same chair as before, the gun in his hand again, the muzzle in his mouth, his teeth biting down on the barrel.

Stunned, he took the .38 out of his mouth and put it on the floor beside the chair. His palm was damp. He blotted it on his slacks.

He got to his feet. His legs were shaky. He broke into a sweat, and the sour taste of half-digested pizza rose in the back of his mouth.

Although he didn't understand what was happening

to him, he knew for certain that he did not have a suicidal urge. He wanted to live. Forever, if possible. He would not have put the barrel of the gun between his lips, not voluntarily, not in a million years.

He wiped one trembling hand down his damp face and—

—was on the chair again, holding the revolver, the muzzle pressed to his right eye, staring into the dark barrel. Five steely inches of eternity. Finger around the trigger.

Sweet Jesus.

His heart knocked so hard that he could feel it in every bruise on his body.

Carefully he put the revolver in his shoulder holster, under his rumpled coat.

He felt as if he were caught in a spell. Magic seemed to be the only explanation for what was happening to him. Sorcery, witchcraft, voodoo – he was suddenly willing to believe in all of it, as long as believing would buy a pardon from the sentence that Ticktock had pronounced on him.

He licked his lips. They were chapped, dry, burning. He looked at his hands, which were pale, and he figured that his face was even paler.

After getting shakily to his feet, he hesitated briefly, then started toward the door. He was surprised to reach it without being returned inexplicably to the chair.

He remembered the four expended bullets that he had found in his shirt pocket after shooting the vagrant four times, and he recalled as well the discovery of the newspaper under his arm as he'd walked out of the convenience store earlier in the night. Finding himself three times in the kitchen chair with no recollection of having gone to it was, he sensed, merely the result of a different application of the same trick that had put those slugs in his pocket and the paper under his arm. An explanation of how the effect was achieved seemed almost within his grasp . . . but remained elusive.

When he edged out of the kitchen without further incident, he decided that the spell was broken. He rushed to the master bedroom, wary of encountering Ticktock, but the vagrant seemed to have gone.

He was afraid of finding Connie dead, her head turned around backward like Ricky's had been, eyes torn out.

She was sitting on the balcony floor in glittering puddles of tempered glass, still alive, thank God, holding her head in her hands and groaning softly. Her short dark hair fluttered in the night breeze, shiny and soft. Harry wanted to touch her hair, stroke it.

Crouching beside her, he said, 'You all right?'

'Where is he?'

'Gone.'

'I want to tear his lungs out.'

Harry almost laughed with relief at her bravado.

She said, 'Tear 'em out and stuff 'em where the sun don't shine, make him breathe through his ass from now on.'

'Probably wouldn't stop him.'

'Slow him down some.'

'Maybe not even that.'

'Where the hell did he come from?'

'Same place he went. Thin air.'

She groaned again.

Harry said, 'You sure you're all right?'

She finally raised her face from her hands. The right corner of her mouth was bleeding, and the sight of her blood made him shiver with rage as much as with fear. That whole side of her face was red, as if she had been slapped hard and repeatedly. It would probably darken with bruises by tomorrow.

If they lived to see tomorrow.

'Man, could I use some aspirin,' she said.

'Me too.'

From his coat pocket, Harry removed the bottle of Anacin that he had borrowed from her medicine cabinet a few hours ago.

'A genuine boy scout,' she said.

'I'll get you some water.'

'I can get it myself.'

Harry helped her to her feet. Bits of glass fell from her hair and clothes.

When they stepped inside from the balcony, Connie paused to look at the painting on the bedroom wall. The headless human corpse. The hungry ghoul with mad, staring eyes.

'Ticktock had yellow eyes,' she said. 'Not like before, outside the restaurant when he panhandled me. Yellow eyes, bright, with black slits for pupils.'

They headed for the kitchen to get water to chase the

Anacin. Harry had the irrational feeling that the ghoul's eyes in the Goya painting turned to watch as he and Connie passed by, and that the monster climbed out of the canvas and crept after them through the dead man's house.

FOUR

·1·

Sometimes when he was weary from exercising his powers, Bryan Drackman grew sullen and petulant. He didn't like anything. If the night was cool, he wanted it warm; if it was warm, he wanted it cool. Ice cream tasted too sweet, corn chips too salty, chocolate far too chocolaty. The feel of clothes against his skin, even a silk robe, was intolerably irritating, yet he felt vulnerable and strange when he was naked. He didn't want to stay in the house, didn't want to go out. When he looked at himself in the mirror, he didn't like what he saw, and when he stood in front of the jars full of eyes, he had the feeling that they were mocking rather than adoring him. He knew he should sleep in order to restore his energy and improve his mood, but he loathed the world of dreams as much as he despised the waking world.

This crabbiness escalated until he became quarrelsome. Because he had no one with whom to quarrel in his seaside sanctum, his temper could not be vented. Irascibility intensified into anger. Anger became blind rage.

Too exhausted to work off his rage in physical activity, he sat naked in his black bed, propped against pillows covered in black silk, and allowed wrath to consume him. He closed his hands into fists on his thighs, squeezed tighter, tighter, until his fingernails dug painfully into his palms and until the muscles in his arms ached from the exertion. He pounded his thighs with his fists, knuckle-first to hurt the most, then his abdomen, then his chest. He twisted strands of hair around his fingers and pulled on it until tears blurred his vision.

His eyes. He hooked his fingers, pressed the nails against his eyelids, and tried to generate enough courage to gouge his eyes out, tear them loose and crush them in his fists.

He didn't understand why he was overcome by the urge to blind himself, but the compulsion was powerful.

Irrationality seized him.

He wailed, tossed his head in anguish and thrashed upon the black sheets, kicked and flailed, screamed and spat, cursed with a fluidity and vehemence that made his tantrum appear to be the work of some spawn of Hell that had possessed him. He cursed the world and himself, but most of all he cursed the bitch, the breeding bitch, the stupid hateful breeding bitch. His mother.

His mother.

Rage abruptly turned to piteous distress, and his furious cries and hate-filled screams shivered into agonized sobs. He curled into the fetal position, hugging his pummeled and aching body, and he wept as intensely as he had shrieked and flailed, as passionate in his self-pity as he had been in his wrath.

It wasn't fair, not fair at all, what was expected of him. He had to Become without the company of a brother, without the guiding hand of a carpenter father, without the tender mercy of his mother. Jesus, while Becoming, had enjoyed the perfect love of Mary, but there was no Holy Virgin this time, no radiant Madonna at his side. This time there was a hag, withered and debilitated by her greedy appetites and self-indulgence, who turned from him in loathing and fear, unable and unwilling to provide comfort. It was so unfair, so bitterly unjust, that he should be expected to Become and remake the world without the adoring disciples who had stood at the side of Jesus, and without a mother like Mary, Queen of Angels.

Gradually his wretched sobbing subsided.

The flow of tears slowed, dried up

He lay in miserable solitude.

He needed to sleep.

Since his most recent nap, he had created a golem to kill Ricky Estefan, built another golem to tie the silver buckle to the rearview mirror of Lyon's Honda, practiced godhood by bringing to life the flying reptile from the sand on the beach, and created yet another golem to terrorize the bigshot hero cop and his partner. He had also used his Greatest and Most Secret Power to put the spiders and snakes in Ricky Estefan's kitchen cabinets, to place the broken head of the religious figurine in Connie Gulliver's tightly clenched hand, and to drive Lyon half crazy by returning him three times to that kitchen chair in various suicidal postures.

Bryan giggled at the memory of Harry Lyon's utter confusion and fear.

Stupid cop. Big hero. Almost peed his pants in terror.

Bryan giggled again. He rolled over and buried his face in a pillow as the giggling built.

Almost peed his pants. Some hero.

Pretty soon he had stopped feeling sorry for himself. He was in a much better mood.

He was still exhausted, needed to sleep, but he was also hungry. He had burned up a tremendous number of calories in the exercise of his power and had lost a couple of pounds. Until he quelled his hunger pangs, he would not be able to sleep.

Pulling on his red silk robe, he went downstairs to the kitchen. He took a package of Malomars, a package of Oreos, and a large bag of onion-flavored potato chips from the pantry. From the refrigerator he got two bottles of Yoo Hoo, one chocolate and one vanilla.

He carried the food through the living room and outside, to the Mexican-tile patio, part of which was overhung by the master-bedroom balcony on the second story. He sat on a lounge chair near the railing, so he could see the dark Pacific.

As Tuesday ticked past midnight and became Wednesday, the breeze off the ocean was cool, but Bryan didn't mind. Grandma Drackman would have nagged him about catching pneumonia. But if it became too chilly, he was able with little effort to make some adjustments in his metabolism and raise his body temperature.

He washed down the whole bag of Malomars with vanilla Yoo Hoo.

He could eat what he wanted.

He could do what he wanted.

Although Becoming was a lonely process, and although it seemed unfair to be without his admiring disciples and his own Holy Mother, all was for the best in the end. While Jesus was a god of compassion and healing, Bryan was meant to be a god of wrath and cleansing; for this reason, it was desirable that he Become in solitude, without having been softened by a mother's love, without being encumbered by teachings of solicitude and mercy.

·2·

So this stinky man, stinkier than rotten oranges dropped off a tree and full of squirming things, stinkier than a three-day-dead mouse, stinkier than anything, stinky enough to make you sneeze when you smell too much of him, goes from street to street and into an alley, trailing clouds of odors.

The dog follows a few steps back, curious, keeping his distance, sniffing out the trace of the-thing-that-will-kill-you which is mixed in with all the other smells.

They stop at the back of a place where people make food.

Good smells, almost stronger than the stinky man,

hungry-making smells, lots of them, lots. Meat, chicken, carrots, cheese. Cheese is good, sticks in the teeth but is real good, much better than old chewing gum from the street which sticks in the teeth but isn't so good. Bread, peas, sugar, vanilla, chocolate, and more to make your jaws ache and your mouth water.

Sometimes he comes to food places like this, wagging his tail, whining, and they give him something good. But most of the time they chase him, throw things, shout, stamp their feet. People are strange about a lot of things, one of which is food. A lot of them guard their food, don't want you to have any – then they throw some of it away in cans where they let it go stinky and sick-making. If you knock over the cans to get the food before it goes all sick-making, people come running and shouting and chasing like they think you're a cat or something.

He is not for fun chasing. Cats are for fun chasing. He is not a cat. He is a dog. This seems so obvious to him.

People can be strange.

Now the stinky man knocks on a door, knocks again, and the door is opened by a fat man dressed in white and all surrounded by clouds of hungry-making smells.

Dear God, Sammy, you're a bigger mess than usual, says the fat man in white.

Just some coffee, says the stinky man, holding out the bottle he's carrying. *Don't want to bother you, really, I feel bad about this, but I need a little coffee.*

I remember when you first started out years ago—
Some coffee to sober me up.

—working with that little ad agency in Newport Beach—

Gotta get sober fast.

—before you moved to the big time in L.A., you were always so sharp, a real dresser, the best clothes.

Gonna die if I don't get sober.

You've spoke the truth there, says the fat man.

Just a thermos of coffee, Kenny. Please.

You're not going to get sober with coffee alone. I'll bag you some food, you promise you'll eat it.

Yeah, sure, sure I will, and some coffee, please.

Step aside there, away from the door. Don't want the boss to see you, realize I'm giving you anything.

Sure, Kenny, sure. I appreciate it, I do, really, 'cause I just gotta get sober.

The fat man looks behind and to one side of the stinky man, and he says, *You got a dog now, Sammy?*

Huh? Me? A dog? Hell, no.

The stinky man turns, looks, is surprised.

Maybe the stinky man would kick at him or chase him away, but the fat man is different. The fat man is nice. Anybody who smells of so many good things to eat must be nice.

The fat man leans forward in the doorway, with light from the food place behind him. In a people-who-will-feed-you voice, he says, *Hey there, fella, how you doin'?*

Just people noises. He doesn't really understand any of this, it's just people noises.

So he wags his tail, which he knows people always like, and he tilts his head and puts on the look that usually makes them go *ahhhhh.*

297

The fat man says, *Ahhhhh, you don't belong on the street, fella. What kind of people would abandon a nice mutt like you? You hungry? Bet you are. I can take care of that, fella.*

Fella is one of the things people call him, the one they call him most often. He remembers being called Prince when he was a puppy, by a little girl that liked him, but that's long ago. The woman and her boy call him Woofer, but Fella is what he hears the most.

He wags his tail harder and whines to show he likes the fat man. And he just sort of quivers all over to show how harmless he is, a good dog, a very good dog, good. People like that.

The fat man says something to the stinky man, then disappears into the food place, letting the door go shut.

Gotta get sober, the stinky man says, but he's just talking to himself.

Time to wait.

Just waiting is hard. Waiting for a cat in a tree is harder. And waiting for food is the hardest waiting of all. The time from when people seem to be going to give you food until when they really do give it to you is always so long that it seems like you could chase a cat, chase a car, sniff out every other dog in the territory, chase your tail until you're dizzy, turn over lots of cans full of sick-making food, and maybe sleep a while and *still* have to wait before they come back with what you can eat.

I've seen things people got to know about, says the stinky man.

Staying away from the man, still wagging his tail, he tries not to smell all the smells that are coming out of the food place, which only make the waiting harder. But the smells keep coming. He can't *not* smell them.

The ratman is real. He's real.

At last the fat man returns with the strange bottle and a bag for the stinky man – and with a plate heaped with scraps.

Wagging his tail, shivering, he thinks the scraps are for him, but he doesn't want to be too bold, doesn't want to go for the scraps and then they aren't for him and then the fat man takes a kick at him or something. He waits. He whines so the fat man won't forget about him. Then the fat man puts the plate down, which means the scraps are for him, and this is good, this is very good, oh, this is the best.

He slinks up to the plate, snatches at the food. Ham. Beef. Chunks of bread soaked in gravy. Yes yes yes yes yes yes yes.

The fat man squats down, wants to pet him, scratch behind his ears, so he lets that happen though he's a little spooked. Some people, they tease you with food, hold it out to you, give it to you, make like they want to pet you, then they swat you on the nose or kick you or worse.

Once he remembers some boys who had food for him, laughing boys, happy boys. Pieces of meat. Hand-feeding him. Nice boys. All of them petting him, scratching behind his ears. He sniffed them, smelled nothing wrong. Licked their hands. Happy boys, smelling like summer sun, sand, sea salt. He stood on his hind legs, and he chased his tail, and he fell over his own feet – all to make them laugh, please them. And they *did* laugh. They wrestled with him. He even rolled on his back. Exposed his belly. Let them rub his belly. Nice boys. Maybe one of them would take him home, feed him every day. Then they grabbed him by the scruff of the neck, and one of them had fire on a little stick, and they were trying to light his fur. He squirmed, squealed, whined, tried to get free. The fire stick went out. They lit another one. He could have bit at them. But that would have been bad. He was a good dog. Good. He smelled burnt fur but didn't quite catch fire, so they had to light another fire stick, and then he got away. He ran out of their reach. Looked back at them. Laughing boys. Smelling of sun, sand, and sea salt. Happy boys. Pointing at him and laughing.

Most people are nice but others are not nice. Sometimes he can smell the not-nice ones right away. They smell . . . like cold things . . . like ice . . . like winter metal . . . like the sea when it's gray and no sun and people all gone from the beach. But other times, the not-nice people smell just like the nice ones. People are the most interesting things in the world. They are also the scariest.

The fat man behind the food place is a nice one. No hitting on the nose. No kicking. No fire. Just good food, yes yes yes yes, and a nice laugh when you lick his hands.

Finally the fat man makes it clear that there is no more food right now. You stand on your hind feet, you whine, whimper, roll over and expose your belly, sit up and beg, do your little dance in a circle, tilt your head, wag wag wag wag your tail, shake your head and flap your ears, do all your little food-getting tricks, but you can't get anything more out of him. He goes inside, closes the door.

Well, you *are* full. Don't need more food.

Doesn't mean you can't *want* more.

So wait anyway. At the door.

He's a nice man. He'll come back. How can he forget you, your little dance and wagging tail and begging whine?

Wait.

Wait.

Wait. Wait.

Gradually he remembers that he was doing something interesting when he came upon the fat man with the food. But what?

Interesting . . .

Then he remembers: the stinky man.

The strange stinky man is at the far end of the alley, at the corner, sitting on the ground between two shrubs, his back against the wall of the food place. He is eating out of a bag, drinking out of a big bottle. Coffee smell. Food.

Food.

He trots toward the stinky man because maybe he can get some more to eat, but then he stops because he suddenly smells the bad thing. On the stinky man. But on the night air too. Very strong again, that scent, cold and terrible, carried on the breeze.

The thing-that-will-kill-you is outside again.

No longer wagging his tail, he turns away from the stinky man and hurries through the night streets, following that one scent among thousands of others, moving toward where the land disappears, where there is only sand and then water, toward the rumbling, cold, dark, dark sea.

·3·

James Ordegard's neighbors, like those of Ricky Estefan, did not acknowledge the commotion next door. The gunfire and shattering glass elicited no response. When Harry opened the front door and looked up and down the street, the night remained calm, and no sirens rose in the distance.

It seemed as if the confrontation with Ticktock had taken place in a dream to which only Harry and Connie were privy. However, they had plenty of proof that the encounter had been real: expended shell casings in their revolvers; broken glass all over the master-bedroom balcony; cuts, scrapes, and various tender spots that would later become bruises.

Harry's first urge – and Connie's too – was to get the hell out of there before the vagrant returned. But they both knew that Ticktock could find them as easily elsewhere, and they needed to learn what they could from the aftermath of their confrontation with him.

In James Ordegard's bedroom again, under the malevolent stare of the ghoul in the Goya painting, Harry looked for one more proof. Blood.

Connie had shot Ticktock at least three times, maybe four, at close range. A portion of his face had been blown away, and there had been a substantial wound in his throat. After the vagrant had thrown Connie through the sliding glass door, Harry had pumped two rounds into his back.

Blood should have been splattered as liberally as beer at a frat-house party. Not one drop of it was visible on the walls or carpet.

'Well?' Connie asked from the doorway, holding a glass of water. The Anacins had stuck in her throat. She was still trying to wash them all the way down. Or maybe she had gotten the pills down easily enough, and something else had stuck in her throat – like fear, which she usually had no trouble swallowing. 'Did you find anything?'

'No blood. Just this . . . dirt, I guess it is.'

The stuff certainly felt like moist earth when he crumbled it between his fingertips, smelled like it too. Clots and sprinkles were scattered across the carpet and the bedspread.

Harry moved around the room in a crouch, pausing at the larger clumps of dirt to poke at them with one finger.

'This night's going too fast,' Connie said.

'Don't tell me the time,' he said without looking up.

She told him anyway. 'Few minutes past midnight. Witching hour.'

'For sure.'

He kept moving, and in one small mound of dirt,

he found an earthworm. It was still moist, glistening, but dead.

He uncovered a wad of decaying vegetable matter, which seemed to be ficus leaves. They peeled apart like layers of filo dough in a Mid-eastern pastry. A small black beetle with stiff legs and jewel-green eyes was entombed in the center of them.

Near one of the nightstands, Harry found a slightly misshapen lead slug, one of the rounds that Connie had pumped into Ticktock. Damp earth clung to it. He picked it up and rolled it between his thumb and forefinger, staring at it thoughtfully.

Connie came farther into the room to see what he had discovered. 'What do you make of it?'

'I don't know exactly . . . though maybe . . .'

'What?'

He hesitated, looking around at the soil on the carpet and the bedspread.

He was recalling certain folk legends, fairy tales of a fashion, although with an even stronger religious over-tone than those of Hans Christian Andersen. Judaic in origin, if he wasn't mistaken. Tales of cabalistic magic.

He said, 'If you gathered up all this dirt and debris, if you packed it together real tight . . . do you think it would be just exactly the right amount of material to fill in the wound in his throat and the hole in the side of his face?'

Frowning, Connie said, 'Maybe. So . . . what're you saying?'

He stood and pocketed the slug. He knew that he didn't have to remind her about the inexplicable pile

304

of dirt in Ricky Estefan's living room – or about the exquisitely sculpted hand and coat sleeve sprouting from it.

'I'm not sure what I'm saying just yet,' Harry told her. 'I need to think about it a little more.'

As they passed through Ordegard's house, they turned off the lights. The darkness they left behind seemed alive.

Outside in the post-midnight world, ocean air washed the land without cleansing it. Wind off the Pacific had always felt crisp and clean to Harry, but no longer. He had lost his faith that the chaos of life was continuously swept into order by the forces of nature. Tonight the cool breeze made him think of unclean things: grave-yard granite, fleshless bones in the eternal embrace of gelid earth, the shiny carapaces of beetles that fed on dead flesh.

He was battered and tired; perhaps exhaustion accounted for this new somber and portentous turn of mind. Whatever the cause, he was drifting toward Connie's view that chaos, not order, was the natural state of things and that it could not be resisted, only ridden in the manner that a surfer rides a towering and potentially deadly wave.

On the lawn, between the front door and the driveway where he had parked the Honda, they almost walked into a large mound of raw earth. It had not been there when they had first gone inside.

Connie got a flashlight from the glove compartment of the Honda, returned, and directed the beam on the mound, so Harry could examine it more closely. First he carefully circled the pile, studying it closely, but he could find no hand or other human feature molded from it. Deconstruction had been complete this time.

Scraping at the dirt with his hands, however, he uncovered clusters of dead and rotting leaves like the wad he had discovered in Ordegard's bedroom. Grass, stones, dead earthworms. Soggy pieces of a mouldering cigar box. Pieces of roots and twigs. Thin parakeet bones, including the fragile calcium lace of one folded wing. Harry wasn't sure what he expected to find: maybe a heart sculpted from mud with all the detail of the hand they had seen in Ricky's living room, and still beating with strange malignant life.

In the car, after he started the engine, he switched on the heater. A deep chill had settled in him.

Waiting to get warm, staring at the black mound of earth on the dark lawn, Harry told Connie about that vengeful monster of legend and folklore – the golem. She listened without comment, even less skeptical about this astonishing possibility than she had been at her apartment, earlier in the night, when he had raved on about a sociopath with psychic abilities and the demonic power to possess other people.

When he finished, she said, 'So he makes a golem and uses it to kill, while he stays safe somewhere.'

'Maybe.'

'Makes a golem out of dirt.'

'Or sand or old brush or maybe just about anything.'

'Makes it with the power of his mind.'

Harry didn't respond.

She said, 'With the power of his mind or with magic like in the folktales?'

'Jesus, I don't know. It's all so crazy.'

'And you still think he can also possess people, use them like puppets?'

'Probably not. No proof of it so far.'

'What about Ordegard?'

'I don't think there's any connection between Ordegard and this Ticktock.'

'Oh? But you wanted to go to the morgue because you thought— '

'I did, but I don't now. Ordegard was just an ordinary, garden-variety, pre-millennium nutcase. When I blew him away in the attic yesterday afternoon, that was the end of it.'

'But Ticktock showed up here at Ordegard's— '

'Because we were here. He knows how to find us somehow. He came here because we were here, not because he has anything to do with James Ordegard.'

A forced stream of hot air poured out of the dash-board vents. It washed over him without melting the ice he imagined he could feel in the pit of his stomach.

'We just ran into two psychos within a couple of hours of each other,' Harry said. 'First Ordegard, then this guy. It's been a bad day for the home team, that's all.'

'One for the record books,' Connie agreed. 'But if Ticktock isn't Ordegard, if he wasn't angry with you for shooting Ordegard, why'd he fixate on you? Why's he want you dead?'

'I don't know.'

'Back at your place, before he burned it down, didn't

307

he say you couldn't shoot *him* and think that was the end of it?'

'Yeah, that's part of what he said.' Harry tried to recall the rest of what the vagrant-golem had thundered at him, but the memory was elusive. 'Now that I think of it, he never mentioned Ordegard's name. I just assumed . . . No. Ordegard's been a false trail.'

He was afraid she was going to ask how they could pick up the real trail, the right one, that would lead them to Ticktock. But she must have realized that he was completely at a loss, because she didn't put him on the spot.

'It's getting too hot in here,' she said.

He lowered the temperature control on the heater.

At the bone, he was still chilled.

In the light from the instrument panel, he noticed his hands. They were coated with grime, like the hands of a man who, buried prematurely, had desperately clawed his way out of a fresh grave.

Harry backed the Honda out of the driveway and drove slowly down through the steep hills of Laguna. The streets in those residential neighborhoods were virtually deserted at that late hour. Most of the houses were dark. For all they knew, they might have been descending through a modern ghost town, where all of the residents had vanished like the crew of the old sailing ship *Mary Celeste*, beds empty in the darkened houses, televisions aglow in deserted family rooms, midnight snacks laid out on plates in silent kitchens where no one remained to eat.

He glanced at the dashboard clock. 12:18.

Little more than six hours until dawn.

'I'm so tired I can't think straight,' Harry said. 'And, damn it, I've *got* to think.'

'Let's find some coffee, something to eat. Get our energy back.'

'Yeah, all right. Where?'

'The Green House. Pacific Coast Highway. It's one of the few places open this late.'

'Green House. Yeah, I know it.'

After a silence during which they descended another hill, Connie said, 'You know what I found weirdest about Ordegard's house?'

'What?'

'It reminded mc of my apartment.'

'Really? How?'

'Don't shine me on, Harry. You saw both places tonight.'

Harry *had* noticed a certain similarity, but he hadn't wanted to think about it. 'He has more furniture than you do.'

'Not a whole damn lot more. No knick-knacks, none of what they call decorative pieces, no family photos. One piece of art hanging in his place, one in mine.'

'But there's a big difference, a huge difference – you've got that sky-diver's eye-view poster, bright, exhilarating, gives you a sense of freedom just to look at it, nothing like that ghoul chewing on human body parts.'

'I'm not so sure. The painting in his bedroom's about death, human fate. Maybe my poster isn't so exhilarating, really. Maybe what it's really about is death, too, about falling and falling and never opening the chute.'

Harry glanced away from the street. Connie wasn't looking at him. Her head was tilted back, eyes closed.

'You're not any more suicidal than I am,' he said.

'How do you know?'

'I know.'

'The hell you do.'

He stopped at a red traffic light at Pacific Coast Highway, and looked at her again. She still hadn't opened her eyes. 'Connie— '

'I've always been chasing freedom. And what is the ultimate freedom?'

'Tell me.'

'The ultimate freedom is death.'

'Don't get Freudian on me, Gulliver. One thing I've always liked about you is, you don't try to psychoanalyze everyone.'

To her credit, she smiled, evidently remembering that she had used those words on him in the burger restaurant after the shooting of Ordegard, when he had wondered if she was as hard inside as she pretended to be.

She opened her eyes, checked the traffic light. 'Green.'

'I'm not ready to go.'

She looked at him.

He said, 'First I want to know if you're just jiving or if you really think you've got something in common with a fruitcake like Ordegard.'

'All this shit I go on about, how you have to love

chaos, have to embrace it? Well, maybe you do, if you want to survive in this screwed-up world. But tonight I've been thinking maybe I used to like surfing on it because, secretly, I hoped it would wipe me out one day.'

'Used to?'

'I don't seem to have the same taste for chaos that I once did.'

'Ticktock give you your fill of it?'

'Not him. It's just . . . earlier, right after work, before your condo was burned down and everything went to hell, I discovered I've got a reason to live that I never knew about.'

The light had turned red again. A couple of cars *whooshed* past on the coast highway, and she watched them go.

Harry said nothing because he was afraid that any interruption would discourage her from finishing what she had begun to tell him. In six months, her arctic reserve had never thawed until, for the briefest moment in her apartment, she had seemed about to disclose something both private and profound. She had quickly frozen again; but now the face of the glacier was cracking. His desire to be let into her world was so intense that it revealed as much about his own need for connections as it did about the extent to which she had heretofore guarded her privacy; he was prepared to expend all of his last six hours of life at that traffic light, if necessary, waiting for her to provide him with a better understanding of the special woman that he believed existed under the hard veneer of the streetwise cop.

'I had a sister,' she said. 'Never knew about her until recently. She's dead. Been dead five years. But she had a child. A daughter. Eleanor. Ellie. Now I don't want to be wiped out, don't want to surf on the chaos any more. I just want to have a chance to meet Ellie, get to know her, see if I can love her, which I think maybe I can. Maybe what happened to me when I was a kid didn't burn love out of me forever. Maybe I can do more than hate. I've got to find out. I can't *wait* to find out.'

He was dismayed. If he understood her correctly, she had not yet felt for him anything like the love he had begun to feel for her. But that was all right. Regardless of her doubts, he knew that she had the ability to love and that she would find a place in her heart for her niece. And if for the girl, why not for him as well?

She met his eyes and smiled. 'Good God, just listen to me, I sound like one of those confessional neurotics spilling their guts on an afternoon TV talkshow.'

'Not at all. I . . . I want to hear it.'

'Next thing you know, I'll be telling you how I like to have sex with men who dress like their mothers.'

'Do you?'

She laughed. 'Who doesn't?'

He wanted to know what she meant when she said *what happened to me when I was a kid*, but he dared not ask. That experience, if not the core of her, was at least what she believed the core to be, and she would be able to reveal it only at her own pace. Besides, there were a thousand other questions he wanted to ask her, ten thousand, and if he started, they really *would* sit at that intersection until dawn, Ticktock, and death.

The traffic light was in their favor again. He entered the intersection and turned right. Two blocks farther north he parked in front of the Green House.

When he and Connie got out of the car, Harry noticed a filthy hobo in the shadows at the corner of the restaurant, by an alleyway that ran toward the back of the building. It was not Ticktock, but a smaller, pathetic-looking specimen. He sat between two shrubs, legs drawn up, eating from a bag in his lap, drinking hot coffee from a thermos, and mumbling urgently to himself.

The guy watched them as they walked toward the entrance to the Green House. His stare was fevered, intense. His bloodshot eyes were like those of many other denizens of the streets these days, hot with paranoid fear. Perhaps he believed himself to be persecuted by evil space aliens who were beaming microwaves at him to muddle his thoughts. Or by the dastardly band of ten thousand and eighty-two conspirators who had *really* shot John F. Kennedy and who had secretly controlled the world ever since. Or by fiendish Japanese businessmen who were going to buy everything everywhere, turn everyone else into slaves, and serve the raw internal organs of American children as side dishes in Tokyo sushi bars. Recently it seemed that half the *sane* population – or what passed for sane these days – believed in one demonstrably ridiculous paranoid conspiracy theory or another. And for the most thoroughly stoned street-wanderers like this man, such fantasies were de rigueur.

To the hobo, Connie said, 'Can you hear me, or are you on the moon somewhere?'

The man glared at her.

'We're cops. You got that? Cops. You touch that car while we're gone, you'll find yourself in a detox program so fast you won't know what hit you, no booze or drugs for three months.'

Forced detoxification was the only threat that worked with some of these squires of the gutter. They were already at the bottom of the swamp, used to being knocked around and chewed up by the bigger animals. They had nothing left to lose – except the chance to stay high on cheap wine or whatever else they could afford.

'Cops?' the man said.

'Good,' Connie said. 'You heard me. Cops. Three months with not a single hit, it'll seem like three centuries.'

Last week, in Santa Ana, a drunken vagrant had taken advantage of their unattended department sedan to make a social protest by leaving his feces on the driver's seat. Or maybe he mistook them for space aliens to whom a gift of human waste was a sign of welcome and an invitation to intergalactic cooperation. In either case, Connie had wanted to kill the guy, and Harry had needed every bit of his diplomacy and persuasiveness to convince her that forced detox was crueller.

'You lock the doors?' Connie asked Harry.

'Yeah.'

Behind them, as they went into the Green House, the vagrant said thoughtfully: 'Cops?'

·4·

Having eaten the cookies and potato chips, Bryan briefly used his Greatest and Most Secret Power to insure total privacy, then stood at the edge of the patio and urinated between railings into the silent sea below. He always got a kick out of doing things like that in public, sometimes right out in the street with people around, knowing that his Greatest and Most Secret Power would insure against discovery. Bladder empty, he started things up again and returned to the house.

Food alone was seldom sufficient to restore his energy. He was, after all, a god Becoming, and, according to the Bible, the first god had needed rest himself on the seventh day. Before he could work more miracles, Bryan would still have to nap, perhaps for as much as an hour.

In the master bedroom, lit only by one bedside lamp, he stood for a while in front of the black-lacquered shelves where eyes of many species and colors floated in preserving fluid. Feeling their unblinking, eternal gazes. Their adoration.

He unbelted his red robe, shrugged out of it, and let it drop to the floor.

The eyes loved him. Loved him. He could feel their love, and he accepted it.

He opened one of the jars. The eyes in it had belonged to a woman who had been thinned from the herd because she was one of those who could vanish from the world without causing much concern.

They were blue eyes, once beautiful, the color faded now and the lenses milky.

Dipping into the pungent fluid, he removed one of the blue eyes and held it in his left hand. It felt like a ripe date – soft but firm, and moist.

Trapping the eye between his palm and chest, he rolled it gently across his body from nipple to nipple, back and forth, not pressing too hard, careful to avoid damaging it, but eager for the dead woman to see him in all his Becoming glory, every smooth plane and curve and pore of him. The small sphere was cool against his warm flesh, and left a trail of moisture on his skin. He shivered deliciously. He eased the slick orb down his flat belly, describing circles there, then held it for a moment in the hollow of his navel.

From the open jar, he extracted the second blue eye. He trapped it under his right hand and allowed both eyes to explore his body: chest and flanks and thighs, up across his belly and chest again, along the sides of his neck, his face, gently rotating the moist and spongy spheres on his cheeks, around, around, around. So satisfying to be the object of adoration. So supremely glorious for the dead woman to be granted this intimate moment with the Becoming god who had judged and condemned her.

Winding tracks of preserving fluid marked each eye's journey over his body. As the fluid evaporated, it was easy to believe that the tracery of coolness was actually a lace of tears upon his skin, shed by the dead woman who rejoiced in this sacrosanct contact.

The other eyes upon the shelves, watching from their

separate glass-walled liquid universes, seemed envious of the blue eyes to which he had granted communion.

Bryan wished that he could bring his mother here and show her all the eyes that adored and cherished him, revered him, and found no aspect of him from which they wished to turn their gazes.

But, of course, she would not look, could not see. The stubborn, withered hag would persist in fearing him. She regarded him as an abomination, though it should be obvious even to her that he was Becoming a figure of transcendent spiritual power, the sword of judgment, instigator of Armageddon, savior of a world infested with an abundance of humanity.

He returned the pair of blue eyes to the open jar, and screwed the lid shut.

He had satisfied one hunger with cookies and chips, satisfied another by revealing his glory to the congregation in the jars and by seeing that they were in awe of him. Now it was time to sleep for a short while and recharge his batteries; dawn was nearer, and he had promises to keep.

As he settled upon the disarranged bed sheets, he reached for the switch on the nightstand lamp, but then decided not to turn it off. The disembodied communicants in the jars would be able to see him better if the room was not entirely dark. It pleased him to think that he would be admired and venerated even while he slept.

Bryan Drackman closed his eyes, yawned, and as always sleep came to him without delay. Dreams: great cities falling, houses burning, monuments collapsing, mass graves of broken concrete and twisted steel stretching to the horizon and attended by flocks of feeding vultures so numerous that, in flight, they blackened the sky.

·5·

He sprints, trots, slows to a walk, and finally creeps warily from shadow to shadow as he draws nearer to the thing-that-will-kill-you. The smell of it is ripe, strong, foul. Not filthy like the stinky man. Different. In its own way, worse. Interesting.

He is not afraid. He is not afraid. Not afraid. He is a dog. He has sharp teeth and claws. Strong and quick. In his blood is the need to track and hunt. He is a dog, cunning and fierce, and he runs from nothing. He was born to chase, not *be* chased, and he fearlessly pursues anything he wants, even cats. Though cats have clawed his nose, bitten and humiliated him, still he chases them, unafraid, for he is a dog, maybe not as smart as some cats, but a *dog*.

Padding along beside a row of thick oleander. Pretty flowers. Berries. Don't eat the berries. Sick-making. You can tell from the smell. Also the leaves. Also the flowers.

Never eat *any* kind of flowers. He tried to eat one once. There was a bee in the flower, then in his mouth, buzzing in his mouth, stinging his tongue. A very bad day, worse than cats.

He creeps onward. Not afraid. Not. Not. He is a dog.

People place. High white walls. Windows dark. Near the top, one square of pale light.

He slinks along the side of the place.

The smell of the bad thing is strong here, and getting stronger. Almost burns in the snout. Like ammonia but not like. A cold smell and dark, colder than ice and darker than night.

Halfway along the high white wall, he stops. Listens. Sniffs.

He is not afraid. He is not afraid.

Something overhead goes *Whoooooooooooo*.

He is afraid. Whipping around, he starts to run back the way he came.

Whoooooooooooo.

Wait. He knows that sound. An owl, swooping through the night above, hunting prey of its own.

He was frightened by an owl. Bad dog. Bad dog. Bad.

Remember the boy. The woman and the boy. Besides . . . the smell, the place, the moment are interesting.

Turning once again, he continues to creep along the side of the people place, white walls, one pale light high above. He comes to an iron fence. Tight squeeze. Not as tight as the drain pipe where you follow the cat and get stuck and the cat keeps going, and you twist and kick and struggle for a long time inside the pipe, you think you're never going to get loose, and then you wonder if maybe the cat is coming back toward you through the darkness of the pipe, is going to claw your nose while you're stuck and can't move. Tight, but not *that* tight. He shakes his rear end, kicks, and gets through.

He comes to the end of the place, starts around the corner, and sees the thing-that-will-kill-you. His vision is not nearly as keen as his smell, but he is able to make out a man, young, and he knows it is the bad thing because it reeks of that strange dark cold smell. Before, it looked different, never a young man, but the smell is the same. This is the thing, for sure.

He freezes.

He is not afraid. He is not afraid. He is a dog.

The young-man-bad-thing is on its way into the people place. It is carrying food bags. Chocolate. Marshmallow. Potato chips.

Interesting.

Even the bad thing eats. It has been outside, eating, and now it is going in, and maybe some of the food is left. A wag of the tail, a friendly whine, the sitting-up-and-begging trick might get something good, yes yes yes yes.

No no no no. Bad idea.

But chocolate.

No. Forget it. The kind of bad idea that gets your nose scratched. Or worse. Dead like the bee in the puddle, the mouse in the gutter.

The thing-that-will-kill-you goes inside, closes the door. Its scary smell isn't so strong now.

Neither is the chocolate smell. Oh well.

Whoooooooooooo.

Just an owl. Who would be afraid of an owl? Not a dog.

He sniffs around behind the people place for a while, some of it grass, some of it dirt, some of it flat stones

that people put down. Bushes. Flowers. Busy bugs
in the grass, different kinds. A couple of things for
people to sit in . . . and beside one of them, a piece
of cookie. Chocolate. Good, good, gone. Sniff around,
under, here, there, but no more to be found.

A little lizard! Zip, so fast, across the stones, get it,
get it, get it, get it. This way, that way, this way, between
your legs, that way, here it comes, there it goes – now
where is it? – over there, zip, don't let it get away, get
it, get it, want it, need it, *bang* an iron fence out of
nowhere.

The lizard is gone, but the fence smells of fresh people
pee. Interesting.

It's the pee of the thing-that-will-kill-you. Not a nice
smell. Not a bad smell. Just interesting. The thing-that-
will-kill-you looks like people, pees like people, so must
be people, even if it's strange and different.

He follows the route the bad thing took when it
stopped peeing and went into the people place, and in
the bottom of the big door he finds a smaller door, more
or less his size. He sniffs it. The smaller door smells like
another dog. Faint, very faint, but another dog. A long
time ago, a dog went in and out this door. Interesting. So
long ago, he has to sniff sniff sniff sniff to learn anything.
A male dog. Not small, not too big. Interesting. Nervous dog . . . or maybe sick. Long time ago. Interesting.

Think about this.

Door for people. Door for dogs.

Think.

So this isn't just a people place. This is a people and
dog place. Interesting.

He pushes his nose against the little cold metal door, and it swings inward. He sticks his head in, lifting the door just far enough to sniff deep and look around.

People food place. Hidden away is food, not out where he can see it but where he can still smell it. Strongest of all, the smell of the bad thing, so strong that it leaves him uninterested in food.

The smell repels and frightens him but also attracts him, and curiosity draws him forward. He squeezes through the opening, the little metal door sliding along his back, along his tail, then falling shut with a faint squeak.

Inside.

Listening. Humming, ticking, a soft clink. Machine sounds. Otherwise, silence.

Not much light. Just little glowing spots up on some of the machines.

He is not afraid. Not, not, not.

He creeps from one dark space to another, squinting into the shadows, listening, sniffing, but he does not find the thing-that-will-kill-you until he comes to the bottom of stairs. He looks up and knows that the thing is in one of the spaces up there somewhere.

He starts up the stairs, pauses, continues, pauses, looks down to the floor below, looks up, continues, pauses, and he wonders the same thing he always wonders at some point while chasing a cat: what is he doing here? If there is not food, if there is not a female in heat, if there is not anyone here to pet and scratch and play with him, why is he here? He doesn't really know why. Maybe it is just the nature of a dog to wonder what is around the next corner, over the next hill. Dogs are special. Dogs are curious. Life is strange and interesting, and he has the feeling that each new place or each new day might show him something so different and special that just by seeing and smelling it, he will understand the world better and be happier. He has the feeling that a wonderful thing is waiting to be found, a wonderful thing he can't imagine, but something even better than food or females in heat, better than petting, scratching, playing, running along a beach with wind in his fur, chasing a cat, or even better than catching a cat if such a thing was possible. Even here, in this scary place, with the smell of the thing-that-will-kill-you so strong he wants to sneeze, he *still* feels that a wonderfulness might be just around the next corner.

And don't forget the woman, the boy. They're nice. They like him. So maybe he can find a way to keep the bad thing from bothering them any more.

He continues to the top of the steps into a narrow space. He pads along, sniffing at doors. Soft light behind one of them. And very heavy, bitter: the thing-that-will-kill-you smell.

Not afraid, not afraid, he is a dog, stalker and hunter, good and brave, good dog, good.

The door is open a crack. He puts his nose to the gap. He could push it open wider, go into the space beyond it, but he hesitates.

Nothing wonderful in *there*. Maybe somewhere else in this people place, maybe around every other corner, but not in there.

323

Maybe he can just leave now, go back to the alley, see if the fat man left out more food for him.

That would be a cat thing to do. Sneaking away. Running. He is not a cat. He is a dog.

But do cats ever get their noses scratched, cut deep, bleeding, sore for days? Interesting thought. He has never seen a cat with a scratched nose, has never gotten close enough to scratch one.

But he is a dog, not a cat, so he pushes against the door. It eases open wider. He goes into the space beyond.

Young-man-bad-thing lying on black cloths, above the floor, not moving at all, making no sound, eyes closed. Dead? Dead bad thing on the black cloths.

He pads closer, sniffing.

No. Not dead. Sleeping.

The thing-that-will-kill-you eats, and it pees, and now it sleeps, so it is like people in many ways, like dogs too, even if it isn't either people or dog.

What now?

He stares at the sleeping bad thing, thinking how he might jump up there with it, bark in its face, wake it up, scare it, so then maybe it won't come around the woman and boy any more. Maybe even bite it, just a little bite, be a bad dog for once, just to help the woman and the boy, bite its chin. Or its nose.

It doesn't look so dangerous, sleeping. Doesn't look so strong or quick. He can't remember why it was scary before.

He looks around the black room and then up,

and light glistens in a lot of eyes floating up there in bottles, people eyes without people, animal eyes without animals. Interesting but not good, not good at all.

Again he wonders what he is doing here. He realizes this place is like a drain pipe where you get stuck, like a hole in the ground where big spiders live that don't like you sticking your snout in at them. And then he realizes that the young-man-bad-thing on the bed is sort of like those laughing boys, smelling of sand and sun and sea salt, who will pet you and scratch behind your ears and then try to set your fur on fire.

Stupid dog. Stupid for coming here. Good but stupid.

The bad thing mumbles in its sleep.

He backs away from the bed, turns, tucks his tail down, and pads out of the room. He goes down the stairs, getting out of there, not afraid, not afraid, just careful, not afraid, but his heart pounding hard and fast.

·6·

Weekdays, Tanya Delaney was the private nurse on the graveyard shift, from midnight until eight o'clock in the morning. Some nights she would rather have worked *in* a graveyard. Jennifer Drackman was spookier than anything Tanya could conceive of encountering in a cemetery.

Tanya sat in an armchair near the blind woman's bed,

silently reading a Mary Higgins Clark novel. She liked to read, and she was a night person by nature, so the wee-hour shift was perfect for her. Some nights she could finish an entire novel and start another one because Jennifer slept straight through.

Other times, Jennifer was unable to sleep, raving incoherently and consumed by terror. On those occasions, Tanya knew the poor woman was irrational and that there was nothing to be afraid of, yet the patient's angst was so intense that it was communicated to the nurse. Tanya's own skin would prickle with gooseflesh, the back of her neck would tingle, she would glance uneasily at the darkness beyond the window as if something waited in it, and would jump at every unexpected noise.

At least the pre-dawn hours of that Wednesday were not filled with shouts and tortured cries and strings of words as meaningless as the manic babble of a religious passionary speaking in tongues. Instead, Jennifer slept but not well, harried by bad dreams. From time to time, without waking, she moaned, grasped with her good hand at the bed rail, and tried without success to pull herself up. With bony white fingers hooked around the steel, atrophied muscles barely defined in her fleshless arms, face gaunt and pale, eyelids sewn shut and concave over empty sockets, she seemed not like a sick woman in bed but like a corpse struggling to rise from a coffin. When she talked in her sleep, she didn't shout but spoke almost in a whisper, with tremendous urgency; her voice seemed to arise from thin air and float through the room with the eeriness of a spirit speaking at a séance: *'He'll kill us all . . . kill . . . he'll kill us all . . .'*

Tanya shivered and tried to concentrate on the suspense novel, though she felt guilty about ignoring her patient. At the least she should pry the bony hand off the railing, feel Jennifer's forehead to be sure she was not feverish, murmur soothingly to her, and attempt to guide her through the stormy dream into calmer shoals of sleep. She was a good nurse, and ordinarily she would rush to comfort a patient in the grip of a nightmare. But she stayed in the armchair with her Clark book because she didn't want to risk waking Jennifer. Once awakened, the woman might slip from the nightmare into one of those frightening fits of shouting, tearless weeping, wailing, and glossolalic shrieking that made Tanya's blood turn to ice.

Came the ghostly voice out of sleep: *'. . . the world's on fire . . . tides of blood . . . fire and blood . . . I'm the mother of Hell . . . God help me, I'm the mother of Hell . . .'*

Tanya wanted to turn the thermostat higher, but she knew the room was already a bit too warm. The chill she felt was within her, not without.

'. . . such a cold mind . . . dead heart . . . beating but dead . . .'

Tanya wondered what the poor woman had endured that had left her in such a dismal state. What had she seen? What had she suffered? What memories haunted her?

·7·

The Green House on Pacific Coast Highway included a large and typical California-style restaurant filled with too many ferns and pothos even for Harry's taste, and a sizable barroom where fern-weary patrons had long ago learned to keep the greenery under control by poisoning the potting soil with a dribble of whiskey every now and then. The restaurant side was closed at that hour.

The popular bar was open until two o'clock. It had been remodeled in a black-silver-green Art Deco style that was nothing like the adjacent restaurant, a strained attempt to be chic. But they served sandwiches along with the booze.

Midst stunted and yellowing plants, about thirty customers drank, talked, and listened to jazz played by a four-man combo. The musicians were performing quirky semi-progressive arrangements of famous numbers from the big-band era. Two couples, who didn't realize the music was better for listening, were gamely dancing to quasi-melodic tunes marked by constant tempo changes and looping extemporaneous passages that would have thwarted Fred Astaire or Baryshnikov.

When Harry and Connie entered, the thirtyish manager-host met them with a dubious look. He was wearing an Armani suit, a hand-painted silk necktie, and beautiful shoes so soft-looking that they might have been made out of a calf fetus. His fingernails were manicured, his teeth perfectly capped, his hair permed. He subtly signaled one of the bartenders, no doubt to help give them the bum's rush back into the street.

Aside from the dried blood at the corner of her mouth and the bruise only beginning to darken one whole side of her face, Connie was reasonably presentable, if slightly rumpled, but Harry was a spectacle. His clothes, baggy and misshapen from having been rain-soaked, were more wrinkled than an ancient mummy's shroud. Formerly crisp and white, his shirt was now mottled gray, smelling of smoke from the house fire he'd barely escaped. His shoes were scuffed, scraped, muddy. A moist bloody abrasion as big as a quarter marred his forehead. He had heavy beard stubble because he hadn't shaved in eighteen hours, and his hands were grimy from pawing through the pile of dirt on Ordegard's lawn. He realized he must appear to be only a treacherous step up the ladder from the hobo outside the bar to whom Connie had just delivered a warning about forced detoxification, even now socially devolving before the scowling host's eyes.

Only yesterday, Harry would have been mortified to appear in public in such a state of dishevelment. Now he didn't particularly care. He was too worried about survival to fret about good grooming and sartorial standards.

Before they could be ejected from the Green House, they both flashed their Special Projects ID.

'Police,' Harry said.

No master key, no password, no blue-blood social register, no royal lineage opened doors as effectively as a badge. Opened them grudgingly, more often than not, but opened them nonetheless.

It also helped that Connie was Connie:

'Not just police,' she said, 'but pissed off police, having a bad day, in no mood to be refused service by some prissy sonofabitch who thinks we might offend his effete clientele.'

They were graciously shown to a corner table that just happened to be in the shadows and away from most of the other customers.

A cocktail waitress arrived at once, said her name was Bambi, crinkled her nose, smiled, and took their orders. Harry asked for coffee and a hamburger medium-well with cheddar.

Connie wanted her burger rare with blue cheese and plenty of raw onions. 'Coffee for me, too, and bring both of us double shots of cognac, Remy Martin.' To Harry she said, 'Technically, we're not on duty any more. And if you feel as crappy as I feel, you need more of a jolt to the system than you're going to get from coffee or a burger.'

While the waitress filled their orders, Harry went to the men's room to wash his grubby hands. He felt as crappy as Connie suspected, and the restroom mirror confirmed that he looked even worse than he felt. He could hardly believe that the grainy-skinned, hollow-eyed, desperation-lined face before him was *his* face.

He vigorously scrubbed his hands, but a little dirt stubbornly remained under his fingernails and in some knuckle creases. His hands resembled those of a car mechanic.

He splashed cold water in his face, but that didn't make him look fresher – or less distraught. The day had taken a toll from him that might forever leave its mark. The loss of his house and all his possessions, Ricky's gruesome death, and the bizarre chain of supernatural events had rattled his faith in reason and order. His current haunted expression might be with him for a long time – assuming he was going to live beyond a few more hours.

Disoriented by the strangeness of his reflection, he almost expected the mirror to prove magical, as mirrors so often were in fairy tales – a doorway to another land, a window on the past or future, the prison in which an evil queen's soul was trapped, a magic talking mirror like the one from which Snow White's wicked stepmother learned that she was no longer the fairest of them all. He put one hand to the glass, warm fingers met cold, but nothing supernatural happened.

Still, considering the events of the past twelve hours, it was not madness to expect sorcery. He seemed to be trapped in a fairy tale of some kind, one of the darker variety like *The Red Shoes*, in which the characters suffer terrible physical tortures and mental anguish, die horribly, and then are finally rewarded with happiness not in this world but in Heaven. It was an unsatisfying plot pattern if you were not entirely sure that Heaven was, in fact, up there and waiting for you.

The only indication that he *hadn't* become imprisoned in a children's fantasy was the absence of a talking animal. Talking animals populated fairy tales even

331

more reliably than psychotic killers populated modern American films.

Fairy tales. Sorcery. Monsters. Psychosis. Children.

Suddenly Harry felt he was teetering on the edge of an insight that would reveal an important fact about Ticktock.

Sorcery. Psychosis. Children. Monsters. Fairy tales. Revelation eluded him.

He strained for it. No good.

He realized he was no longer lightly touching his fingertips to their reflection, but was pressing his hand against the mirror hard enough to crack the glass. When he took his hand away, a vague moist imprint remained for a moment, then swiftly evaporated.

Everything fades. Including Harry Lyon. Maybe by dawn.

He left the restroom and walked back to the table in the bar where Connie was waiting.

Monsters. Sorcery. Psychosis. Fairy tales. Children.

The band was playing a Duke Ellington medley with a modern jazz interpretation. The music was crap. Ellington simply didn't need improvement.

On the table stood two steaming coffee cups and two brandy snifters with Remy glowing like liquid gold.

'The burgers'll be a few minutes,' Connie said as he pulled out one of the black wooden chairs and sat down.

Psychosis. Children. Sorcery.

Nothing.

He decided to stop thinking about Ticktock for a

while. Give the subconscious a chance to work without pressure.

'I Gotta Know,' he said, giving Connie the title of a Presley song.

'Know what?'

'Tell Me Why.'

'Huh?'

'It's Now or Never.'

She caught on, smiled. 'I'm a fanatical Presley fan.'

'So I gathered.'

'Came in handy.'

'Probably kept Ordegard from throwing another grenade at us, saved our lives.'

'To the king of rock-'n'-roll,' she said, raising her brandy snifter.

The band stopped torturing the Ellington tunes and took a break, so maybe there was a God in Heaven after all, and blessed order in the universe.

Harry and Connie clinked glasses, sipped. He said, 'Why Elvis?'

She sighed. 'Early Elvis – he was something. He was all about freedom, about being what you want to be, about not being pushed around just because you're different. "Don't step on my blue suede shoes." Songs from his first ten years were already golden oldies when I was just seven or eight, but they spoke to me. You know?'

'Seven or eight? Heavy stuff for a little kid. I mean, a lot of those songs were about loneliness, heartbreak.'

'Sure. He was that dream figure – a sensitive rebel, polite but not willing to take any shit, romantic and cynical at the same time. I was raised in orphanages, foster homes, so I knew what loneliness was all about, and my heart had some cracks of its own.'

The waitress brought their burgers, and the busboy refreshed their coffee.

Harry was beginning to feel like a human being again. A dirty, rumpled, aching, weary, frightened human being, but a human being nonetheless.

'Okay,' he said, 'I can understand being crazy for the early Elvis, memorizing the early songs. But later?'

Shaking ketchup onto her burger, Connie said, 'In its way, the end's as interesting as the beginning. American tragedy.'

'Tragedy? Winding up a fat Vegas singer in sequined jumpsuits?'

'Sure. The handsome and courageous king, so full of promise, transcendent – then because of a tragic flaw, he takes a tumble, a long fall, dead at forty-two.'

'Died on a toilet.'

'I didn't say this was Shakespearean tragedy. There's an element of the absurd in it. That's what makes it *American* tragedy. No country in the world has our sense of the absurd.'

'I don't think you'll see either the Democrats or Republicans using that line as a campaign slogan anytime soon.' The burger was delicious. Around a mouthful of it, he said, 'So what was Elvis's tragic flaw?'

'He refused to grow up. Or maybe he wasn't able.'

'Isn't an artist supposed to hold onto the child within him?'

She took a bite of her sandwich, shook her head. 'Not

the same as perpetually *being* that child. See, the young Elvis Presley wanted freedom, had a passion for it, just like I've always had, and the way he got total freedom to do anything he wanted was through his music. But when he got it, when he could've been free forever . . . well, what happened?'

'Tell me.'

She had clearly thought a lot about it. 'Elvis lost direction. I think maybe he fell in love with fame more than freedom. Genuine freedom, freedom with responsibility not from it – that's a worthy adult dream. But fame is just a cheap thrill. You'd have to be immature to really enjoy fame, don't you think?'

'I wouldn't want it. Not that I'm likely to *get* it.'

'Worthless, fleeting, a trinket only a child would mistake for diamonds. Elvis, he looked like a grownup, talked like one— '

'Sure as hell sang like a grownup when he was at his best.'

'Yeah. But emotionally he was a case of arrested development, and the grownup was just a costume he wore, a masquerade. Which is why he always had a big entourage like his own private boy's club, and ate mostly fried banana sandwiches with peanut butter, kids' food, and rented whole amusement parks when he wanted to have fun with his friends. It's why he wasn't able to stop people like Colonel Parker from taking advantage of him.'

Grownups. Children. Arrested development. Psychosis. Fame. Sorcery. Fairy tales. Arrested development. Monsters. Masquerade.

Harry sat up straighter, his mind racing.

Connie was still talking, but her voice seemed to be coming from a distance: '. . . so the last part of Elvis's life shows you how many traps there are . . .'

Psychotic child. Fascinated by monsters. With a sorcerer's power. Arrested development. Looks like a grownup but masquerading.

'. . . how easy it is to lose your freedom and never find your way back to it . . .'

Harry put down his sandwich. 'My God, I think maybe I know who Ticktock is.'

'Who?'

'Wait. Let me think about this.'

Shrill laughter erupted from a table of noisy drunks near the bandstand. Two men in their fifties with the look of wealth about them, two blondes in their twenties. They were trying to live their own fairy tales: the aging men dreaming of perfect sex and the envy of other men; the women dreaming of riches, and happily unaware that their fantasies would one day seem dreary, dull, and tacky even to them.

Harry rubbed his eyes with the heels of his hands, struggled to order his thoughts. 'Haven't you noticed there's something childish about him?'

'Ticktock? That ox?'

'That's his golem. I'm talking about the real Ticktock, the one who makes the golems. This seems like a game to him. He's playing with me the way a nasty little boy will pull the wings off a fly and watch it struggle to get airborne, or torture a beetle with matches. The deadline at dawn, the taunting attacks, childish, as if he's some playground bully having his fun.'

He remembered more of what Ticktock had said as he had risen from the bed in the condo, just before he'd started the fire: . . . *you people are so much fun to play with . . . big hero . . . you think you can shoot anyone you like, push anyone around if you want . . .*

Push anyone around if you want . . .

'Harry?'

He blinked, shivered. 'Some sociopaths are made by having been abused as children. But others are just born that way, bent.'

'Something screwed up in the genes,' she agreed.

'Suppose Ticktock was born bad.'

'He was never an angel.'

'And suppose this incredible power of his doesn't come from some weird lab experiment. Maybe it's also a result of screwed-up genes. If he was born with this power, then it separated him from other people the way fame separated Presley, and he never learned to grow up, didn't need or want to grow up. In his heart he's still a child. Playing a child's game. A mean little child's game.'

Harry recalled the bearish vagrant standing in his bedroom, red-faced with rage, shouting over and over again: *Do you hear me, hero, do you hear me, do you hear me, do you hear me, DO YOU HEAR ME, DO YOU HEAR ME . . .?* That behavior had been terrifying because of the hobo's size and power, but in retrospect it distinctly had the quality of a little boy's tantrum.

337

Connie leaned across the table and waved one hand in front of his face. 'Don't go catatonic on me, Harry. I'm still waiting for the punchline. Who is Ticktock? You think maybe he actually *is* a child? Are we looking for some grade-school boy, for God's sake? Or girl?'

'No. He's older. Still young. But older.'

'How can you be sure?'

'Because I've met him.'

Push anyone around if you want . . .

He told Connie about the young man who had slipped under the crime-scene tape and crossed the sidewalk to the shattered window of the restaurant where Ordegard had shot up the lunchtime crowd. Tennis shoes, jeans, a Tecate beer T-shirt.

'He was staring inside, fascinated by the blood, the bodies. There was something eerie about him . . . he had this faraway look . . . and licking his lips as if . . . as if, I don't know, as if there was something erotic about all that blood, those bodies. He ignored me when I told him to get back behind the barrier, probably didn't even hear me . . . like he was in a trance . . . licking his lips.'

Harry picked up his brandy snifter and finished the last of his cognac in one swallow.

'Did you get his name?' Connie asked.

'No. I screwed up. I handled it badly.'

In memory, he saw himself grabbing the kid, shoving him across the sidewalk, maybe hitting him and maybe not – had he jammed a knee into his crotch? – jerking and wrenching him, bending him double, forcing him under the crime-scene tape.

'I was sick about it later,' he said, 'disgusted with

myself. Couldn't believe I'd roughed him up that way. I guess I was still uptight about what had happened in the attic, almost being blown away by Ordegard, and when I saw that kid getting off on the blood, I reacted like . . . like . . .'

'Like me,' Connie said, picking up her burger again.

'Yeah. Like you.'

Although he had lost his appetite, Harry took a bite of his sandwich because he had to keep his energy up for what might lie ahead.

'But I still don't see how you can be so damn sure this kid is Ticktock,' Connie said.

'I *know* he is.'

'Just because he was a little weird— '

'It's more than that.'

'A hunch?'

'A lot better than a hunch. Call it cop instinct.'

She stared at him for a beat, then nodded. 'All right. You remember what he looked like?'

'Vividly, I think. Maybe as young as nineteen, no older than twenty-one or so.'

'Height.'

'An inch shorter than me.'

'Weight?'

'Maybe a hundred and fifty pounds. Thin. No, that's not right, not thin, not scrawny. Lean but muscular.'

'Complexion?'

'Fair. He's been indoors a lot. Thick hair, dark brown or black. Good-looking kid, a little like that actor, Tom Cruise, but more hawkish. He had unusual eyes. Gray. Like silver with a little tarnish on it.'

339

Connie said, 'What I'm thinking is, we go over to Nancy Quan's house. She lives right here in Laguna Beach— '

Nancy was a sketch artist who worked for Special Projects and had a gift for hearing and correctly interpreting the nuances in a witness's description of a suspect. Her pencil sketches often proved to be astonishingly good portraits of the perps when they were at last cornered and hauled into custody.

'—you describe this kid to her, she draws him, and we take the sketch to the Laguna police, see if they know the little creep.'

Harry said, 'What if they don't?'

'Then we start knocking on doors, showing the sketch.'

'Doors? Where?'

'Houses and apartments within a block of where you ran into him. It's possible he lives in that immediate area. Even if he doesn't live there, maybe he hangs out there, has friends in the neighborhood— '

'This kid has no friends.'

'—or relatives. Someone might recognize him.'

'People aren't going to be real happy, we go knocking on their doors in the middle of the night.'

Connie grimaced. 'You want to wait for dawn?'

'Guess not.'

The band was returning for their final set.

Connie chugged the last of her coffee, pushed her chair back, got up, took some folding money from one coat pocket, and threw a couple of bills on the table.

'Let me pay half,' Harry said.

340

'My treat.'

'No, really, I should pay half.'

She gave him an are-you-nuts look.

'I like to keep accounts in balance with everyone. You know that,' he explained.

'Take a walk on the wild side, Harry. Let the accounts go out of balance. Tell you what – if dawn comes and we wake up in Hell, you can buy breakfast.'

She headed for the door.

When he saw her coming, the host in the Armani suit and hand-painted silk tie scurried into the safety of the kitchen.

Following Connie, Harry glanced at his wristwatch. It was twenty-two minutes past one o'clock in the morning.

Dawn was perhaps five hours away.

·8·

Padding through the night town. People in their dark places all drowsy around him.

He yawns and thinks about lying under some bushes and sleeping. There's another world when he sleeps, a nice world where he has a family that lives in a warm place and welcomes him there, feeds him every day, plays with him anytime he wants to play, calls him Prince, takes him with them in a car and lets him put his head out the window in the wind with his ears flapping – feels good, smells coming at him dizzy-fast, yes yes yes – and never kicks him. It's a

341

good world in sleep, even though he can't catch the cats there, either.

Then he remembers the young-man-bad-thing, the black place, the people and animal eyes without bodies, and he isn't sleepy any more.

He's got to do something about the bad thing, but he doesn't know what. He senses it is going to hurt the woman, the boy, hurt them bad. It has much anger. Hate. It would set their fur on fire if they had fur. He doesn't know why. Or when or how or where. But he must do something, save them, be a good dog, good.

So . . .

Do something.

Okay.

So . . .

Until he can think what to do about the bad thing, he might as well look for some more food. Maybe the smiling fat man left more good scraps for him behind the people food place. Maybe the fat man is still there in the open door, looking this way and that way along the alley, hoping to see Fella again, thinking he would like to take Fella home, give him a warm place, feed him every day, play with him anytime he wants to play, take Fella for rides in cars with his head sticking out in the wind.

Hurrying now. Trying to smell the fat man. Is he out in the open? Waiting?

Sniffing, sniffing, he passes a rust-smelling, grease-smelling, oil-smelling car parked in a big empty space, and then he smells the woman, the boy, even through the closed windows. He stops, looks up. Boy sleeping, can't be seen. Woman leaning against door, head against window. Awake, but she does not see him.

Maybe the fat man will like the woman, the boy, will have room for all of them in his nice warm people place, and they can play together, all of them, eat when they want, go for rides in cars with their heads sticking out windows, smells coming at them dizzy-fast. Yes yes yes yes yes yes. Why not? In the sleep world, there is a family. Why not in this world too?

He is excited. This is good. This is really good. He feels the wonderful thing around the corner, wonderful thing coming that he always knew was out there some where. Good. Yes. Good. Yes yes yes yes yes.

The people food place with the fat man waiting is not far from the car, so maybe he should bark to make the woman see him, then lead her and the boy to the fat man.

Yes yes yes yes yes yes.

But wait, wait, it could take too long, too long, getting them to follow him. People are so slow to understand sometimes. The fat man might go away. Then they get there, the fat man is gone, they're standing in the alley, and they don't know why, they think he's just a stupid dog, stupid silly dog, humiliated like when the cat is up in the tree looking down at him.

No no no no no. The fat man can't go away, can't. Fat man goes away, they won't be together in a nice warm place or in a car with the wind.

What to do, what to do? Excited. Bark? Don't bark? Stay, go yes, no, bark, don't bark?

Pee. Got to pee. Lift the leg. Ah. Yes. Strong-smelling pee. Steaming on the pavement, steaming. Interesting.

Fat man. Don't forget the fat man. Waiting in the alley. Go to the fat man first, before he goes inside and is gone forever, get him and bring him back here, yes yes yes yes, because the woman and the boy are not going anywhere.

Good dog. Smart dog.

He trots away from the car. Then runs. To the corner. Around. A little farther. Another corner. The alley behind the people food place.

Panting, excited, he runs up to the door where the fat man gave out scraps. It is closed. The fat man is gone. No more scraps on the ground.

He is surprised. He was so sure. All of them together like in the sleep world.

He scratches at the door. Scratches, scratches.

The fat man doesn't come. The door stays closed.

He barks. Waits. Barks.

Nothing.

Well. So. Now what?

He is still excited, but not as much as before. Not so excited that he has to pee, but too excited to be still. He paces in front of the door, back and forth across the alley, whining in frustration and confusion, beginning to be a little sad.

Voices echo to him from the far end of the alley, and he knows one of them belongs to the stinky man who smells like everything bad at once, including like the touch of the thing-that-will-kill-you. He can smell the stinky man really well even from a distance. He doesn't know who the other voices belong to, can't smell those people so much because the stinky man's odor covers them.

Maybe one is the fat man, looking for his Fella.

Could be.

Wagging his tail, he hurries to the end of the alley, but when he gets there he finds no fat man, so he stops wagging. Only a man and a woman he's never seen before, standing near a car in front of the people food place with the stinky man, all of them talking.

You really cops? says the stinky man.

What'd you do to the car? says the woman.

Nothing. I didn't do anything to the car.

There's any crap in this car, you're a dead man.

No, listen, for God's sake.

Forced detox, you scumbag.

How could I get in the car, with it locked?

So you tried, huh?

I just wanted to nose around, see were you really cops.

I'll show you are we really cops or not, you hairball.

Hey, let go of me!

Jesus, you stink!

Let me go, let me go!

Come on, let him go. All right, easy now, says the man who isn't so stinky.

Sniffing, sniffing, he smells something on this new man that he smells on the stinky man, too, and it surprises him. The touch of the thing-that-will-kill you. This man has been around the bad thing not long ago.

You smell like a walking toxic waste dump, says the woman.

She also has on her the smell of the thing-that-will-kill-you. All three of them. Stinky man, man, and woman. Interesting.

He moves closer, sniffing.

Listen, please, I've got to talk to a cop, says the stinky man.

So talk, says the woman.

My name's Sammy Shamroe. I got a crime to report.

Let me guess — somebody stole your new Mercedes.

I need help!

So do we, pal.

All three of them not only have the touch of the bad thing on them, but they smell of fear, the same fear he has smelled on the woman and the boy who call him Woofer. They are afraid of the bad thing, all of them.

Someone's going to kill me, says the stinky man.

Yeah, it's gonna be me if you don't get out of my face.

Easy. Easy now.

The stinky man says, *And he's not human, either. I call him the ratman.*

Maybe these people should meet the woman and the boy in the car. All of them afraid separately. Together, maybe not afraid. Together, all of them, they might live in a warm place, play all the time, feed him every day, all of them go places in a car — except the stinky man would have to run behind unless he stopped being stinky enough to make you sneeze.

I call him the ratman 'cause he's made out of rats,

he falls apart and he's just a bunch of rats running everywhichway.

But how? How to get them together with the woman and the boy? How to make them understand, people being so slow sometimes?

·9·

When the dog came sniffing around their feet, Harry didn't know if it was with the bum, Sammy, or if it was just a stray on its own. Depending on how obstreperous the vagrant became, if they had to use force with him, the dog might take sides. It didn't look dangerous, but you never could tell.

As for Sammy, he appeared to be more of a threat than the dog. He was wasted from life on the street and from whatever had put him there, worse than skinny, spindly, Salvation Army giveaway clothes hanging so loosely on him that you expected to hear bones rattling together when he moved, but that didn't mean he was weak. He was twitchy with excess energy. His eyes were so wide open, the lids seemed to have been stretched back and pinned out of the way. His face was tight with tension lines, and his lips repeatedly skinned back from his bad teeth in a feral snarl that might have been meant to be an ingratiating smile but was alarming instead.

'The ratman, see, is what I call him, not what he calls himself. Never heard him call himself anything. Don't know where the hell he comes from, where he's hiding his ship, he's just all of a sudden *there*, just there, the sadistic bastard, one scary son of a bitch— '

In spite of how weak he appeared to be, Sammy might be like a robotic mechanism receiving too much power, circuits overloading, on the trembling verge of exploding, disintegrating into a shrapnel of gears and springs and burst pneumatic tubes that would kill everyone within a block. He might have a knife, knives, even a gun. Harry had seen shaky little guys like this who looked as if a strong gust of wind would blow them all the way to China; then it turned out that they were stoned on PCP, which could transform kittens into tigers, and three strong men were required to disarm and subdue them.

'—see, maybe I don't care if he kills me, maybe that would be a blessing, just get totally drunk and let him kill me, so wasted I'd hardly notice when he does me,' Sammy said, crowding them, moving to the left when they moved in that direction, to the right when they tried that way, insisting on a confrontation. 'But then tonight, when I was deep in the bag, sucking down my second double liter, I realized who the ratman has to be, I mean *what* he has to be – one of the aliens!'

'Aliens,' Connie said disgustedly. 'Aliens, always aliens with you dim bulbs. Get out of here, you greasy hairball, or I swear to God I'm gonna— '

'No, no, listen. We've always known they're coming, haven't we? Always known, and now they're here, and they've come to me first, and if I don't warn the world, then everyone's going to die.'

As he took hold of Sammy's arm and tried to maneuver him out of their way, Harry was almost as leery of Connie as he was of the bum. If Sammy was an overwound clockwork mechanism ready to explode, then Connie was a nuclear plant heading for a meltdown. She was frustrated that the vagrant was delaying them from getting to Nancy Quan the police artist, acutely aware that dawn was rushing toward them from the East. Harry was frustrated too, but with him, unlike with Connie, there was no danger that he might knee Sammy in the crotch and pitch him through one of the nearby restaurant windows.

'—don't want to be responsible for aliens killing the whole world, I've already got too much on my conscience, too much, can't stand the idea of being responsible, I've let so many people down already— '

If Connie thumped the guy, they would never get to Nancy Quan or have a chance to locate Ticktock. They would be tied up here for an hour or longer, arranging for Sammy's arrest, trying not to choke to death on his body odor, and struggling to deny police brutality (a few bar patrons were watching them, faces to the glass). Too many precious minutes would be lost.

Sammy grabbed at Connie's jacket sleeve. 'Listen to me, woman, you listen to me!'

Connie jerked loose of him, cocked her fist.

'No!' Harry said.

Connie barely checked herself, almost threw the punch.

Sammy was spraying spittle as he ranted: '—it gave me thirty-six hours to live, the ratman, but now it must be twenty-four or less, not sure— '

Harry tried to hold Connie back with one hand as she reached for Sammy again, while simultaneously pushing Sammy away with the other hand. Then the dog jumped up on him. Grinning, panting, its tail wagging. Harry twisted away, shook his leg, and the dog dropped back onto the sidewalk on all fours.

Sammy was babbling frantically, now clutching with both hands at Harry's sleeve and tugging for attention, as if he didn't have it already: '—his eyes like snake eyes, green and terrible, terrible, and he says I got thirty-six hours to live, ticktock, ticktock— '

Fear and amazement quivered through Harry when he heard that word, and the breeze off the ocean seemed suddenly colder than it had been.

Startled, Connie stopped trying to get at Sammy. 'Wait a minute, what'd you say?'

'Aliens! Aliens!' Sammy shouted angrily. 'You're not listening to me, damn it.'

'Not the aliens part,' Connie said. The dog jumped on her. Patting its head and pushing it away, she said, 'Harry, did he say what I think he said?'

'I'm a citizen, too,' Sammy shrieked. His need to give testimony had escalated into a frenzied determination. 'I got a right to be listened to sometimes.'

'Ticktock,' Harry said.

'That's right,' Sammy confirmed. He was pulling on Harry's sleeve almost hard enough to tear it off. '"Ticktock, ticktock, time is running out, you'll be dead by dawn tomorrow, Sammy." And then he just dissolves into a pack of rats, right before my eyes.'

Or a whirlwind of trash, Harry thought, or a pillar of fire.

'All right, wait, let's talk,' Connie said. 'Calm down, Sammy, and let's discuss this. I'm sorry for what I said, I really am. Just get calm.'

Sammy must have thought she was insincere and merely trying to humor him into letting his guard down, because he didn't respond to the new respect and consideration she accorded him. He stamped his feet in frustration. His clothes flapped on his bony body, and he looked like a scarecrow shaken by a Halloween wind. 'Aliens, you stupid woman, aliens, aliens, aliens!'

Glancing at the Green House, Harry saw that half a dozen people were at the barroom windows now, peering out at them.

He realized what a singular spectacle they were, all three of them bedraggled, tugging and pulling at each other, shouting about aliens. He was probably in the last hours of his life, pursued by something paranormal and incredibly vicious, and his desperate fight for survival had been transformed, at least for a moment, into a piece of slapstick street theater.

Welcome to the '90s. America on the brink of the millennium. Jesus.

Muffled music filtered to the street: the four-man combo was playing some West Coast swing now, 'Kansas City,' but with weird riffs.

The host in the Armani suit was one of those at the

bar windows. He was probably silently berating himself for being fooled by what he now surely believed were phony badges, and would go any second to call the real police.

A passing car slowed down, driver and passenger gawking.

'Stupid, stupid, stupid woman!' Sammy shouted at Connie.

The dog took hold of the right leg of Harry's trousers, nearly jerked him off his feet. He staggered, kept his balance, and managed to pull free of Sammy, though not the dog. It squirmed backward, striving with canine tenacity to drag Harry along with it. Harry resisted, then almost lost his balance again when the mutt abruptly let go of him.

Connie was still trying to soothe Sammy, and the bum was still telling her that she was stupid, but at least neither was trying to hit the other.

The dog ran south along the sidewalk for a few steps, skidded to a halt in the downfall of light from a street lamp, looked back, and barked at them. The breeze ruffled its fur, fluffed its tail. It dashed a little farther south, halted in shadows this time, and barked again.

Seeing that Harry was distracted by the dog, Sammy became even more outraged at his inability to get serious consideration. His voice became mocking, sarcastic: 'Oh, sure, that's it, pay more attention to a damn dog than to me! What am I, anyway, just some piece of street garbage, less than a dog, no reason to listen to trash like me. Go on, Timmy, go on, see what Lassie wants, maybe Dad's trapped under an overturned tractor down on the fucking south forty!'

Harry couldn't help laughing. He would never have expected a remark like that out of someone like Sammy, and he wondered who the man had been before he'd wound up as he was now.

The dog squealed plaintively, cutting Harry's laugh short. Tucking its bushy tail between its legs, pricking up its ears, raising its head quizzically, it turned in a circle and sniffed at the night air.

'Something's wrong,' Connie said, worriedly looking around at the street.

Harry felt it too. A change in the air. An odd pressure. Something. Cop instinct. Cop and *dog* instinct.

The mutt caught a scent that made it yelp in fear. It spun around on the sidewalk, biting at the air, then rushed back toward Harry. For an instant he thought it was going to barrel into him and knock him on his ass, but then it angled toward the front of the Green House, plunged into a planting bed full of shrubbery, and lay flat on its belly, hiding among azaleas, only its eyes and snout visible.

Taking his cue from the dog, Sammy turned and sprinted toward the nearby alleyway.

Connie said, 'Hey, no, wait,' and started after him.

'Connie,' Harry said warningly, not sure what he was warning her about, but sensing that it was not a good idea for them to separate just then.

She turned to him. 'What?'

Beyond her, Sammy disappeared around the corner.

That was when everything stopped.

Growling uphill in the southbound lane of the coast highway, a tow truck, evidently on the way to help a stranded motorist, halted on the proverbial dime but without a squeal of brakes. Its laboring engine fell silent from one second to the next, without a lingering chug, cough, or sputter, though its headlights still shone.

Simultaneously a Volvo about a hundred feet behind the truck also stopped and fell mute.

In the same instant, the breeze died. It didn't wane gradually or sputter out, but ceased as quickly as if a cosmic fan had been switched off. Thousands upon thousands of leaves stopped rustling as one.

Precisely in time with the silencing of traffic and vegetation, the music from the bar cut off mid-note.

Harry almost felt he had gone stone deaf. He'd never known a silence as profound in a controlled interior environment, let alone outdoors where the life of a town and the myriad background noises of the natural world produced a ceaseless atonal symphony even in the comparative stillness between midnight and dawn. He could not hear himself breathe, then realized that his own contribution to the preternatural hush was voluntary; he was simply so stunned by the change in the world that he was holding his breath.

In addition to sound, motion had been stolen from the night. The tow truck and Volvo were not the only things that had come to a complete standstill. The curbside trees and the shrubbery along the front of the Green House seemed to have been flash-frozen. The leaves had not merely stopped rustling, but had entirely ceased moving; they could not have been more still if sculpted from stone. Overhanging the windows of the Green House, the scalloped valances on the canvas awnings had been fluttering in the breeze, but they had gone rigid in mid-flutter; now they were as stiff as if formed from sheetmetal. Across the street, the blinking arrow on a neon sign had frozen in the on position.

Connie said, 'Harry?'

He started, as he would have at any sound except the intimate muffled thumping of his own racing heart.

He saw his own confusion and anxiety mirrored in her face.

Moving to his side, she said, 'What's happening?'

Her voice, aside from having an uncharacteristic tremor, was vaguely different from what it had been, slightly flat in tone and marginally less inflective.

'Damned if I know,' he told her.

His voice sounded much like hers, as though it issued from a mechanical device that was extremely clever – but not quite perfect – at reproducing the speech of any human being.

'It's got to be him doing it,' she said.

Harry agreed. 'Somehow.'

'Ticktock.'

'Yeah.'

'Shit, this is crazy.'

'No argument from me.'

She started to draw her revolver, then let the gun slide back into her shoulder holster. An ominous mood infused the scene, an air of fearful expectation. But for the moment, at least, there was nothing at which to shoot.

'Where is the creep?' she wondered.

'I have a hunch he'll show up.'

'No points for that one.' Indicating the tow truck out in the street, she said, 'For God's sake . . . look at that.'

At first he thought Connie was just remarking on the fact that the vehicle had mysteriously halted like everything else, but then he realized what sight had pushed the needle higher on her astonishment meter. The air had been just cool enough to cause vehicle exhaust (but not their breath) to condense in pale plumes; those thin puffs of mist hung in mid-air behind the tow truck, neither dispersing nor evaporating as vapor should have done. He saw another but barely visible gray-white ghost suspended behind the tail pipe of the more distant Volvo.

Now that he was primed to look for them, similar wonders became evident on all sides, and he pointed them out to her. A few pieces of light debris – gum and candy wrappers, a splintered portion of a popsicle stick, dry brown leaves, a tangled length of red yarn – had been swept up by the breeze; although no draft remained to support the items, they were still aloft, as if the air had abruptly turned to purest crystal around them and had trapped them motionless for eternity. Within arm's reach and just a foot higher than his head, two late-winter moths as white as snowflakes hung immotive, their wings soft and pearl-smooth in the glow of the street lamp.

Connie tapped her wristwatch, then showed it to Harry. It was a traditional-style Timex with a round dial and hands, including not only hour and minute hands but a red second hand. It was stopped at 1:29 plus sixteen seconds.

Harry checked his own watch, which had a digital readout. It also showed 1:29, and the tiny blinking dot that took the place of a second hand was burning steadily, no longer counting off each sixtieth of a minute.

'Time has . . .' Connie was unable to finish the sentence. She surveyed the silent street in amazement, swallowed hard, and finally found her voice: 'Time has stopped . . . just stopped. Is that it?'

'Say what?'

'Stopped for the rest of the world but not for us?'

'Time doesn't . . . it can't . . . just stop.'

'Then what?'

Physics had never been his favorite subject. And though he had some affinity for the sciences because of their ceaseless search for order in the universe, he was not as scientifically literate as he should have been in an age when science was king. However, he had retained enough of his teachers' lectures and had watched enough PBS specials and had read enough bestseller-list books of popularized science to know that what Connie had said did not explain numerous aspects of what was happening to them.

For one thing, if time had really stopped, why were they still conscious? How could they be aware of the phenomenon? Why weren't they frozen in that last moment of forward-moving time just as the airborne litter was, as the moths were?

'No,' he said shakily, 'it's not that simple. If time stopped, *nothing* would move – would it? – not even subatomic particles. And without subatomic movement . . . molecules of air . . . well, wouldn't molecules of air be as solid as molecules of iron? How would we be able to breathe?'

Reacting to that thought, they both took deep and grateful breaths. The air did have a faint chemical taste, as slightly odd in its way as the timbre of their voices, but it seemed capable of sustaining life.

'And light,' Harry said. 'Light waves would stop moving. No waves to register with our eyes. So how could we see anything but darkness?'

In fact, the effect of time coming to a stop probably would be infinitely more catastrophic than the stillness and silence that had descended on the world that March night. It seemed to him that time and matter were inseparable parts of creation, and if the flow of time were cut off, matter would instantly cease to exist. The universe would implode – wouldn't it? – crash back in on itself, into a tiny ball of extremely dense . . . well, whatever the hell dense stuff it was before it had exploded to create the universe.

Connie stood on her toes, reached up, and gently pinched the wing of one of the moths between thumb and forefinger. She settled back on her heels and brought the insect in front of her face for a closer inspection.

Harry had not been sure if she would be able to alter the bug's position or not. He wouldn't have been surprised if the moth had hung immovably on the dead-calm air, as fixed in place as a metal moth welded to a steel wall.

'Not as soft as a moth should be,' she said. 'Feels like it's made out of taffeta . . . or starched fabric of some kind.'

When she opened her fingers, letting go of the wing, the moth hung in the air where she had released it.

Harry gently batted the bug with the back of his hand, and watched with fascination as it tumbled a few inches before coming to rest in the air again. It was as motionless as it had been before they had toyed with it, just in a new position.

The ways in which they affected things appeared to be pretty much normal. Their shadows moved when they did, though all other shadows were as unmoving as the objects that cast them. They could act upon the world and pass through it as usual but couldn't really interact *with* it. Connie had been able to move the moth, but touching it had not brought it into their reality, had not made it come alive again.

'Maybe time hasn't stopped,' she said. 'Maybe it just slowed way, way down for everyone and everything else except us.'

'That's not it either.'

'How can you be sure?'

'I can't. But I think . . . if we're experiencing time at such a tremendously faster rate, enough faster to make the rest of the world appear to be standing still, then every move we make has *incredible* comparative velocity. Doesn't it?'

'So?'

'I mean, a lot more velocity than any bullet fired from any gun. Velocity is destructive. If I took a bullet in my hand and threw it at you, it wouldn't do any damage. But at a few thousand feet per second, it'll punch a substantial hole in you.'

She nodded, staring thoughtfully at the suspended moth. 'So if it was just a case of us experiencing time a lot faster, the swat you gave that bug would've disintegrated it.'

'Yeah. I think so. I'd have probably done some damage to my hand too.' He looked at his hand. It was unmarked. 'And if it was just that light waves are traveling slower than usual . . . then no lamps would be as bright as they are now. They'd be dimmer and . . . reddish, I think, almost like infra-red light. Maybe. And air molecules would be sluggish . . .'

'Like breathing water or syrup?'

He nodded. 'I think so. I don't really know for sure. Hell's bells, I'm not sure even Albert Einstein would be able to figure this if he was standing right here with us.'

'The way this is going, he might show up any minute.'

No one had gotten out of either the tow truck or the Volvo, which indicated to Harry that the occupants were as trapped in the changed world as were the moths. He could see only the shadowy forms of two people in the front seat of the more distant Volvo, but he had a better view of the man behind the wheel of the tow truck, which was almost directly across the street from them. Neither the shadows in the car nor the truck driver had moved a fraction of an inch since the stillness had fallen. Harry supposed that if they had *not* been on the same time track as their vehicles, they might have exploded through the windshields and tumbled along the highway the instant that the tires precipitously stopped rotating.

At the barroom windows of the Green House, six people continued to peer out in precisely the postures they had been in when the Pause had come. (Harry thought of it as a Pause rather than a Stop because he assumed that sooner or later Ticktock would start things up again. Assuming it was Ticktock who had called the halt. If not him, who else? God?) Two of them were sitting at a window table; the other four were standing, two on each side of the table.

Harry crossed the sidewalk and stepped between the shrubs to examine the onlookers more closely. Connie accompanied him. They stood directly in front of the glass and perhaps a foot below those inside the barroom.

In addition to the gray-haired couple at the table, there was a young blonde and her fiftyish companion, one of the couples who had been sitting near the bandstand, making too much noise and laughing too heartily. Now they were as quiet as the residents of any tomb. On the other side of the table stood the host and a waiter. All six were squinting through the window, leaning slightly forward toward the glass.

As Harry studied them, not one blinked an eye. No face muscles twitched. Not a single hair stirred. Their clothes draped them as if every garment had been carved from marble.

Their unchanging expressions ranged from amusement to amazement to curiosity to, in the case of the host, perturbation. But they were not reacting to the incredible stillness that had befallen the night. Of that, they were oblivious because they were a part of it. Rather, they were staring over Harry's and Connie's heads, at the place on the sidewalk where the two of them had last been standing after Sammy and the dog had fled. Their facial expressions were in reaction to that interrupted bit of street theater.

Connie raised one hand above her head and waved it in front of the window, directly in the line of view of the onlookers. The six did not respond to it in any way whatsoever.

'They can't see us,' Connie said wonderingly.

'Maybe they see us standing out there on the sidewalk, in the instant that everything stopped. They could be frozen in that split second of perception and not have seen anything we've done since.'

Virtually in unison, he and Connie looked over their shoulders to study the dead-still street behind them, equally apprehensive of the unnatural quietude. With astonishing stealth, Ticktock had appeared behind them in James Ordegard's bedroom, and they had paid with pain for not anticipating him. Here, he was not yet in sight, although Harry was sure that he was coming.

Returning her attention to the gathering inside the bar, Connie rapped her knuckles against a pane of glass. The sound was slightly tinny, differing from the *right* sound of knuckles against glass to the same small but audible degree that their current voices differed from their real ones.

The onlookers did not react.

To Harry, they seemed to be more securely imprisoned than the most isolated man in the deepest cell in the world's worst police state. Like flies in amber, they were trapped in one meaningless moment of their lives. There was something horribly vulnerable about their helpless suspension and their blissful ignorance of it.

Their plight, although they were almost certainly unaware of it, sent a chill along Harry's spine. He rubbed the back of his neck to warm it.

'If they still see us out on the sidewalk,' Connie said, 'what happens if we go away from here, and then everything starts up again?'

'I suppose, to them, it'll appear as if we vanished into thin air, right before their eyes.'

'My God.'

'It'll give them a jolt, all right.'

She turned away from the window, faced him. Worry lines creased her brow. Her dark eyes were haunted, and her voice was somber to an extent not fully attributable to the change in its tone and pitch. 'Harry, this bastard isn't just some spoon-bending, fortune-telling, sleight-of-hand, Vegas lounge act.'

'We already knew he had real power.'

'Power?'

'Yes.'

'Harry, this is more than power. The word just doesn't convey, you hear me?'

'I hear you,' he said placatingly.

'Just by willing it, he can stop time, stop the engine of the world, jam the gears, do whatever the fuck it is he's done. That's more than power. That's . . . being God. What chance do we have against someone like that?'

'We have a chance.'

'*What* chance? How?'

'We have a chance,' he insisted stubbornly.

'Yeah? Well, I think this guy can squash us like bugs any time he wants, and he's just been stalling because he enjoys watching bugs suffer.'

'You don't sound like the Connie Gulliver I know,' Harry said more sharply than he had intended.

'Well, maybe I'm not.' She put one thumb to her mouth and used her teeth to trim off a full crescent of the nail.

He had never seen her bite her nails before, and he was almost as astonished by that revelation of nervousness as he would have been if she had broken down and cried.

She said, 'Maybe I tried to ride a wave too big for me, got dumped bad, lost my nerve.'

It was inconceivable to Harry that Connie Gulliver could lose her nerve over anything at all, not even over something as strange and frightening as what was happening to them. How could she lose her nerve when she was *all* nerve, one hundred and fifteen pounds or so of solid *nerve*?

She turned away from him, swept the street with her gaze again, walked to some azalea bushes and parted them with one hand, revealing the hiding dog.

'These don't feel quite like leaves. Stiffer. More like thin cardboard.'

He joined her, stooped, and petted the dog, which was as frozen by the Pause as were the bar patrons. 'His fur feels like fine wire.'

'I think he was trying to tell us something.'

'So do I. Now.'

'Because he sure knew something was about to happen when he hid in these bushes.'

Harry remembered the thought he'd had in the men's room of the Green House: *The only indication that I haven't become imprisoned in a fairy tale is the absence of a talking animal.*

Funny, how hard it was to break a man's grasp on his sanity. After a hundred years of Freudian analysis, people were conditioned to believe that sanity was a fragile possession, that everyone was a potential victim of neuroses or psychoses caused by abuse, neglect, or even by the ordinary stresses of daily life. If he had seen the events of the past thirteen hours as the plot of a movie, he'd have found it unbelievable, smugly certain that the male lead – himself – would have cracked from the strain of so many supernatural events and encounters combined with so much physical abuse. Yet here he was, with aches in most of his muscles and pains in half his joints, but with his wits intact.

Then he realized that perhaps he could not assume his wits were intact. Unlikely as it was, he might already be strapped down on a bed in a psychiatric ward, with a rubber wedge in his mouth to keep him from biting off his tongue in a mad frenzy. The silent and unmoving world might be only a delusion.

Sweet thought.

When Connie let go of the azalea branches that she had moved, they did not fall back into place. Harry had to press gently on them to force them to drape the dog once more.

They rose to their feet and scrutinized the visible length of Pacific Coast Highway, the shoulder-to-shoulder businesses on both sides, the narrow dark gaps between buildings.

The world was a huge clockwork mechanism with a bent key, broken springs, and rust-locked gears. Harry tried to tell himself that he was growing accustomed to this weird state of affairs, but he was not convincing. If he'd gotten so mellow about it, why was there a cold sweat on his brow, under his arms, and down the small of his back? The totally becalmed night exerted no tranquilizing influence, for there was spring-taut violence and sudden death under its peaceful façade; instead, it was deeply eerie and growing more so with the passage of each non-second.

'Enchantment,' Harry said.

'What?'

'Like in a fairy tale. The whole world has fallen under an evil enchantment, a spell.'

'So where the hell is the witch who did it? That's what I want to know.'

'Not witch,' Harry corrected. 'That's female. A male witch is a warlock. Or sorcerer.'

She was fuming. 'Whatever. Damn it, where is he,

why is he toying with us like this, taking so long to show his face?'

Glancing at his wristwatch, Harry confirmed that the red second indicator had not resumed blinking and that the time on the readout was still 1:29. 'Actually, how much time he's taking depends on how you look at it. I guess you could say that he hasn't taken any time at all.'

She noted the 1:29 on her watch. 'Come on, come on, let's get this over with. Or do you think he's waiting for us to go looking for him?'

Elsewhere in the night, there arose the first sound, since the Pause, that they had not made themselves. Laughter. The low, gravelly laughter of the golem-vagrant who had burned like a tallow candle in Harry's condo and later reappeared to hammer on them in Ordegard's house.

Again, out of habit, they reached for their revolvers. Then both remembered the uselessness of guns against this adversary, and left their weapons holstered.

South of them, at the uphill end of the block, on the other side of the street, Ticktock turned the corner, wearing his all-too-familiar vagrant identity. If anything, the golem seemed bigger than before, well over seven feet tall instead of six and a half, with a greater tangle of hair and wildness of beard than when they'd seen him last. Leonine head. Tree-trunk neck. Massive shoulders. Impossibly broad chest. Hands as big as tennis rackets. His black raincoat was as voluminous as a tent.

'Why the hell was I so impatient for him?' Connie wondered, voicing Harry's identical thought.

His troll-mean laughter fading, Ticktock stepped off the far curb and started to cross the street diagonally, coming straight toward them.

'What's the plan?' Connie asked.

'What plan?'

'There's always a plan, damn it.'

Indeed, Harry was surprised to realize they had stood waiting for the golem without giving a thought to a course of action. They had been cops for so many years, and had worked as partners long enough, that they knew how best to respond in every situation, to virtually any threat. Usually they didn't actually have to put their heads together on strategy; they just acted instinctively, each of them confident that the other would make all the right moves as well. On the rare occasions when they needed to talk out a plan of action, a few one-word sentences sufficed, the shortspeak of partners in sync. However, confronted by a nearly invulnerable adversary made of bloodless mud and stones and worms and God-knew-what-else, by a fierce and relentless fighter who was but one of an endless army that their *real* enemy could create, they seemed bereft of both instinct and brains, able only to stand paralyzed and watch him approach.

Run, Harry thought, and was about to take his own advice when the towering golem stopped in the middle of the street, about fifty feet away.

The golem's eyes were different from anything Harry had seen before. Not just luminous but blazing. Blue. The hot blue of gas flames. Dancing brightly in his sockets. His eyes cast images of flickering blue fire on

his cheekbones and made the frizzy ends of his beard
look like thin filaments of blue neon.

Ticktock spread his arms and raised his enormous
hands above his head in the manner of an Old Testament
prophet standing on a mountain and addressing his fol-
lowers below, relaying messages from beyond. Tablets
of stone containing a *hundred* commandments could
have been concealed within his generous raincoat.

'In one hour of real time the world starts up again,'
Ticktock said. 'I'll count to fifty. A headstart. Survive one hour, and I'll let you live, never torment
you again.'

'Dear sweet Jesus,' Connie whispered, 'he really *is* a
child playing nasty games.'

That made him at least as dangerous as any other
sociopath. More so. Some young children, in their
innocence of empathy, had the capacity to be extremely
cruel.

Ticktock said, 'I'll hunt you fair and square, use none
of my tricks, just my eyes,' and he pointed to his blazing
blue sockets, 'my ears,' and he pointed to one of those,
'and my wits.' He tapped the side of his skull with one
thick forefinger. 'No tricks. No special powers. More
fun that way. One . . . two . . . better run, don't you
think? Three . . . four . . . five . . .'

'This can't be happening,' Connie said, but she turned
and ran anyway.

Harry followed her. They sprinted to the alley and
around the side of the Green House, almost colliding
with the bony hobo who had called himself Sammy
and who was now frozen precariously on one foot in

mid-stride. Their feet made curious, hollow slapping sounds on the blacktop as they exploded past Sammy and raced deeper into the dark backstreet, almost the sound of running footsteps but not quite. The echoes, too, were not precisely like echoes in the real world, less reverberant and too short-lived.

As he ran, wincing at a hundred separate pains that flared with each footfall, Harry struggled to devise some strategy by which they might survive the hour. But, like Alice, they had crossed through the looking glass, into the kingdom of the Red Queen, and no plans or logic would work in that land of the Mad Hatter and Cheshire Cat, where reason was despised and chaos embraced.

FIVE

·1·

'Eleven . . . twelve . . . you're dead if I find you . . .
thirteen . . .'

Bryan was having so much fun.

He sprawled naked on the black silk sheets, busily
creating and gloriously Becoming, while the votive eyes
adored him from their glass reliquaries.

Yet a part of him was in the golem, which was also
exhilarating. He had constructed the creature bigger
this time, made it a fierce and unstoppable killing
machine, the better to terrorize the bigshot hero and
his bitch. Its immense shoulders were *his* shoulders,
too, and its powerful arms were his to use. Curling those
arms, feeling the inhuman muscles flex and contract and
flex, was so thrilling that he could barely contain his
excitement over the hunt before him.

'. . . sixteen . . . seventeen . . . eighteen . . .'

He had made this giant from dirt and clay and sand,
given its body the appearance of flesh, and animated it –
just as the first god had created Adam from lifeless mud.
Although his destiny was to be a more merciless divinity
than any who had come before him, he could create as

well as destroy; no one could say that he was less a god than others who had ruled, no one. No one.

Standing in the middle of Pacific Coast Highway, *towering* there, he gazed out upon the still and silent world, and was pleased with what he had wrought. This was his Greatest and Most Secret Power – the ability to stop everything as easily as a watchmaker could stop a ticking timepiece merely by opening the casing and applying the proper tool to the key point in the mechanism.

'. . . twenty-four . . . twenty-five . . .'

This power had arisen within him during one of his psychic growth surges when he was sixteen, though he had been eighteen before he had learned to use it well. That was to be expected. Jesus, too, had needed time to learn how to turn water into wine, how to multiply a few loaves and fishes to feed multitudes.

Will. The power of the will. That was the proper tool with which to remake reality. Before the beginning of time and the birth of this universe, there had been one will that had brought it all into existence, a consciousness that people called God, though God was no doubt utterly different from all the ways that humankind had pictured Him – perhaps only a child at play who, as a game, created galaxies like grains of sand. If the universe was a perpetual-motion machine created as an act of will, it also could be altered by sheer will, remade or destroyed. All that was needed to manipulate and edit the first god's creation was power and understanding; both had been given to Bryan. The power of the atom was a dim light when compared to the blindingly brilliant power of the mind. By applying his will, by intently focusing thought and desire, he found that he could make fundamental changes in the very foundations of existence.

'. . . thirty-one . . . thirty-two . . . thirty-three . . .'

Because he was still earnestly Becoming and was not yet the new god, Bryan was able to sustain these changes only for short periods, usually no more than one hour of real time. Occasionally he grew impatient with his limits, but he was certain the day would arrive when he could alter current reality in ways that would be permanent if he so wished. In the meantime, as he continued to Become, he satisfied himself with amusing alterations that temporarily negated all the laws of physics and, at least for a short while, tailored reality to his desire.

Although it would appear to Lyon and Gulliver that time had ground to a halt, the truth was more complicated than that. By the application of his extraordinary will, almost like *wishing* before blowing out the candles on a birthday cake, he had re-conceived the nature of time. If it had been an ever-flowing river of dependable effect, he transformed it into a series of streams, large placid lakes, and geysers with a *variety* of effects. This world now lay in one of the lakes where time advanced at such an excruciatingly slow rate that it appeared to have stopped flowing – yet, also at his wish, he and the two cops interacted with this new reality much as they had with the old, experiencing only minor changes in most of the laws of matter, energy, motion, and force.

'. . . forty . . . forty-one . . .'

As if making a birthday wish, as if wishing on

a star, as if wishing to a fairy godmother, wishing, wishing, wishing with all his considerable might, he had created the perfect playground for a spirited game of hide-and-seek. And so what if he had bent the universe to make a toy of it?

He was aware that he was two people of widely disparate natures. On the one hand he was a god Becoming, exalted, with incalculable authority and responsibility. On the other hand, he was a reckless and selfish child, cruel and prideful.

In that respect he fancied that he was like humankind itself – only more so.

'. . . forty-five . . .'

In fact, he believed he had been anointed precisely because of the kind of child he had been. Selfishness and pride were merely reflections of ego and, without a strong ego, no man could have the confidence to create. A certain amount of recklessness was required if one hoped to explore the limits of one's creative powers; taking chances, without regard for consequences, could be liberating and a virtue. And, as he was to be the god who would chasten humankind for its pollution of the earth, cruelty was a requirement of Becoming. His ability to remain a child, to avoid spending his creative energy in the senseless breeding of more animals for the herd, made him the perfect candidate for divinity.

'. . . forty-nine . . . fifty!'

For a while he would keep his promise to hunt them down only with the aid of ordinary human senses. It would be fun. Challenging. And it would be good to experience the severe limitations of their existence, not in order to develop compassion for them – they did not deserve compassion – but to enjoy more fully, by comparison, his own extraordinary powers.

In the body of the hulking vagrant, Bryan moved from the street into the fabulous amusement park that was the dead-still, whisperless town.

'Here I come,' he shouted, 'ready or not.'

·2·

A dangling pine cone, like a Christmas ornament suspended by a thread from the bough above, had been arrested in mid-drop by the Pause. An orange and white cat had been stilled while leaping from a tree branch to the top of a stucco wall, airborne, forepaws reaching, back legs sprung out behind. A rigid, unchanging filigree of smoke curled from a fireplace chimney.

As she and Harry ran farther into the strange, unbeating heart of the paralyzed town, Connie did not believe that they would escape with their lives; nonetheless she frantically conceived and discarded numerous strategies to elude Ticktock for one hour. Under the hard shell of cynicism that she had nurtured so lovingly for so long, like every poor fool in the world, she evidently treasured the hope that she was different and would live forever.

She should have been embarrassed to find within herself such a stupid, animal faith in her own immortality.

Instead, she embraced it. Hope could be a treacherous kind of confidence, but she couldn't see how their predicament could be made worse by a little positive thinking.

In one night she had learned so many new things about herself. It would be a pity not to live long enough to build a better life on those discoveries.

For all of her fevered thinking, only pathetic strategies occurred to her. Without slowing, between increasingly ragged gasps for breath, she suggested they change streets often, turning this way and that, in the feeble hope that a twisting trail would somehow be harder to follow than one that was arrow-straight. And she guided them along a downhill route where possible because they could cover more ground in less time if they weren't fighting a rising grade.

Around them, the inert residents of Laguna Beach were oblivious to the fact that they were running for their lives. And if she and Harry were caught, no screams would wake these enchanted sleepers or bring help.

She knew why Ricky Estefan's neighbors had not heard the golem exploding up through his hallway floor and beating him to death. Ticktock had stopped time in every corner of the world except inside that bungalow. Ricky's torture and murder had been conducted with sadistic leisure – while no time at all was passing for the rest of humanity. Likewise, when Ticktock had accosted them in Ordegard's house and had thrown Connie through the glass sliding door onto the master-bedroom balcony, neighbors had not responded to the crash or to the gunshots that had preceded it because the entire confrontation had taken place in non-time, in a dimension one step removed from reality.

As she ran at her top speed, she counted to herself, trying to maintain the slow rhythm in which Ticktock had been counting. She reached fifty much too soon, and doubted they had put half enough ground between them and him to be safe.

If she had continued counting, she might have reached a hundred before, finally, they had to stop. They leaned against a brick wall to catch their breath.

Her chest was tight, and her heart seemed to have swelled to the point of bursting. Each breath felt searingly hot, as if she were a fire-eater in a circus, exhaling ignited gasoline fumes. Her throat was raw. Calf and thigh muscles ached, and the increased circulation renewed the pain in all of the bumps and bruises she'd gotten during the night.

Harry looked worse than she felt. Of course, he had received more blows in more encounters with Ticktock than she had sustained, and had been on the run longer.

When she could speak, she said, 'Now what?'

At first each word puffed from him explosively. 'What. About. Using. Grenades?'

'Grenades?'

'Like Ordegard.'

'Yeah, yeah, I remember.'

'Bullets don't work on a golem— '

She said, 'I noticed.'

'—but if we blew the damn thing to pieces— '

'Where we going to find grenades? Huh? You know a friendly neighborhood explosives shop around here?'

'Maybe a National Guard armory, someplace like that.'

'Get real, Harry.'

'Why? The rest of the world isn't.'

'We blow one of these damn things to smithereens, he just scoops up some mud and makes another.'

'But it'll slow him down.'

'Maybe two minutes.'

'Every minute counts,' he said. 'We've just got to get through one hour.'

She looked at him with disbelief. 'Are you saying you think he'll keep his promise?'

With his coat sleeve, Harry wiped sweat off his face. 'Well, he might.'

'Like hell.'

'He might,' Harry insisted.

She was ashamed of herself for wanting to believe.

She listened to the night. Nothing. That didn't mean Ticktock wasn't nearby.

'We've got to get going,' she said.

'Where?'

No longer needing to lean against the wall for support, Connie looked around and discovered they were in the parking lot beside a bank. Eighty feet away, a car was stopped near the twenty-four-hour automatic teller. Two men stood at the machine in the bluish glow from an overhead security lamp.

Something about the postures of the two was wrong.

Not just that they were as still as statues. Something else.

Connie started across the parking lot toward the odd tableau.

'Where you going?' Harry asked.

'Check this out.'

Her instinct proved reliable. The Pause had hit in the middle of a robbery.

The first man was using his bank card to get three hundred dollars from the machine. He was in his late fifties with white hair, a white mustache, and a kind face now lined with fear. The packet of crisp bills had begun to slide out of the dispenser and into his hand when everything had stopped.

The perp was in his late teens or early twenties, blond, good looking. In Nikes, jeans, and a sweatshirt now, he was one of those beach-boy types who could be found all summer long, on every street of downtown Laguna, wearing sandals and cutoffs, flat-bellied, with a mahogany tan, white-haired from the sun. To look at him as he was at that moment or as he would be when summer came, you might suspect that he lacked ambition and had a talent for leisure, but you would not imagine that anyone so wholesome in appearance could harbor criminal intentions. Even in the act of robbery he appeared to be cherubic, and had a pleasant smile. He was holding a .32-caliber pistol in his right hand, the muzzle jammed against the older man's spine.

Connie moved around the pair, studying them thoughtfully.

'What're you doing?' Harry asked.

'We've got to deal with this.'

'We don't have time.'

'We're cops, aren't we?'

Harry said, 'We're being hunted, for God's sake!'

'Who else is going to keep the world from going to Hell in a handbasket, if we don't?'

'Wait a minute, wait a minute,' he said. 'I thought you were in this line of work for the thrill, and to prove something to yourself. Isn't that what you said earlier?'

'And aren't *you* in it to preserve order, protect the innocent?'

Harry took a deep breath, as if to argue, then let it out in an explosive sigh of exasperation. It wasn't the first time during the past six months that she had elicited that reaction from him.

She thought he was sort of cute when he was exasperated; it was such a pleasing change from his usual equanimity, which got boring because it was so constant. In fact, Connie even liked the way he looked tonight, rumpled and in need of a shave. She had never seen him this way, had never *expected* to see him this way, and thought he seemed more rough than seedy, more dangerous than she would have believed he could look.

'Okay, okay,' he said, stepping into the robbery tableau to inspect the perp and victim more closely. 'What do you want to do?'

'Make a few adjustments.'

'Might be dangerous.'

'That velocity business? Well, the moth didn't disintegrate.'

Cautiously, she touched one finger to the perp's face. His skin felt leathery, and his flesh was somewhat firmer than it should have been. When she took her finger away, she left a shallow dimple in his cheek, which evidently would not disappear until the Pause ended.

Staring into his eyes, she said, 'Creep.'

In no way whatsoever did he acknowledge her presence. She was invisible to him. When time resumed its usual flow, he would not be aware that she had ever been there.

She pulled back on the perp's gun arm. It moved but with stiff resistance.

Connie was patient because she worried that time might begin to move forward again when she least expected it, that her presence might startle the reanimated gunman, and that he might accidentally pull the trigger. Conceivably she could cause him to blow the older man away, although his original intention might have been only to commit a robbery.

When the muzzle of the .32 was no longer pressed against the victim's spine, Connie slowly pushed it to the left until it was not pointed at him at all but aimed harmlessly into the night.

Harry carefully pried the gunman's fingers off the pistol. 'It's like we're kids playing with life-size action figures.' The .32 stayed precisely where it had been when the perp's hand had encircled it, suspended in mid-air.

Connie found that the gun could be moved more easily than the gunman, although it still offered some resistance. She took it to the man at the automatic teller, pressed it into his right hand, and closed his fingers tightly around it. When the Pause ended, he would find a pistol in his hand where none had been a fraction of a second previously, and would have no idea how it had gotten there. From the pay-out tray of the machine, she removed the banded packet of twenties and put it in the customer's left hand.

'I see how the ten-dollar bill ended up magically back in my hand after I gave it to that hobo,' she said.

Surveying the night uneasily, Harry said, 'And how the four bullets I pumped into him ended up in my shirt pocket.'

'The head of that religious statue in my hand, from Ricky Estefan's shrine.' She frowned. 'Gives you the creepy crawlies to think we were like these people, frozen in time, and the bastard played with us that way.'

'You done here?'

'Not quite. Come on, help me turn the guy away from the machine.'

Together, they rocked him around a hundred and eighty degrees, as if he were a garden statue carved from marble. When they were finished, the victim not only had the pistol but was covering the perp with it.

Like set dressers in a wax museum handling extremely realistic mannequins, they had redesigned the scene and given it a new kind of drama.

'Okay, now let's get out of here,' Harry said, and started to move away from the bank, across the parking lot.

Connie hesitated, examining their handiwork.

He looked back, saw she wasn't following him, and turned to her. 'Now what?'

Shaking her head, she said, 'This is too dangerous.'

'The good guy has the gun now.'

'Yes, but he'll be surprised when he finds it in his hand. He might drop it. The creep here might get hold of it again, probably will, and then they're right back where we found them.'

Harry returned, an apoplectic look on his face. 'Have you forgotten a certain dirty, demented, scar-faced gentlemen in a black raincoat?'

'I don't hear him yet.'

'Connie, for God's sake, he could stop time for *us*, too, then take however damn long he wants to walk up to us, wait until he was right in front of us before letting us back into the game. So you *wouldn't* hear him until he tore your nose off and asked you if you'd like a handkerchief.'

'If he's going to cheat like that— '

'Cheat? Why *wouldn't* he cheat?' Harry demanded exasperatedly, though two minutes ago he had been arguing that there was a chance Ticktock would keep his promise and play fair. 'We aren't talking about Mother Teresa here!'

'—then it doesn't matter whether we finish our work or run. Either way, he'll get us.'

The keys to the white-haired bank patron's car were in the ignition. Connie took them out and unlocked the trunk. The lid did not pop up. She had to lift it as if she was raising the lid on a coffin.

'This is anal-retentive,' Harry told her.

'Oh? Like *you* might ordinarily be expected to handle it, huh?'

He blinked at her.

Harry took the perp under the arms, and Connie grabbed him by the feet. They carried him to the back of the car and gently lowered him into the trunk. The body seemed somewhat heavier than it would have been in real time. Connie tried to slam the lid, but in this altered reality, her push didn't give it the momentum to go all the way down; she had to lean on it to make the latch click into place.

When the Pause ended and time started up again, the perpetrator would find himself in the trunk of the car with no memory whatsoever of how he had wound up in that unhappy position. In the blink of an eye he would have gone from being assailant to prisoner.

Harry said, 'I think I understand how I wound up three times in the same chair in Ordegard's kitchen, with the barrel of my own gun in my mouth.'

'He kept taking you out of real time and putting you there.'

'Yeah. A child playing pranks.'

Connie wondered if that was also how the snakes and tarantulas had gotten into Ricky Estefan's kitchen. During a previous Pause, had Ticktock gathered them from pet shops, laboratories, or even from their nests in the wild, and then put them in the bungalow? Had he started time up again – at least for Ricky – startling the poor man with the sudden infestation?

Connie walked away from the car, into the parking

lot, where she stopped and listened to the unnatural night.

It was as if everything in the world had suddenly died, from the wind to all of humanity, leaving a planetwide cemetery where grass and flowers and trees and mourners were made from the same granite as the tombstones.

At times in recent years, she had considered chucking police work and moving to some cheap shack on the edge of the Mojave, as far away from people as she could get. She lived so Spartanly that she had substantial savings; living as a desert rat, she could make the money last a long time. The barren, peopleless expanses of sand and scrub and rock were immensely appealing when compared to modern civilization.

But the Pause was far different from the peace of a sun-baked desert landscape, where life was still a part of the natural order and where civilization, sick as it was, still existed somewhere over the horizon. After only about ten non-minutes of silence and stillness as deep as death, Connie longed for the flamboyant folly of the human circus. The species was too fond of lying, cheating, envy, ignorance, self-pity, self-righteousness, and utopian visions that always led to mass murder – but until and if it destroyed itself, it harbored the potential to become nobler, to take responsibility for its actions, to live and let live, and to earn the stewardship of the earth.

Hope. For the first time in her life, Connie Gulliver had begun to believe that hope, in itself, was a reason to live and to tolerate civilization as it was.

But Ticktock, as long as he lived, was the end of hope.

'I hate this son of a bitch like I've never hated anyone,' she said. 'I want to get him. I want to waste him so bad I can hardly stand it.'

'To get him, first we have to stay alive,' Harry reminded her.

'Let's go.'

·3·

Initially, staying on the move in that motionless world seemed to be the wisest thing they could do. If Ticktock was faithful to his promise, using only his eyes and ears and wits to track them, their safety increased in direct proportion to the amount of distance they put between him and them.

As Harry ran with Connie from one lonely street to another, he suspected there was a better than even chance that the psycho would keep his word, stalking them only by ordinary means and releasing them unharmed from the Pause if he could not catch them in one hour of real time. The bastard was, after all, demonstrably immature in spite of his incredible power, a child playing a game, and sometimes children took games more seriously than real life.

Of course, when he released them, it would still be twenty-nine minutes past one in the morning when clocks finally started ticking again. Dawn remained five hours away. And while Ticktock might play this particular game-within-a-game strictly according to the rules he had outlined, he would still intend to kill them by dawn. Surviving the Pause would only win them the slim chance to find him and destroy him once time started up again.

And even if Ticktock broke his promise, using some sixth sense to track them, it was smart to keep moving. Perhaps he had pinned psychic tags on them, as Harry had speculated earlier; in which case, if he *did* cheat, he could find them regardless of where they went. By remaining on the move, at least they were safe unless and until he could catch them or get ahead by anticipating their next turn.

From street to alley to street, across yards and between silent houses they ran, clambering over fences, through a school playground, footfalls vaguely metallic, where every shadow seemed as permanent as iron, where neon lights burned steadier than any Harry had ever seen before and painted eternal rainbows on the pavement, past a man in a tweed coat walking his Scottie dog and both of them as motionless as bronze figures.

They sprinted along a narrow stream bed where runoff from the storm earlier in the day was time-frozen but not at all like ice: clearer than ice, black with reflections of the night and marked by pure silver highlights instead of frost-white crystallization. The surface was not flat, either, like a frozen winter creek, but rippled and runneled and spiraled by turbulence. Where the stream splashed over rocks in its course, the air was hung with unmoving sprays of glittering water resembling elaborate sculptures made from glass shards and beads.

Though staying on the move was desirable, continued flight soon became impractical. They were already tired and stiff with pain when they began their run; each additional exertion took a geometrically greater toll from them.

Although they seemed to move as easily in this petrified world as in the one to which they were accustomed, Harry noticed that they did not create a wind of their own when they ran. The air parted around them like butter around a knife, but no turbulence arose from their passage, which indicated that the air was objectively denser than it appeared subjectively. Their speed might be considerably less than it appeared to them, in which case movement required more effort than they perceived.

Furthermore, the coffee, brandy, and hamburger that Harry had eaten churned sourly in his stomach. Acidic flares of indigestion burned through his chest.

More important, block by block as they fled through that town-size mausoleum, an inexplicable inversion of biological response increased their misery. Although such strenuous activity should have left them over-heated, they grew steadily colder. Harry couldn't work up a sweat, not even an icy one. His toes and fingers felt as if he had slogged across an Alaskan glacier, not a southern California beach resort.

The night itself felt no colder than before the Pause. Indeed, perhaps not quite as cool, since the crisp breeze off the ocean had fallen into stillness with everything else. The cause of the queer internal chill was evidently other than the air temperature, more mysterious and profound – and frightening.

It was as if the world around them, its abundant energy trapped in stasis, had become a black hole of sorts, relentlessly absorbing their energy, sucking it out of them, until degree by degree they would become as inanimate as everything else. He suspected it was imperative that they begin to conserve what resources they had left.

When it became incontrovertibly clear that they would have to stop and find a promising place to hide, they had left a residential neighborhood and entered the east end of a canyon with scrub-covered slopes. Along the three-lane service road, lit by rows of sodium-vapor arc lamps that transformed the night into a two-tone black and yellow canvas, the flat ground was occupied by semi-industrial businesses of the type that image-conscious towns like Laguna Beach carefully tucked away from primary tourist routes.

They were walking now, shivering. She was hugging herself. He turned up his collar and pulled the halves of his sport coat tight together.

'How much of the hour has passed?' Connie asked.

'Damned if I know. I've lost all time sense.'

'Half an hour?'

'Maybe.'

'Longer?'

'Maybe.'

'Less?'

'Maybe.'

'Shit.'

'Maybe.'

To their right, in a sprawling recreational-vehicle storage yard behind heavy-duty chain-link fence crowned with razor wire, motor homes stood side by side in the gloom, like row after row of slumbering elephants.

'What're all these cars?' Connie wondered.

They were parked on both sides of the road, half on the narrow shoulders and half on the pavement, squeezing the three-lane street to no more than two lanes. It was curious, because none of those businesses would have been open when the Pause hit. In fact, all of them were dark, and had closed up seven to eight hours earlier.

On their right, a landscape-maintenance company occupied a concrete-block building behind which a tree and shrub nursery was terraced halfway up the canyon wall.

Directly under one of the pole lamps, they came upon a car in which a young couple was necking. Her blouse was open, and his hand was inside, marble palm cupping marble breast. As far as Harry was concerned, their frozen expressions of ardent passion, tinted sodium-yellow and glimpsed through the car windows, was about as erotic as a couple of corpses tumbled together on a bed.

They passed two automobile-repair shops on opposite sides of the three-lane, each specializing in different foreign makes. The businesses fronted their own parts junkyards heaped with cannibalized vehicles and fenced with high chain-link.

Cars continued to line the street, blocking driveways to the businesses. A boy of about eighteen or nineteen, shirtless in jeans and Rockports, as thoroughly gripped by the Pause as everyone they had seen thus far, was sprawled across the hood of a black '86 Camaro, arms out to his sides and palms up, staring at the occluded sky as if there was something to see up there, a stupid expression of drugged-out bliss on his face.

'This is weird,' Connie said.

'Weird,' Harry agreed, flexing his hands to keep the knuckles from growing too stiff with the cold.

'But you know what?'

'Familiar somehow,' he said.

'Yeah.'

Along the final length of the three-lane blacktop, all of the businesses were warehouses. Some were built of concrete block covered with dust-caked stucco, stained with rust from water pouring off corrugated metal roofs during countless rainy seasons. Others were entirely of metal, like Quonset huts.

The parked cars grew more numerous in the final block of the street, which dead-ended in the crotch of the canyon. In some places they were doubled up, narrowing the road to one lane.

At the end of the street, the last of all the buildings was a large warehouse unidentified by any company name. It was one of the stucco-coated models with a corrugated steel roof. A giant FOR RENT banner was strung across the front, with a Realtor's phone number.

Security lights shone down the face of the structure,

across metal roll-up doors large enough to admit big tractor-and-trailer rigs. At the southwest corner of the building was a smaller, man-size door at which stood two tough-looking guys in their early twenties, steroid-assisted physiques bulked up beyond what weight-lifting and diet alone could achieve.

'Couple of bouncers,' Connie said as they approached the Pause-frozen men.

Suddenly the scene made sense to Harry. 'It's a rave.'

'On a weekday?'

'Must be someone's special party, birthday or something.'

Imported from England a few years ago, the rave phenomenon appealed to teenagers and those in their early twenties who wanted to party nonstop until dawn, beyond the eye of all authorities.

'Smart place to hide?' Connie wondered.

'As smart as any, I guess, and smarter than some.'

Rave promoters rented warehouses and industrial buildings for a night or two, moving the event from one spot to another to avoid police detection. Locations of upcoming raves were advertised in underground newspapers and in fliers handed out at record stores, nightclubs, and schools, all written in the code of the subculture, using phrases like 'The Mickey Mouse X-press,' 'American X-press,' 'Double-Hit Mickey,' 'Get X-rayed,' 'Dental Surgery Explained,' and 'Free Balloons for the Kiddies.' Mickey Mouse and X were nicknames for a potent drug more commonly known as Ecstasy, while references to dentistry and balloons meant that nitrous oxide – or laughing gas – would be for sale.

Avoidance of police detection was essential. The theme of every illegal rave party – as opposed to tamer imitations in the legitimate rave nightclubs – was sex, drugs, and anarchy.

Harry and Connie walked past the bouncers, through the door, and into the heart of chaos, but a chaos to which the Pause had brought a tenuous and artificial order.

The cavernous room was lit by half a dozen red and green lasers, perhaps a dozen yellow and red spots, and strobes, all of which had been blinking and sweeping over the crowd until the Pause stilled them. Now lances of colorful, fixed light found some partiers and left others in shadows.

Four or five hundred people, mostly between eighteen and twenty five, but some as young as fifteen, were frozen in either the act of dancing or just hanging out. Because the disc jockeys at raves invariably played highly energized techno dance music with a rapidly pounding bass that could shake walls, many of the young celebrants had been Paused in bizarre poses of flailing and gyrating abandon, bodies contorted, hair flying. The men and boys were for the most part dressed in jeans or chinos with flannel shirts and baseball caps worn backward, or with preppy sport coats over T-shirts, though some were decked out all in black. The girls and young women wore a wider variety of clothes, but every outfit was provocative – tight, short, low-cut, translucent, revealing; raves were, after all, celebrations of the carnal. The silence of graves had replaced the booming music, as well as the screams and shouts of the partiers; the eerie light combined with the stillness to impart an anti-erotic cadaverous quality to the exposed curves of calves, thighs, and breasts.

As he and Connie moved through the crowd, Harry noticed that the dancers' faces were stretched in grotesque expressions which probably had conveyed excitement and hopped-up gaiety when they were animated. In freeze-frame, however, they were eerily transformed into masks of rage, hatred, and agony.

In the fiery glow produced by the lasers and spots, and by the psychedelic images that film projectors beamed onto two huge walls, it was easy to imagine that this was no party, after all, but a diorama of Hell, with the damned writhing in pain and wailing for release from their excruciating torment.

By seining out the rave's noise and movement, the Pause might have captured the truth of the event in its net. Perhaps the ugly secret, beneath the flash and thunder, was that these revelers, in their obsessive search for sensation, were not truly having fun on any fundamental level, but were suffering private miseries from which they frantically sought relief that eluded them.

Harry led Connie out of the dancers into the spectators who were gathered around the perimeter of the enormous vaulted chamber. A few had been caught by the Pause in small groups, in the midst of shouted conversations and exaggerated laughter, faces strained and muscles corded in their necks as they had struggled to compete with the thunderous music.

But most seemed to be alone, disengaged from those around them. Some were slack-faced and staring vacuously into the crowd. Others were as taut as stretched wire, with unnervingly feverish stares.

Perhaps it was the Halloween lighting and the stark shadows, but in either case, whether hollow-eyed or glaring, the petrified ravers on the sidelines reminded Harry of movie zombies paralyzed in the middle of some murderous task.

'It's a regular creepshow,' Connie said uneasily, evidently also perceiving a quality of menace in the scene that might not have been so obvious if they had wandered into it before the Pause.

'Welcome to the '90s.'

A number of the zombies on the periphery of the dance floor were holding balloons in an array of bright colors, though not attached to strings or sticks. Here was a red-haired, freckled boy of seventeen or eighteen, who had stretched the neck of a canary-yellow balloon and wrapped it around his index finger to prevent deflation. And here was a young man with a Pancho Villa mustache, firmly pinching the neck of a green balloon between thumb and forefinger, as was a blond girl with empty blue eyes. Those who didn't use their fingers seemed to employ the type of hinged binder clips that could be bought by the box at stationery stores. A few ravers had the necks of their balloons between their lips, taking hits of nitrous oxide, which they had bought from a vendor who was no doubt working out of a van behind the building. With all the vacant or intense stares and the bright balloons, it was as if a pack of the walking dead had wandered into a children's birthday party.

Although the scene was made infinitely strange and fascinating by the Pause, it was still drearily familiar to Harry. He was, after all, a homicide detective, and sudden deaths occasionally occurred at raves.

Sometimes they were drug overdoses. No dentist would sedate a patient with a concentration of nitrous oxide higher than eighty percent, but the gas available at raves was often pure, with no oxygen mixed in. Take too many hits of the pure stuff in too short a time, or suck too long on one toke, you might not merely make a giggling spectacle of yourself but induce a stroke that killed you; or, worse, one that was not fatal but caused irreparable brain damage and left you flopping like a fish on the floor, or catatonic.

Harry spotted a loft overhanging the entire width of the back of the warehouse, twenty feet above the main floor, with wooden steps leading to it from both ends.

'Up there,' he told Connie, pointing.

They would be able to see the entire warehouse from that high deck – and quickly spot Ticktock if they heard him enter, no matter which door he used. The two staircases ensured an escape route regardless of the direction from which he came at them.

Moving deeper into the building, they passed two bosomy young women in tight T-shirts on which was printed 'Just Say NO,' a rave joke on Nancy Reagan's anti-drug campaign, which meant these two said *yes* to nitrous oxide, NO, if not to anything else.

They had to step around three girls lying on the floor

near the wall, two of them holding half-deflated balloons and Paused in fits of red-faced giggles. The third was unconscious, mouth open, a fully deflated balloon on her chest.

Near the back, not far from the right-hand stairs, an enormous white X was painted on the wall, large enough to be visible from every corner of the warehouse. Two guys in Mickey Mouse sweatshirts – and one of them in a mouse-ear hat – had been frozen in the middle of bustling commerce, taking twenty-dollar bills from customers in return for capsules of Ecstasy or for disco biscuits saturated with the same stuff.

They came to a teenager, no more than fifteen, with guileless eyes and a face as innocent as that of a young nun. She was wearing a black T-shirt with a picture of a shotgun under the words PUMP ACTION. She had Paused in the process of putting a disco biscuit into her mouth.

Connie plucked the cookie from the girl's stiff fingers and slipped it out from between her parted lips. She threw it to the floor. The cookie didn't have quite enough momentum to carry it all the way down, halting inches above the concrete. Connie pushed it the rest of the way with the toe of her shoe and crushed it underfoot. 'Stupid kid.'

'This isn't like you,' Harry said.

'What?'

'Being a stuffy adult.'

'Maybe someone's got to.'

Methylenedioxymethamphetamine, or Ecstasy, an

amphetamine with hallucinogenic effects, could radically energize the user and induce euphoria. It could
also generate a false sense of profound intimacy with
any strangers in whose company the user happened to
be when high.

Although other drugs sometimes appeared at raves,
NO and Ecstasy were far and away predominant. NO
was just nonaddictive giggle juice – wasn't it? – and
Ecstasy could bring you into harmony with your fellow
human beings and put you in tune with Mother Nature.
Right? That was its rep. The chosen drug of ecologically
minded peace advocates, well consumed at rallies to
save the planet. Sure, it was dangerous for people with
heart conditions, but there was no recorded death from
its use in the entire United States. True, scientists had
recently discovered that Ecstasy caused pin-size holes
in the brain, hundreds or even thousands of them from
continued use, but there was no proof that these holes
resulted in diminished mental capacity, so what they
probably did, see, was let the cosmic rays shine in better
and assist enlightenment. Right?

Climbing to the loft, Harry could look down between
the steps, which had treads but no risers, and see
couples frozen in makeout postures in the shadows
under the staircase.

All the sex education in the world, all the graphic
pamphlets on condom use, could be swept aside by
one tab of Ecstasy if the user experienced an erotic
response, as so many did. How could you remain
concerned about disease when the stranger you'd just
met was such a soulmate, the yin to your yang, radiant

and pure to your third eye, so in tune to your every need and desire?

When he and Connie reached the loft, the light was dimmer than on the main level, but Harry could see couples lying on the floor or sitting together with their backs against the rear wall. They were making out more aggressively than those beneath the stairs, Paused in tongue duels, blouses unbuttoned, jeans unzipped, hands seeking within.

Two or three of the couples, in an Ecstasy rush, might even have lost such complete touch with where they were and with common propriety that they were actually *doing* it in one fashion or another, when the Pause hit.

Harry had no desire to confirm that suspicion. Like the sad circus on the main floor, the scene in the loft was only depressing. It was not in the least erotic to any voyeur with minimum standards, but provoked as many somber thoughts as any Hieronymus Bosch painting of hellacious realms and creatures.

As Harry and Connie moved between the couples toward the loft railing where they could look down on the main floor, he said, 'Be careful what you step in.'

'You're disgusting.'

'Only trying to be a gentleman.'

'Well, that's unique in this place.'

From the railing, they had a good view of the frozen throng below, partying eternally.

Connie said, 'God, I'm cold.'

'Me too.'

Standing side by side, they put their arms around each other at the waist, ostensibly sharing body heat.

Harry had rarely in his life felt as close to anyone as he felt to her at that moment. Not close in an amorous sense. The stoned and groping couples on the floor behind them were sufficiently anti-romantic to assure against any romantic feelings rising in him just then. The atmosphere wasn't right for it. What he felt, instead, was the platonic closeness of friend to friend, of partners who had been pushed to their limits and then beyond, who were very probably going to die together before dawn – and this was the important part – without either of them ever having decided what he really wanted out of life or what it all meant.

She said, 'Tell me not all kids these days go to places like this, saturate their brains with chemicals.'

'They don't. Not all of them. Not even most of them. Most kids are reasonably together.'

'Because I wouldn't want to think this crowd is typical of "our next generation of leaders," as they say.'

'It isn't.'

'If it is,' she said, 'then the *post*-millennium cotillion is going to be even nastier than what we've been living through these last few years.'

'Ecstasy causes pin-size holes in the brain,' he said.

'I know. Just imagine how much more inept the government would be if the Congress was full of boys and girls who like to ride the X-press.'

'What makes you think it isn't already?'

She laughed sourly. 'That would explain a lot.'

The air was neither cold nor warm, but they were shivering worse than ever.

The warehouse remained deathly still.

'I'm sorry about your condo,' she said.

'What?'

'It burned down, remember?'

'Well.' He shrugged.

'I know how much you loved it.'

'There's insurance.'

'Still, it was so nice, cozy, everything in its place.'

'Oh? The one time you were there, you said it was "the perfect self-constructed prison" and that I was "a shining example to every anal-retentive nutcase fussbudget from Boston to San Diego."'

'No, I didn't.'

'Yes, you did.'

'Really?'

'Well, you were angry with me.'

'I must have been. About what?'

He said, 'That was the day we arrested Norton Lewis, he gave us a little run for our money, and I wouldn't let you shoot him.'

'That's right. I *really* wanted to shoot him.'

'Wasn't necessary.'

She sighed. 'I was really up for it.'

'We nailed him anyway.'

'Could've gone bad, though. You were lucky. Anyway, the son of a bitch deserved shooting.'

'No argument there,' he said.

'Well, I didn't mean it – about your condo.'

'Yes, you did.'

'Okay, I did, but I have a different take on it now. It's a screwed-up world, and we all need to have a way of coping. Yours is better than most. Better than mine, in fact.'

'You know what I think's happening here? I think maybe this is what the psychologists call "bonding."'

'God, I hope not.'

'I think it is.'

She smiled. 'I suspect that already happened weeks or months ago, but we're just getting around to admitting it.'

They stood in companionable silence for a while.

He wondered how much time had passed since they'd fled from the counting golem on Pacific Coast Highway. He felt as if he had surely been on the run for an hour, but it was difficult to tell real time when you were not living in it.

The longer they were stuck in the Pause, the more inclined Harry was to believe their enemy's promise that the ordeal would only last one hour. He had a feeling, perhaps at least partly cop instinct rather than entirely wishful thinking, that Ticktock was not as all-powerful as he seemed, that there were limits to even his phenomenal abilities, and that engineering the Pause was so draining, he could not long sustain it.

The growing inner cold that troubled both him and Connie might be a sign that Ticktock was finding it increasingly difficult to exempt them from the enchantment that had stilled the rest of the world. In spite of their tormentor's attempt to control the altered reality that he had created, perhaps Harry and Connie were gradually being transformed from movable game pieces to permanent fixtures on the game board itself.

He remembered the shock of hearing the gravelly voice speak to him out of his car radio last evening, when he had been speeding between his burning condo in Irvine and Connie's apartment in Costa Mesa. But until now he had not realized the importance of the words the golem-vagrant had spoken: *Gotta rest now, hero . . . gotta rest . . . tired . . . a little nap . . .* More had been said, mostly threats, the raspy voice gradually fading into static, silence. However, Harry suddenly understood that the most important thing about the incident was not the fact that Ticktock could somehow control the ether and speak to him out of a radio, but the revelation that even this being of godlike abilities had limits and needed periodic rest like any ordinary mortal.

When Harry thought about it, he realized that each of Ticktock's more flamboyant manifestations was always followed by a period of an hour or longer when he didn't come around to continue his torments.

Gotta rest, hero . . . tired . . . a little nap . . .

He remembered telling Connie, earlier at her apartment, that even a sociopath with enormous paranormal powers was certain to have weaknesses, points of vulnerability. During the intervening hours, as he had seen Ticktock perform a series of tricks, each of which was more amazing than the one before it, he had grown more pessimistic about their chances. Now optimism blossomed again.

Gotta rest, hero . . . tired . . . a little nap . . .

He was about to share these hopeful thoughts with Connie when she suddenly stiffened. His arm was still around her waist, so he also felt her shivering abruptly stop. For an instant he was afraid that she had been too deeply chilled, surrendered to entropy, and become part of the Pause.

Then he saw that she had tilted her head in response to some faint sound that he, in his woolgathering, had not heard.

It came again. A click.

Then a low scrape.

A much louder clatter.

The sounds were all flat, truncated, like those they themselves had made during their long run from the coast highway.

Alarmed, Connie slipped her arm from around Harry's waist, and he let go of her as well.

Down on the main floor of the warehouse, the golem-vagrant moved through iron shadows and revealing shafts of frozen light, between the zombie spectators and among the petrified dancers. Ticktock had entered through the same door they had used, following their trail.

·4·

Connie's instinct was to step back from the loft railing, so the golem would not look up and see her, but she overcame that reflexive urge and remained motionless. In the fathomless stillness of the Pause, even the

404

whispery friction of shoe sole against floor, or the softest creak of a board, would instantly draw the creature's unwanted attention.

Harry was also quick enough to slam a lock on his instinctual reaction, remaining almost as still as any of the ravers caught in the Pause. Thank God.

If the thing looked up, it probably would not see them. Most of the light was below, and the loft hung in shadows.

Connie realized she was clinging to the stupid hope that Ticktock really was trailing them only with ordinary senses, keeping his promise. As if any sociopathic serial killer, paranormally empowered or not, could be trusted to keep a promise. Stupid, not worthy of her, but she clung to the possibility anyway. If the world could fall under an enchantment as profound as any in a fairy tale, who was to say that her own hopes and wishes did not also have at least some power?

And wasn't *that* an odd idea coming from her of all people, who had given up hope as a child, who had never in memory wished for any gift or blessing or surcease?

Everyone can change, they said. She had never believed it. For most of her life, she had been unchanging, expecting nothing from the world that she did not earn twice over, taking perverse solace from the fact that her expectations were never exceeded.

Life can be as bitter as dragon tears. But whether dragon tears are bitter or sweet depends entirely on how each man perceives the taste.

Or woman.

Now she felt a stirring within, an important change, and she wanted to live to see how it played out.

But below prowled the golem-vagrant, hunting.

Connie breathed through her open mouth, slowly and quietly.

Moving among the fossilized dancers, the massive creature turned its burly head left and then right, methodically scanning the crowd. It changed color as it passed through frozen lasers and spotlights, red to green, green to yellow, yellow to red to white to green, gray and black when it moved between shafts of light. But always its eyes were blue, radiant and strange.

When the space between dancers narrowed, the golem shoved aside a young man in jeans and a blue corduroy jacket. The dancer toppled backward, but the resistance of all Paused things prevented him from completing the fall. He stopped at a forty-five-degree angle to the floor and hung there precariously, still poised mid-dance, with the same celebratory expression on his face, ready to complete the fall in the first fraction of a second after time started up again, if it ever did.

Moving from front to back of the cavernous room, the hulking golem shoved other dancers aside, into falls and spins and stumbles and head-butting collisions that would not be completed until the Pause ended. Getting out of the building safely when real time kicked in again would be a challenge, because the startled ravers, never having seen the beast pass among them while they were Paused, would blame those around them for being knocked down and shoved. A dozen fights would erupt in the first half-minute, pandemonium would break out, and confusion would inevitably give way to panic. With lasers and spotlights sweeping the crowd, the throbbing bass of the techno music shaking the walls, and violence inexplicably erupting at every turn, the rush to get out would pile people up at the doors, and it would be a miracle if a number of them were not trampled to death in the mêlée.

Connie had no special sympathy for the mob on the dance floor, since defiance of the law and policemen was one of the motivations that brought them to a rave in the first place. But as rebellious and destructive and socially confused as they might be, they were nonetheless human beings, and she was outraged at the callousness with which Ticktock was bulling through them, without a thought for what would happen to them when the world suddenly shifted into gear again.

She glanced at Harry beside her and saw a matching anger in his face and eyes. His teeth were clenched so tight that his jaw muscles bulged.

But there was nothing they could do to stop what was happening below. Bullets had no effect, and Ticktock was not likely to respond to a heartfelt request.

Besides, by speaking out, they would only be revealing their presence. The golem-vagrant had not once glanced toward the loft, and as yet there was no reason to think either that Ticktock was using more than ordinary senses to search for them or that he knew they were in the warehouse.

Then Ticktock perpetrated an outrage that made it clear he fully *intended* to cause bedlam and leave bloody tumult in his wake. He stopped in front of a raven-haired girl of twenty, whose slender arms were raised above her head in one of those rapturous expressions of the joy that rhythmic movement and primitive driving music could sometimes bring to a dancer even without the assistance of drugs. He loomed over her for a moment, studying her, as if taken with her beauty. Then he grabbed one of her arms in both his monstrous hands, wrenched with shocking violence, and tore it out of her shoulder socket. A low, wet laugh escaped him as he threw the arm behind him, where it hung in the air between two other dancers.

The mutilation was as bloodless as if he had merely disconnected the arm of a mannequin, but of course blood would not begin to flow until time itself flowed again. Then the madness of the act and its consequences would be all too apparent.

Connie squeezed her eyes shut, unable to watch what he might do next. As a homicide cop, she had seen countless acts of mindless barbarity – or the consequences of them – and she had collected stacks of newspaper stories about crimes of positively fiendish brutality, and she had seen the damage this particular psychotic bastard had done to poor Ricky Estefan, but the fierce savagery of the act he committed on the dance floor rocked her as nothing had before.

The *utter* helplessness of this young victim might have been the difference that knocked the wind out of Connie and left her shaking not from any inner or outer chill but with icy horror. All victims were helpless to one degree or another; that was why they became targets for the savages among them. But this pretty young woman's helplessness was of an infinitely more terrible nature, for she had never seen her assailant coming, would never see him go or know his identity, would be stricken as suddenly as any innocent field mouse pierced by the razor claws of a swooping hawk which it had never seen diving from on high. Even after she had been maimed, she remained unaware of the attack, frozen in the last moment of pure happiness and worry-free existence that she might ever know, a laugh still painted on her face though she had been forever crippled and perhaps condemned to death, not even permitted to know her loss or to feel the pain or to scream until her attacker had returned to her the ability to feel and react.

Connie knew that, to this monstrous enemy, she was as shockingly vulnerable as the young dancer below. Helpless. No matter how fast she could run, regardless of the cleverness of her strategies, no defense would be adequate and no hiding place secure.

Although she had never been particularly religious, she suddenly understood how a devout fundamentalist Christian might tremble at the thought that Satan could be loosed from Hell to stalk the world and wreak Armageddon. His awesome power. His relentlessness. His hard, gleeful, merciless brutality.

Greasy nausea slithered in her guts, and she was afraid she might throw up.

Beside her, the softest hiss of apprehension escaped Harry, and Connie opened her eyes. She was determined to meet her death face to face with all the resistance she could muster, useless as resistance might be.

On the floor of the warehouse below, the golem-vagrant reached the foot of the same set of stairs up which she and Harry had climbed to the loft. He hesitated there, as if considering whether to turn and walk away, search elsewhere.

Connie dared to hope that their continued silence, in spite of every provocation to cry out, had encouraged Ticktock to believe that they could not possibly be hiding anywhere in the rave.

Then he spoke in that rough demonic voice. 'Fee, fie, fo, fum,' he said, starting up the stairs, 'I smell the blood of hero cops.'

His laugh was as cold and inhuman as any sound that might issue from a crocodile – yet contained an eerily recognizable quality of childlike delight.

Arrested development.

A psychotic child.

She remembered Harry telling her that the burning vagrant, in the process of destroying the condominium, had said, *You people are so much fun to play with*. This was his private game, played by his rules, or without rules at all if he wished, and she and Harry were nothing but his toys. She had been foolish to hope that he would keep his promise.

The crash of each of his heavy footsteps reverberated across the wood treads and up through the entire structure. The floor of the loft shook from his ascent. He was climbing fast: BOOM, BOOM, BOOM, BOOM!

Harry grabbed her by the arm. 'Quick, the other stairs!'

They turned away from the railing and toward the

opposite end of the loft from where the golem was ascending.

At the head of the second set of stairs stood a second golem identical to the first. Huge. Mane of tangled hair. Wild beard. Raincoat like a black cape. He was grinning broadly. Blue flames flickering brightly in deep sockets.

Now they knew one more thing about the extent of Ticktock's power. He could create and control at least two artificial bodies at the same time.

The first golem reached the top of the stairs to their right. He started toward them, ruthlessly kicking a path through the tangled lovers on the floor.

To their left, the second golem approached with no greater respect for the Paused people in his way. When the world started up again, cries of injury and outrage would arise from end to end of the wide loft.

Still gripping Connie's arm, pulling her back against the railing, Harry whispered, '*Jump!*'

BOOM-BOOM-BOOM-BOOM-BOOM the thud of the twin golems' footsteps shook the loft, and BOOM-BOOM-BOOM-BOOM the pounding of her heart shook Connie, and the two sounds became indistinguishable from one another.

Following Harry's example, she put her hands behind her on the railing, pushed up to sit on the handrail.

The golems kicked more viciously at the human obstacles between them and their prey, closing in faster from both sides.

She lifted her legs and swung around to face the warehouse. At least a twenty-foot drop to the floor.

411

Far enough to break a leg, crack open her skull? Probably.

Each of the golems was less than twenty feet away, coming toward her with all the irresistible force of freight trains, gas-flame eyes burning as hot as any fires in Hell, reaching for her with massive hands.

Harry jumped.

With a cry of resignation, Connie pushed with her feet against the balusters and her hands against the handrail, launching herself into the void—

—and fell only six or seven feet before coasting to a full stop in mid-air, beside Harry. She was facing straight down, legs and arms spread in an unconscious imitation of the classic skydiving position, and below her were the frozen dancers, all of them as oblivious of her as they were of everything else beyond the instant when they had been spellbound.

The deepening chill in her bones and the rapid depletion of her energy as they fled through Laguna Beach had indicated that she was not making her way through the Paused world as easily as it seemed, certainly not as easily as she moved through the normal world. The fact that they did not create their own wind when they ran, which Harry also noticed, seemed to support the idea that resistance to their motion was present even if they were not conscious of it, and now the arrested fall proved it. As long as they exerted themselves, they could keep moving, but they could not rely on momentum or even the pull of gravity to carry them far when exertion ceased.

Looking over her shoulder, Connie saw that she had

managed to launch herself outward only five feet from
the loft railing, though she had shoved away from it with
all her might. However, combined with a five- or six-foot
vertical drop, she had gone far enough to be beyond the
reach of the golems.

They stood at the loft railing, leaning out, reaching
down, grasping for her but coming up only with handsful
of empty air.

Harry shouted at her: 'You can move if you try!'

She saw that he was using his arms and legs somewhat
in the manner of a swimmer doing a breaststroke,
angled toward the floor, pulling himself downward by
agonizing inches, as if the air wasn't air at all but some
curious form of extremely dense water.

She quickly realized she was unfortunately not weightless like an astronaut in orbit aboard the space shuttle,
and enjoyed none of the motive advantages of a
gravity-free environment. A brief experiment proved
she couldn't propel herself with an astronaut's ease or
change direction on a whim.

When she imitated Harry, however, Connie found
that she *could* pull herself down through the gluey air
if she was methodical and determined. For a moment it
seemed even better than skydiving because the period
of the dive when you had the illusion of flying like a bird
was at comparatively high altitudes; and with features
on the ground rapidly enlarging, the illusion was never
fully convincing. Here, on the other hand, she was right
over the heads of other people and airborne within a
building, which even under the circumstances gave her
an exhilarating sense of power and buoyancy, rather like

one of those blissful dreams of flying that too seldom informed her sleep.

Connie actually might have enjoyed the bizarre experience if Ticktock had not been present in the form of the two golems and if she had not been fleeing for her life. She heard the BOOM-BOOM-BOOM-BOOM of their heavy hurried footsteps on the wooden loft, and when she looked back over her shoulder and up, she saw they were headed for opposite sets of stairs.

She was still ten or eleven feet from the warehouse floor and 'swimming' downward at an infuriatingly slow speed, inch by grinding inch through the colorful fixed beams of the spotlights and party lasers. Gasping for breath from the exertion. Getting rapidly colder now, colder.

If there had been something solid for her to push against, such as a nearby wall or roof-supporting column, she'd have been able to achieve greater propulsion. But there was nothing besides the air itself off which to launch – almost like trying to lift herself entirely by her own bootstraps.

To her left, Harry was about a foot ahead of her but making no better time than she was. He was farther along only because he had started sooner.

Kick. Pull the arms. Struggle.

Her sense of freedom and buoyancy swiftly gave way to a feeling of being trapped.

BOOM-BOOM-BOOM-BOOM-BOOM, the footfalls of their pursuers echoed flatly through the huge chamber.

She was perhaps nine feet off the floor, moving

toward a clear space among the dancers. Kick. Pull. Kick and pull. Keep moving, moving. So cold.

She glanced over her shoulder again, even though she was afraid that the act of doing so would slow her down.

At least one of the golems had reached the head of one set of stairs. He descended the steps two at a time. In his cloaklike raincoat, shoulders hunched, burly head lowered, leaping down in the rollicking manner of an ape, he reminded her of an illustration in a long-forgotten storybook, a picture of an evil troll from some medieval legend.

Struggling so fiercely that her heart felt as if it might explode, she drew herself within eight feet of the floor. But she was angled head-first; she would have to pull herself laboriously all the way to the concrete, which would provide the first solid surface against which she could regain her equilibrium and scramble to her feet.

BOOM-BOOM-BOOM-BOOM.

The golem reached the bottom of the stairs.

Connie was exhausted. Freezing.

She heard Harry cursing the cold and the resisting air.

The pleasant dream of flying had become the most classic of all nightmares, in which the dreamer could flee only in slow motion, while the monster pursued with terrifying speed and agility.

Concentrating on the floor below, seven feet from it now, Connie nevertheless saw movement from the corner of her left eye and heard Harry cry out. A golem had reached him.

A darker shadow fell across the shadow-layered floor directly below her. Reluctantly, she turned her head to the right.

Suspended in mid-air, with her feet above and behind her, like an angel swooping down to do battle with a demon, she found herself face to face with the other golem. Regrettably, unlike an angel, she was not armed with a fiery sword, a bolt of lightning, or an amulet blessed by God and capable of knocking demons back into the fires and boiling tar of the Pit.

Grinning, Ticktock gripped her throat. The golem's hand was so enormous that the thick fingers overlapped the fat thumb where they met at the back of her head, completely encircling her neck, though it did not immediately crush her windpipe and cut off her breath.

She remembered how Ricky Estefan's head had been turned backward on his shoulders, and how the raven-haired dancer's slender arm had been ripped so effortlessly from her body.

A flash of rage burned away her terror, and she spat in the huge and terrible face. 'Let go of me, shithead.'

A foul exhalation washed over her, making her grimace, and the scar-faced golem-vagrant said, 'Congratulations, bitch. Time's up.'

The blue-flame eyes burned brighter for an instant, then winked out, leaving deep black sockets beyond which it seemed that Connie could see to the end of eternity. The vagrant's hideous face, writ large on this oversize golem, was abruptly transformed from flesh and hair into a highly detailed monochromatic brown countenance that appeared to have been sculpted from clay or mud. An elaborate web of hairline cracks formed from the bridge of his nose, swiftly spinning in a spiral pattern across his face, and in a wink his features crumbled.

The giant vagrant's entire body dissolved, and with a shattering detonation of techno music that resumed full-blast in mid-note, the world started up again. No longer suspended in the air, Connie fell the last seven feet to the warehouse floor, face-first into the moist mound of dirt and sand and grass and rotting leaves and bugs that had been the golem's body, cushioned from injury by the now-lifeless mass but gagging and spitting in disgust.

Around her, even above the pounding music, she heard screams of shock, terror, and pain.

·5·

'Game's over – for now,' the golem-vagrant said, then obligingly dissolved. Harry dropped out of the air. He sprawled on his stomach in the remains, which smelled strongly of nothing more than rich damp earth.

In front of his face was a hand formed entirely of dirt, similar to – but larger than – the one they had seen in Ricky's bungalow. Two fingers twitched with a residue of supernatural energy and seemed to reach toward his nose. He slammed one fist into that disembodied monstrosity, pulverizing it.

Screaming dancers stumbled into him and collapsed

across his back and legs. He scrambled out from under the falling bodies, onto his feet.

An angry boy in a Batman T-shirt rushed forward and took a swing at him. Harry ducked, threw a right into the kid's stomach, planted a left uppercut under his chin, stepped over him when he fell, and looked around for Connie.

She was nearby, dropping a tough-looking teenage girl with a karate kick, and then swiveling on one foot to drive her elbow into the solar plexus of a muscle-bound youth who looked surprised as he went down. He obviously thought he was going to polish his shoes with her and throw her away.

If she felt as rotten as Harry did, she might not be able to hold her own. His joints still ached with the cold that had seeped into them during the Pause, and he felt tired, as if he had carried a great weight on a journey of many miles.

Joining up with her, screaming to be heard above the music and other noise, Harry said, 'We're too old for this crap! Come on, let's get out of here!'

For the most part, on every side, the dancing had given way to fighting, or at least to vigorous pushing and shoving, thanks to the tricks Ticktock had played earlier on his way through the Paused crowd. However, not all of the partiers seemed to understand that the rave had devolved into a dangerous brawl, because some of the pushers and shovers were laughing as if they believed they had merely been caught up in a boisterous, relatively good-natured slam dance.

Harry and Connie were too far from the front of the

building to make it out that way before an understanding of the true nature of the situation swept the crowd. Though there was nothing as immediately threatening as a fire, the tendency of a panicked crowd would be to react to the violence as if flames had been seen. Some of them would even believe they *had* seen fire.

Harry grabbed Connie's hand to keep them from being separated in the turmoil, and led her toward the nearer rear wall, where he was sure there would have to be other doors.

In that chaotic atmosphere, it was easy to understand why the revelers would confuse real violence for make-believe, even if they hadn't been on drugs. Spotlights swung back and forth and swooped across the metal ceiling, intensely colored laser beams slashed complex patterns across the room, strobes flashed, phantasmagoric shadows leaped-twisted-twirled through the energetic crowd, young faces were strange and mysterious behind ever-changing carnival masks of reflected light, psychedelic film images pulsed and writhed over two big walls, the disc jockey pumped up the volume on the manic music, and the crowd noise alone was loud enough to be disorienting. The senses were overloaded and apt to mistake a glimpse of violent confrontation for an exhibition of high good spirits or something even more benign.

Far behind Harry a scream rose unlike any of the others, so shrill and hysterical that it pierced the background roar and called attention to itself even in that cacophony. No more than a minute had passed since the Pause had ended, if that long. Harry figured the new screamer was either the black-haired girl coming out of shock and discovering that her shoulder ended in a gory stump – or the person who had suddenly found himself confronted by the grisly detached arm.

Even if that heart-stopping wail didn't draw attention, the crowd would not party on in ignorance much longer. There was nothing like a punch in the face to dislodge fantasy and snap reality into place. When the change in the mood penetrated to a majority of the ravers, the rush to the exits would be potentially deadly, even though there was no fire.

A sense of duty and a policeman's conscience encouraged Harry to turn back, find the girl who had lost an arm, and try to administer first-aid. But he knew that he would probably not be able to find her in the churning throng, and that he wouldn't have a chance to help even if he did manage to locate her, not in that growing human maelstrom, which already seemed to have reached the equivalent of hurricane force.

Holding tight to Connie's hand, Harry pushed out of the dancers and through the now-clamorous onlookers with their bottles of beer and balloons of nitrous oxide, all the way to the back wall of the warehouse, which was deep under the loft. Beyond the reach of the party lights. Darkest place in the building.

He looked left, right. Couldn't see a door.

That wasn't surprising, considering a rave was essentially an illegal drug party staged in a deserted warehouse, not a chaperoned prom in a hotel ballroom where there would be well-lighted red exit signs. But, Jesus, it would be so pointless and stupid to survive the

Pause and the golems, only to be trampled to death by hundreds of doped-up kids frantically trying to squeeze through a doorway all at once.

Harry decided to go right, for no better reason than that he had to go one way or the other. Unconscious kids were lying on the floor, recovering from long hits of laughing gas. Harry tried not to step on anyone, but the light under the loft was so poor that he didn't see some of those in darker clothes until he'd stumbled over them.

A door. He almost passed by without spotting it.

In the warehouse behind him, the music continued to thump as ever, but a sudden change occurred in the quality of the crowd noise. It became a less celebratory roar, darkened into an uglier rumble shot through with panicky shrieks.

Connie was gripping Harry's hand so tightly, she was grinding his knuckles together.

In the gloom Harry pushed against the door. Pushed with his shoulders. Wouldn't budge. No. Must be an outside door. Pull inward. But that didn't work either.

The crowd broke toward the outer walls. A wave of screaming swelled, and Harry could actually feel the heat and terror of the oncoming mob that was surging even toward the back wall. They were probably too disoriented to remember where the main entrances were.

He fumbled for the door handle, knob, push-bar, whatever, and prayed it wasn't locked. He found a vertical handle with a thumb latch, pressed down, felt something click.

The first of the escaping crowd rammed into them

from behind, Connie cried out, Harry shoved back at them, trying to keep them out of the way so he could pull the door open – *please God don't let it be a restroom or closet we'll be crushed smothered* – kept his thumb down hard on the latch, the door popped, he pulled it inward, shouting at the crowd behind him to wait, wait, for God's sake, and then the door was torn out of his grasp and slammed all the way open, and he and Connie were carried outside into the cool night air by the desperate tide of people behind them.

More than a dozen ravers were in a parking area, gathered around the back of a white Ford van. The van was draped with two sets of green and red Christmas-tree lights, which operated off its battery and provided the only illumination in the deep night between the back of the building and the scrub-covered canyon wall. One long-haired man was filling balloons from a pressure tank of nitrous oxide that was strapped to a handtruck behind the van, and a totally bald guy was collecting five-dollar bills. All of them, both merchants and customers, looked up in amazement as screaming and shouting people erupted through the back door of the warehouse.

Harry and Connie separated, by-passing everyone behind the van. She went around to the passenger-side door, and Harry went to the driver's side.

He jerked open the door and started to climb in behind the steering wheel.

The guy with the shaved head grabbed his arm, stopped him and pulled him out. 'Hey, man, what do you think you're doing?'

As he was being dragged backward out of the van, Harry reached under his coat and drew his revolver. Turning, he jammed the muzzle against his adversary's lips. 'You want me to blow your teeth out the back of your head?'

The bald man's eyes went wide, and he backed up fast, raising both hands to show he was harmless. 'No, hey, no, man, cool it, take the van, she's yours, have fun, enjoy.'

Distasteful as Connie's methods might be, Harry had to admit there was a certain time-saving efficiency when you handled problems her way.

He climbed behind the steering wheel again, pulled the door shut, and holstered his revolver.

Connie was already in the passenger seat.

The keys were in the ignition, and the engine was running to keep the battery charged up for the Christmas lights. Christmas lights, for God's sake. Festive bunch, these NO dealers.

He released the handbrake, switched on the headlights, threw the van in gear, and tramped hard on the accelerator. For a moment the tires spun and smoked, squealing like angry pigs on the blacktop, and all the ravers scattered. Then the rubber bit in, the van shot toward the back corner of the warehouse, and Harry hammered the horn to keep people out of his way.

'The road out of here's going to jam tight in two minutes,' Connie said, bracing herself against the dashboard as they rounded the corner of the warehouse not quite on two wheels.

'Yeah,' he said, 'everyone trying to get away before the cops show up.'

'Cops are such party poopers.'

'Such numbnuts.'

'Never any fun.'

'Prudes.'

They rocketed down the wide driveway alongside the warehouse, where there was no exit door and therefore no panicked people to worry about. The van handled well, real power and a good suspension. He supposed it had been modified for quick escapes when the police showed up.

Out in front of the warehouse, the situation was different, and he had to use the brake and the horn, weaving wildly to avoid fleeing partiers. More people had escaped the building more quickly than he had imagined possible.

'Promoters were smart enough to roll up one of the big truck doors to let people out,' Connie said, turning in her seat to look out the side window as they went past the place.

'Surprised it even works,' Harry said. 'God knows how long the place has stood empty.'

With the pressure inside so quickly relieved, the death toll – if there was one – would be substantially smaller.

Hanging a hard left into the street, Harry clipped a parked car with the rear bumper of the van but kept going, blowing the horn at the few ravers who had made it that far and were running down the middle of the street like terrified people in one of those Godzilla movies fleeing from the giant thunderlizard.

Connie said, 'You pulled your gun on that bald guy.'

'Yeah.'

'I hear you tell him you'd blow his head off?'

'Something like that.'

'Didn't show him your badge?'

'Figured he'd have respect for a gun, none at all for a badge.'

She said, 'I could get to like you, Harry Lyon.'

'No future in it – unless we get past dawn.'

In seconds they were past all of the partiers who had left the warehouse on foot, and Harry tramped the accelerator all the way to the floor. They shot by the nursery, body shops, and recreational-vehicle storage lot that they had passed on the way in, and were soon beyond the partiers' parked cars.

He wanted to be long gone from the area when the Laguna Beach Police arrived, which they would – and soon. Being caught in the aftermath of the rave débâcle would tie them up too long, maybe just long enough so they would lose their one and only chance at getting the drop on Ticktock.

'Where're you going?' Connie asked.

'The Green House.'

'Yeah. Maybe Sammy's still there.'

'Sammy?'

'The bum. That was his name.'

'Oh, yeah. And the talking dog.'

'Talking dog?' she said.

'Well, maybe he doesn't talk, but he's got something to tell us we need to know, that's for damn sure, and maybe he *does* talk, what the hell, who knows any more, it's a crazy world, a crazy damn night. There are talking animals in fairy tales, why not a talking dog in Laguna Beach?'

Harry realized he was babbling, but he was driving so fast and recklessly that he didn't want to take his eyes off the road even to glance at Connie and see if she was giving him a skeptical look.

She didn't sound worried about his sanity when she said, 'What's the plan?'

'I think we've got a narrow window of opportunity.'

'Because he has to rest now and then. Like he told you on the car radio.'

'Yeah. Especially after something like this. So far there's always been an hour or more between his . . . appearances.'

'Manifestations.'

'Whatever.'

After a few turns they were back in residential neighborhoods, working through Laguna toward the Pacific Coast Highway.

A police car and an ambulance, emergency beacons flashing, shot past them on a cross street, almost certainly answering a call to the warehouse.

'Fast response,' Connie said.

'Someone with a car phone must have dialled 911.'

Maybe help would arrive in time to save the girl who had lost an arm. Maybe the arm could even be saved, sewn back on. Yeah, and maybe Mother Goose was real.

Harry had been buoyant because they had escaped

the Pause and the rave. But his adrenaline high faded swiftly as he recalled, too vividly, how savagely the golem had torn off the young woman's slender arm.

Despair crept back in at the edges of his thoughts.

'If there's a window of opportunity while he rests or even sleeps,' Connie said, 'how can we possibly find him fast enough?'

'Not with one of Nancy Quan's portraits, that's for sure. No time for that approach any more.'

She said, 'I think next time he manifests, he'll kill us, no more playing around.'

'I think so too.'

'Or at least kill me. Then you the time after that.'

'By dawn. That's one promise our little boy will keep.'

They were both silent for a moment, somber.

'So where does that leave us?' she asked.

'Maybe the bum in front of the Green House— '

'Sammy.'

'—maybe he knows something that will help us. Or if not . . . then . . . hell, I don't know. It looks hopeless, doesn't it?'

'No,' she said sharply. 'Nothing's hopeless. Where there's life, there's hope. Where there's hope, it's always worth trying, worth going on.'

He wheeled around another corner from one street full of dark houses to another, straightened out the van, let up on the accelerator a little, and looked at her in astonishment. 'Nothing's hopeless? What's happened to you?'

She shook her head. 'I don't know. It's still happening.'

·6·

Although they had spent at least half of the hour-long Pause on the run before they had wound up in the warehouse at the end of that canyon, they didn't need nearly as long to get back to where they had started from. According to Connie's wristwatch, they reached the coast highway less than five minutes after commandeering the nitrous-oxide dealers' wheels, partly because they took a more direct return route and partly because Harry drove fast enough to scare even her.

In fact, when they slid to a stop in front of the Green House, with some still-unbroken Christmas lights clinking noisily along the sides of the van, the time was just thirty-five seconds past 1:37 in the morning. That was little more than eight minutes since the Pause had both begun and ended at 1:29, which meant they had taken about three minutes to fight their way out of the crowded warehouse and seize their transportation at gunpoint – though it sure had seemed a lot longer.

The tow truck and the Volvo, which had been frozen in the southbound lane, were gone. When time had started up again, their drivers had continued on with no realization that anything unusual had happened. Other traffic was moving north and south.

Connie was relieved to see Sammy standing on the sidewalk in front of the Green House. He was gesticulating wildly, arguing with the permed host in the Armani suit and hand-painted silk tie. One of the waiters was standing in the doorway, apparently prepared to help the boss if the confrontation got physical.

When Connie and Harry got out of the van, the host saw them and turned away from Sammy. 'You!' he said. 'My God, it's you!' He came toward them purposefully, almost angrily, as if they had left without paying their check.

Bar patrons and other employees were at the windows, watching. Connie recognized some of them as the people who had been watching her and Harry with Sammy and the dog, and who had been frozen there, staring fixedly, after the Pause hit. They were no longer as rigid as stone, but they were still watching with fascination.

'What's going on here?' the host asked as he approached, an edge of hysteria in his voice. 'How did that happen, where did you go? What is this . . . this . . . this van!'

Connie had to remind herself that the man had seen them vanish in what seemed to him a split second. The dog had yelped and nipped the air and plunged for the shrubbery, alerting them that something was happening, which had spooked Sammy into sprinting for the alley. But Connie and Harry had remained on the sidewalk in full view of the people at the restaurant windows, the Pause had hit, they had been forced to run for their lives, then the Pause had ended without them where they originally had been on the sidewalk, and to the onlookers it had seemed as if two people had vanished into thin air. Only to turn up eight minutes later in a white van decorated with strings of red and green Christmas lights.

The host's exasperation and curiosity were understandable.

If their window of opportunity for finding and dealing with Ticktock had not been so small, if the ticking seconds had not been leading them inexorably closer to sudden death, the uproar in front of the restaurant might even have been funny. Hell, it *was* funny, but that didn't mean she and Harry could take the time to laugh at it. Maybe later. If they lived.

'What is this, what happened here, what's going on?' the host demanded. 'I can't make heads or tails out of what your raving lunatic over there is telling me.'

By 'raving lunatic,' he meant Sammy.

'He's not our raving lunatic,' Harry said.

'Yes he is,' Connie reminded Harry, 'and you better go talk to him. I'll handle this.'

She was half afraid that Harry – as painfully aware of their time limit as she was – might pull his revolver on the host and threaten to blow his teeth out the back of his head if he didn't shut up and get inside. As much as she approved of Harry taking a more aggressive approach to certain problems, there was a proper time and place for aggression, and this was not it.

Harry went off to talk with Sammy.

Connie put one arm around the host's shoulders and escorted him up the walkway to the front door of his restaurant, speaking in a soft but authoritative voice, informing him that she and Detective Lyon were in the middle of important and urgent police business, and sincerely assuring him that she would return to explain everything, even what might seem to him inexplicable, 'just as soon as the ongoing situation is resolved.'

Considering that it was traditionally Harry's job to calm and placate people, her job to upset them, she had a lot of success with the restaurateur. She had no intention of ever returning to explain anything whatsoever to him, and she had no idea how he thought she could explain people vanishing into thin air. But he calmed down, and she persuaded him to go inside his restaurant with the bodyguard-waiter who was standing in the doorway.

She checked the shrubbery but confirmed what she already knew: the dog was not hiding there any more. He was gone.

She joined Harry and Sammy on the sidewalk in time to hear the hobo say, 'How should I know where he lives? He's an alien, he's a long way from his planet, he must have a spaceship hidden around here somewhere.'

More patiently than Connie expected, Harry said, 'Forget that stuff, he's no alien. He— '

A dog barked, startling them.

Connie spun around and saw the flop-eared mutt. He was uphill, just turning the corner at the south end of the block. Following him were a woman and a boy of about five.

As soon as the dog saw that he had gotten their attention, he snatched hold of one cuff of the boy's jeans, and with his teeth impatiently pulled him along. After a couple of steps he let go, ran toward Connie,

431

stopped halfway between his people and hers, barked at her, barked at the woman and boy, barked at Connie again, then just sat there looking left and right and left again, as if to say, *Well, haven't I done enough?*

The woman and the boy appeared to be curious but frightened. The mother was attractive in a way, and the child was cute, neatly and cleanly dressed, but they both had the wary and haunted look of people who knew the streets too well.

Connie approached them slowly, with a smile. When she passed the dog, he got off his butt and padded along at her side, panting and grinning.

There was a quality of mystery and awe about the moment, and Connie knew that whatever connection they were about to make was going to mean life or death to her and Harry, maybe to all of them.

She had no idea what she was going to say to them until she was close enough to speak: 'Have you had . . . *also* had . . . a strange experience lately?'

The woman blinked at her in surprise. 'Strange experience? Oh, yes. Oh my, yes.'

Part Three

A SCARY LITTLE COTTAGE IN THE WOODS

Faraway in China,
the people sometimes say,
life is often bitter
and all too seldom gay.
Bitter as dragon tears,
great cascades of sorrow
flood down all the years,
drowning our tomorrows.

Faraway in China,
the people also say,
life is sometimes joyous
if all too often gray.
Although life is seasoned
with bitter dragon tears,
seasoning is just a spice
within our brew of years.
Bad times are only rice,
tears are one more flavor,
that gives us sustenance,
something we can savor.

—The Book of Counted Sorrows

SIX

·1·

Now they know.

He is a good dog, good dog, good.

They are all together now. The woman and the boy, the stinky man, the not-so-stinky man, and the woman without a boy. All of them smelling of the touch of the thing-that-will-kill-you, which is why he knew they had to be together.

They know it too. They know why they are together. They stand in front of the people food place, talking to each other, talking fast, all excited, sometimes all talking at once, while the women and the boy and the not-so-stinky man are always sure to keep the stinky man up-wind from them.

They keep stooping down to pet him and scratch behind his ears and tell him he's a good dog, good, and they say other nice things about him that he can't really understand. This is the best. It is so good to be petted and scratched and liked by people who will, he is pretty sure, not set his fur on fire, and by people who do not have any cat smell on them, none.

Once, long after the little girl who called him Prince,

there were some people who took him into their place and fed him and were nice to him, called him Max, but they had a cat. Big cat. Mean. The cat was called Fluffy. Max was nice to Fluffy. Max never once chased Fluffy. In those days Max never chased cats. Well, hardly ever. Some cats, he liked. But Fluffy did not like Max and did not want Max in the people place, so sometimes Fluffy stole Max's food, and other times Fluffy peed in Max's water bowl. During the day when the nice people were gone from their place to some other place, Max and Fluffy were left alone, and Fluffy would screech, all crazy and spitting, and scare Max and chase him around the place. Or jump off high things onto Max. Big cat. Screeching. Spitting. Crazy. So Max understood that it was Fluffy's place, not Max's and Fluffy's place, just Fluffy's, so he went away from the nice people and was just Fella again.

Ever since, he worries that when he finds nice people who want to take him into their place and feed him forever, they will have cat smell on them, and when he goes to their place with them and walks in the door with them, there will be Fluffy. Big. Mean. Crazy.

So now it is nice that *none* of these people has any cat smell, because if one of them wants to be a family with him, he will be safe, and he won't have to worry about pee in his water bowl.

After a while, they are so excited talking to each other that they aren't petting him so much and saying how good he is, so he gets bored. Yawns. Lies down. Might sleep. He is tired. Busy day, being a good dog.

But then he sees the people in the food place, looking out the windows of the food place. Interesting. At the windows, looking out. Looking at him.

Maybe they think he is cute.

Maybe they want to give him food.

Why *wouldn't* they want to give him food?

So he gets up and pads to the food place. Head high. Prance a little. Wag the tail. They like that.

At the door, he waits. Nobody opens it. He puts one paw on it. Waits. Nobody. He scratches. Nobody.

He goes out where the people at the window can see him. He wags his tail. He tilts his head, pricks up one ear. They see him. He knows they see him.

He goes to the door again. Waits. Waits.

Waits.

Scratches. Nobody.

Maybe they don't know he wants food. Or maybe they're scared of him, think he's a bad dog. He doesn't look like a bad dog. How could they be scared? Don't they know when to be scared, when not? He would never jump off high places on top of them or pee in their water bowls. Stupid people. Stupid.

Finally he decides he's not going to get any food, so he goes back to the nice people he brought together. On his way he keeps his head up, prances, wags his tail, just to show the people at the window what they're missing.

When he gets back to the women and the boy and the stinky man and the not-so-stinky man, something is wrong. He can feel it and smell it.

They are scared. This is not new. They have all been

scared since he first smelled each of them. But this is a different scared. Worse scared.

And they have a little trace of the just-lie-down-and-die smell. Animals get that smell sometimes, when they're old, when they're very tired and sick. People, not so often. Though he knows a place where people have that smell. He was there earlier in the night with the woman and the boy.

Interesting.

But bad interesting.

He is worried that these nice people have even a little bit of the just-lie-down-and-die smell. What is wrong with them? Not sick. Maybe the stinky man, sick a little, but not the rest of them. Not old either.

Their voices are different too. A little excited, not so much as before. Tired, a little. Sad, a little. Something else . . . What? Something. What? What?

He sniffs around their feet, one at a time, sniffs sniffs sniffs sniffs, even the stinky man, and suddenly he knows what's wrong with them, and he can't believe it, can't.

He is amazed. Amazed. He backs away, looks at them, amazed.

All of them have the special smell that says do-I-chase-it-or-does-it-chase-me?-do-I-run-or-do-I-fight?-am-I-hungry-enough-to-dig-something-out-of-its-hole-and-eat-it-or-should-I-wait-and-see-if-people-will-give-me-something-good? It is the smell of not knowing what to do, which is sometimes a different kind of fear smell. Like now. They are afraid of the thing-that-will-kill-you, but they are also afraid because they don't know what to do next.

He is amazed because *he* knows what to do next, and he is not even a people. But sometimes they can be so slow, people.

All right. He will show them what to do next.

He barks, and of course they all look at him because he's not a dog that barks much.

He barks again, then runs past them, downhill, runs, runs, and then stops and looks back and barks again.

They stare at him. He is amazed.

He runs back to them, barks, turns, runs downhill again, runs, runs, stops, looks back, barks again.

They're talking. Looking at him and talking. Like maybe they get it.

So he runs a little farther, turns, looks back, barks.

They're excited. They get it. Amazing.

·2·

They did not know how far the dog was going to lead them, and they were agreed that the five of them would be too conspicuous on foot, as a group, at almost two o'clock in the morning. They decided to see if Woofer would be as eager to run ahead and lead the van as he was to lead them on foot, because in the vehicle they would be considerably less of a spectacle.

Janet helped Detective Gulliver and Detective Lyon quickly take the Christmas-tree lights off the van. They were attached with metal clips in some places and with pieces of masking tape in others.

It seemed doubtful that the dog was going to lead

them directly to the person they were calling Ticktock. Just in case, however, it made a lot of sense not to draw attention to themselves with strings of red and green lights.

While they worked, Sammy Shamroe followed them around the Ford, telling them, not for the first time, that he had been a fool and a fallen man, but that he was going to turn over a new leaf after this. It seemed important to him that they believe he was sincere in making a commitment to a new life – as if he needed other people to believe it before he would be convinced himself.

'I never really thought I had anything the world really needed,' Sammy said, 'thought I was pretty much worthless, just a hype artist, smooth talker, empty inside, but now here I am saving the world from an alien. Okay, not an alien, actually, and not saving the world all by myself, but *helping* to save it damn sure enough.'

Janet was still astonished by what Woofer had done. No one was quite sure how he knew that the five of them were living under the same bizarre threat or that it would be useful for them to be brought together. Everyone knew that animals' senses were in some respects weaker than those of human beings but in many respects stronger, and that beyond the usual five senses they might have others that were difficult to understand. But after *this*, she would never look at another dog – or any animal, for that matter – in quite the same way that she had regarded them before.

Taking the dog into their lives and feeding him when

she could least afford it had turned out to be perhaps the smartest thing she had ever done.

She and the two detectives finished removing the lights, rolled them up, and put them in the back of the van.

'I've quit drinking for good,' Sammy said, following them to the rear door. 'Can you believe it? But it's true. No more. Not one drop. Nada.'

Woofer was sitting on the sidewalk with Danny, in the fall of light under a street lamp, watching them, waiting patiently.

Initially, when she learned that Ms Gulliver and Mr Lyon were police detectives, Janet had almost grabbed Danny and run. After all, she had left a dead husband, killed by her own hand, mouldering under desert sands in Arizona, and she had no way of knowing if the hateful man was still where she had left him. If Vince's body had been found, she might be wanted for questioning; there might even be a warrant for her arrest.

More to the point, no authority figure in her life had been a friend to her, with the possible exception of Mr Ishigura at Pacific View Care Home. She thought of them as a different breed, people with whom she had nothing in common.

But Ms Gulliver and Mr Lyon seemed reliable and kind and well-meaning. She did not think they were the type of people who would let Danny be taken away from her, though she had no intention of telling them she'd killed Vince. And Janet certainly did have things in common with them – not least of all, the will to live and the desire to get Ticktock before he got them.

She had decided to trust the detectives largely because she had no choice; they were all in this together. But she also decided to trust them because the dog trusted them.

'It's five minutes till two,' Detective Lyon said, checking his wristwatch. 'Let's get moving, for God's sake.'

Janet called Danny to her, and he got into the back of the van with her and Sammy Shamroe, who pulled the rear door shut after them.

Detective Lyon climbed into the driver's seat, started the engine, and switched on the headlights.

The rear of the van was open to the front compartment. Janet, Danny, and Sammy crowded forward to look over the front seat and through the windshield.

Serpentine tendrils of thin fog were beginning to slither across the coast highway from the ocean. The headlights of an oncoming car, the only other traffic in sight, caught the lazily drifting mist at just the right angle and created a horizontal ribbon of rainbowlike colors that began at the right-hand curb and ended at the left-hand curb. The car drove through the colors, carrying them off into the night.

Detective Gulliver was still standing out on the sidewalk with Woofer.

Detective Lyon released the handbrake and put the van in gear. Raising his voice slightly, he said, 'Okay, we're ready.'

On the sidewalk, Detective Gulliver could hear him because the van's side window was open. She talked to the dog, made a shooing motion with her hands, and the dog studied her quizzically.

Realizing that they were asking him to lead them

where he had wanted to lead them just a couple of minutes ago, Woofer took off downhill, north along the sidewalk. He ran about one third of a block, stopped, and looked back to see if Detective Gulliver was following. He seemed pleased to discover that she was staying with him. He wagged his tail.

Detective Lyon took his foot off the brake and let the van drift downhill, close behind Detective Gulliver, keeping pace with her, so the dog would get the idea that the vehicle was also following him.

Though the van was not moving fast, Janet gripped the seat behind Detective Lyon's head to steady herself, and Sammy clutched the headrest behind the empty passenger seat. With one hand, Danny held fast to Janet's belt, and stood on his tiptoes to try to see what was happening outside.

When Detective Gulliver had almost caught up with Woofer, the dog took off again, sprinted to the end of the block and stopped at the intersection to look back. He watched the woman approaching him, then studied the van for a moment, then the woman, then the van. He was a smart dog; he would get it.

'Wish he'd just talk to us and tell us what we need to know,' Detective Lyon said.

'Who?' Sammy asked.

'The dog.'

After Detective Gulliver followed Woofer across the intersection and halfway along the next block, she stopped and let Detective Lyon catch up to her. She waited until Woofer was looking at her, then opened the passenger door and got into the van.

The dog sat down and stared at them.

Detective Lyon let the van drift forward a little.

The dog pricked up his ears lopsidedly.

The van drifted.

The dog got up and trotted farther north. He stopped, looked back to be sure the van was still coming, then trotted farther.

'Good dog,' Detective Gulliver said.

'Very good dog,' Detective Lyon said.

Danny said proudly, 'He's the best dog there is.'

'I'll second that,' said Sammy Shamroe, and rubbed one hand on the boy's head.

Turning his face into Janet's side, Danny said, 'Mama, the man really stinks.'

'Danny!' Janet said, appalled.

'It's okay,' Sammy said. He was inspired to launch into another of his earnest but rambling assurances of repentance. 'It's true. I stink. I'm a mess. Been a mess for a long time, but that's over now. You know one reason I was a mess? Because I thought I knew everything, thought I understood exactly what life was about, that it was meaningless, that there was no mystery to it, just biology. But after this, after tonight, I have a different view on things. I don't know everything, after all. It's true. Hell, I don't know diddly-squat! There's *plenty* of mystery in life, something more than biology for sure. And if there's something more, who needs wine or cocaine or anything? Nope. Nothing. Not a drop. Nada.'

One block later, the dog turned right, heading east along a steeply rising street.

Detective Lyon turned the corner after Woofer, then glanced at his wristwatch. 'Two o'clock. Damn, time's just going too fast.'

Outside, Woofer rarely turned his head to glance at them any more. He was confident that they would stay with him.

The sidewalk along which he padded was littered with bristly red blooms from the large bottle-brush trees that lined the entire block. Woofer sniffed at them as he proceeded east, and they made him sneeze a couple of times.

Suddenly Janet thought she knew where the dog was taking them. 'Mr Ishigura's nursing home,' she said.

Detective Gulliver turned in the front seat to look at her. 'You know where he's going?'

'We were there for dinner. In the kitchen.' And then: 'My God, the poor blind woman with no eyes!'

Pacific View Care Home was in the next block. The dog climbed the steps and sat at the front door.

·3·

After visiting hours, no receptionist was on duty. Harry could look through the glass in the top of the door and see the dimly lighted and totally deserted public lounge.

When he rang the bell, a woman's voice responded through the intercom. He identified himself as a police officer on urgent business, and she sounded concerned and eager to cooperate.

He checked his wristwatch three times before she appeared in the lounge. She didn't take an extraordinarily long time; he was just remembering Ricky Estefan and the girl who had lost an arm at the rave, and each second blinked off by the red indicator light on his watch was part of the countdown to his own execution.

The nurse, who identified herself as the night supervisor, was a no-nonsense Filipino lady, petite but not in the least fragile, and when she saw him through the portal in the door, she was less sanguine than she had been over the intercom. She would not open up to him.

First of all, she didn't believe he was a police officer. He couldn't blame her for being suspicious, considering that after all he had been through during the past twelve or fourteen hours, he looked as if he lived in a packing crate. Well, actually, Sammy Shamroe lived in a packing crate, and Harry didn't look quite *that* bad, but he certainly looked like a flophouse dweller with a long-term moral debt to the Salvation Army.

She would only open the door the width of the industrial-quality security chain, so heavy it was surely the model used to restrict access to nuclear-missile silos. At her demand, he passed through his police ID wallet. Although it included a photograph that was sufficiently unflattering to resemble him in his current battered and filthy condition, she was unconvinced that he was an officer of the law.

Wrinkling her cute nose, the night supervisor said, 'What else have you got?'

He was sorely tempted to draw his revolver, shove

it through the gap, cock the hammer, and threaten to blow her teeth out through the back of her head. But she was in her middle to late thirties, and it was possible that she had grown up under – and been toughened by – the Marcos regime before emigrating to the US, so she might just laugh in his face, stick her finger in the barrel, and tell him to go to hell.

Instead, he produced Connie Gulliver, who was for once a more presentable police officer than he was. She grinned through the door glass at the pint-sized Gestapo Florence Nightingale, made nice talk, and passed her own credentials through the gap on demand. You would have thought they were trying to get into the main vault at Fort Knox instead of a pricey private nursing home.

He checked his watch. It was 2:03 A.M.

Based on the limited experience they'd had with Ticktock, Harry guessed that their psychotic Houdini required as little as an hour but more commonly an hour and a half of rest between performances, recharging his supernatural batteries in about the same amount of time that a stage magician needed to stuff all the silk scarves and doves and rabbits back up his sleeves to get ready for the late show. If that was the case, then they were safe at least until two-thirty and probably until three o'clock.

Less than an hour at the outside.

Harry was so intently focused on the blinking red light of his watch that he lost track of what Connie said to the nurse. Either she charmed the lady or came up with an incredibly effective threat, because the security chain was removed, the door was opened, their ID wallets were returned to them with smiles, and they were welcomed into Pacific View.

When the night supervisor saw Janet and Danny, who had been out of sight on the lower front steps, she had second thoughts. When she saw the dog, she had third thoughts, even though he was wagging his tail and grinning and, quite clearly, being intentionally cute. When she saw – and smelled – Sammy, she almost became intractable again.

For policemen, as well as for house-to-house salesmen, the supreme difficulty was always getting through the door. Once inside, Harry and Connie were no easier to dislodge than the average vacuum-cleaner salesman intent on scattering all manner of sample filth on the carpet to demonstrate the superior suction of his product.

When it became clear to the Filipino nurse that resistance to them was going to disturb the home's patients more than would cooperation, she spoke a few musical words in Tagalog, which Harry assumed was a curse on their ancestors and progeny, and led them through the facility to the room of the patient they sought.

Not surprisingly, in all of Pacific View's accommodations, there was only one eyeless woman with lids sewn shut over empty sockets. Her name was Jennifer Drackman.

Mrs Drackman's handsome but 'distant' son – they were told in whispered confidence while in transit – paid for three shifts of the finest private nurses, seven days a week, to care for his 'mentally disoriented' mother.

She was the only patient in Pacific View provided with such 'suffocating' ministrations on top of the already 'extravagant' care that the facility offered in its minimum package. With those and a number of other loaded words, the night supervisor made it clear, ever so politely, that she didn't care for the son, felt the private nurses were unnecessary and an insult to the staff, and thought the patient was creepy.

The private nurse on the graveyard shift was an exotically beautiful black woman named Tanya Delaney. She was not sure of the propriety and wisdom of letting them disturb her patient at such an ungodly hour, even if some of them were police officers, and briefly she threatened to be even more of a barrier to their survival than the night supervisor had been.

The gaunt, mealy, bony woman in the bed was a ghastly sight, but Harry could not look away from her. She compelled attention because within the horror of her current condition there was a tragically faint but undeniable ghost of the beauty that had once been, a specter that haunted the ravaged face and body and, by refusing to relinquish entire possession of her, allowed a chilling comparison between what she most likely had been in her youth and what she had become.

'She's been sleeping.' Tanya Delaney spoke in a whisper, as they all did. She stood between them and the bed, making it clear that she took nursing seriously. 'She doesn't sleep peacefully very often, so I wouldn't like to wake her.'

Beyond the piled pillows and the patient's face,

on a nightstand that also held a cork-bottom tray with a chrome carafe of ice-water, stood a simple black-lacquered picture frame with a photograph of a good-looking young man of about twenty. An aquiline nose. Thick dark hair. His pale eyes were gray in the black-and-white photo and were surely gray in reality, the precise shade of slightly tarnished silver. It was the boy in blue jeans and a Tecate T-shirt, the boy licking his lips with a pink tongue at the sight of James Ordegard's blood-soaked victims. Harry remembered the hateful glare in the boy's eyes after he'd been forced back behind the yellow crime-scene tape and humiliated in front of the crowd.

'It's him,' Harry said softly, wonderingly.

Tanya Delaney followed his gaze. 'Bryan. Mrs Drackman's son.'

Turning to meet Connie's eyes, Harry said, 'It's him.'

'Doesn't look like the ratman,' Sammy said. He had moved to the corner of the room farthest from the patient, perhaps remembering that the blind supposedly compensated for their loss of sight by developing better hearing and a sharper sense of smell.

The dog mewled once, briefly, quietly.

Janet Marco pulled her sleepy boy tighter against her side and stared worriedly at the photograph. 'Looks a little like Vince . . . the hair . . . the eyes. No wonder I thought Vince was coming back.'

Harry wondered who Vince was, decided it wasn't a priority, and said to Connie, 'If her son really does pay all of her bills— '

'Oh, yes, it's the son,' said Nurse Delaney. 'He takes such good care of his mother.'

'—then the business office here will have an address for him,' Connie finished.

Harry shook his head. 'That night supervisor won't let us look at the records, no way. She'll guard them with her life until we come back with a warrant.'

Nurse Delaney said, 'I really think you should go before you wake her.'

'I'm not asleep,' said the white scarecrow in the bed. Her permanently shut eyelids didn't even twitch, lay slack, as if the muscles in them had atrophied over the years. 'And I don't want his photo here. He forces me to keep it.'

Harry said, 'Mrs Drackman— '

'Miss. They call me Mrs but I'm not. Never was.' Her voice was thin but not frail. Brittle. Cold. 'What do you want with him?'

'Miss Drackman,' Harry continued, 'we're police officers. We need to ask you some questions about your son.'

If they had the opportunity to learn more than Ticktock's address, Harry believed they should seize it. The mother might tell them something that would reveal some vulnerability in her exceptional offspring, even if she had no idea of his true nature.

She was silent a moment, chewing on her lip. Her mouth was pinched, her lips so bloodless they were almost gray.

Harry looked at his watch.

2:08.

451

The wasted woman raised one arm and hooked her hand, as lean and fierce-looking as a talon, around the bed rail. 'Tanya, would you leave us alone?'

When the nurse began to voice a mild objection, the patient repeated the request more sharply, as a command.

As soon as the nurse had gone, closing the door behind her, Jennifer Drackman said, 'How many of you are there?'

'Five,' Connie said, failing to mention the dog.

'You aren't all police officers, and you aren't here just on police business,' Jennifer Drackman said with perspicacity that might have been a gift she'd been given to compensate for the long years of blindness.

Something in her tone of voice, a curious hopefulness, induced Harry to answer her truthfully. 'No. We're not all cops, and we're not here just as cops.'

'What has he done to you?' the woman asked.

He had done so much that no one could think how to put it into words succinctly.

Interpreting the silence correctly, the woman said, 'Do you know what he is?' It was an extraordinary question, and revealed that the mother was aware, at least to some degree, of the son's difference.

'Yes,' Harry said. 'We know.'

'Everyone thinks he's such a nice boy,' the mother said, her voice tremulous. 'They won't listen. The stupid fools. They won't listen. All these years . . . they won't believe.'

'We'll listen,' Harry said. 'And we already believe.'

A look of hope flickered across the ravaged face, but

hope was an expression so unfamiliar to those features that it could not be sustained. She raised her head off the pillows, a simple act that made the cords go taut with strain under the sagging skin of her neck. 'Do you hate him?'

After a moment of silence, Connie said, 'Yes. I hate him.'

'Yes,' Janet Marco said.

'I hate him almost as much as I hate myself,' the invalid said. Her voice was now as bitter as bile. For a moment the ghost of beauty past was no longer visible in her withered face. She was sheer ugliness, a grotesque hag. 'Will you kill him?'

Harry was not sure what to say.

Bryan Drackman's mother was at no such loss for words: 'I'd kill him myself, kill him . . . but I'm so weak . . . so weak. Will you kill him?'

'Yes,' Harry said.

'It won't be easy,' she warned.

'No, it won't be easy,' he agreed. He glanced at his watch again. 'And we don't have much time.'

·4·

Bryan Drackman slept.

His was a deep, satisfying sleep. Replenishing.

He dreamed of power. He was a conduit for lightning. Though it was daylight in the dream, the heavens were almost night-dark, churning with the black clouds of Final Judgment. From that storm to end all storms, great surging rivers of electric current flowed into him, and from his hands, when he willed them, flashed lances and balls of lightning. He was Becoming. When that process was someday concluded, he would *be* the storm, a great destroyer and cleanser, washing away what had been, bathing the world in blood, and in the eyes of those who were permitted to survive, he would see respect, adoration, love, love.

·5·

Through the eyeless night came blind hands of fog, seeking. White vaporous fingers pressed inquisitively against the windows of Jennifer Drackman's room.

Lamplight glimmered in the cold beads of sweat on the water carafe, and burnished the stainless steel.

Connie stood with Harry at the side of the bed. Janet sat in the nurse's chair, holding her sleeping boy on her lap, the dog lying at her feet with its head upon its paws. Sammy stood in the corner, wrapped in shadows, silent and solemn, perhaps recognizing a few elements of his own story in the one to which they listened.

The withered woman in the bed appeared to shrivel further while she spoke, as though she needed to burn her very substance for the requisite energy to share her dark memories.

Harry had the feeling that she'd held fast to life all these years only for this moment, for an audience that would not merely listen patronizingly but would believe.

In that voice of dust and corrosion, she said, 'He's only twenty years old. I was twenty-two when I became pregnant with him . . . but I should begin . . . a few years before his . . . conception.'

Simple calculation revealed she was now only forty-two or forty-three. Harry heard small startled sounds and nervous fidgeting from Connie and the others as the awareness of Jennifer's relative youth swept through them. She looked more than merely old. Ancient. Not prematurely aged by ten or even twenty years, but by *forty*.

As thickening cataracts of fog formed over the night windows, the mother of Ticktock spoke of running away from home when she was sixteen, sick to death of school, childishly eager for excitement and experience, physically mature beyond her years since she'd been thirteen but, as she would later realize, emotionally underdeveloped and not half as smart as she thought she was.

In Los Angeles and later in San Francisco, during the height of the free-love culture of the late '60s and early '70s, a beautiful girl had a choice of like-minded young men with whom to crash and an almost infinite variety of mind-altering chemicals with which to experiment. After several jobs in head shops, selling psychedelic posters and lava lamps and drug paraphernalia, she went for the main chance and started selling drugs themselves. As a dealer and a woman who was romanced by suppliers for both her sales ability and her good looks, she had the opportunity to sample a lot of exotic substances that were never widely distributed on the street.

'Hallucinogens were my main thing,' said the lost girl still wandering somewhere within the ancient woman on the bed. 'Dehydrated mushrooms from Tibetan caves, luminescent fungus from remote valleys of Peru, liquids distilled from cactus flowers and strange roots, the powdered skin of exotic African lizards, eye of newt, and anything that clever chemists could concoct in laboratories. I wanted to try it all, much of it over and over, anything that would take me places I'd never been, show me things that no one else might ever see.'

In spite of the depths of despair into which that life had led her, a frigorific wistfulness informed Jennifer Drackman's voice, an eerie longing.

Harry sensed that a part of Jennifer would want to make all the same choices if given a chance to live those years again.

He had never entirely rid himself of the chill that had seeped into him during the Pause, and now coldness spread deeper into the marrow of his bones.

He checked his watch. 2:12.

She continued, speaking more quickly, as if aware of his impatience. 'In 1972, I got myself knocked up . . .'

Not sure which of three men might be the father, nevertheless she had at first been delighted by the prospect of a baby. Although she could not coherently have defined what the relentless ingestion of so many mind-altering chemicals had taught her, she felt that she had a great store of wisdom to impart to her offspring. It was then one small step of illogic to decide that continued – even increased – use of hallucinogens during pregnancy would result in the birth of a child of heightened consciousness. Those were strange days when many believed that the meaning of life was to be found in peyote and that a tab of LSD could provide access to the throne room of Heaven and a glimpse of the face of God.

For the first two to three months of her term, Jennifer had been aglow with the prospect of nurturing the perfect child. Perhaps he would be another Dylan, Lennon or Lenin, a genius and peacemaker, but more advanced than any of them because his enlightenment had begun in the womb, thanks to the foresight and daring of his mother.

Then everything had changed with one bad trip. She could not recall all of the ingredients of the chemical cocktail that marked the beginning of the end of her life, but she knew that among other things it had contained LSD and the powdered carapace of a rare Asian beetle. In what she had believed to be the highest state of consciousness that she had ever achieved, a series of luminous and uplifting hallucinations had suddenly turned terrifying, filling her with a nameless but crippling dread.

Even when the bad trip ended and the hallucinations of death and genetic horrors had passed, the dread remained with her – and grew day by day. She did not at first understand the source of her fear, but gradually she focused on the child within and came to understand that in her altered state of mind she had been sent a warning: her baby was no Dylan, but a monster, not a light unto the world but a bringer of darkness.

Whether that perception was in fact correct or merely

drug-induced madness, whether the child inside her was already a mutant or still a perfectly normal fetus, she would never know, for as a result of her overwhelming fear, she set out upon a course of action that in itself might have introduced the final mutagenic factor which, enhanced by her pharmacopeia of drugs, made Bryan what he was. She sought an abortion, but not from the usual sources, for she was afraid of midwives with their coathangers and of back-alley doctors whose alcoholism had driven them to operate beyond the law. Instead, she resorted to strikingly untraditional and, in the end, riskier methods.

'That was in '72.' She clutched the bed rail and squirmed under the sheets to pull her half-paralyzed and wasted body into a more comfortable position. Her white hair was wire-stiff.

The light caught her face from a slightly new angle, revealing to Harry that the milk-white skin over her empty eye sockets was embroidered with a network of thread-fine blue veins.

His watch. 2:16.

She said, 'The supreme court didn't legalize abortion until early '73, when I was in the last month of my term, so it wasn't available to me until it was too late.'

In fact, had abortion been legal, she still might not have gone to a clinic, for she feared and distrusted all doctors. She first tried to rid herself of the unwanted child with the help of a mystic Indian homeopathic practitioner who operated out of an apartment in Haight-Ashbury, the center of the counter-culture in San Francisco at that time. He had first given her a series of herb potions known to affect the walls of the uterus and sometimes cause miscarriages. When those medications did not work, he tried a series of potent herbal douches, administered with increasing pressure, to flush the child away.

When those treatments failed as well, she turned in desperation to a quack offering a briefly popular radium douche, supposedly not radioactive enough to harm the woman but deadly to the fetus. That more radical approach was equally unsuccessful.

It seemed to her as if the unwanted child was consciously aware of her efforts to be free of it and was clinging to life with inhuman tenacity, a hateful thing already stronger than any ordinary unborn mortal, invulnerable even in the womb.

2:18.

Harry was impatient. She had told them nothing, thus far, that would help them deal with Ticktock. 'Where can we find your son?'

Jennifer probably felt she would never have another audience like this one, and she was not going to tailor her story to their schedule, regardless of the cost. Clearly, in the telling there was some form of expiation for her.

Harry could barely stand the sound of the woman's voice, and could no longer tolerate the sight of her face. He left Connie by the bed and went to the window to stare out at the fog, which looked cool and clean.

'Life became, like, really a bad trip for me,' Jennifer said.

Harry found it disorienting to hear this pinched and haggard ancient use such dated slang.

She said her fear of the unborn was worse than anything she had experienced on drugs. Her certainty that she harbored a monster only increased daily. She needed sleep but dreaded it because her sleep was troubled by dreams of shocking violence, human suffering in infinite variety, and something unseen but terrible moving always in shadows.

'One day they found me in the street, screaming, clawing at my stomach, raving about a beast inside of me. They put me in a psychiatric ward.'

From there she had been brought to Orange County, under the care of her mother, whom she'd deserted six years earlier. Physical examinations had revealed a scarred uterus, strange adhesions and polyps, and wildly abnormal blood chemistry.

Although no abnormalities were detectable in the unborn child, Jennifer remained convinced that it was a monster, and became more hysterical by the day, the hour. No secular or religious counseling could calm her fears.

Hospitalized for a closely monitored delivery that was necessitated by the things she had done to be rid of the child, Jennifer had slipped beyond hysteria, into madness. She experienced drug flashbacks rife with visions of organic monstrosities, and developed the irrational conviction that if she merely looked upon the child she was bringing into the world, she would be at once damned to Hell. Her labor was unusually difficult and protracted, and due to her mental condition, she was restrained through most of it. But when her restraints were briefly loosened for her comfort, even as the stubborn child was coming forth, she gouged out her eyes with her own thumbs.

At the window, staring into the faces that formed and dissolved in the fog, Harry shuddered.

'And he was born,' Jennifer Drackman said. 'He was born.'

Even eyeless, she knew the dark nature of the creature to which she had given birth. But he was a beautiful baby, and then a lovely boy (so they told her), and then a handsome young man. Year after year no one would take seriously the paranoid ravings of a woman who had put out her own eyes.

Harry checked his watch. 2:21.

At most they had forty minutes of safe time remaining. Perhaps substantially less.

'There were so many surgeries, complications from the pregnancy, my eyes, infections. My health went steadily downhill, a couple of strokes, and I never returned home with my mother. Which was good. Because *he* was there. I lived in a public nursing home for a lot of years, wanting to die, praying to die, but too weak to kill myself . . . too weak in many ways. Then, two years ago, after he killed my mother, he moved me here.'

'How do you know he killed your mother?' Connie asked.

'He told me so. And he told me how. He describes his power to me, how it grows and grows. He's even shown me things . . . And I believe he can do everything he says. Do you?'

'Yes,' Connie said.

'Where does he live?' Harry asked, still facing the fog.

'In my mother's house.'

'What's the address?'

'My mind's not clear on a lot of things . . . but I remember that.'

She gave them the address.

Harry thought he knew approximately where the place was. Not far from Pacific View.

He checked his watch yet again. 2:23.

Eager to get out of that room, and not merely because they urgently needed to deal with Bryan Drackman, Harry turned away from the window. 'Let's go.'

Sammy Shamroe stepped out of the shadow-hung corner. Janet rose from the nurse's chair, holding her sleeping child, and the dog got to his feet.

But Connie had a question. It was the kind of personal question Harry ordinarily would have asked and that until tonight would have made Connie scowl with impatience because they had already learned the essentials.

'Why does Bryan keep coming here to see you?' Connie inquired.

'To torture me in one way or another,' the woman said.

'That's all – when he has a world full of people to torture?'

Letting her hand slide off the bed rail, which she had

been grasping all this time, Jennifer Drackman said, 'Love.'

'He comes because he loves you?'

'No, no. Not him. He's incapable of love, doesn't understand the word, only thinks he does. But he wants love from me.' A dry, humorless laugh escaped the skeletal figure in the bed. 'Can you believe he comes to *me* for this?'

Harry was surprised that he could feel a grudging pity for the psychotic child who had entered the world, unwanted, from this disturbed woman.

That room, though warm and comfortable enough, was the last place in creation to which anyone should go in search of love.

·6·

Fog poured off the Pacific and embraced the night coast, dense and deep and cool. It flowed through the sleeping town, like the ghost of an ancient ocean with a high-tide line far above that of the modern sea.

Harry drove south along the coast highway, faster than seemed wise in that limited visibility. He had decided that the risk of a rear-end collision was outweighed by the danger of getting to the Drackman house too late to catch Ticktock before he had recovered his energy.

The palms of his hands were damp on the steering wheel, as if the fog had condensed on his skin. But there was no fog inside the van.

2:27.

Almost an hour had passed since Ticktock had gone away to rest. On the one hand, they had accomplished a lot in that brief time. On the other hand, it seemed that time was not a river, like the song said, but a crashing avalanche of minutes.

In the back, Janet and Sammy rode in uneasy silence. The boy slept. The dog seemed restless.

In the passenger seat, Connie switched on the small overhead map-reading lamp. She cracked open the cylinder of her revolver to be sure there was a round in every chamber.

That was the second time she had checked.

Harry knew what she must be thinking: What if Ticktock had awakened; had stopped time since she had last checked her weapon; had removed all the cartridges; and when she had the chance to shoot him, what if he only smiled while the hammer fell on empty chambers?

As before, in the revolver, a full complement of case heads gleamed. All chambers loaded.

Connie snapped the cylinder shut. Clicked off the light.

Harry thought she looked extremely tired. Face drawn. Eyes watery, bloodshot. He worried that they were going to have to stalk the most dangerous criminal of their careers at a time when they were exhausted. He knew *he* was far off his usual form. Perceptions dulled, reactions slow.

'Who goes into his house?' Sammy asked.

'Harry and me,' Connie said. 'We're the professionals. It's the only thing that makes sense.'

'And us?' Janet asked.

'Wait in the van.'

'Feel like I should help,' Sammy said.

'Don't even think about it,' Connie said sharply.

'How will you get in?'

Harry said, 'My partner here carries a set of lock picks.'

Connie patted one jacket pocket to be sure the folding packet of burglary tools was still there.

'What if he's not sleeping?' Janet asked.

Checking the names on the street signs as he drove, Harry said, 'He will be.'

'But what if he's not?'

'He *has* to be,' Harry replied, which pretty much said all that could be said about how frighteningly limited their options were.

2:29. Damn. Time stopped, now going too fast.

The name of the street was Phaedra Way. Letters on the Laguna Beach street signs were too small, hard to read. Especially in the fog. He leaned over the wheel, squinting.

'How can he be killed?' Sammy asked worriedly. 'I don't see how the ratman can be killed, not him.'

'Well, we can't just risk wounding him, that's for damned sure,' Connie said. 'He might be able to heal himself.'

Phaedra Way. Phaedra. Come on, come on.

'But if he's got healing power,' Harry said, 'it comes from the same place all his other power comes from.'

'His mind,' Janet said.

Phaedra, Phaedra, Phaedra . . .

Letting the van slow because he was sure they were in the area where Ticktock's street ought to be, Harry said, 'Yeah. Will power. Mind power. Psychic ability is the power of the mind, and the mind is seated in the brain.'

'Headshot,' Connie said.

Harry agreed. 'At close range.'

Connie looked grim. 'It's the only way. No jury trial for this bastard. Damage the brain instantly, kill him instantly, and he doesn't have a chance to strike back.'

Remembering how the golem-vagrant had hurled fireballs around his condo bedroom and how instantly white-hot flames erupted from the things he torched, Harry said, 'Yeah. For sure, before he has a chance to strike back. Hey! There. Phaedra Way.'

The address they had gotten from Jennifer Drackman was less than two miles from Pacific View Care Home. They located the street at 2:31, slightly more than one hour after the Pause had begun and ended.

It was actually more of a long driveway than a short street, serving only five homes with ocean views, though now the Pacific was lost in fog. Because, from spring through autumn, the entire coastal area was crawling with tourists seeking parking spaces near beaches, a sign was posted at the entrance, sternly announcing PRIVATE – VIOLATORS WILL BE TOWED, but no security gate restricted access.

Harry didn't make the turn. Because the street was so short and because the van would be loud enough to wake the sleeping and draw attention at that dead hour of the morning, he drove past the turnoff and coasted to a stop two hundred feet farther along the highway.

* * *

Everything better, everyone together, so maybe they can all be a family and want a dog to feed and all live in a people place, warm and dry – and then suddenly everything wrong, wrong.

Deathcoming. The woman who has no boy. The not-so-stinky man. Sitting up front in the van, and deathcoming all around them.

He smells it on them, yet it is not an odor. He sees it on them, yet they look no different. It makes no sound, yet he hears it when he listens to them. If he licked their hands, their faces, deathcoming would have no taste of its own, yet he would know it was on them. If they petted or scratched him, he would feel it in their touch, deathcoming. It is one of those few things he senses without really knowing how he knows. Deathcoming.

He is shaking. He cannot stop shaking.

Deathcoming.

Bad. Very bad. The worst.

He must do something. But what? What what what what?

He doesn't know when the deathcoming will be or where it will be or how it will be. He doesn't know whether deathcoming will be to both of them or only to one of them. It could be only to one of them, and he senses it on both of them only because it will happen when they are together. He cannot sense

467

this thing as clearly as he can sense the countless odors of the stinky man or the fear on all of them, because it is not really something to be smelled or tasted so much as just felt, a coldness, a dark, a deepness. Deathcoming.

So . . .

Do something.

So . . .

Do something.

What what what?

* * *

When Harry switched off the engine and doused the headlights, the silence seemed almost as deep as it had been during the Pause.

The dog was agitated, sniffing and whining. If he began to bark, the walls of the van would muffle the sound. Besides, Harry was confident that they were too far from the Drackman house for Ticktock to be disturbed by any sound the dog could make.

Sammy said, 'How long before we should figure . . . you know . . . you didn't get him, he got you? Sorry, but I had to ask. When should we run?'

'If he gets us, you won't have a chance to run,' Connie said.

Harry turned to look at them in the shadowy rear compartment. 'Yeah. He's going to wonder how the hell we found him, and after he kills us, there'll be another Pause, immediately, while he checks out all of you, everything, trying to figure it out. If he gets us, you'll know it, because just a few seconds later in real time, one of his golems will probably appear right here in the van with you.'

Sammy blinked owlishly. He wetted his cracked lips with his tongue. 'Then, for God's sake, be sure you kill him.'

Harry opened his door quietly, while Connie left the van on her side. When he stepped out, the dog slipped between the front seats and followed him before he realized what was happening.

He made a grab at the mutt as it brushed past his legs, but he missed.

'Woofer, no!' he whispered.

Ignoring him, the dog padded to the back of the van.

Harry went after him.

The dog broke into a sprint, and Harry ran several steps in pursuit, but the dog was faster and vanished into the heavy fog, heading north along the highway in the general direction of the turnoff to the Drackman house.

Harry was cursing under his breath when Connie joined him.

'He can't be going there,' she whispered.

'Why can't he?'

'Jesus. If he does anything to alert Ticktock . . .'

Harry checked his watch. 2:34.

Maybe they had twenty, twenty-five minutes. Or maybe they were already too late.

He decided they couldn't worry about the dog.

'Remember,' he said, 'headshot. Quick and up close. It's the only way.'

When they reached the entrance to Phaedra Way, he glanced back toward the van. It had been swallowed by the fog.

SEVEN

·1·

He is not afraid. Not. Not afraid.

He is a dog, sharp teeth and claws, strong and quick.

Creeping, he passes thick, high oleander. Then the people place where he's been before. High white walls. Windows dark. Near the top, one square of pale light.

The smell of the thing-that-will-kill-you is heavy on the fog. But like all smells in fog, not as sharp, not as easy to track.

The iron fence. Tight. Wriggle. Through.

Careful at the corner of the people place. The bad thing was out there last time, behind the place, with bags of food. Chocolate. Marshmallow. Potato chips. Didn't get any. But almost got caught. So put just the nose past the corner this time. Sniff sniff sniff. Then the whole head for a look. No sign of the young-man-bad-thing. Was there, not now, safe so far.

Behind the people place. Grass, dirt, some flat stones that people put down. Bushes. Flowers.

The door. And in the door the little door for dogs.

Careful. Sniff. Young-man-bad-thing smell, very strong. Not afraid. Not, not, not, not. He is a dog. Good dog, good.

Careful. Head in, lifting the dog door. It makes a faint squeak. People food place. Dark. Dark.

Inside.

* * *

The softly fluorescent fog refracted every ray of ambient light on Phaedra Way, from the low mushroom-shaped Malibu lamps along the front walk at one house to the lighted numerals of the address on another, seeming to brighten the night. But, in fact, its slowly churning, amorphous luminosity was deceptive; it revealed nothing and obscured much.

Harry could see little of the houses past which they walked, except that they were large. The first of them was modern, sharp angles looming out of the fog in several places, but the others seemed to be older Mediterranean-style homes from a more graceful era of Laguna's history than the end of the millennium, sheltered by mature palms and ficuses.

Phaedra Way followed the shoreline of a small promontory that jutted out into the sea. According to the prematurely aged woman at Pacific View, the Drackman house was the farthest out, at the point of the bluff.

Considering how much of his ordeal had seemed to be based upon the darker elements of fairy tales, Harry would not have been at all surprised if they had found a small but preternaturally dark forest at the end of the

472

promontory, filled with lantern-eyed owls and slinking wolves, the Drackman house tucked therein, decidedly gloomy and brooding, in the finest tradition of the residences of witches, warlocks, sorcerers, trolls, and the like.

He almost hoped that was the kind of house he would find. It would be a comforting symbol of order.

But when they reached the Drackman place, only the eerie pall of fog upheld the tradition. In both its landscaping and architecture, it was less menacing than the scary little cottage in the woods for which folk and fairy tales had long prepared him.

Like the neighboring houses, it had palm trees in its shallow front yard. Even in the cloaking mist, masses of bougainvillea vines were visible climbing one white stucco wall and spreading onto the red tile roof. The driveway was littered with their bright blossoms. A nightlight to one side of the garage door illuminated the house number, its glow reflected in beads of dew on the hundreds of bright bougainvillea blossoms that glimmered like jewels on the driveway.

It was too pretty. He was irrationally angry at its prettiness. Nothing was as it ought to be any more, all hope of order gone.

They quickly checked the north and south sides of the house for signs of occupancy. Two lights.

One was upstairs on the south side, toward the back. A single window, not visible from the front. It might have been a bedroom.

If the light was on, Ticktock must have awakened from his nap, or had never gone to sleep. Unless . . .

some children wouldn't sleep without a light on, and in many ways Ticktock was a child. A twenty-year-old, insane, vicious, exceedingly dangerous child.

The second light was on the north side, first floor at the rear – or west – corner. Because it was at ground level, they were able to look inside and see a white-on-white kitchen. Deserted. One chair was turned half-away from the glass-topped table, as if someone had been sitting there earlier.

2:39.

Since both lights were toward the back of the house, they did not attempt to gain entrance on the west – or rear – side. If Ticktock was in the upstairs room with the light, awake or asleep, he would be more likely to hear even the furtive noises they would make if they were directly beneath him.

Because Connie had the set of picks, they didn't even try the windows, but went straight to the front door. It was a big oak slab with raised panels and a brass knocker.

The lock might have been a Baldwin, which was good but not a Schlage. In that gloom, it was difficult to tell the make.

Flanking the door were wide leaded-glass sidelights with beveled panes. Harry put his forehead against one to study the foyer beyond. He could see through the foyer and down a shadowy hallway because of light leaking through a partially open door at the end, which had to be the kitchen.

Connie opened the packet of lock picks. Before starting to work, she did what any good burglar did first – tried the door. It was unlocked, and she let it swing open a few inches.

She jammed the picks into one pocket without bothering to fold up the packet. From the shoulder holster under her corduroy jacket, she withdrew her revolver.

Harry pulled his weapon too.

When Connie hesitated, he realized that she had broken open the cylinder. She did a Braille check to be sure that cartridges still filled all the chambers. He heard a soft, soft *snick* as she closed it, evidently satisfied that Ticktock had not been playing any of his tricks.

She crossed the threshold first because she was nearer to it. He followed her.

They stood in the marble-floored foyer for twenty seconds, half a minute, very still, listening. Both hands on their guns, sights just below their lines of vision, Harry covering the left side, Connie covering everything on the right.

Silence.

The Hall of the Mountain King. Somewhere a sleeping troll. Or not sleeping. Maybe just waiting.

Foyer. Not much light, even with that second-hand fluorescent glow leaking down the hall from the kitchen. Mirrors to the left, dark images of themselves in the glass, shadowy forms. To the right was a doorway to either a closet or a den.

Ahead and to the right, a switchback staircase led to a landing, shrouded in shadows, then to an unseen second-floor hall.

Directly ahead, the first-floor hall. Archways and

dark rooms off both sides, the kitchen door at the end ajar maybe four or five inches with light beyond.

Harry hated this. He had done it scores of times. He was practiced and skilled. He still hated it.

Silence continuing. Only inner noise. He listened to his heart, not bad yet, fast but steady, not crashing yet, in control.

They were committed now, so he eased the front door shut behind them with no more noise than a padded coffin lid being lowered for the last time in the velvet-curtained hush of a funeral parlor.

* * *

Bryan woke from a fantasy of destruction, into a world that offered the satisfaction of real victims, real blood.

For a moment he lay naked on the black sheets, staring at the black ceiling. He was still dream-sodden enough to be able to imagine that he was adrift in the night, out over the lightless sea, beneath a starless sky, weightless, floating.

Levitation was not a power he possessed, nor was he particularly skilled at telekinesis. But he was sure that the ability to fly and to manipulate all matter in all imaginable ways would be his when he had fully Become.

Gradually he became aware of wrinkled folds of silk that were pressing uncomfortably against his back and buttocks, the coolness of the air, a sour taste in his mouth, and a hunger that made his stomach growl. Imagination was foiled. The Stygian sea became only ebony sheets, the starless sky became only a ceiling painted with black semigloss, and he had to admit that gravity still exerted a claim on him.

He sat up, swung his legs over the side of the bed, and stood. He yawned and stretched luxuriously, studying himself in the wall of mirrors. Someday, after he had thinned the human herd, there would be artists among those he spared, and they would be inspired to paint him, portraits infused with awe and reverence, like those that featured Biblical figures and hung now in the great museums of Europe, apocalyptic scenes on cathedral ceilings where he would be shown as a Titan dealing punishment to the wretched masses who died at his feet.

Turning from the mirrors, he faced the black-lacquered shelves on which stood the array of Mason jars. Because he had left one bedside lamp on while he slept, the votive eyes had watched him in his dreams of godhood. They watched him still, adoring.

He recalled the pleasure of blue eyes captured between the palms of his hands and his body, the smooth damp intimacy of their loving inspection.

His red robe lay at the foot of the shelves, where he had dropped it. He picked it up, slipped into it, cinched and knotted the belt.

All the while, he scanned the eyes, and none of them regarded him with scorn or rejected him.

Not for the first time, Bryan wished that his mother's eyes were part of his collection. If he possessed those eyes of all eyes, he would allow her communion with every convexity and concavity of his well-proportioned body, so she could understand the beauty of him, which she had never seen, and could know that her fears of hideous mutation had been foolish and that her sacrifice of vision had been so pointless, stupid.

If he had her eyes before him now, he would take one gently into his mouth and let it rest upon his tongue. Then he would swallow it whole, so she might see that his perfection was internal as well as external. Thus enlightened, she would lament her misguided act of self-mutilation the night of his birth, and it would be as if the intervening years of estrangement had never happened. The mother of the new god would then come willingly and supportively to his side, and his Becoming would be easier and would move more rapidly toward completion, toward his Ascension to the throne and the beginning of the Apocalypse.

But the hospital staff had disposed of her damaged eyes long ago, in whatever manner they dealt with all dead tissue from tainted blood to an excised appendix.

He sighed with regret.

* * *

Standing in the foyer, Harry tried not to look toward the light at the end of the hall where the kitchen door was ajar, so his eyes would adjust to the darkness quicker. It was time to move on. But they had choices to make.

Ordinarily he and Connie would conduct an interior search together, room by room, but not always. Good partners had a reliable and mutually understood routine for every basic situation, but they were also flexible.

478

Flexibility was essential because there were some situations that weren't basic. Like this one.

He didn't think it was a good idea to stay together because they were up against an adversary who had weapons better than guns or submachine guns or even explosives. Ordegard had almost taken out both of them with a grenade, but *this* scumbag could waste them with ball lightning that he shot off his fingertips or some other bit of magic they hadn't seen yet.

Welcome to the '90s.

If they stayed widely separated, say one of them searching the first floor while the other took the rooms upstairs, they would not only save time when time was at a premium, but they would double their chances of surprising the geek.

Harry moved to Connie, touched her shoulder, put his lips to her ear, and barely breathed the words: 'Me upstairs, you down.'

From the way she stiffened, he knew she didn't like the division of labor, and he understood why. They had already looked through the first floor window into the lighted kitchen and knew it was deserted. The only other light in the house was upstairs, so it was more likely than not that Ticktock was up in that other room. She wasn't worried that Harry would botch the job if he went up alone; it was just that she had a big enough hate-on for Ticktock that she wanted to have an equal chance to be the one who put the bullet in his head.

But there was no time for debate in these circumstances, and she knew it. They couldn't plan this one. They had to ride the wave. When he moved

479

across the foyer toward the stairs, she didn't stop him.

* * *

Bryan turned away from the votive eyes. He crossed the room toward the open door. His silk robe rustled softly as he moved.

He was always aware of the time, the second and minute and hour, so he knew dawn was still a few hours away. He needn't be in a rush to keep his promise to the bigshot hero cop, but he was eager to locate him and see to what depths of despair the man had plummeted after experiencing the stoppage of time, the world frozen for a game of hide and seek. The fool would know, now, that he was up against immeasurable power, and that escape was hopeless. His fear, and the awe with which he'd now regard his persecutor, would be enormously satisfying and worth relishing for a while.

First, however, Bryan had to satisfy his physical hunger. Sleep was only part of the restorative he needed. He knew that he had lost a few pounds during the most recent creative session. The use of his Greatest and Most Secret Power always took a toll. He was famished, in need of sweets and salties.

Stepping out of his bedroom, he turned right, away from the front of the house, and hurried along the hallway toward the back stairs that led directly down to the kitchen.

Enough light spilled from his open bedroom door to allow him to observe himself in motion both to his left and right, reflections of the young god Becoming, a spectacle of power and glory, striding purposefully to infinity in swirls of royal red, royal red, red upon red upon red.

* * *

Connie did not want to split off from Harry. She was worried about him.

In the old woman's room at the nursing home, he had looked like death warmed over and served on a paper plate. He was desperately tired, a walking mass of contusions and abrasions, and he had seen his world fall apart in little more than twelve hours, losing not merely possessions but cherished beliefs and much of his self-image.

Of course, aside from the part about lost possessions, much the same could be said of Connie. Which was another reason she did not want to separate to search the house. Neither of them had his usual sharp edge, yet considering the nature of this perp, they needed a greater advantage than usual, so they *had* to separate.

Reluctantly, as Harry moved toward the steps and then started up, Connie turned to the door on the right, off the foyer. It had a lever handle. She eased it down with her left hand, revolver in her right and in front of her. Faintest click of the latch. Ease the door inward and to the right.

Nothing for it but to cross the threshold, clearing the doorway as fast as possible, doorways always being the most dangerous, and slipping to the left as she entered, both hands on the gun in front of her, arms straight and locked. Keeping her back to the wall. Straining her eyes to see in the deep darkness, unable to find and use the light switch without giving away the game.

A surprising plenitude of windows in the north and east and west walls – *not so many windows on the exterior, were there?* – offered only minor relief from the darkness. Vaguely luminous fog pressed against the panes, like cloudy gray water, and she had the queer feeling of being under the sea in a bathysphere.

The room was wrong. Didn't feel right somehow. She didn't know what it was that she sensed, what wrongness, but it was there.

Something was also odd about the wall at her back when she brushed against it. Too smooth, cold.

She let go of the gun with her left hand, and felt behind her. Glass. The wall was glass but it wasn't a window because it was the wall shared with the foyer.

For a moment Connie was confused, thinking frantically because anything inexplicable was frightening under the circumstances. Then she realized it was a mirror. Her fingers slid across a vertical seam, onto another big sheet of glass. Mirrored. Floor to ceiling. Like the south wall of the foyer.

When she looked behind her, at the wall along which she had been slipping so stealthily, she saw reflections of the north-side windows and the fog beyond. No wonder there were more windows than there should have been. The windowless south and west walls were mirrored, so half the windows she saw were only reflections.

And she realized what bothered her about the room. Although she had kept on the move to the left, putting herself at changing angles to the windows, she hadn't seen silhouettes of any furniture between her and the grayish rectangles of glass. She hadn't bumped against any piece of furniture set with its back to the south wall either.

Both hands on the gun again, she eased toward the center of the room, wary of knocking something over and drawing attention. But inch by inch, cautious step by step, she became convinced there was nothing in her way.

The room was empty. Mirrored and empty.

As she neared the center, in spite of the unrelenting gloom, she was able to see a dim image of herself to her left. A phantom with her form, moving across the reflection of the fog-gray east-facing window.

Ticktock was not here.

* * *

A chaos of Harrys moved along the upstairs hall, gun-bearing clones in dirty rumpled suits, unshaven faces gray with stubble, tense and scowling. Hundreds, thousands, an uncountable army, they advanced abreast in a single slightly curved line, stretching forever to the left and right. In their mathematical symmetry and perfect choreography, they should have been the apotheosis of order. Even glimpsed with peripheral vision, however, they disoriented Harry, and he could not look directly either left or right without risking dizziness.

Both walls were mirrored floor to ceiling, as were all of the doors to the rooms, creating an illusion of infinity, bouncing his reflection back and forth, reflecting reflections of reflections of reflections.

Harry knew he should check room by room as he advanced, leaving no unexplored territory behind him, from which Ticktock might be able to move in on his back. But the sole light on the second floor was ahead, spilling out of the only open door, and chances were that the bastard who had murdered Ricky Estefan was in that lighted room and no other.

Although he was so tired that his cop instinct had deserted him, and simultaneously so jumped-up with adrenaline that he did not trust his reactions to be calm and measured, Harry decided to hell with traditional procedure, go with the flow, ride the wave, and let unexplored rooms at his back. He went directly to the doorway with the light beyond, on his right.

The mirrored wall opposite the open door would give him a look at part of the room before he had to step into the doorway and across the threshold, committing himself. He halted beside the door with his back to the mirrored wall, looking at an angle toward the wedge of the room's interior that was reflected across the hallway in another length of mirror.

All he could see was a confusion of black planes and angles, different black textures revealed by lamplight, black shapes against black backgrounds, all of it cubistic and strange. No other color. No Ticktock.

Suddenly he realized that, because he was seeing only part of the room, anyone standing in an unrevealed portion of it but looking toward the door might be at such an angle as to see *his* infinite reflections bouncing from wall to wall.

He stepped into the doorway and crossed the threshold, staying low and moving fast, his revolver held out in front of him with both hands. The hallway carpet did not continue into the bedroom. There was black ceramic tile on the floor instead, against which his shoes made noise, a click-scrape-click, and he froze within three steps, hoping to God he hadn't been heard.

* * *

Another dark room, much larger than the first, what should have been a living room, off the downstairs hall. More windows on the pearly luminescent fog and more reflections of windows.

Connie had a feel for that special oddness now, and wasted less time there than she had in the den off the foyer. The three walls without windows were mirrored, and there was no furniture.

Multiple reflections of her silhouette kept perfect time with her in the dark reflective surfaces, like ghosts, like other Connies in alternate universes briefly overlapping and barely visible.

Ticktock evidently liked to look at himself.

She would like to get a look at him too, but in the flesh.

Silently she returned to the downstairs hall and moved on.

* * *

The big walk-in pantry off the kitchen was filled with cookies, hard candies, taffy, chocolates of all kinds, caramels, red and black licorice, tins of sweet biscuits and exotic cakes imported from every corner of the world, bags of cheese popcorn, caramel popcorn, potato chips, tortilla chips, cheese-flavored tortilla chips, pretzels, cans of cashews, almonds, peanuts, mixed nuts, and millions of dollars in cash stacked in tight bundles of twenty- and hundred-dollar bills.

While he examined the sweets and salties, trying to make up his mind what he most wanted to eat, what would be the least like a meal of which Grandma Drackman would have approved, Bryan idly picked up a packet of hundred-dollar bills and riffled the crisp edges with one thumb.

He had acquired the cash immediately after he had killed his grandmother, stopping the world with his Greatest and Most Secret Power and wandering at his leisure into all the places where money was kept in large quantities and protected by steel doors and locked gates and alarm systems and armed guards. Taking whatever he wanted, he had laughed at the uniformed fools with all their guns and their somber expressions, who were oblivious of him.

Soon, however, he'd realized that he had little need of money. He could use his powers to take *anything*, not merely cash, and to alter sales and public records to create extensive legal support for his ownership if he were ever questioned. Besides, if ever he *were* questioned, he had only to eliminate those idiots who dared to be suspicious of him, and alter *their* records to ensure no further investigation.

He had stopped piling up cash in the pantry, but he still liked to riffle it under his thumb and listen to the crisp flutter, smell it, and play games with it sometimes. It felt so good to know that he was different from other people in this way, too: he was beyond money, beyond concerns related to things material. And it was fun to think that he could be the richest person in the world if he wanted, richer than Rockefellers and Kennedys, could pile up cash to fill room after room, cash and emeralds if he wanted emeralds, diamonds and rubies, anything, anything, like pirates of old in their lairs and surrounded by treasure.

He tossed the packet of currency back on the shelf from which he'd taken it. From the side of the pantry where he kept food, he took down two boxes of Reese's peanut-butter cups and a family-size bag of Hawaiian-style potato chips, which were a lot oilier than ordinary chips. Grandma Drackman would've had a stroke at the very *thought*.

* * *

Harry's heart knocked so hard and fast that his ears were filled with doubletime drumming that would probably drown out the sound of approaching footsteps.

In the black bedroom, on black shelves, scores of eyes floated in clear fluid, slightly luminous in the amber lamplight, and some were animal eyes, had to be because they were so strange, but others were human eyes, oh shit, no doubt at all about that, some brown and some black, blue, green, hazel. Unhooded by lids or lashes, they all looked scared, perpetually wide with fright. Crazily he wondered if, by looking closely enough, he would be able to see reflections of Ticktock in all the lenses of those dead eyes, the last sight each victim had seen in this world, but he knew that was impossible, and he had no desire to look that close anyway.

Keep moving. The insane sonofabitch was here. In the house. Somewhere. Charles Manson with psychic power, for God's sake.

Not in the bed, sheets tossed and rumpled, but somewhere.

Jeffrey Dahmer crossed with Superman, John Wayne Gayce with a sorcerer's spells and magics.

And if not in the bed, awake, oh Jesus, awake and therefore more formidable, harder to get close to.

Closet. Check it. Just clothes, not many, mostly jeans and red robes. Move, move.

The little creep was Ed Gein, Richard Ramirez, Randy Kraft, Richard Speck, Charles Whitman, Jack the Ripper, all the homicidal sociopaths of legend rolled into one and gifted with paranormal talents beyond measure.

The adjoining bathroom. Through the door, no light, find it, just mirrors, more mirrors on all walls *and* the ceiling.

Back in the black bedroom, heading toward the door, stepping as silently as possible on the black ceramic tiles, Harry didn't want to look again at the floating eyes but couldn't stop himself. When he glanced at them again, he realized Ricky Estefan's eyes must be among those in the jars, though he couldn't identify which pair they were, couldn't, under the current circumstances, even remember what color Ricky's eyes had been.

He reached the door, crossed the threshold, into the upstairs hall, dizzied by infinite images of himself, and from the corner of his eye he saw movement to his left. Movement that was not another Harry Lyon. Coming straight at him and not from out of a mirror, either, coming low. He swiveled toward it, bringing the revolver around, pressure on the trigger, telling himself it had to be a headshot, a headshot, only a headshot would be sure to stop the bastard.

It was the dog. Tail wagging. Head cocked.

He almost killed it, mistaking it for the enemy, almost alerted Ticktock that someone was in the house. He let up on the trigger a fraction of an ounce short of the pressure needed to squeeze off a shot, and would have made the mistake of cursing the dog aloud if his voice hadn't caught in his throat.

* * *

Connie kept listening for gunfire from the second floor, hoping Harry had found Ticktock asleep and would scramble his brain with a couple of rounds. The continued silence was beginning to worry her.

After quickly checking out another mirrored chamber opposite the living room, Connie was in what she assumed would have been the dining room in an ordinary house. It was easier to inspect than the other areas she'd been through, because a band of fluorescent-quality light came under the door from the adjoining kitchen, dispelling some of the gloom.

One wall featured windows, and the other three were mirrored. No furniture, not one stick. She supposed he never ate in the dining room, and he was certainly not the sort of sociable guy who would entertain a lot.

She started to return through the archway to the downstairs hall, then decided to go directly to the kitchen from the dining room. Having looked into the kitchen from an outside window, she knew Ticktock wasn't there, but she had to sweep it again, just to be sure, before joining Harry upstairs.

*　*　*

Carrying two boxes of Reese's peanut-butter cups and one bag of chips, Bryan left the light burning in the pantry and went into the kitchen. He glanced at the table but didn't feel like eating there. Heavy fog pressed at the windows, so if he went outside to the patio, he would have no view of the breaking surf on the beach below, which was the best reason for eating out there.

He was happiest, anyway, when the votive eyes watched him; he decided to go upstairs and eat in the bedroom. The glossy white-tile floor was sufficiently polished to reflect the red of his robe, so it seemed as if he walked through a thin, constantly evaporating film of blood as he crossed the kitchen toward the rear stairs.

* * *

After pausing to wag his tail at Harry, the dog hurried past him to the end of the hall. It stopped and peered down into the back stairwell, very alert.

If Ticktock was in any of the upstairs rooms that Harry had not yet checked, the dog surely would have shown interest in that closed door. But he had trotted by all of them to the end of the hall, so Harry joined him there.

The narrow stairwell was an enclosed spiral, curving down and around and out of sight like stairs in a lighthouse. The concave wall on the right was paneled with tall narrow mirrors that reflected the steps immediately in front of them; because each was angled slightly toward the one before it, every subsequent panel also partly reflected the reflection in the previous one. Because of the weird funhouse effect, Harry saw his full reflection in the first couple of panels on the right, then fractionally less of himself in each succeeding panel, until he did not appear at all in the panel just this side of the first turn in the stairwell.

He was about to start down the steps when the dog stiffened and nipped a mouthful of trouser cuff to restrain him. By now he knew the dog well enough to understand that the attempt to hold him back meant there was danger below.

But he was hunting danger, after all, and had to find it before it found him; surprise was their only hope. He tried to jerk loose of the dog without making any noise or causing it to bark, but it held fast to his cuff.

Damn it.

* * *

Connie thought she heard something just before she entered the kitchen, so she paused on the dining-room side of the door and listened closely. Nothing. Nothing.

She couldn't wait forever. It was a swinging door. Cautiously, she pulled it toward her, easing around it, rather than pushing the door in where it would block part of her view.

The kitchen appeared deserted.

* * *

Harry tugged again, with no better result than he'd gotten before; the dog held tight.

Glancing nervously down the mirrored stairs again, Harry had the terrible feeling that Ticktock *was* down there and was going to get away, or more likely encounter Connie and kill her, all because the dog wouldn't let him slip down and behind the perp. So he rapped the dog smartly on the top of the head with the barrel of his revolver, risking its yelp of protest.

Startled, it let go of him, thankfully didn't bark, and Harry stepped out of the hallway, onto the first stair. Even as he started to descend, he saw a flash of red in the mirror at the farthest curve of the first spiral, another red flash, a billow of red fabric.

Before Harry could register the meaning of what he had seen, the dog shot past him, nearly knocking him off his feet, and it plunged into the stairwell. Then Harry saw more red like a skirt and a red sleeve and part of a bare wrist and a hand, a man's hand, holding something, somebody coming up, maybe Ticktock, and the dog hurtling toward him.

* * *

Bryan heard something, looked up from the boxes of candy in his hands, and saw a pack of snarling dogs erupting toward him, down the staircase, all identical dogs. Not a pack, of course, only one dog reflected repeatedly in the angled mirrors, revealed in advance of its attack, not yet even visible in the flesh. But he only had time to gasp before the beast flew around the curve in front of him. It was moving so fast that it lost its footing and bounced off the concave outer wall. Bryan dropped the candy, and the dog regained enough purchase on the stairs to launch itself at him, crashing into his chest and face, both of them falling backward, the dog snapping and snarling, end over end.

* * *

Snarling, a startled cry, and the thump-crash of falling bodies caused Connie to turn away from the open pantry door where shelves were stacked with bundles of cash. She spun toward the arch beyond which the back stairs curved upward out of sight.

The dog and Ticktock spilled onto the kitchen floor, Ticktock flat on his back and the dog on top of him, and for an instant it looked as if the dog was going to tear out the kid's throat. Then the dog squealed and was flung away from the kid, not thrown by hands or booted with a foot, but *sent* with a pale flash of telekinetic power, hurled across the room.

It was going down, holy God, right there and then, but going down all wrong. She wasn't close enough to jam the muzzle of her revolver against his skull and pull the trigger, she was about eight feet away, but she fired just the same, once even as the dog was in the air, again as the dog slammed into the front of the refrigerator. She hit the perp both times, because he didn't even realize she was in the kitchen until the first shot took him, maybe in the chest, the second in the leg, and he rolled off his back, onto his stomach. She fired again, the bullet *spanged* off the tile, spraying up ceramic chips, and from his prone position Ticktock held one hand toward her, the palm spread, that strange flash as with the dog, and she felt herself airborne, then slammed into the kitchen door hard enough to shatter all the glass in it and send shockwaves of pain up her spine. Her gun flew out of her hand, and her corduroy jacket was suddenly on fire.

* * *

As soon as the snarling dog exploded past Harry and scrambled-bounced-leaped out of sight around the first curve in the narrow spiral staircase, Harry followed, taking the steps two at time. He fell before he reached the turn, cracked one of the mirrors with his head, but didn't tumble all the way to the bottom, came up wedged at the midpoint of the well, with one leg twisted under him.

Dazed, he looked around frantically for his weapon, discovered it was still clutched in his hand. He clambered to his feet and continued down, dizzy, one hand braced against the mirrors to keep his balance.

The dog squealed, gunshots boomed, and Harry spiraled down, into the last turn, to the foot of the stairs in time to see Connie catapulted backward, crashing into the door, on fire. Ticktock was lying on his stomach, directly in front of the stairs, facing out toward the kitchen, and Harry leaped off the last step, landed hard on red silk stretched taut across the kid's back, jammed the muzzle hard against the base of the kid's skull, saw the gunmetal suddenly glow green and felt the start of what might have been a swift and terrible heat in his hand, but pulled the trigger. The explosion was muffled, like firing into a pillow, the green glow disappeared in the instant it first arose, and he squeezed the trigger again, both rounds into the troll's brain. That was surely enough, had to be enough, but you never knew with magic, never knew in this pre-millennium cotillion, these wild '90s, so he squeezed the trigger again. The skull was coming apart like chunks of rind from a cantaloupe hit with a hammer, and still Harry pulled the trigger, and a fifth time, until there was a terrible spreading mess on the floor and no more rounds in the revolver, the hammer snapping against expended casings with a dry *click, click, click, click, click*.

·2·

Connie had stripped off the burning jacket and stamped out the fire by the time Harry realized his gun was empty, climbed off the dead troll, and managed to reach her. It was amazing she'd been able to act fast enough to avoid going up like a torch, because shedding the jacket had been complicated by the fact that her left wrist was broken. She'd suffered a minor burn on the left arm, as well, but nothing serious.

'He's dead,' Harry said, as if it needed saying, and then he put his arms around her, held her as tightly as he could without touching her injuries.

She returned his hug fiercely, one-armed, and they stood that way for a while, unable to talk, until the dog came sniffing around. He was lame, holding his right rear leg off the floor, but he seemed otherwise all right.

Harry realized that Woofer had not, after all, been the cause of a disaster. In fact, if he hadn't plunged down those stairs and knocked Ticktock ass over tea-kettle, thereby preserving the surprise of Connie's and Harry's presence in the house for just a few vital additional seconds, they would be dead on the floor, the golem-master alive and grinning.

A shiver of superstitious dread swept through Harry. He had to let go of Connie and return to the body, look at it again, just to be sure Ticktock was dead.

·3·

They built houses better in the 1940s, with thick walls and lots of insulation, which might have explained why none of the neighbors responded to the gunfire and why no oncoming sirens wailed in the fogbound night.

Suddenly, however, Connie wondered if, in his last moment of life, Ticktock had thrown the world into another Pause, exempting only his own house, figuring to disable them and then kill them at his leisure. And if he died with the world stopped, would it ever start up again? Or would she and Harry and the dog wander through it alone, among millions of once-living mannequins?

She raced to the kitchen door and through it to the night outside. A breeze, cool on her face, ruffling her hair. Fog swirling, not suspended like a cloud of glitter in an acrylic paperweight. The rumble of waves on the shore below. Beautiful, beautiful sounds of a world alive.

·4·

They were police officers with a sense of duty and justice, but they were not foolish enough to follow prescribed procedures in the aftermath of this one. No way could they call the local authorities and explain the true circumstances. Dead, Bryan Drackman was just a twenty-year-old man, and there was nothing about him to prove that he'd possessed astonishing powers. To tell the truth would be a ticket to institutionalization.

The jars of eyes, however, floating blindly on the shelves in Ticktock's bedroom, and the mirrored strangeness of his house would be evidence enough that they had crossed paths with a homicidal psychopath, even if no one ever produced the bodies from which he had removed the eyes. They were able to provide one body, anyway, to support a charge of brutal murder: Ricky Estefan down in Dana Point, eyeless, with snakes and tarantulas.

'Somehow,' Connie said, as they stood in the pantry staring at the shelves laden with cash, 'we've got to concoct a story to cover everything, all the holes and weirdnesses, the reason why we broke procedures on this case. We can't just close the door and walk away because too many people at Pacific View know we were there tonight, talking to his mother, seeking his address.'

'Story?' he said blearily. 'Dear God in Heaven, what kind of story?'

'I don't know,' she said, wincing from the pain in her wrist. 'That's up to you.'

'Me? Why me?'

'You've always liked fairy tales. Make one up. It has to cover the burning of your house, Ricky Estefan, and this. At least that much.' He was still gaping at her when she pointed to all the piles of cash. 'This is only going to complicate the story. Let's just simplify things by getting it out of here.'

'I don't want his money,' Harry said.

'Neither do I. Not a dollar of it. But we'll never know who it was stolen from, so it'll only go to the government, the same damn government that's given us this pre-millennium cotillion, and I can't tolerate the idea of giving it more to waste. Besides, we both know a few people who could sure use it, don't we?'

'God, they're still waiting in the van,' he said.

'Let's bag this cash and take it out to them. Then Janet can drive them away in the van, with the dog, so they don't get wrapped up in it. Meanwhile, you'll be putting together a story, and by the time they're gone, we'll be ready to call in.'

'Connie, I can't possibly— '

'Better start thinking,' she said, pulling a plastic garbage bag from a box of them on one shelf.

'But this is crazier than— '

'Not much time,' she said warningly, opening the bag with her one good hand.

'All right, all right,' he said exasperatedly.

'Can't wait to hear it,' she said, scooping bundles of currency into the first open bag as he opened a second. 'It should be highly entertaining.'

·5·

Good day, good day, good. Sun shining, breeze blowing through his fur, interesting bugs busy in the grass, interesting smells on people's shoes from faraway interesting places, and no cats.

Everyone there, all together. Ever since this morning early, Janet doing delicious-smelling things in the food room of the people place, the people and *dog* place, their place. Sammy in his garden, cutting tomatoes off vines, pulling carrots out of the ground – interesting, must've buried them in the ground like bones – and then bringing them into the food room for Janet to do delicious things. Then Sammy washing off the stones that people put down over part of the grass behind their place. Washing stones with the hose, yes yes yes yes yes, the hose, splattering water, cool and tasty, everyone laughing, dodging, yes yes yes yes. And Danny there, helping to put the cloth on the table that stands on the stones, arrange the chairs, plates and things. Janet, Danny, Sammy. He knows their names now because they have been together long enough for him to know them, Janet and Danny and Sammy, all together at the Janet-and-Danny-and-Sammy-and-Woofer place.

He remembers being Prince, sort of, and Max because of the cat who peed in his water, and he remembers Fella from everyone for so long, but now he only answers to Woofer.

The others come too, driving up in their car, and he knows their names almost as well because they're around so much, visiting so much. Harry, Connie, and Ellie, Ellie who is Danny's size, all of them coming over to visit from the Harry-and-Connie-and-Ellie-and-Toto place.

Toto. Good dog, good dog, good. Friend.

He takes Toto straight to the garden, where they

aren't allowed to dig – bad dogs if they dig, bad dogs, bad – to show him where the carrots were buried like bones. Sniff sniff sniff sniff. More of them buried here. Interesting. But don't dig.

Playing with Toto and Danny and Ellie, running and chasing and jumping and rolling in the grass, rolling.

Good day. The best. The best.

Then food. Food! Bringing it out of the people food room and piling it up on the table that stands on the stones in the shade of the trees. Sniff sniff sniff sniff, ham, chicken, potato salad, mustard, cheese, cheese is good, sticks to the teeth but is good, and more, much more food, up there on the table.

Don't jump up. Be good. Be a good dog. Good dogs get more scraps, usually not just scraps, whole big pieces of things, yes yes yes yes yes.

Cricket jumps. Cricket! Chase, chase, get it, get it, get it, got to have it, Toto too, leaping, jumping, this way, that way, this way, cricket . . .

Oh, wait, yes, the food. Back to the table. Sit. Chest puffed out. Head cocked. Tail wagging. They love that. Lick your chops, give them the hint.

Here it comes. What what what what? Ham. A piece of ham to start. Good, good, good, gone. A delicious start, a very good start.

Such a good day, a day like he always knew would come, one of lots of good days, one after another, for a long time now, because it happened, it really happened, he went around that one more corner, looked in that one more strange new place, and he found the wonderful thing, the wonderful thing that he always knew was out there waiting for him. The wonderful thing, the wonderful thing, which is this place and this time and these people. And here comes a slice of chicken, thick and juicy!

A NOTE TO MY READERS

All of the outrages to which Connie and Harry refer as items in her collection of atrocities from the 'pre-millennium cotillion' are true crimes that really happened. No one as powerful as Ticktock walks the real world, of course, but his capacity for evil is not unique to fiction.

Hideaway

Dean Koontz

Although accident victim Hatch Harrison dies en route to the hospital, a brilliant physician miraculously resuscitates him. Given this second chance, Hatch and his wife Lindsey approach each day with a new appreciation of the beauty of life – until a series of mysterious and frightening events brings them face to face with the unknown. Although Hatch was given no glimpse of an After-Life during the period when his heart had stopped, he has reason to fear that he has brought a terrible Presence back with him ... from the land of the dead.

When people who have wronged the Harrisons begin to die violently, Hatch comes to doubt his own innocence – and must confront the possibility that this life is just a prelude to another, darker place.

'Fiercely exciting' *Kirkus reviews*

'Brilliant' *Mystery Scene*

'A wonderful story. His prose sparkles as it speaks' *Daily Mail*

0 7472 3815 4

headline

The Key to Midnight

Dean Koontz

Who is Joanna Rand?

Alex Hunter hasn't come to Japan to fall in love. But Joanna Rand is the most beautiful, exciting woman he has ever met.

Yet, Joanna is not who she thinks she is. Ten years before, and halfway across the world, a brutally bizarre experiment recreated her mind. A violation so hideous that her dreams are filled with terror and her memories are a lie.

If they are ever to be free, Alex and Joanna have to reopen the dangerous door into the nightmare past. Somehow they have to find the key to midnight . . .

0 7472 3646 1

headline

Now you can buy any of these other bestselling
books by **Dean Koontz** from your bookshop
or *direct from his publisher*.

FREE P&P AND UK DELIVERY
(Overseas and Ireland £3.50 per book)

From the Corner of His Eye	£6.99
False Memory	£6.99
Seize the Night	£6.99
Fear Nothing	£6.99
Sole Survivor	£6.99
Intensity	£6.99
Dark Rivers of the Heart	£6.99
Mr Murder	£6.99
Dragon Tears	£6.99
Hideaway	£6.99
Cold Fire	£6.99
The Bad Place	£6.99
Midnight	£6.99
Lightning	£6.99

TO ORDER SIMPLY CALL THIS NUMBER

01235 400 414

or e-mail orders@bookpoint.co.uk

Prices and availability subject to change without notice.